PRAISE FOR ELAINE FOX!

UNTAMED ANGEL

"In this innovative take on the Pygmalion plot, Elaine Fox demonstrates a virtuoso understanding of American class divisions and attitudes. This one's carefully created romance, every bit as entertaining as 'My Fair Lady.'"

—*Romantic Times*

TRAVELER

"A delightful heroine, a dream of a hero and a timeless love combine for a charming debut! Elaine Fox's *Traveler* is a winner!"

—Nora Roberts

"Hurray! There's a vibrant new voice in romance, and her name is Elaine Fox. Time-travel romance at its absolute best—a stunning debut from an exciting new talent!"

—Patricia Gaffney

THE ROAD TO RUIN

Melisande sat back against a bale of hay and touched her lips with her fingertips. She'd been kissed before, once or twice in a dark corner of a balcony at a ball, but never a slow, sensual kiss like the one she'd just gotten. And never had she been lying down, her hair loose around her, and her body pressed hotly against a man's as his hands moved over her.

Her hand drifted down her neck. His palm had held her breast, his thumb had touched her bare skin. She felt again the tingling of pleasure that started at her core and melted downward. For a moment, at the edge of waking, she had wanted that hand to move inside her clothing. For a moment, her entire body had longed to push up against the hard, male body next to hers, to feel him along her torso, her limbs, to clutch his back and pull him into her.

She felt again his hand in her hair, the way he'd cupped the back of her head, and his warm breath along her neck. Spine-tingling sensations of pleasure wound through her again now, as they had when he had been here.

She shook her head roughly and jumped to her feet. This was terrible. He'd put her under some sort of spell, some sort of sensual spell. This was why unmarried women were not supposed to be alone with unmarried men.

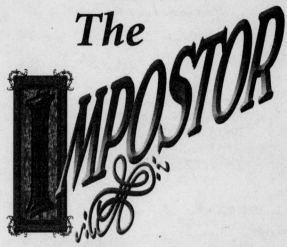

The IMPOSTOR

ELAINE FOX

LEISURE BOOKS NEW YORK CITY

For Jacquelyn,
What would I do without you?

A LEISURE BOOK®

June 1999

Published by

Dorchester Publishing Co., Inc.
276 Fifth Avenue
New York, NY 10001

ISBN 0-8439-4523-0

Chapter One

Dorset, England
January 1998

Flynn Patrick stepped off the curb and into a puddle. Water penetrated his shoe and seeped into his sock, and he swore, jumping sideways out of the moat. He shook his drenched foot, then continued through the downpour around the back of the huge black cab to the driver's window.

"Excuse me," he said to the bent gray head inside.

No response.

He knocked sharply on the glass and repeated, louder, *"Excuse me."*

The driver jerked, glanced up at him, and rolled down the window. "Sorry, guv. Didn't see you there," he said in the thick indecipherable accent that frustrated Flynn to death. Sure, it was English they spoke in this godforsaken—or he should say, *sun*forsaken—country, but who could understand them? Their pronunciation was at best inventive, most often incomprehensible. "What kind of doof are you?" the driver asked.

Flynn stared at him. *"What?"*

"I said, what can I do for you?"

"Oh." Flynn shoved his hands in his pockets. "I need to go to Merestun, ah, estate or something. You know the place?"

"Oh, aye," the man answered, notching Flynn's irritation down slightly. "Everybody knows Merestun. Quite a stunner, that one. You going for the party?"

Flynn heaved a sigh as the rain pecked at his head. It couldn't be that far if the man knew of the wedding taking place this weekend. After the six-hour flight Thursday night and the train trip this morning, he was ready for the short leg of this journey. "Yes. Those are our bags on the platform there." He pulled up his collar and started back toward the covered entry to the train station.

"But I can't be goin' there now," the man interjected just before Flynn was out of earshot. *But my cat be hoyden there, nah,* Flynn heard.

He turned. "What's that?"

"No, sir," the wiry man said from his dry seat inside the car. "I can't be goin' that far now."

"What do you mean? You're a cab, I'll pay you to go there."

"I got me mum comin' for tea and the wife'll have me hide if I'm late. The two o' them don't exactly get on, if you understand my meanin'."

Rain pummeled the top of Flynn's head and trickled down the inside of his Burberry's collar. He shot his arm out to look at his watch. Rain speckled the crystal face. "It's only four. You'll be back in plenty of time for tea." Not that he knew when tea was. He pushed his hand back into his pocket, hunched his shoulders against the chill, and moved back to the man's window, bending to look him dead in the eye. "It's close by, right? I'll pay you double the going rate."

The man continued to shake his head. "Sorry, sir. It's nigh on an hour to Merestun."

"An *hour*. *Jesus Christ*." Flynn straightened and looked around in desperation. The place was deserted, not another cab in sight. Water dragged his hair onto his forehead and ran into his eyes. He blinked and pushed it back, glancing toward the platform in front of the station where his girlfriend, Nina James, peered out from beneath a Russian sable hat. Her chin was tucked into the bushy fur collar of her coat, and her foot tapped at the pavement with nervous energy. *She* would not be happy with the prospect of another hour on the road, he knew, and he wished he weren't the one who had to tell her. She'd been complaining since they'd landed at Heathrow that they should have left a day earlier so she could have rested along the way.

He had the brief, uncharitable thought that Nina should be the one standing in the downpour instead of him—dressed as she was to face far worse elements than a simple, if annoying, rain.

He turned back to the cabbie. "Okay, if you won't take us, do you have a suggestion about how we can get there? I don't see another cab and something tells me there's not a Hertz anywhere near here.''

''Jules'll come after I'm done. And I finish in . . .''
He pulled a chrome watch on a chain from a knob on
the dash. ''About three-quarters of an hour now.''

Flynn blew his cheeks out in despair, and glanced
again at Nina. ''Forty-five minutes, you say?'' He
imagined walking through the mine field of puddles
to the platform and Nina. Then he imagined explaining to her that she had to wait in this rain because
this man couldn't miss tea with his wife and mother.
She'd have a fit.

''So you're telling me we have to wait here nearly
an hour because you don't feel like driving us to Merestun?'' he asked. He was being obnoxious, he knew,
but he did not want to end this conversation because
then he would have to deliver the bad news to Nina.

''It's not that I don't want to drive you, sir.'' The
man seemed anxious not to offend. ''It's just a bit out
of my way, is all.''

''You're a *cab*,'' Flynn pointed out. ''It's your *job*
to drive out of your way.''

''You could have a cup of tea inside the station,''
the cabbie suggested with a gap-toothed grin. ''Just
tell the stationmaster Reg sent you in. He'll share a
pinch o' the pekoe with you.''

Flynn could have sworn the rain came down harder
at that moment, sliding through his hair like fingers.
His shoes were soaked and the bottoms of his pants
clung to his ankles.

''This weekend is going to be hell,'' he muttered,
looking around again for—what?—some kind of authority who could explain to the cabbie about the cus-
tomer always being right. Did they even have a Better

Business Bureau in England? "Look, we can't just sit around and drink tea. I don't mean to be unreasonable but you've got to understand. We have plans—a wedding, for God's sake. We can't be late." *Not to mention I'd kill for a shower and something a lot stronger than tea to drink.*

The man nodded at him with an expression of pity. "Aye, that's a tough one."

Flynn laughed incredulously. "This is crazy. Can't you call another cab to come get us? What's the phone number? I'll do it." He scanned the black car for markings, a company name, an identifying number—anything. "How do you guys stay in business with only one of you out here at a time?"

The man shrugged. "Most times we don't need more than one. I'd sorely like to help you but like I said, the wife would flay me alive. Not married, are you, son?"

Flynn glanced involuntarily at Nina, where she stood shifting from one foot to the other on the dry platform. "Not yet," he said, frowning. The rain shifted to slap him across his left cheek. "Look . . ." He turned back to the driver. "It's forty degrees out here and my—"

"Well, lookit here," the cabbie interrupted, gazing into his rearview mirror. "Ain't that a happy thing? Jules is early."

Flynn lifted his head to see another large black car creep toward them. He'd have been a whole lot happier to see it, he thought morosely, if the damn things didn't look so much like hearses.

The car eased behind the cab where Flynn stood and turned off its lights.

Elaine Fox

"Thank God." Flynn turned away from the man to the new car.

"Enjoy your weekend," the cabbie called after him.

"Thanks," he said automatically. Right. Enjoy it, Flynn thought. He'd be lucky if he lived through it. The weekend was going to be endless. Sheer torture. The three-day wedding of a man he hadn't seen in fifteen years to a woman he'd never met. He didn't have time for it, he thought for the hundredth time, and he planned to hate every minute of it.

The worst part about it was the fact that it would send Nina back up on her soapbox about marriage. He sighed as he slogged through another pool of water. And he'd had about enough of that argument for one weekend.

"I'm going to Merestun," Flynn said as he reached the new driver's window. "Can you take me?"

The cabbie, a burly man with thick, wild eyebrows, stubbed a cigar out against the side of the car on a spot that had obviously been used for the purpose before. "That's my job."

"Thank God." Flynn waved Nina over. "You're a lifesaver, you know? If you hadn't shown up early I'd be walking to Merestun right now," he remarked. "Those bags on the platform are ours."

"That'd be quite a walk. 'Ticularly in this weather."

The burly man hefted himself out of his seat as Nina tiptoed through the rain to the car. She pulled open the huge back door and flopped into the seat as Flynn slid in beside her.

"Thanks for getting the door," she snapped, slamming it hard behind her. "What in the world took you so long?" She looked out the back window at the cabbie retrieving their bags. "I hope you remembered to tell him the black case is fragile."

Flynn glanced back and grimaced as the big man hurled the black bag from the platform to the ground near the passenger door. "Sorry." He turned back and shook the water off his coat sleeves. "God, I'm drenched."

"Watch what you're doing," Nina protested, brushing at a portion of skirt exposed in the gap of her coat. "This is silk."

"I know." Flynn pushed both hands through his sopping hair and closed his eyes. "I warned you not to wear it."

Nina grabbed her purse and pulled a hand mirror from its considerable depths. "Damn," she spat, poking at the wisps of hair that protruded from her hat. A curl had dared to erupt in the straight blond cut.

"I hope to God we've got time to shower when we get there," he said, thinking a good steaming shower was the only thing that would get rid of the chill. That and a healthy shot of whiskey.

"You mean bathe," she corrected. "How can these people stand never taking a shower? Those handheld things just soak the whole room."

"I think they're supposed to be relaxing," he said. "Showers are for people in a hurry."

"And baths are for people who enjoy wallowing in their own filth."

Flynn grimaced. "That's a disgusting way of putting it." He examined the spots of water he'd shaken onto his silk tie. It was the only tie his mother had ever given him that he could stand. And she'd given him a lot of ties.

Flynn reached for his briefcase, then remembered he'd left it with the rest of the bags. He twisted to look again out the window. The driver was just hefting the last bag—one of Nina's enormous suitcases—into the trunk. The car dipped with the impact. Puffing out his cheeks, Flynn sat back in the seat and exhaled. No getting it now.

The car dipped again when the beefy driver returned to the front seat, apparently unperturbed by the rain in his slicker and cap. "Merestun, you say?" the driver asked, starting the car. The engine growled, and the cab pulled away from the curb. "No one sent a car for you then?"

"Apparently not," Nina snapped, shooting Flynn a condemning look.

Cuthbert "Cubby" Lytton, the groom at this weekend's dreaded affair, had claimed all the cars were needed to pick up his future in-laws arriving on an earlier train. Nina had been outraged when Flynn had explained it to her, but he'd figured it wouldn't make much difference. A cab or a limo, they were the same thing, essentially.

At her reaction, Flynn had been tempted for the hundredth time to turn around and head home—except he didn't want to face the wrath of his mother if he didn't show. She rarely asked a thing of him, but when she did, it was a doozie.

"I'd've thought they'd send a car for the guests, it being such a distance and all," the driver continued. "Could be quite dear, a ride all the way out there. . . ."

14

"Don't worry, you'll be paid," Flynn said, pushing damp hair off his forehead again. "We've got the cash."

The hell with Cubby Lytton, he thought. Sure, he'd known him as a child, but did that obligate them to keep in touch forever? According to his mother, yes.

The cabbie laughed. "Oh, I can tell that. All's I'm sayin' is—"

"The fact is they didn't send a car," Nina said irritably, looking pointedly at Flynn again. "Bad for us, good for you. Let's just get on with it."

"Whatever you say, ma'am," the driver murmured.

Flynn leaned back in the seat, yanking his tie off with a surly glance at the spots and balling it in his fist. It was going to be one hell of a long ride with Nina in this mood. If he could have gotten some work done, the time wouldn't have been a total loss. As it was, they'd be nearly an hour driving through this slop and his laptop was in the trunk. If he didn't finish the NOW speech for Kincaid before Monday, all hell would break loose. It wouldn't matter how inspired his rhetoric was on Tuesday.

Beside him Nina applied more lipstick, ignoring him.

Sulking, he thought. She'd been mad at him since they'd gotten on the plane and he'd snapped at her that he really wished she had stayed home. Nina had talked the entire way about his *feelings,* about their *plans,* about what the *future* might, should, could, or would hold for them. Then she'd started in on weddings and how they should consider having *their own* someday. Then she'd talked about how she was going

15

to take notes at this one, as she had at the last several she'd been to, because she wanted hers to be perfect. She'd gone on and on about it so long that he'd finally told her he had no desire to even think about a wedding at this time.

That had bought him several hours of quiet.

He'd tried, once they were on the ground at Heathrow, to jolly her out of the mood, telling her she'd caught him in a foul mood and that they could talk about it *later*. But if there was one thing Nina excelled at it was holding a grudge.

Well, he conceded, it wasn't as if it would be the end of the world if he and Nina split after this weekend. He did not want to marry her—honestly hadn't realized she'd wanted to marry *him* so badly until recently—and they were not enjoying themselves as they had in the beginning. It was time, he thought, to put them both out of this misery.

But not yet. Not until they were home. Until then he would have to suffer, and it was his own fault for letting her come. His own fault completely.

Flynn loosened his grip on the tie and put it on the seat beside him. Looking out the rain-spattered window his eyes followed a bird, little more than a black spot on the gray horizon, flying parallel to the car. It seemed to be going the same speed as the car, neither veering off nor dropping behind.

He sighed and rubbed his hands over his face, leaning his head back on the seat. In the first place, he told himself, he should not have let his mother make him feel guilty unless he came. And in the second, he should have held firm against Nina's pleas to accompany him. But in a moment of weakness he'd felt pity for his mother, and he'd compounded his error with a momentary belief that it might be a good thing if Nina came with him.

Instead of offering him a simple distraction from what could be a stressful trip, however, she'd increased the level of strain tenfold. He closed his eyes, tension creeping up his spine and gripping him across the back of the neck.

He deserved it, however. He'd committed one of the cardinal sins of bachelorhood: He'd brought a girlfriend to a wedding with no intention of giving her one of her own.

He opened his eyes and turned his head back to the window. The fingers of one hand tapped against his thigh. The bird still kept pace with the cab, its wings flapping slow and steady against the pelting rain.

Flynn watched it. In Washington it had seemed a remote possibility that his past would come up, but now that he was here he realized how stupid that assumption had been. His connection to Merestun was the link between himself and Cubby, virtually the only one, and Nina was sure to ask about it. For some reason he did not care to identify, he didn't want her delving into that part of himself.

But, he told himself, Cubby probably didn't even remember Flynn's connection to the place. It had been too many years. It was only Flynn's mother who wouldn't let him forget it. And forget it he would, given half a chance.

Flynn's eyes dropped from the bird to the dark backdrop of trees across a barren field. He'd had a bird once, he thought.

"Doesn't it *ever* stop raining in this damn country?'' Flynn demanded, suddenly sick of the tinny sound on the roof and hiss of the tires on wet blacktop. He glanced at Nina. She was here as a distraction—why didn't she distract him?

Nina, who'd removed her hat and was still fussing with her hair, dropped her hands to her lap and looked over at him. Her eyes, Jell-O green through the miracle of contacts, narrowed. ''We could be in the Caribbean, you know.''

Flynn regarded her steadily. ''*You* could be. I have a wedding I have to go to.''

She rolled her eyes. ''You didn't *have* to come. You could have said no to your mother. You have before. And I know *I'd* rather be on a beach.''

He rolled the window partway down, felt the rain sting his face, and rolled it back up to just a crack. ''Then you shouldn't have insisted on coming.''

Nina threw her comb to the floor of the cab and gave him a steely look.

''Fine. You can take me right back to the train station. Driver!'' She leaned forward. ''Driver, turn around, I'm going back to the train.''

The car slowed as the driver took his foot off the accelerator.

''Don't be ridiculous,'' Flynn snapped. ''Keep going, cabbie. For Christ's sake, sit back, Nina.''

The cab picked up speed.

Folding her arms across her chest, she glared at him. ''No, I won't. You've been a perfect bastard since we started this trip. Back to the station, driver.''

The car slowed.

''*Sit back,*'' Flynn ordered through clenched teeth. ''We're only going to be here for two days. *Two.* You

18

can tell everyone what a bastard I am when we get there, that should make you happy. Keep going," he instructed the driver.

The cabbie hit the accelerator again.

Nina collapsed back in her seat with a pout. "You know I hate it when you get this way."

"That's ridiculous. *I* haven't gotten any way. You're the one who's all bent out of shape," Flynn argued. Why were women always telling him how he was, or how he wasn't, or worst of all how he *ought* to be?

"Everything's ridiculous," she said. "This whole weekend's ridiculous. Why are we here? You don't even like this guy, you said it yourself."

Flynn frowned and gazed out the window. Barren fields slid by in a wet haze. "I don't like him. But his family did me a big favor once."

Nina snorted. "So we've traveled halfway around the world to go to this wedding as a favor? That doesn't seem like you at all, Flynn. Or does this have some sort of journalistic angle I'm missing?"

Flynn shot her a dry look. "I'm not a journalist anymore, remember? I'm a speechwriter." After a moment he added, "But he is president of NatWest Bank. I guess that could be helpful at some point."

Nina made an annoyed sound, flipped open a compact, and pressed powder across the bridge of her nose. "You're despicable, you know that? Using people who think they're your friends like that."

"He doesn't think he's my friend."

Nina closed the compact and put it back in her bag, her mouth pursed. "Then why did he do you a favor?"

"He didn't," Flynn said. "His parents did. Thirty years ago. The Lyttons were friends with my parents, so my mother asked me to come. I couldn't say no."

Nina turned to him, her icy eyes speculative. "Because of him, right? Your father? She's still not over his death, is she?"

Flynn scoffed to himself, wondering how she could think anyone would have a hard time getting over his father's death. His mother might put on a show of mourning, but Flynn knew better. The old bastard's death had been a godsend for her.

Flynn kept his voice bland. "Right."

Nina's clinical voice emerged. "I see."

He sighed, and looked out the window again. The bird was still there. He began to wonder if it was something stuck on the glass, and brought a hand up to the fogged glass. But the bird was there, in the distance, just parallel to them.

"Fine." Nina zipped her bag closed. "Be a grouch about it, then. God, you can be a jerk sometimes." Her perfectly chiseled profile was sharp and clear against the background of fogged glass and rain. Pale, nearly blue-veined skin, professionally straightened nose, health-club-firm chin and neck.

"Like father like son," he muttered.

The ride progressed in silence. Flynn felt more uncomfortable with every passing mile. He wished again he had his laptop to divert him—anything rather than stare out the window—but that would require stopping the car, and the one thing he wanted more than distraction was arrival.

A strange mixture of dread and anticipation amassed within him as he watched the passing landscape. There was no denying it, the place disturbed him. He would have thought after so many years he'd have no feelings about it, but apparently that was not so. He folded his arms over his chest. Ridiculous, he thought again, to allow any emotion about a place he could not even remember. It must be stress, he thought. His new job was getting to him.

Outside, under the curtain of rain, the scene of neatly parceled farms was a pastoral taunt to his anxiety. He should not have come, he thought again, barely holding back a wave of unexpected desperation. Their increasing proximity to Merestun settled around his head like a personal storm cloud. No matter how much his mother had insisted, he should have told her no. He had too much to do, too much to think about, without this ill-timed interruption. And he sure as hell didn't need this displaced feeling, this knowledge without memory.

Jet lag, he told himself. He was exhausted. And he was tired of dealing with Nina's moods. That was all.

So why was he seized with dread when he looked out the window? Why did he find himself trying to imagine what was just down the road? Why did he fear how he'd feel when the house came into view?

He hated farmland, he decided. Too barren. Too treeless. No place to hide, he thought idly, then started at the idea. *No place to hide?*

He closed his eyes and ran a hand over his face, noticing as he did so that his other hand was clenched in a tight fist. He unfurled his fingers and looked at them, stiff from the grip.

Shifting his eyes from his hand, he gazed back out at the passing farms. Occasionally he thought he saw a little cabin or cottage tucked into the trees between the fields, but when he concentrated there was nothing there. Once he thought he saw a man standing on the back of a plow pulled by a horse, but that turned out to be a mound of deadwood. Nobody would be plowing this time of year anyway, he told himself, and certainly not with a horse.

Though he kept his eyes focused out the window, the landscape didn't look familiar. He expected it to and it didn't. Yet it should.

It should, he thought reluctantly.

They rounded a line of trees and came upon the house so suddenly it almost seemed to have materialized out of thin air.

Flynn felt the sight in his gut, a shock of airlessness and an immediate tightening in his chest.

Across a cultured lawn the sprawling, fanciful structure rose stalwart in the rain. Turrets and gables, round pointed rooftops that looked as eccentric as circus tents, stone dressings and mellow red brick, all made the place look like some medieval mansion.

Inside himself he had the sensation of taking off in a plane—a lightness, an excitement—did he actually remember seeing this house before or did its resemblance to a castle make it familiar? He must have had a book on it as a child, he decided, for his eyes drank in the sight with an appreciation for unchanged detail he could not otherwise have felt.

In front of the house, in the wide, circular drive, stood a big black carriage and four dancing horses. A man in peacock blue livery sat tall on the box, the whip straight as a fishing rod beside him.

"It's incredible," Nina breathed beside him.

"Truly magical. It looks as if a someone conjured it up with a magic wand!"

Flynn glanced back at her as if she'd just appeared beside him, saw the expression of awe on her face, and felt confused that the place seemed to be affecting her strangely too.

He could not resist the image of the house for long, however, and he turned back to examine it hungrily. The carriage was gone. His eyes searched the circular drive, but it was nowhere to be seen. It must have gone back around to the carriage house, he thought then. It had probably just dropped off the bride.

The bird, which had mirrored their course with its flight, began an easy glide, coasting lower and lower, until it disappeared behind the house.

It had been coming here too, he thought with a chill. The black bird and himself.

Nina's laughter brought him up short.

"You're *speechless*!" she squealed.

He snapped his mouth shut and turned to her, somehow surprised again by her presence. But as before, he could only manage to look at her for moment before his gaze was drawn back to the house. The apprehension that had colored his view of the countryside was gone, replaced by a wonder he hadn't felt in years. He was transfixed by the sight.

"Incredible." He realized he'd voiced the thought aloud only when Nina answered.

"Isn't it?" she whispered. "I just wish it weren't raining. Imagine this place on a sunny day! And look, there's a pond."

His eyes flicked to the pond off to the side of the house. "That's new," he murmured.

"What do you mean? It looks like it's been here forever. Look at the size of that willow tree."

The feelings blossoming inside Flynn were unaccountable, yet so buoyant he could not suppress them. "Nina," he said, his voice hushed, "I know this place. I *know* it."

She looked at him quizzically. "You've been here before?"

The question reverberated in his head as he drank in the view, his mind overpowered by images of stone hearths and staid portraits, ornately carved woodwork and lavish furnishings. His heart beat erratically.

"Yes," he said quietly. "Yes, I was born here."

Chapter Two

Dorset, England
January 1815

"I had another of the dreams last night," Melisande St. Claire announced, gazing into the mirror on the table in front of her.

Behind her, a maid drew a silver-handled brush through Melisande's hair with long, slow strokes. In the light of the candles, red highlights shone in the dark skein and Melisande frowned. They had angered her mother, she recalled, who had warned her time and again to stay out of the sun. The lightening of her hair had been further proof that if she wasn't careful, her skin would turn brown as a gypsy's.

"Ooh, another dream," the maid said, her blue eyes alight with relish. "Shall I go and fetch Miss Juliette? She wouldn't want to miss it, you know."

Melisande sighed and toyed with the fringe of the dressing-table cover, noting as she lifted it the fine heft and weight of the material. The whole bedroom consisted of such appointments—sumptuous, refined—but then, one could expect no less in a ducal home, and Merestun was one of the finest.

"No need, Daphne. Juliette needs to finish getting dressed. Mother's allowing her to join us for dinner. I will tell her later."

The maid leaned forward, her face beaming in the candlelight, her crooked teeth exposed in a delighted grin. "Which dream was it this time? Another with the prince?"

Melisande's lips curved. "Yes, he was there. Though this time it was strange. . . ." Her smile waned and she gazed into her own dark eyes in the mirror, wondering again if the odd dreams reflected anything more serious than a peculiar imagination. "This time, I felt . . ." She paused, remembering the rush of feeling, the terror, the loss and pain. "This time I felt afraid."

Daphne drew back. "Afraid! With the prince there? Didn't he protect ye?"

Melisande's brows drew together. "That was the odd part. He was there, and then he wasn't. He simply disappeared before my very eyes."

"Aye, that'll happen in dreams." Daphne nodded knowingly.

Melisande's hands gripped the edge of the table and she leaned forward, looking at Daphne's eyes in the mirror. "But this was so *real*. And when he left, I felt such pain of loss—it was almost a physical pain. A force as if someone stood upon my heart."

One of the candles flickered and Daphne's hands stopped their work, one hand holding the heavy length of Melisande's hair, the other holding the brush over her own heart. "Was the prince in danger?"

Melisande shook her head. "I don't know. He must have been. But he looked sad, not afraid." She tried to remember what he had said, but couldn't. She hadn't understood what he'd meant anyway, though she'd understood the words. "He held my hand," she added, remembering the surge of certainty she'd felt at the contact. "And then he disappeared."

"Do ye suppose the prince is really Lord Bellingham?" Daphne asked dreamily. "Imagine if when ye finally meet the earl tonight before the ball, he's got eyes of blue steel and hair black as jet, just like the prince. Ooh, such a handsome man. Did he look the same in the dream last night?"

"Yes," Melisande murmured. "He looked just the same."

Handsome. Perplexing. Dangerous.

Melisande had invented the prince for Juliette and Daphne. That is, she'd invented the part about his *being* a prince. The man was real. Too real, for a dream. As Daphne remembered so clearly, he had eyes the color of a finely tempered blade and hair dark as a crow's wing, frequently dipping low over one eye. As she thought about it again, she had a sudden vision of him pushing the lock back with one hand. Such a familiar movement for a man from a dream. . . .

What she liked best, though, was when he'd smile at her, with straight white teeth and warmth in his eyes just for her. But then he would say the strangest things.

But as Daphne said, that was the way of dreams. Melisande knew they didn't always make sense. The fact that these were so consistent—always the same man and always in disturbing situations—was the part that troubled her. And those emotional elements were ever-present—great desire, great fear, and an overpowering feeling that she was not sure was love, though of course she told Daphne and Juliette it was.

That was why she'd made up the part about him being a prince. Dreaming about a prince come to save her made much more sense than conjuring a strange man come to torment her with confusion.

"I think it'll be Lord Bellingham," Daphne asserted, drawing the brush through Melisande's hair again. "It's got t' be him. Why else would ye dream of him so much and only recently, when ye're in his house and about t' be betrothed to him?"

"It's not really his house," Melisande corrected. "Not yet anyway. Only after the old duke dies."

"Och, well, I hear Lord Merestun's sickly. Before you know it your Earl of Bellingham will be the next Duke of Merestun. And you a duchess—imagine!"

Melisande tried summon the triumph she'd felt upon agreeing to marry the notorious Lord Bellingham—and couldn't. She'd never met him, but he was known across the country for wealth, social position, and imminent rank. He'd also been known to have said he would never marry, and therefore had been the most sought after bachelor in England. With everyone saying only the most beautiful, respectable, and deserving lady in the country could win him,

Melisande was so carried away by her success when he proposed that she could not say no.

Now that she had done it, however, she dreaded what she had achieved. The closer she got to sealing her fate with him, the more worried she felt. How could she have agreed to marry someone without even laying eyes on him? How could she have thought the triumph of an instant would sustain her through the rest of her life?

She swallowed to calm the now-familiar roiling of her stomach. Once her father and the earl had agreed on terms three weeks ago, her father had been out of his head with excitement. The Earl of Bellingham— a true lord, a peer of the realm, and a *future duke*! His pride and pleasure in his daughter had been enough to convince her it was the right decision. But now . . . now that she was about to meet the earl for the first time, she was not so sure.

Their betrothal was to be announced this evening at a ball given in their honor by no less a figure than the reigning Duke of Merestun. As the future Duchess of Merestun, Melisande's presence at the estate had been mandatory so she could be formally accepted by the old duke, who was said to be a prickly fellow more concerned with heirs than wealth. Though she came with a sizeable fortune, she imagined he wanted to judge her potential as breeding stock, examining more closely the size of her hips than her pocketbook. Perhaps her fate was not so inexorably sealed after all, she pondered grimly.

"I suppose the prince could be Lord Bellingham," Melisande said. A swift thrill of pleasure skated along her nerves at the prospect. Then she frowned and narrowed her eyes at Daphne in the mirror. "But the prince doesn't have the same look ... the way they say Bellingham is."

Daphne concentrated on the brush in her hand. "And what're ye talkin' about? Have ye heard tell of Bellingham's looks then?"

Melisande opened a silver-topped jar and drew from it a feathered puff of powder. "No, not his looks, though they say he's nearly forty. And the prince hasn't any gray hair."

"Och, what's a gray hair or two? I've a couple meself now, and I'm only nine and twenty. And anyway, Bellingham's rich as Croesus, as ye know, so he could look like a prince. They say he surely dresses like one."

Melisande leaned forward and dabbed the powder around her face. "But they say he's ... he's promiscuous." Feeling a blush creep into her cheeks, she dropped the puff to her chest and powdered the pale expanse above her chemise, pausing thoughtfully.

Daphne pursed her lips and brushed more roughly. "That's that nasty little maid talking again, isn't it. Jenny, she calls herself. I wouldn't trust her at all, miss, not even with telling the time of day. Now, what else happened in the dream?" She twisted one side of Melisande's hair up and pinned it with a comb.

"Ouch! Daphne, you needn't pull so hard." Melisande pulled away.

Daphne smiled ruefully and took up the other side with more care. "Sorry, miss. I just don't like people speaking ill o' the prince, is all."

Melisande leaned back in her seat with a short laugh. "Well, my goodness, it's not as if he's real.

Anyway, this time it wasn't a long dream. Not like the one where I met him by the fountain. And he wasn't so argumentative in this one either. He was quite gentle.''

"Hmmm," Daphne murmured, a satisfied smile on her lips.

"He must have given me some sort of potion, because he told me to go to sleep and when I awoke, he'd be back and then he would take care of me."

Yet she'd been frightened despite his words; and so she wondered, was he an evil man after all?

"Well, of course he would take care of ye. He's done that all along, in all yer adventures.'' Daphne pinned up the side and began braiding the long tresses in back.

"Do you suppose he could have meant Norfolk?" Melisande asked. "Father said I'm to go with Bellingham to Norfolk after the winter ball in February, to stay with his mother and brother. Then we're to be married in the spring in London."

Daphne nodded, her lips pressed together. "A spring wedding, to be sure, is ideal. But I don't understand why ye must go and stay with Lady Bellingham first. I've heard tell she's mean as a bitch in season.''

"Daphne!" But Melisande giggled through the reprimand. "You're so bad. I'm to learn to run the house, though I don't see why I should have to go to Lytton Hall for that. It's no bigger than Browerly and has the same number of servants. But Mother says I must show Lady Bellingham respect even if she teaches me nothing."

Daphne snorted. "From all I've heard, *you* should

31

be teaching *her*. A more pampered lady you'll never meet, is the way they tell it. Ye can be sure *I've* no wish to be under her command.''

Melisande turned in her seat and fixed her maid with a hard look. ''You won't be. You're *my* maid and you'll answer only to *me*, do you understand? I don't care what that old witch has to say about it.''

Daphne drew back and looked at her in surprise. ''Yes, miss, of course. And if ye can manage such a tone with her ladyship, I'm sure she'll understand as well.''

Melisande dropped her eyes and smiled. ''I'm sorry. It's just that I've heard so much about Lady Bellingham and what I'm expected to do and to say and how I'm supposed to act that I feel like canceling the entire arrangement.''

''Canceling!'' Daphne dropped her hands and gave Melisande a scandalized look. ''What, and have ye gone and lost yer mind then?''

Melisande turned rebellious eyes on her. ''It's not yet official. I could still change my mind.''

''Change yer mind!''

Panic surged in Melisande's breast at the look on her maid's face. She *was* trapped. It hit her with the force of a thousand gales. The wedding was not the moment of finality, she realized—the *promise* had been. The *promise* she had already made.

Tears sprang to her eyes as she stared at her maid in sudden horror. ''Why, certainly,'' she said in a choked voice. ''Daphne! Don't look at me so. Certainly I could—I could break—''

Daphne squatted, her form even stouter in the position, and wiped a coarse thumb across her mistress's damp cheek. "Come now, Miss Melisande," she chided. "Ye're to be a duchess! You would be a fool to give that up now."

Melisande closed her eyes and gritted her teeth, willing away the onslaught of fear and regret.

"We're always afraid of what we don't know," the maid continued. "But ye just wait and see. I'll bet Lord Bellingham is as kind and handsome as your prince, and before the night's through all your worries'll be over."

Melisande drew in a long, unsteady breath, cursing the weakness that made her want to sink her head into her hands and sob. "It doesn't matter." Her voice emerged controlled. "I made my decision and—and it was the right one. Who could refuse a duke, after all?"

Daphne smoothed back her hair, her merry eyes somber now. "Of course it was the right decision. No doubt he'll be the duke 'ere long, and I'm sure he'll be the perfect husband—"

"No." Melisande shook her head. "He might not be perfect. But it matters not, does it? I shall be happy no matter what he is like. Isn't that right?"

"Miss Melisande, I've never met a lady stronger than yerself."

"Oh, but I'm *not*, Daphne," Melisande protested almost angrily, swiping the back of her hand across her nose. "That's my terrible secret. I'm false and full of bravado. I'm not strong."

Daphne took Melisande's chin between two sturdy fingers. "Ye *are* strong, ye just don't know it. Ye haven't had to use it yet, is all. But when ye do, it'll be there, mark my words."

Daphne's eyes held Melisande's without compromise.

Melisande forced a smile. "How did you get so wise in just twenty-nine years?" She took a deep breath. "All right. Yes. I must not be so uncertain. I just hope he's intelligent," she said. "You know I can't abide a stupid man."

Daphne smiled and rose to her feet, patting Melisande's cheek before turning back to her braiding. "Stupid men don't sit in the House of Lords, miss."

The gown Melisande wore was made completely of lace with a pink satin underslip that hugged her form when she walked. It had cost her father more than anything else in her extensive wardrobe, but he wanted to be sure that on the night of her betrothal to an earl she looked the part of a St. Claire, daughter of one of the oldest, wealthiest families in England. The alliance was a victory, he'd said on more than one occasion, and there would be hundreds in attendance at the ball where the news was to be announced. Not that it was going to be a surprise to anyone. The gossips had gotten wind of the information weeks ago, and invitations to the ball had been in high demand.

Melisande held her head like a queen as she moved through the gallery on her way to the great chamber where she was to meet her fiancé. Her slippered footsteps sounded hollowly in the marble hall as she passed busts of Roman emperors and portrait after portrait of somber Merestun ancestors, all seeming to project across the ages their approval as yet another future duchess sacrificed silly romantic dreams to take her place in history.

Sacrificed? She mentally chastised herself. As if it were any true sacrifice to marry a duke. Or a future duke, at any rate. How many friends had she seen march down the aisle with some ugly or old man without nearly the rank of Bellingham? How many times had she bolstered their courage with false words of encouragement? She'd said the very things Daphne had said to her just an hour ago. Be strong. Everything will be fine. You can do it. But now she understood why her friends had clung to the words so desperately, as if she might possibly know a thing about marriage. She, a maiden, just as Daphne was.

She reached the end of the long gallery and turned resolutely toward the great chamber.

He might be kind or even clever. He could be handsome. Or funny. Or any of a thousand positive things—so why did she dwell so on her fears?

She arrived at the door to the great chamber and halted, taking a deep, strengthening breath. He was in there, with her parents. She could just barely make out the sound of voices. She would enter, their eyes would meet . . . would she succumb to the fright that lay just below the surface? Or would she smile into eyes of sheerest blue? The eyes of her prince.

She stared at the ornately carved door. Her breath came rapidly and her heart struggled to escape her chest. Don't be a fool, she told herself. You made the prince up. This marriage is by far the most successful one you could have made. Indeed, women all over England were lamenting their lost chances with the Earl of Bellingham. This *was* a triumph.

She took another deep breath and closed her eyes. Immediately, a vision of the prince assailed her. As if emerging from a mist, his hard, lean face appeared, his gaze rich with some emotion that turned her knees to jelly. She heard his laughter in the hall, sharp and free. Whipping her eyes open, she looked around.

Voices still murmured behind the high door. The hallway was empty. The prince, if he had ever been there, was gone.

Flynn Patrick laughed. "Don't tell me you're jealous of a painting, now, Nina," he said, gazing at the portrait hanging on the wall. They stood in what Cubby had referred to as the gallery during their earlier tour, but it was more like a wide hallway with portrait after portrait of humorless souls all long dead lining the walls.

The picture that had caught his attention was of a young woman, undeniably beautiful, and the only woman in the hall. But it was the expression on her face that had captivated him. Her dark eyes looked positively sultry, and she gazed out of the painting with such sensuality that he felt as if she beckoned him to her.

"Well, you seem to be inordinately fascinated by *this* one," Nina said.

He laughed again. "Well, look at her. She's gorgeous. And it's the first time I've ever felt like a portrait was undressing me with its eyes."

Nina didn't laugh, but turned him away from the picture and wound her arm through his. "Now that I've got you alone," she began, sending tendrils of dread through Flynn's chest. "I thought we could do some serious talking."

"Hey, take a look at this old guy," Flynn said, desperately trying to avoid the subject he knew was coming. He pointed to a painting of an old man with a chess set beside him. "What's he holding?" He leaned closer. "Oh, it's a pocketwatch. Look at that little thing, it's weird."

Nina didn't stop. "I don't care. I want to continue our conversation from this afternoon."

Flynn sighed, and they edged toward another painting across the hall, an innocuous oil of an enormous vase of flowers on a wooden table. For some reason the picture reminded him of something, and he leaned toward it.

"Are you listening to me?" Nina demanded.

"Of course," he said, reaching forward and finding the spot he somehow knew was there. Just near the signature, a small tear had been repaired.

"I wanted to talk about *us*—"

Footsteps sounded at the end of the hall and the groom appeared, drink in hand.

"Cubby," Flynn said, happy to escape what he was sure would have turned out to be another uncomfortable conversation about his future with Nina. "How's married life so far? Now that you're, what . . ." He turned up his wrist to check the hour. "Ninety minutes into it?"

"So far so good," Cubby boomed. Flynn could see he was already well on his way to being what the English might term "in his cups." "I saw you met Carruthers earlier. Pretty savvy about your political system, what? You know, of course, he teaches American political science at the U. of London. Were the two of you talking shop?"

Flynn lifted his drink in a mild shrug as Nina piped up. "Flynn picked a fight with him." She grinned, and her eyes narrowed in catlike delight.

"I didn't pick a fight. His ideas were more suited to the nineteenth century than the twentieth, is all," Flynn said, polishing off his drink. "I tried to change the subject."

"Really. How interesting," Cubby said, looking much more interested in Nina than anything Carruthers had thought about the American political system.

"It's true," Nina said, latching on to Cubby's interest and drawing him in like a fish on a line. "You really should have been there. I guess the guy wanted to show off what he thought he knew. He should have picked somebody nicer to argue with."

"Hey, I was nice. I told him there are as many theories on politics as there are politicians," Flynn said, irritated by Nina's behavior. He shot her a hard look.

Cubby, displaying uncharacteristic perception, took Flynn by the arm and started to lead him back to the party. "I'm sure Carruthers'll live through a minor dispute. Every once in a while those academics need a tussle with reality. But come back to the party, old man, and let me introduce you around." The three of them returned to the overcrowded ballroom, where Nina was promptly snagged by a man she'd met earlier.

"Freshen your drink?" Cubby asked Flynn, scanning the room for a server. "Charles! Freshen Flynn's scotch, would you? Straight up, yes? Good show!

Why dilute the stuff? He'll be right around with it, don't worry. Good man, Charles.''

Flynn deposited his empty glass on a table as they passed, wondering if Charles would be able to track them through the throng.

"Jolly good party, eh, what?" Cubby continued. "It's not every day a man gets married, you know. Sure as bloody hell isn't something *I* intend to do every day, I'll tell you. Once is enough. So what do you think of Carol?"

Flynn eyed a passing woman in a form-fitting black sheath. Diamonds sparkled at her ears, neck, and wrists. Nice figure, he thought. Expensive face.

"She's a great girl, Cubby. You couldn't have done better."

Cubby Lytton strangled a laugh and took the drink Charles, miraculously, held out to him. Throwing back half of it, he wiped his mouth with the back of his hand and winked at Flynn. "No, I couldn't have done better. She's worth more money than you and I both will ever make. She's a Haverford, you know. And what's a few extra stone when you're talking *millions* of pounds, I ask you." He belched, laughed loudly, and squeezed Flynn's shoulders with one viselike arm.

Flynn managed a smile, and took the drink Charles offered him. "She seems nice enough."

Cubby's laughter exploded across the room, his face flushed and his red-rimmed eyes watering. A few curious gazes turned toward them, then politely turned away. "Yes, she's nice *enough,*" he wheezed, laughing. "And what about you, eh? That's a pretty little piece you've brought with you. Perhaps there's a wedding bell tolling in your future, hm?''

At the same moment, Flynn caught sight of Nina weaving through the throng toward them, her pale blond hair a beacon in the dark-suited crowd.

"It's a distant bell," Flynn said. "Barely audible, really. Listen, Cubby, don't bring it up with Nina, all right? I'm suffering enough about the whole issue as it is. I should never have brought her with me," he added, more to himself, and shook his head.

Cubby's brows rose, and he clapped Flynn on the back. "Oh, got you, right. I understand. Leave it to me."

"*There* you are," Nina said accusingly, as if he'd deliberately ditched her. The fact was, the place was enormous and teeming with people. He couldn't have avoided losing her if he'd wanted to.

Nina wore a white sequined dress that barely covered her breasts and descended to cover only about four inches of thigh. In between, it clung to her model-thin frame, revealing a body that contained not an ounce of fat, and a chest that cost thousands.

Cubby's gaze latched onto her cleavage, and a cynical smile curved Flynn's lips. So much for ninety minutes of marriage.

"I'm sorry, Nina," Flynn said, drawing her in to his body with an arm around her waist. Her hair, cut straight to the line of her jaw, was soft as he kissed her cheek. She looked surprised, then glowed with satisfaction at his unexpected affection.

"Miss James," Cubby said. "I didn't get a chance to tell you earlier, ah, in the receiving line—it's a lovely frock you're wearing this evening."

Nina smiled and extended her hand. "Thanks. It's

an original. Flynn bought it for me in Paris."

"I paid for it," Flynn clarified. "I didn't buy it."

"Well, yes, I can see why you would." Cubby smiled and winked at Flynn. "Yes, sir, I can certainly see why. Our Flynn's quite a chap, isn't he?"

Nina turned a skeptical look upon Flynn. "Most of the time."

Flynn smiled, his eyes drifting to a dark-haired woman behind her, and opted not to answer.

"So, having a nice time, are you?" Cubby asked Nina. "I mean, the food good and all? Got enough to drink?"

"Oh, it's great. I just love weddings," Nina said.

"Excellent, wonderful." Cubby colored and looked at Flynn, who rolled his eyes. "I mean, well, they're not all they're cracked up to be, you know. Bloody lot of work. Wouldn't have gone through it if I hadn't known Carol forever. Simply forever, several lifetimes, you know. So how long have you and Flynn—that is to say, have you, just by the by, met up recently?"

Flynn wanted to sink his head into his hands. So much for avoiding the dreaded topic. He attempted diversion. "Cubby, are you two going to live—"

"Eight months," Nina cut in. "We met eight months ago next Thursday. At The Priory."

Cubby looked momentarily nonplussed. "Good lord, a priory?"

"It's a bar," Flynn informed him.

"Eight months," Nina repeated. "It's long enough." She squeezed Flynn's arm and gave him a significant look.

He grimaced and looked back at the dark-haired

woman, who met his gaze with sultry eyes.

"Good heavens, *no*. Eight months—*ha*—not nearly long enough," Cubby said. At Nina's glacial look, however, he added, "Well, that is, *perhaps* it's not. After all, Carol and I've known each other so long we know every bloody thing about each other. You probably haven't gotten even a tenth of Flynn's story out of him yet."

Nina's red lips imitated a smile. "Oh, I think I have. I know all I need to."

Flynn downed the rest of his drink and said, "Cavalier words, my dear."

Trying to stop her now would be a mistake, he knew. She'd had just enough alcohol to become belligerent if crossed. All he could do was avoid hearing the argument one more time. Let her convince Cubby they should marry. The two of them could plot his marital demise while he drank himself into a stupor.

"Well, the truth of the matter is, it's good to know *everything* about each other," Cubby continued. "And that sort of thing takes *years,* take it from me. The secrets people have about themselves . . . sometimes you don't find out the most vile things until it's too late." He threw up his hands and sloshed half his drink down the back of a nearby man's tux. Fortunately, the bystander didn't realize it.

Nina settled herself on one hip and drilled Cubby with her now-robin's-egg-blue eyes. Flynn concentrated on trying to remember what color her eyes really were.

"Well, *you've* known him his whole life," Nina challenged. "Flynn tells me he was born here. What terrible secrets are there that I don't know about?"

Flynn flagged Charles for another drink. "That's an area I don't think we need to get into—"

"I'll take one of those too, Charles." Cubby waved his empty glass in the direction of the man. Turning back to Nina he said, "Of course, we're not sure just *where* he was born, though it's fairly certain to have been somewhere around here."

Flynn groaned.

"Not sure?" Nina asked.

With his hand on her waist, Flynn could feel her practically quiver with curiosity through the tight material of her dress.

Cubby gave Flynn an inscrutable look. "Well, yes. He must have told you. You see, we can only *assume* he was born around here, but it's hard to say with foundlings, you know."

Nina's mouth dropped open. *"Foundlings?"* she repeated.

Flynn grabbed at the drink Charles brought him and swallowed half of it before looking around for some-one—*anyone*—to draw into the conversation and, hopefully, change the subject.

An old sense of shame threatened the edges of his confidence, shame that his parentage was unknown, shame that though his father had chosen him for a son, he'd never lived up to the man's expectations.

"Neil Patrick wasn't really your father?" Nina asked, stepping out of the circle of his arm and laying stunned eyes on him.

Flynn assumed a bland expression. "Don't look so surprised, Nina. In fact, if I were you I'd be relieved."

"People in the village claimed the gypsies left him," Cubby offered with a chuckle. "Can you imag-

43

ine? Though, by God, in some ways he looks like he could be a gypsy, don't you think?"

Nina and Cubby turned to scrutinize him, Nina's expression conveying no small degree of repugnance.

Flynn eyed them back and wondered whether they'd both go away if he drenched one of them with his drink. "I don't think this is necessary," he said. "If you don't mind, I consider my past a private matter."

"Not with those eyes," Nina said. "Gypsies have dark eyes. His are too blue, too pale. Men always get the most beautiful eyes," she added dourly.

"But the hair, nearly black, I tell you," Cubby said, gesturing with his drink. "He could be a gypsy, I think. Part gypsy, maybe."

"This is pointless," Flynn said. He should have known he couldn't count on these two to be tactful. "I'm going to get something to eat. Nina, do you want to come with me or should I leave you here to exploit my past without me?"

"I always assumed he was Irish, like his fa—like Neil Patrick," Nina said, focused on Cubby with a look of fresh appreciation for his sudden status as informer. "So he's not *really* Neil Patrick's son?"

"Did you know Neil?" Cubby asked. For the first time he looked more interested in her words than what she wore.

"Did anyone *really* know Neil?" Flynn muttered rhetorically. "Let's talk about *his* past, shall we? The crook."

"No, I never met him," she said. "He died just before I met Flynn. Terrible. I was such an admirer of his, ever since his early days as a senator in Washington. I would have given anything to meet him. A great man, truly.''

Cubby and Flynn both snorted at once. Then Cubby flushed and downed the rest of his drink. ''Sorry, old chap,'' he muttered to Flynn. ''It's true he was a brilliant man. Brilliant. Single-handedly managed to help my father hang on to the old ancestral estate here. Been in the Lytton family since the 1800's. Weren't for him, Merestun would be a bloody bed-and-breakfast by now and we'd all be living in some go-dawful villa somewhere in Italy. No doubt none of us would have made a *farthing* there, mark my words.''

''So,'' Nina persisted, looking concerned, ''Flynn was a *foundling*. What exactly does that mean? He was left on a doorstep in a basket?''

Cubby's brows furrowed in thought—much to Nina's dismay, Flynn could tell.

''I don't think so,'' Cubby said. ''No, I seem to remember he was too old for that. Just an orphan, I believe. We should ask my mother, she'd remember the story.'' He turned and gazed halfheartedly into the crowd.

''This is fascinating,'' Nina said, looking closer to horrified than fascinated.

''Actually, it was Dorrie Patrick who wanted him,'' Cubby continued, obviously relishing her attention. ''She and Neil were visiting my parents here at the time. Flynn wasn't a baby, though. Seems to me he was five or six, somewhere thereabouts. Tried for months to track down his folks but no one claimed him—so the Patricks adopted him.''

''How incredible,'' Nina said. ''Five or six? Then you must remember something about your real parents, don't you, Flynn? Good heavens, you were probably illegitimate. Do you remember how you got here?''

Flynn polished off the rest of his latest drink. They didn't deserve it, but he gave them the one memory he had of that time, the one memory he simultaneously treasured and reviled. "I remember a woman in a blue dress with a white apron serving me an apricot tart for breakfast.''

Nina scoffed. "That's *it*? You remember a woman in a blue dress and an apricot tart? No wonder they couldn't find your real parents. That's not much in the way of clues.''

Flynn blinked slowly. "That's all I've got, sorry,'' he said, suddenly having to work to keep the words from slurring. He put his glass down on a nearby table.

"Oh, come now,'' Nina chided. "Nothing? Or is it just too embarrassing?'' She was apparently enjoying being nasty.

Flynn looked around for Charles. Perhaps the man fetched water too. "Other than that,'' Flynn said, "my earliest memory is of my father presenting me with a swing set.'' Damn, it was hot in here.

"Here? Or in the States?'' Nina pressed.

"What?'' He refocused his eyes on her.

"Which father? Here?'' She sounded annoyed.

"No, the States,'' he said. "Neil gave it to me.'' He struggled to place the memory, though his head was descending into an uncomfortable fog. "I remember I didn't know what the hell it was.''

"Didn't know what it was? I guess that would confirm the gypsy theory,'' Nina said with a hard laugh.

"Poor little gypsy adopted by the rich Americans. Truly a rags-to-riches story. What a lap of luxury you landed in."

"Took a lot of finagling too," Cubby added. "Neil parted with a good sum of cold hard cash for you, Flynn, arranging an international adoption like that. No doubt more than a few palms were greased. Mother said the authorities didn't want to let you leave the country. He must have really wanted a son."

Flynn ran a hand across his forehead. "Yeah, well, he got one."

The room was unbearably stuffy. Flynn looked around. A group of men by the bar had lit up cigars, and the cloud of smoke over their heads began to drift outward.

"I can't *believe* you never told me this, Flynn," Nina scolded in an unamused voice. "All these months . . . And to think, everyone talks about how much you look like Neil."

A burst of laughter came from the cigar smokers. Flynn looked over at them as they toasted each other with thick short glasses of amber liquid, the very sight of which made Flynn think he was going to be sick.

For a second he thought he saw one of them stand up on a chair to make a toast wearing knickers and a ponytail. But the room was smoky and the man disappeared when he blinked.

"I think I need some air," Flynn said. His head swam as the smell of cigars wended its way through the crowd.

"Wait a minute," Nina said, laying her hand on his arm and turning to Cubby. "Didn't you say earlier something about Flynn being very like his father?"

Cubby laughed and swallowed more of his drink. Flynn watched his lips close over the rim of the glass, saw his Adam's apple rise and fall as the liquid descended. Flynn's own stomach roiled at the sight. Christ, maybe he was coming down with something.

"I meant in business," Cubby said with a pointed smile. "Both of them can be heartless bastards when they want to be."

Ignoring Nina's clutching hand, Flynn tore himself free and lurched toward the French doors. He fumbled with the knob, his throat closing as if he were suffocating.

Locked. Panic sluiced through him.

He had to get out of this room. Sound roared around him suddenly, indistinguishable and loud. He moved to the next set of doors, wondering if he'd have to go all the way down the line of them before escaping. He grabbed the handle, the left side swung open, and he stumbled out onto the patio, slamming the door behind him.

Misty rain sprayed him, bathing his hot face with a cold, bracing drizzle. He inhaled deeply, the crisp air cleansing his smoke-clogged lungs.

Wet tendrils of hair drooped to his forehead, but Flynn didn't budge. He stood motionless on the glistening flagstones, letting the rain slide down his face and drench his wool suit.

What sort of weird episode was that? he wondered, taking another deep breath, then another.

After a minute he opened his eyes and pushed the hair back off his forehead. He turned to look back inside. The party seethed inside the densely packed room. Sleek women in black and glitter, solid men in dark suits, polished animals grouping, dispersing, re-grouping . . . all of them generating heat.

Smoke made the room a gauzy cocoon, a cradle of silk ties and diamonds.

Flynn turned away. The sight made him nauseous. He pressed his palms to the sides of his head, willing the last of the fuzziness away, then slid them back through his hair. He was soaked, but he did not want to return to the ballroom.

In the center of the patio stood a shallow stone pool, lit from beneath by yellow lamps that glowed eerily green through the floating plants and algae. A short stone wall around the pool showed serious signs of neglect. Crumbled rock and mortar lay around its base, and weeds sprang up between the terrace and the wall.

Flynn approached it and sat down, holding his head in his hands. His body felt hot despite the rain, the damp stone upon which he sat comfortingly cool. He was suddenly extremely tired. Maybe this had something to do with jet lag.

With another deep breath he lifted his head and gazed across the terrace to the French doors. Inside, chandeliers glittered like giant snowdrops and the sweet strains of a string quartet—which he hadn't noticed earlier—tinkled like icicles. He hoped they'd just started playing, but he suspected he had simply been too drunk to notice the sound before.

Nina talked with a group of men he didn't recognize. They ogled her slim, sparkling body as though it were a sideshow, one of them staring blatantly at her body while she spoke to another. She looked like a snowflake amongst coals, he thought, particularly when she melted onto one of the men's arms and looked up at him with her slanted cat-eyes. She'd probably asked him to get her a drink, Flynn speculated, and smiled in grim satisfaction as the man disengaged himself from the group and threaded his way through the crowd.

She was beautiful, she was smart, and she wanted to get married, he thought, and felt fatigue descend onto him again like a pile of old blankets. Maybe he could stay out here forever, he mused, let the rain sculpt him into stone, erode him to the shape of these time-worn rocks upon which he sat. He closed his eyes and imagined himself made of stone—maybe one of those pissing boys in the center of a fountain.

He chuckled at the thought, and the laughter echoed as if in a hollow chamber. Flynn's eyes flew open and he swayed on the short wall. Then the whole terrace pitched like the deck of a ship. He grabbed for the wall, but his fingers slipped off the slick stone and he lost his balance.

He crashed backwards into the pool, his shoulders slapping the icy water before the basin swallowed him up.

The brief thought that he must look pretty damned silly crossed his mind before the slimy stems of the water plants twined around his limbs, dragging him deeper into the water. Flynn groped behind him, expecting any moment to feel the bottom of the pool; but he felt nothing—only water and more weeds, thick leafy tendrils waving insidiously and clinging to his grasping fingers like skeletal hands.

Flynn clamped his mouth and eyes shut, kicked his legs out in search of the wall upon which he'd just sat, but felt nothing. He was surrounded by water with nothing solid in reach. It was insane. The pool simply wasn't that big.

Bound by the plants, he tried to swim upward and couldn't. He grabbed hold of the stems and pulled downward in the hope of hitting bottom and pushing up to the surface. But they came free in his hands, pulled out of the murk to cling to his fingers like cobwebs.

He stroked blindly forward, but his hands would move only in slow motion. Plants caressed his face.

With his lungs bursting, his mouth instinctively opened to suck in nothing but water and muck. He gagged, inhaling water through his nose. Panic exploded in his chest.

He was drowning.

Chapter Three

Melisande bowed her head and said a quick prayer. *Lord, let him at least be intelligent.* With a deep breath, she opened the door.

"Here she is," her father said. He came toward her, his hands outstretched and a benevolent smile upon his face. "You look lovely, my dear. Does she not look lovely, Elinor?"

"She does indeed," her mother said.

Melisande took her father's hands and smiled up at him, at once gratified and intimidated by the pride on his face. "Thank you, Papa. Mama."

She turned until her eyes found her mother's. She too radiated pride and beamed at her daughter. The approval on their faces had never been so complete, Melisande thought, and felt the web tighten around her.

She could not help but feel the presence of the man

near the mantel. Whether he loomed large because of the situation or his own air, she could not say, but she could not even glance at him, not until she knew she would not falter. He was tall and ominously still, she sensed, and for a moment she worried that her knees would not support her.

Understanding in her eyes, her mother approached as her father stepped away, toward Bellingham. Her mother's cool hands took Melisande's damp ones and squeezed tightly as she kissed her cheek. "Come, meet Lord Bellingham." Her words were light, but her tone spoke much more. She understood, Melisande knew, even sympathized. Her mother had met her father on their wedding day.

At last Melisande turned and gazed upon the man with whom she was to spend the rest of her life.

Shrewd black eyes studied her from beneath gray brows. He was tall and lean, with gray hair that curled nearly to his shoulders. His face was austere and thin, and a hooked nose cut between the high planes of his cheekbones.

He was not ugly, she saw at once; and he was not, she was very sure, stupid. But there was absolutely nothing in his face of kindness.

She had a moment of wishing she could revise her quick prayer—intelligence was clearly not the quality of most import. This man looked as he ate small children for breakfast.

"Miss St. Claire," he said, his voice neither high nor low, but rather sharp, cleaving straight through her composure. "You are more beautiful than I was led to believe."

The words did not feel like a compliment. He approached and bowed over her hand.

She forced stiff knees to bend into a curtsy. "Good evening, Lord Bellingham." Her voice, thankfully, had not betrayed her fear, though it emerged lower than normal.

They rose. His hand lingered on hers and his eyes glittered. He smiled a smile that did nothing to lessen the carnality of his gaze.

"You look every inch a duchess tonight, my dear," he said, his hand still clasping hers. His thumb traced a path across her skin. "His Grace will be impressed, I am certain."

She tried to regulate her breathing as she watched his gaze drop to and linger on the décolletage of her gown. Resisting the urge to cover herself with her free hand, she murmured, "I hope so, my lord. I look forward to meeting the illustrious Duke of Merestun."

"Yes . . . I believe everyone will be impressed with you." He let go of her hand and turned to her parents. "Everything is in order then. For my part, I am quite satisfied."

Her father glowed, but the smile diminished as the earl held one finger aloft.

"Except . . ." Bellingham arched a gray brow.

Her father stood motionless, his chest still puffed out in suddenly precarious pride.

"I would like," the earl continued, "to spend a few minutes alone with my intended." He inclined his head. "If, of course, it meets with your approval, sir. I think it important that we be at ease with one another this evening. To present the most reassuring image of impending bliss, you understand."

Melisande's blood thundered in her ears as she turned to her parents, her eyes pleading for refusal of this request.

Her father, with obvious relief, bobbed his head and grinned. "Of course, of course," he said. "You're to be alone soon enough, and for a long time, eh?"

"Cornelius," her mother chided softly. "Perhaps it would not be the best—"

"Nonsense!" her father burbled, blushing. "We shall see you at dinner in half an hour, Bellingham."

Bellingham bowed as they left, her father's hand firm on her mother's arm, his face forbidding.

Melisande curtsied as they passed, and watched until the door closed behind them. The *click* of the latch sounded loud.

She turned. Regarding her like a hawk from a high tree branch, the earl stood motionless. His stillness unnerved her. She had never felt more like a mouse.

"My dear." He held out one hand to her. "Come, let me get a better look at you."

She gave him her hand, and he held it out from her side as he looked her up and down. She clasped her skirt in her other hand, unsure what to do.

While he studied her, she noted the rich tailoring of his clothes, the conservative cut, the gold monocle, and the ivory-topped cane that leaned against the mantel behind him. She could not meet his eyes, however, those dark, hot orbs with their unsettling glitter.

"Lovely," he murmured. "So pure to look at." He touched a curl that lay on her shoulder. "I wonder," he added speculatively, "are you as innocent as you seem?"

Melisande's breath caught. She raised her brows, certain she'd misunderstood him. "My lord?"

He grasped her chin between two fingers and turned her head first one way, then the other, as if he were about to paint her portrait. "Hmm, yes. You are a classic beauty, as I'd heard. Classic." Melisande's lips parted, and he grazed one finger illicitly across them.

"My lord!" She took a step backward, but he still gripped her hand. His fingers were hot, his gaze impure. She was suddenly, quite irrationally, afraid of him.

Trembling, she forced her head high and kept her gaze forthright.

He smiled. "I'm sorry. I've been in society so long it's easy for me to forget how delicate young, well-protected ladies can be. Your father tells me you've only spent one season in London?"

"That's correct, sir," she replied. She pressed her lips together. The feel of his thumb tracing patterns on the back of her hand disturbed her. "I did not enjoy London overmuch."

"Is that so?" he asked. "And why was that?"

His fingers moved from her hand up her arm. Repressed shudders slid down Melisande's spine. She raised her chin as his hand cupped her elbow.

"Because . . ." She took a deep breath. "I did not enjoy being trotted out like a horse at an auction."

His black eyes bored holes into her face. His hand gripped her arm. "But you have been claimed now, Melisande," he said quietly.

She opened her mouth to retort and tensed her muscles to jerk her arm away, but instinct took over and bade her hold her temper. She stilled. She could not offend him. Even if she lost her senses and begged her father to terminate the betrothal, she should not shame the earl now.

If he was to be her husband he should be allowed a certain amount of familiarity, she reminded herself. So he spoke forcefully and took a few more liberties than she had been subjected to before. These things were hardly grounds for canceling the engagement. Indeed, she would be a fool to renege on the arrangement. Lord Bellingham was to be a *duke,* she could almost hear her father exclaiming. She would never do better than that— never. If she were to renounce the opportunity now, her father would surely disown her.

Lord Bellingham's hand moved to her shoulder, to the bare skin of her collarbone, and brushed aside a lock of hair.

"Skin soft as sable," he murmured. "Tender, so tender." His fingers, like his eyes, moved to the smooth expanse above the bodice of her dress.

"Lord Bellingham, I beg you," she said, striving not to recoil. She kept her voice even. " 'Tis unseemly so soon. . . ."

His fingers on her hand tightened. "My dear, we're to be married. We're to share the most . . . revealing intimacies. I hope you are prepared for that." His finger traced the line of her bodice. "Though I vow you do blush most prettily," he murmured.

She struggled to gather breath. "We are not married *yet,* sir." She pushed his hand away and stepped back, unable to restrain herself longer.

His black eyes snapped to her face, riveting her where she stood. "No. You're quite right," he said after a moment. "I am gratified to find you're as innocent as you've been presented. You see, one must be careful, very careful, these days." His lips thinned and his tone hardened. "I will not have that which another man has had before me."

Melisande jerked her hand from his grip without thinking, breathless with the implication of his words. "I resent your suspicions, sir. Do you accuse me?"

He rubbed his hands together, ridding them of the feel of her anger, she thought. "Of course not. Your indignity is all to your credit, my dear. You've been, at the very least, well-coached. Now, enough of this dalliance. Shall we join your parents for dinner?"

Melisande gaped at him, her limbs shaking with rage. He took two unconcerned steps toward the door, then turned to look upon her. No shame marred his features, no awareness that he had even offended her. He was unmoved.

With great effort, she bowed her head and moved swiftly past him toward the door. When she reached it, Lord Bellingham's arm snaked around her to grasp the knob. She jumped at the contact and drew away.

With a short bow, he smiled, and she thought she saw a flash of amusement in his eyes.

Averting her gaze, she stepped over the threshold, and immediately thought she heard it again. That sound. But it was not really a sound—more of a sensation. She stopped abruptly and raised her head.

Lord Bellingham stopped short behind her. "Miss St. Claire? What is it?"

She held up one hand. There. Distant and dreamlike. The prince again. Only this time he wasn't laughing.

*   *   *

Images flashed behind Flynn's eyelids like slides. His father's raging face—blood-red with fury, lips distorted around hateful words. His mother, pale and calm, and perfectly still at his father's funeral. He saw Nina, cool and sharp; his friend Bill, rumpled and sad-eyed. He saw his apartment as he wandered it at night—deep in shadows so that only the most subtle light caught the chrome and glass.

And he felt cold.

With a jerk, Flynn realized what was happening. He'd given up. *For God's sake, was he ready to die?* With what felt like superhuman effort, he yanked one arm outward and felt the slippery stems that bound him give way. As if in concert, the rest loosened their hold and Flynn floated free. He twisted, gathered his legs under him, and pushed.

His teeth slammed together as his feet hit bottom and he heaved out of the pool. Water careened outward and over the short stone wall, slapping onto the flagstones. He gasped. Choked. Gasped again. Water sloshed around his legs.

Clutching his arms to his chest he gagged, coughed water, then drew his head back with a long, desperate gasp. He coughed again and heard the sound echo around him. He started to flip his hair out of his eyes, but promptly fell forward, dizzy.

Fear clutched at his heart as he imagined descending once again into the depths of the murky pool. He grabbed the closest object—a marble sculpture on a pedestal in the center of the pool. Still choking, he embraced the statue with both arms, the stone cold on his cheek.

God, did no one inside hear him? Water continued

to churn around his legs, slapping out of the pool with every backward wave.

Finally, though the air rushed over a catch in his throat, he was able to take one, then two, three steady breaths.

Maybe it was best no one had witnessed the spectacle, he thought after a minute of unencumbered breathing. Wounded pride returned with each degree of clarity. How stupid could he be, falling into the fountain? He could not even fathom how it had happened. The damn thing must be spring-fed to be so deep. They should have a sign up, some kind of warning, he thought indignantly.

Telling himself he only needed a minute more to catch his breath, he clung to the statue. The music had become louder, he noted, the buzz of conversation now background to what sounded like an entire orchestra.

He straightened and pushed the hair from his face with a pathetically shaking hand. Drawing one clear, calming breath, then another, he eyed the statue to which he clung. He hadn't noticed it before. In fact, he could picture the pool as it had looked when he'd come outside—shallow and well-lit. No statue.

And now, no lights.

He pushed back and looked at the thing to which he clung for balance. A pissing boy! He would have laughed if he hadn't simultaneously noticed that the water he stood in barely reached his knees. His gaze fell, and he extended one foot outward to feel for where the bottom dropped off. Maybe the pool had once been a well—that would explain the unexpected depth. But despite further exploration he found only the solid floor of the pool.

Flynn turned from the statue and took a tentative step toward the wall. His muscles quivered with adrenaline and his knees threatened to collapse beneath him. At least the rain had stopped, he reflected in an effort to ignore the fact that he had just nearly drowned in a foot and a half of water.

He slid his feet forward, making sure with each tiny step that he encountered firm ground before transferring his weight. The slimy weeds waved around his legs. At last he let go of the statue and lurched toward the wall, bending to grab it with his hands before drawing one sodden leg over the lip to the flagstones below.

When he'd succeeded in getting both feet out of the pool, he dropped to the ground beside it and leaned back against the wall. His sodden clothes slapped the pavement as he sat. The air was warmer than before, he thought. Maybe it was the absence of that chilling rain. He leaned his head back and closed his eyes.

His suit was drenched, his hair dripped water into his face, and his shoes felt clammy and tight. But despite the absurdity of the situation, he felt lucky to be alive. For a moment he had honestly believed he might die. *In eighteen inches of water.* The absurdity of it was the most frightening aspect of all.

Had it been the scotch? Jesus, he'd never gotten so drunk as to even stumble before. How, in little more than an hour, had he gotten so inebriated he'd fallen into a fountain and nearly drowned? The very thought of it caused his insides to shake.

What if he'd died?

He imagined Nina wondering where he'd gone. Cubby would tell her not to worry, probably believing he'd picked up some other woman and was doing her in the coatroom. His reputation had always been far worse than the reality. One of those men with whom Nina flirted would invite her to share his room. Nina would demur in the skilled way she had of keeping all her options open. . . .

He closed his eyes. Maybe she would remember he'd said he was going outside. Maybe she would look for him, step out onto the terrace, see something floating in the pool. . . .

Would she care? he wondered. Well, of course she would *care*. No one wanted to find a dead body in a fountain, no matter who it was. But thinking about it now, he was struck by the conviction that she wouldn't grieve.

The image of his mother at his father's funeral sprang to mind—the same vision he'd had as he'd lain in the pool. So pale and so calm, she'd *looked* bereaved—while inside he knew she felt only relief.

He shook his head. No, Nina might be selfish, but she would not be relieved by his death. Just inconvenienced. He smiled at the thought. Her independence was the thing he'd always liked best about her. Soon enough she would find someone else, another man with the right look and connections. And she would ultimately get what she wanted—if not from him, from another just like him. He was the *kind* of man she wanted, not anyone she couldn't live without.

Which was ridiculous, he told himself, because there was no one person that another couldn't live without. Love was a function of want, and wants changed to suit need, and need was nothing more than a manifestation of weakness.

He pushed himself up straight and thought about getting up. Another minute, he told himself. Just another minute.

Flynn shivered. It hadn't warmed up, he realized, raising his head and opening his eyes. In fact, he believed it was colder. His body must have been in some sort of shock, because now he could see his breath.

He had to get back inside. Resolved, he pushed himself to his feet and stopped, eyes riveted to the French doors across the terrace. Frost lined the window panes making the room look dimmer. The music was louder, though, and he could still see the crowd. Only it was a different crowd. Different-looking. He took a step and stopped. Had they all changed clothes?

He edged forward, clapping his hands to his soaked shoulders in an effort to get warm. Maybe it was just the bridal party dancing, he reasoned. He crept closer to the door, eyes peeled for Nina's short white sequins, or Cubby in his penguin suit.

Oh, hell, he thought with a grimace as he made out the people closest to the doors. He hated affairs like this; they'd turned it into a goddamn costume party.

As he neared the door, he heard a snap overhead and something struck him in the face. He flinched and put a hand to his cheek, glancing at the ground. A twig had broken off and hit him in the face. He looked up to see where it had come from, and immediately stepped back, mouth agape.

Above him, a woman in a long dress climbed out of an upstairs window. Dark stockings and a long heavy gown swathed her legs. The dress swung outward as she brought her second leg from the sill to join the first one planted in the thick vines along the wall. Her foot probed for purchase as the woman dangled from her waist out the window.

Flynn watched, fascinated.

She hung there for a minute, perhaps catching her breath, and then one leg waved upward as she leaned back inside. A second later she pushed something large from the sill, and a bag plummeted to the terrace, narrowly missing him.

The night was dark, but from where Flynn stood he could see the woman slide from the ledge on her stomach until the vines upon which she stood held her weight. Her hands gripped the sill. She looked like a vampire scaling the wall.

What in God's name did she plan on doing? Those vines would never support her all the way down, he thought.

She moved slightly, one foot slipping out of control before she stopped it against the brick. She grabbed at the ivy, holding the sill with one hand now. More twigs clattered to the stones below. She froze, then as quiet descended again, she continued.

Whoever she was, she was not doing this in an attempt to get attention. Stealth cloaked her every movement.

Flynn stepped back again as she found another toehold and let go of the ledge. As he watched her, his heart was in his throat.

She was, he decided, out of her mind.

"Hey!" he called.

The woman started. Her hands clutched at the dried leaves, and one foot slid through the ivy before hitting a substantial vine and stopping. Flynn heaved a deep sigh as she regained a dubious balance and turned her face outward.

"Are you *nuts*?" he managed over his thundering heart. "You're going to kill yourself."

"*Silence!*" she hissed. Her face was pale in the darkness, surrounded by dark hair pinned up on her head. She wore a long cape with a hood that lay flat against her back.

Flynn shook his head, shivered, and stomped his feet. He considered leaving the crazy woman to herself and getting inside to one of the fireplaces. But the way things were going, he didn't feel he could leave her to splatter onto the pavement without first doing what he could to help her.

What he could do to help her, however, was exactly nothing.

"You must be crazy," he called, realizing as he said it the less than helpful nature of the statement. He should suggest something practical. Then again, he realized, practicality might wasted on someone climbing out a second-story window dressed like a pilgrim. "Why don't you go back inside and come down the stairs like a normal person?" he offered.

She slid another short distance, hands grasping at twigs and her dress riding up over thick petticoats. He took a step to be beneath her, wondering at the same time what the hell he thought he'd do if she actually fell.

His heart slowed its violent pace as she steadied

herself, found another vine, and lowered herself farther. She was doing a pretty good job of it, he conceded after a minute, considering all she had to hold on to were some ancient ivy vines and the odd outcropping of brick.

"I cannot go back inside, you fool," she whispered back, once she was closer to him and the ground. "Can you not keep quiet?"

"What for?"

He wasn't sure, in the dark, but he thought she rolled her eyes. Which was pretty damn obnoxious considering he wasn't the lunatic climbing down a wall. He rubbed his hands along the sopping-wet sleeves of his suit.

"Because, you imbecile," she ground out, "I do not want my departure made known."

Flynn cocked his head and watched her. She looked like something off the cover of one of those silly novels his mother was always reading. *The Mad Maiden of Merestun.*

"If they call the paramedics now," he suggested, "maybe they'll get here before you crack your fool head open."

"Keep your voice down!" In her agitation she grabbed a weak vine and lurched backwards as the branch cracked.

"Holy sh—" He stopped himself, shifting again to be beneath her, his arms extended. She swung outward, one hand holding a secure vine and one foot lodged in the vee of diverging boughs. She was going to fall, he thought angrily, and they'd both break their damn necks. She was too far down to consider going

back up, but she was not close enough to the ground to jump.

This had to be the weirdest night of his life. First, he nearly drowned in a foot and a half of water, then he met a woman in a Halloween costume crawling out a window. If he weren't so damn cold it might have been funny. As it was, the macabre danger of the events gave him the creeps.

Flynn glanced around in desperation. If he could find a ladder or something similar, he could help her. But true to the grand nature of the estate, the storage sheds were all unobtrusively out of sight. The gardener was probably the only one who could even find them. God knows Cubby wouldn't have a clue about finding a ladder—or any tool for that matter, Flynn was sure.

With an effort, the girl reached her left hand back to the wall, grabbed at the leaves, and continued to descend. Flynn held his breath, at once marveling over her coordination and cursing her stupidity. Once she got within reach, he grabbed her by the waist and lifted her down.

She was light, slim-waisted, and *warm,* he noted as the folds of her cape covered his frigid fingers. She was also dressed like a hostess from historic Williamsburg.

The second her feet hit the ground she whirled on him.

"Who the devil are you?" she demanded, her English accent crisp and commanding despite her lowered voice.

"Flynn Patrick," he answered automatically. "Who the hell are you?"

She glared at him, then lowered her gaze to scald him with an appraisal of his sodden state. Her hair was dark, flecked now with bits of leaf, and her face was pale. Her skirt hitched up in the front, but still, her shadowed eyes flashed over him like a physical slap. Her displeasure was palpable. Flynn was sure his disheveled appearance projected none of the dignity hers did.

"Are you a servant here?" she insisted.

He laughed. "Are you Batgirl?"

It crossed his mind that she might be one of those singing-telegram people who show up in costume, only to strip during the course of a song. But that usually went on at the bachelor party, not the wedding; and they were usually dressed like a cop or a businesswoman, not a colonial housewife. Then again, he thought, in England, who knows?

She didn't smile. "Surely you're not a guest." The words bristled with condescension.

"Of course I am." Flynn drew himself up, uncomfortably aware of his ridiculous appearance. "I've known the groom since childhood. And I've told you my name, so who are you? For all I know you're some kind of burglar. Maybe I should check your bag for jewels."

Her eyes darted to the bag and back again, alarmed. "I've stolen nothing. I take only what is my own." She raised her chin and glared down her nose at him. "You have a very unpleasant way of speaking."

Flynn looked at her, amazed that the insult stung. "So what?" he retorted, quick-witted as a basset hound. "You have an unpleasant way of acting. I was

68

trying to save your goddamn neck and this is what I get.''

Her eyes narrowed. "There, you see? You're very coarse. No gentleman would swear in front of a lady.''

"No *lady* would climb out a window," Flynn retorted. Take that, he thought, disgusted. He had to get out of here and into some dry clothes. Maybe near-death experiences made people stupid.

The woman lowered her eyes. "You're right, of course. I am no lady, just a lady's maid.''

With the daunting heat of her gaze off him, Flynn could not help noticing the delicacy of her face. Against the dark of her lashes her cheeks appeared moonlight pale. Her hair swept up from her temples and nape, and looked thick, accenting high cheekbones and a long, slim neck. Yet for all her fragile beauty and downcast eyes, her posture was arrogant.

"A maid, huh?" he said.

She glanced to the side, then back at him. "Do you try to stop me?''

He shrugged and lifted his hands. "Hey, I only tried to stop you from killing yourself. Now that you're on the ground I don't care what you do." He shivered, then scowled at the weakness it showed. She was a nut, he told himself. Beautiful, but unbalanced. Let her go, his sane side warned.

She nodded and bent to pick up her bag, eyeing him as if he might snatch it up before she could take it. "Then . . . then I shall be going.''

Flynn stepped back, suppressing another shiver. For all her arrogance, she seemed afraid of him, of what he might do. Well, it was nothing to him if

Cubby liked his maids in colonial garb. And it was nothing to him if one of them decided to quit in the middle of the night.

"Fine," he said. "Don't let me hold you up. I'm just the one who tried to keep you from splitting your head open." He glanced again at her dress. Weird, but it flattered her, he thought. Lithe body and high breasts. He tried to remember what her legs had looked like, then discarded the thought. He wasn't here to pick up women, especially not crazy women. But as she turned to leave, it occurred to him to ask why suddenly everyone at the wedding was dressed so strangely. "Wait—just tell me one thing before you go. If you don't mind."

She turned back and inclined her head. "Go on."

The gesture irritated him, made him feel like a flea. "Why are you dressed like that?"

She raised her brows, shot his own suit an ironic look, and said, "I'm traveling. It's winter."

"Traveling?" he repeated with a laugh. "By horse and buggy?"

Her brows drew together. "I don't believe you need to know how."

One corner of his mouth kicked up. "What do you think I'm going to do, turn the dogs out on you?"

Her eyes widened. "Dogs?"

"Hounds, whatever. All right, then tell me this. Why are all of *them* dressed like that?" He flung a hand toward the French doors, through which the dancers who strayed close were sporadically visible. "Is there some sort of costume thing going on that I don't know about? Because I'll tell you, I don't have my knickers with me."

She smiled slowly, amused in a wary sort of way, and gave his clothing a pointed look. "I wouldn't point that out to anyone. But I believe you made the right choice of dress. It suits you. If, as you say, you are a guest, then I suggest you go back inside. I'm sure they shall welcome you in *that* exquisite costume. But tell me," she added with what could only be interpreted as a delicate sneer, "isn't it a bit late in the season for bathing?"

Flynn forced his arms to stay at his sides, instead of clutching themselves to keep warm. "I slipped," he said, and gestured vaguely to the pool behind him.

"Into the fountain?" Her laughter bubbled into the frigid air, bouncing off the walls of the mansion, before she clapped a hand over her mouth. Her eyes glinted over her fingers.

So that's what is meant by *infectious laugh,* Flynn thought, and found himself smiling in response. Maybe it was the outlandish costume, but the woman exuded something irresistible.

"Go ahead and laugh," he said. "I'm sure it'll be all over Dorset tomorrow how the stupid American nearly drowned in the fountain."

She sobered. "American? You're from America?"

"You couldn't tell? Or are you just trying to make me feel better? Most people here seem to spot us the second they lay eyes on us. And they don't seem particularly happy at the sight."

She looked thoughtful. "That explains your peculiar accent. Where are you from in America?"

Flynn warmed under the woman's interested gaze. "I'm from D.C. Listen, you're learning an awful lot about me and I don't even know your name."

"Deecee," she murmured. "I have not heard of it."

"Washington, D.C.?" he repeated, surprised. "The nation's capital?"

"Ah, you mean the District of Columbia."

"Yeah, right." Flynn's teeth chattered and he clenched them together. For reasons he did not analyze, he didn't want this woman to leave thinking him the biggest fool on the planet.

"Why don't you come inside and I'll tell you all about it. I'm going to catch pneumonia out here, and you could enjoy a little more of the party before you go."

She jerked her eyes back to his. "No, I must go."

"Just one drink?" He flashed his most winning smile. But it must have lost something with the chatter of his teeth, for she turned away.

"I must go," she said again, and hefted the drawstring bag over her shoulder. "Please," she said, looking back at him, "say nothing to anyone about seeing me."

He frowned. "I don't even know who you are. Why, are you avoiding someone? Do you have a car? Let me at least call you a cab."

She eyed him apprehensively. "Is that what people wear in America?" She motioned toward his scrunched suit.

"Trust me, when it's dry it's a very good suit. Armani. A hundred-percent winter-weight wool." That's impressive, he told himself sarcastically, wow her with your wardrobe. "Really, I look great in it," he added with a grin.

"Hm." She looked him over another minute, then

glanced at the pool. At that moment, her eyes widened and her mouth dropped open.

He took a step toward her. "Is something wrong?"

She looked at him with what appeared to be fright. "What is your name again?"

"Flynn," he told her. "Flynn Patrick. Now I've told you twice and you still haven't told me yours."

"Flynn . . ." She took a step backwards and turned her head so she looked at him from the corner of her eyes. "The name is not known to me."

"Nor is yours to me." *Nor is yours to me?* He'd be speaking like Masterpiece Theater before he knew it. Anything to impress the girl.

"Where are you from?" she asked again.

"Washington."

She nodded slowly, looking unnerved.

"D.C." he added again, and she bit her lip. "The District of Columbia, remember?"

The girl looked positively panicked. "And what are you doing here?"

He gave her a half-smile that faded at her solemnity. "I came for the wedding."

Her eyes narrowed. "The betrothal, you mean."

"Whatever you call it here. Cubby and I have known each other for years."

"Cubby?"

"Yeah, Lytton. The groom."

She swallowed and raised her chin, her eyes now wide with certain fear. "The groom, you say. You've known the groom since childhood."

"That's right." Was she dim-witted?

She opened her mouth to speak, but at the same moment a door creaked open and she jumped. He heard her quick intake of breath, and she sank back into the shadow of the wall.

Flynn turned and saw a tall, thin man in knickers, sporting a cane and long gray hair, escort a feather-and-lace-clad woman in an startlingly low-cut dress onto the terrace.

"It's too cold, my lord," the young woman protested. Her cultured British accent held a slightly nasal twang.

"Do not fear. You won't be cold for long, my sweet." Flynn recognized the man's tone—he intended to seduce the girl, the lecherous old coot. "Come, let me warm you."

The woman smiled and brought a fan to her face, snapping it open as smoothly as any BBC-trained actress. "But my lord, what about your lovely fiancée?"

Intrigued, Flynn watched as despite her words the woman moved toward the man.

"She need never know. . . ." the lecher murmured, with a smile in the words that made Flynn sorry for whoever his fiancée was.

They came together in an embrace, and Flynn started to chuckle, throwing a glance back at the woman from the window. But she was gone. He spun, looking around, and spotted her running down a path off the terrace. The bag bounced heavily off her backside, making her gait awkward, and one hand held her long skirt up in front.

"Hey!" he called after her. He even took two running steps toward her, then stopped.

"Who is it?" he heard the seductress behind him say in a stage whisper.

Flynn watched the strange woman disappear into

the garden, swallowed up by boxwoods and darkness. An almost unignorable impulse implored him to follow, to run off into the dark with her. But he stood rooted to the spot.

He had to get inside. He needed dry clothing. He couldn't go charging around the countryside in a sopping-wet suit.

His heart pounded with the desire to follow. His legs itched to move.

Still, he stood motionless.

Good lord, he'd nearly died. He couldn't possibly go chasing after some girl in the dead of night after nearly losing his life. He probably needed medical attention.

His eyes strained against the darkness, reaching out to . . . nothing. She was gone.

Still, he took one step in her direction before reality hit him. Jesus, he was here with a date. He had to find Nina. Despite all the sleazy things he'd been accused of in his life, he'd never ditched one date for another on the same night.

He turned reluctantly back to the party, wishing he'd gotten the window woman's name, and found himself face-to-face with the man in the knickers.

The fact that the guy had curls in his hair and eyed him through a monocle wasn't the oddest part. Oh, no. The oddest part was when the man plucked up his cane, yanked off the round top, and with a flourish unsheathed a three-foot blade that he pointed directly at Flynn's chest.

"State your purpose in spying upon us, sir," the man challenged, "or I shall be obliged to run you through."

Chapter Four

Flynn took a moment to assess the situation. He'd fallen into a fountain, come out soaking wet to find a beautiful woman climbing out a window. Then when she'd run off, he'd come face-to-face with a man in tights wielding a sword.

He knew he shouldn't have come to this wedding.

"Get that thing away from me." He swiped the blade away with his hand and stepped forward with one finger pointed at the man's chin. "And don't threaten me. I've had a *really* bad day."

The man fixed Flynn with an icy stare, which was remarkably effective considering the ridiculous clothes he wore, and said, "I'm sorry to be the one to inform you, sir, but it is about to become worse. Come with me." He sheathed his sword, or cane, and turned toward the patio doors.

Flynn scoffed. "Gladly. Are we going to find Lytton? Because I have a thing or two to say to him about his guests and what they're allowed to bring to his parties. I'm sure it was just an oversight that it wasn't actually printed on the invitation to check your weapon at the door.''

The man stopped abruptly at Flynn's words and turned on him with sudden interest. ''Did you say Lytton?''

''I did. The groom.'' Flynn felt a trickle of something moist drip down his finger. ''The owner of this . . . *bizarre* place.'' He extended a hand to encompass the estate house and noticed a cut, burgeoning with blood, across the center of his palm. The damn blade had been sharp as a razor. What kind of costume was this idiot wearing?

''Did you say *bizarre*?'' the stuffy jerk asked.

Flynn wiped the blood from his palm with his handkerchief and determined that the cut was not dangerously deep, though it certainly could have been.

He looked up. The man was actually smiling at the sight of Flynn's blood.

''Yes, bizarre,'' Flynn said heatedly. ''For one thing, he could get sued if he doesn't fix that damn fountain. So could you for wielding that party-favor of a knife you've got. For another, someone just climbed out an upstairs window with a bag full of something, probably the family jewels. And for a third thing, he's got a lot of nerve inviting people to a wedding and then changing the dress code halfway through.'' Flynn looked the man up and down disdainfully. ''Not that I'd be caught dead in something like that.''

Frost should have materialized on the man's eyelashes, so cold was his glare.

"*I* am Lord Lytton, you peasant, so your lies and insults will not help you out of this predicament. And it's a pity you didn't desist with your abusive talk when you were apprehended, as there was a minute possibility I might have been persuaded to deal with you leniently. As it is, however, you have angered me." He turned to his companion. "Lady Carmine, please go and summon my men. Tell them I have someone here who has referred to them all as 'a bunch of nancy-girls.' I believe they'll deal appropriately with him in that case. And with the utmost expedience, I'd wager."

"Look," Flynn said, his patience for this playacting expiring rapidly, "I don't know what the hell you're talking about, but in case you haven't noticed, I'm soaking wet here. I'm going upstairs to change and then I'm going to find Lytton. *Cubby* Lytton. You and your nancies do what you want."

Flynn shouldered his way around the man and grasped the door handle, flinging the door wide. He strode through and slammed it firmly behind him.

Inside was thick and airless. All around him people were dressed in the same type of elaborate costumes the man on the patio wore, and the chandeliers had been replaced with hundreds of candles that choked the air with smoke and heat. He actually felt as if his drenched suit were beginning to steam.

As he elbowed his way through the crowd, he found himself more and more fascinated with the costumes everyone wore. He wasn't one to notice clothes ordinarily, but these weren't your average rent-a-

Cinderella-costume deals—they looked like they belonged on a movie set. Which was a thought that made him glance around the room to be sure no one was filming and he hadn't accidentally wandered into the wrong part of the house.

No cameras in sight, he noted. And this had to be the same ballroom he'd left, because he'd come in the same door he'd gone out. His eyes searched the crowd—who also appeared to be regarding him—but he didn't recognize anyone. Then again, he wouldn't, necessarily. He was a virtual stranger at this wedding. So he kept his eyes peeled for Nina, who in this crowd would stick out as dramatically as if she were nude.

He didn't see her. Likewise, Cubby, whom he couldn't picture, but would have loved to see, in a getup like the one worn by the man on the patio.

He made it all the way through the ballroom to the great hall, where he stopped in the cool, empty air. An eerie feeling rolled in the pit of his stomach. Here, where earlier there had been area rugs on the bright white marble floors, white walls, and upholstered couches and chairs set up in intimate "conversation corners," there was now intricately carved paneling on the walls, bare marble floors, and a long dining table burdened with food in the center of the floor. He looked slowly around, feeling clammy, his heart rate accelerating.

They could not possibly have done all of this redecorating in the time he'd been out on the patio. Further, if he really thought about it, the whole assembly of people could not possibly have gotten out of their tuxes and cocktail dresses and into those elaborate costumes in that amount of time either.

And yet, this *was* the same house. He knew it for too many reasons to count, but in particular the obvious one that he had never left it. He looked at his watch. 10:45. He'd gone outside about 10:00. He knew because they had cut the cake at 9:30 and he'd already eaten his. So, in approximately forty-five minutes the entire crowd had either changed clothes and redecorated, or something truly weird had happened.

He wondered if he was dreaming. But he'd never had a dream in which he wondered if he was dreaming. Besides, he was still wet from the fountain. And he had the beginnings of a headache from all the alcohol he'd consumed.

Maybe he was hallucinating, he thought with senseless cheer. Yes! Someone had slipped something into his drink and he was now probably making a complete ass of himself in front of everyone. No doubt it was that buffoon of a political science teacher. Though he didn't exactly look the type to be carrying around hallucinogenics on the off chance that someone annoyed him. No matter. It was the only explanation. With any luck Flynn was actually passed out in a bedroom somewhere and this was some kind of drug-induced illusion.

Speaking of which, he was soaking wet and needed to find his room. He should go upstairs and change. Yeah, that'd show 'em, he thought. He'd make everyone watch the guy who'd gotten the mickey strip naked.

"*There* he is. I knew he wouldn't have gone far. The man is quite obviously deranged."

Flynn spun at the sound of the patio man's voice. Beside him, and charging forward, were six other enormous men in brightly colored clothes with what looked like billy clubs and huge old-fashioned pistols.

Sure, it was probably a joke. And he was most likely being made the fool and would rue his reaction for the rest of his life. But because once this wedding was over he was leaving this godforsaken country and never coming back, he took off for the front doors.

The thugs, who looked all too real, with real mean looks on their faces and real weapons in their hands, took off after him.

Flynn didn't have any desire to find out how much more real this dream could get. He reached the tall, heavy-looking doors and with strength born of desperation, grabbed the metal rings and pulled them both open. They careened inward on oiled hinges and crashed into the stone walls behind them. Flynn darted into the rain.

He had no time to think, no time to ponder where he was, he simply charged down the stone stoop and beat feet for the back of the house, hoping to find the garage and his car. Or anyone's car. *Something* to get him the hell out of Dodge.

The garage was there, he saw with relief. Huddled under the rain like a troll under a bridge. He sprinted for it, trying to amuse himself with the thought that he was ahead of the game because he was already wet. But when he got closer to the garage, he saw that it was not the same one he'd seen earlier—the doors were too narrow for one thing, and for another there was the overpowering smell of manure.

He opened the main door anyway and disappeared inside.

Sure enough, the deep snuffling and hay-shuffling of horses were immediately apparent, the pungent, sweet smell almost enough to make him gag. He paused.

Outside he heard voices, and some footfalls thudded near the stable door. Flynn glanced in the nearest stall, pulled open the gate, and stepped inside, crouching below the door in the dark, trying hard to quiet his breathing but fearing he'd pass out from the effort.

He heard the same door open that he had entered, and then the drumming of men's feet on the wooden floor.

"Search the stalls!" one of them called.

"Are ye sure 'e came this way?" another asked.

"Yessir. I saw 'im. 'E slipped in a moment before we did. I'm sure 'e's in 'ere somewhere."

They sounded strangely authentic, Flynn thought. No crowd of onlookers snickered in the background. Nobody seemed to think it was a joke at all. Flynn's uneasiness unfolded into a blanket of dread.

What in God's name could have happened? It sure didn't feel like a dream. And it didn't feel like a drug. It felt surreal as hell, like . . . like . . . like a horse breathing down the back of his neck.

Flynn froze. There was a horse in this stall. *Damn.* When he'd glanced in he'd thought it was empty. But it was dark. And now the huge goddamn beast was standing right behind him, breathing down his neck. The thing couldn't have felt more demonic if it'd been trying.

The horse snorted, and Flynn only just resisted the

urge to leap up and scale the stall wall. Damn, he hated horses. Always had, though the subject had not come up all that often. But now, with the thing standing right behind him, practically threatening him with its hot breath and heavy hooves, he felt his blood race. Big, stupid, mean, ugly animals, he thought, wondering if he might be able to psychically cause the death of a horse simply by hating it at extremely close range. No, he'd more likely just enrage it.

The horse snorted again and pawed at the hay-strewn floor.

"I don't see 'im," someone said, his voice tinged with despair.

"Me either."

"Nope."

A deep voice grunted. "God 'elp 'im if 'e's in wi' old Bones."

The others chuckled malevolently.

Flynn leaned his head against the wooden wall of the stall and closed his eyes. He could only assume he was, in fact, in with old Bones as no one had checked this stall.

"Someone go get Frish. 'E's the only one who can 'andle Bones. We got to open up that last one and devil take me if I'll do it wi' out someone got a 'old a that godless beast."

"I'll go." Footsteps ran past the stall toward the door and out.

Flynn felt the godless beast nudge him in the back. The horse pawed the ground again.

"Aye, 'e's interested in somethin' in there," one of the thugs said, then laughed.

Minutes ticked past. Flynn kept his eyes closed and

his breathing even. If this horse really was the devil they seemed to think, maybe when they opened the stall the thing would go so berserk he could get out in the confusion. He tried not to think about what would happen if he were the one the horse went berserk on.

Old Bones nipped at Flynn's hair.

Flynn ducked his head and covered it with his hands. His feet were starting to fall asleep.

Bones nipped at his shoulder and pulled his jacket up. When Flynn didn't respond, the horse dropped it and pushed at him with his snout. Then he snorted a blast of warm, wet air onto Flynn's hands.

There was shuffling outside the stable door, and then, apparently, Frish arrived.

"I don't know," an old man's voice was saying, moving closer. "If he's in there with Bones there's gonna be hell to pay with the master tomorrow. He don't like anybody messing with old Bones. And Bones's the type to get all wrought up, like, and not be fit riding for a week. That won't make the master happy. We had him here nigh on two weeks now, and I never yet seen no one ride him 'cept the master." The reedy voice approached the stall. "He'll let me put a lead on him, take him outside a spell, but he ain't one to tinker with. I hope he's not too riled up now. I'd hate to have to call the master, and him getting ready to announce his betrothal and all."

"Well, it aren't us who be messing 'im up," the gruff one said. "It's the damned infiltrator who's in that stall. 'Iding, 'e is."

"The infiltrator?"

"That's right. Lord Lytton found 'im tryin' to bust

into the party and then 'e escaped. Only we got 'im now—don't we, ye sorry bastard?'' This last was said loudly, and followed with appreciative laughter by all present.

Flynn had two choices. Sit there and wait to see what happened when they opened the stall. Or start something himself and hope to take them by surprise.

As the latch rose and time ran out, Flynn's muscles made the decision. Without thought, he sprang up, shouted an obscenity, and grabbed the stall gate to pull it between him and the horse.

Bones responded immediately by rearing up on his hind legs and punching the air with his front hooves. With an ear-splitting sound the horse bounced on the ground and reared up again, hooves hitting the gate on the way down again. The gate slammed back and Flynn's body hit the wall, the breath knocked out of him.

Shouts of "Whoa!" and "Grab 'im!" filled the room, but all Flynn could see were flailing hooves over the top of the wooden gate. Wild whinnying screeched through the enclosure, and the thunder of hooves meeting wood and then earth made Flynn feel as if the horse had jarred the whole world.

The men sounded closer. Maybe they were going to try to corner the beast and rope him that way. Flynn didn't know. All he knew was that he had to make his move, and fast.

He grabbed the wooden bars that served as the upper wall between stalls, and scrambled up until his foot found the top of the gate. Turning swiftly, he saw the three men squeezed into the stall, only one of whose attention was on him. The others focused on the fighting horse and the lethal hooves that whistled through the air just in front of them.

Flynn flattened himself against the bars and stared at the horse, whose body bumped the gate upon which he stood. He clung to the wooden bars, bracing himself for the next blow to his foothold.

Eventually, the big guy, the leader, noticed him too. His dark eyes narrowed and he backed out of the gateway. Flynn knew immediately what he intended. The man could grab him through the bars and either push him into the wild animal's frantically battling hooves, or lash him to the bars to keep him there until they got the horse calmed. Then they could do whatever they wanted to him.

There was no time to think.

With a muttered curse, Flynn pushed off the gate and landed square on the back of the demonic animal. The horse screamed in protest and reared up again. Flynn twisted his fingers through the mane and pressed every ounce of strength he had into his legs, squeezing the body of the horse between them to hang on, his body prone on the animal's neck.

The horse shot forward. Men fell backwards, pitching headlong to the floor and into the hay for cover as the giant black horse leapt toward the exit. Over the threshold and into the aisle it sprang, taking just a second to breathe before rearing and taking off for the open door to freedom.

For one wild moment Flynn felt exhilarated. As the horse galloped headlong into the darkness, he was half-tempted to sit up and look back over his shoulder at the scattered, terrified thugs. He imagined their anger and frustration as he let out a whoop of triumph, followed by a maniacal laugh.

But reality quickly set in, and he realized he was clinging to the back of a speeding bullet with no control, little balance, and more fear than was healthy for a red-blooded American male.

The horse didn't waver in indecision. He flat-out galloped a beeline from the stables toward the road in the opposite direction of the house, which was the only good thing about the situation at this point. Flynn considered throwing himself off the horse when he got to a field, or someplace that looked like a soft landing, but when he dared glance down at the ground, it seemed to be moving past inordinately fast.

"Whoa," he tried softly, thinking to calm the horse with his voice. But it came out "Wuh-oh-uh-ohhh" as the motion of the horse beneath him jerked the air from his lungs. His perch along Bones's neck moved rhythmically up and down, and after the first few minutes it actually wasn't that rough a ride, for all the speed they had. Flynn was damned if he'd try to move, however. He had no desire to hit the ground at this pace, and using his voice had been enough of a dare.

They sped through the dark until they came to a dirt road and the horse veered to the right. Flynn slid sideways, his heart lodging in his throat, but he managed to maintain his hold and slid back upward fractionally.

God knows where he'd end up, Flynn thought fatalistically, but it had to be better than where he'd been.

*   *   *

Melisande wasn't sure whether she first heard or felt the thundering hooves behind her, but when she realized what was happening, her heart felt as if it had stopped dead in the middle of her chest.

They were chasing her.

She dashed into the forest by the road and crunched into the underbrush. The cold of frost seeped through her boots, but she continued into the trees until she felt she was far enough that she would not be detected. Crouching low, she peered through the foliage toward the road.

Sure enough, moments later a horse thundered by. A great, dark animal with one white hoof. Melisande gasped. The rider crouched low over the beast's neck, but she was sure she knew who it was.

Bellingham. He'd come after her.

As she'd walked and the night had gotten colder, she'd been having second thoughts. Could she make it to London before scandal broke? Would her aunt help her out of this dreadful situation? Would her father ever speak to her again? But the fear she felt at seeing Bellingham on that charging steed, racing after her for all the world as if he would sweep her up, lock her in his dungeon, and throw away the key, made her realize again that she could never be married to him.

It wasn't just that he'd been cold, nor was it his rude behavior when they met, or his reputation for lechery. It wasn't even significant that he was seducing Lady Carmine on the terrace when Melisande had met that strange man as she'd left. It was the startling, awful discovery that he'd been responsible for the death of one of his servants.

Daphne had told her, reluctantly, after supper, and she'd had it straight from Bellingham's valet. Apparently Bellingham had had the poor girl lashed to a tree in the dead of winter for disobeying. No one was really sure precisely what she'd done—though the valet alluded to the girl's purity and the likelihood that she'd denied the earl her favors—but in any case nothing deserved such harsh punishment, the valet had stated. The poor maid had died of exposure.

Of course Melisande couldn't marry someone like that. Though she was not one to listen to idle gossip, she felt sure this story was true. She could sense it. So could Daphne. The man had cruelty running through his veins; she'd known it the moment she'd seen him.

Melisande sat still in the underbrush, waiting for the inevitable search party to come galloping after Bellingham's prize-winning stallion. But no one came. She listened hard, even put a palm to the ground, but heard and felt nothing.

Slowly, she crept out of the forest and onto the road, dragging her bag behind her. Once again she knelt and placed her palm flat on the ground. Nothing. Silence ruled the air. She exhaled slowly. Her breath fogged in the cold.

This was odd. Decidedly, unaccountably odd. She rose to her feet and looked back down the road from whence the rider had come. It was a pitch-black corridor in both directions.

Surely he wouldn't have come alone, she thought, confused. Perhaps it hadn't been him. But she'd know that horse anywhere. She'd heard him described. A gorgeous, untamed animal that Bellingham abused so that no one else could ride him. Black as coal except for that one white stocking. It had to have been Marlyebone.

She was just turning back for the road to the London coach when, like the devil incarnate, something huge and black hurtled from the trees on her left to the road in front of her.

Melisande screamed and the horse reared up in front of her. *Marlyebone*. Melisande dropped her bag and ran for the forest. Tree limbs whipped her face and grabbed at her skirts as she plunged into the depths of the forest. Behind her she heard the horse charge after her.

"Go away!" she screamed, her voice disappearing into the dark. "Leave me, please!"

"Wait!" a man's voice yelled, imbuing her with the energy to continue.

She charged onward. If Bellingham was capable of lashing a servant girl to a tree for disobeying, what would he do to a woman who spurned him before the world?

Fear kissed her heart and blood pounded through her veins. The deeper into the forest she plunged the darker it became, until she was no longer sure which direction she headed, nor even if the rider still pursued her. She knew only that she had to keep running.

Her lungs near to bursting, she took a sharp right turn away from a snarl of bushes, caught her toe on a root, and tumbled headlong down a steep embankment. Rolling, rolling, rolling, she felt her hair pull free from its pins and her cloak wrapped around her legs. As her hands and arms scrabbled for purchase, the ground scratched them to ribbons. Just when she thought she might finally be slowing, a sharp rock dug into her ribs and another caught her in the temple.

The already dark night went black.

She awoke some time later to a blast of warm breath on her neck. It was still dark and above her stood Marlyebone. Muscles protesting, Melisande tried to rise, and felt a sharp pain in her ribs and a dizzying fog in her head. Nevertheless, she pushed herself up.

The horse pawed the ground beside her, his head hanging docilely. She reached out a hand to stroke his face, but he pulled back a step.

"There, there, Marlyebone," she whispered. "Where's your master, eh? Did you leave him behind?"

The horse wore no bridle or saddle. Even a halter was absent. She tried to picture Lord Bellingham riding the stallion bareback, and couldn't. He was such a stickler for appearance, she thought. To be riding without tack, like a savage, would be quite out of character.

But then who had been clinging to the stallion's back when she'd seen him on the road? And who had pursued her so persistently through the woods? On the one hand it made sense that it was someone other than Bellingham, for surely if he were looking for her he would have amassed a search party. Unless he was ashamed of her flight and wished to keep it a secret. But she could not imagine him offering this stallion to anyone to ride for any purpose.

Melisande rose slowly to her feet, wincing with every movement, and looked carefully around. No one stood watching or waiting. Whoever had been on Marlyebone's back had disappeared.

She stood and gazed at the horse. If she left him, would he find his way back? She couldn't take him with her. That would be stealing.

She started to climb the hill she'd rolled down, in an attempt to go back the way she'd come, but the pain in her side and her head made the exertion impossible. Instead she took a deep breath, chose another direction, and started walking.

At first the horse simply watched her go. But after a minute she heard his slow, plodding footfalls behind her.

She hadn't gone far when she came upon a path. Choosing a direction at random, she continued on, this time with more hope; a path generally led somewhere. She had walked perhaps a quarter of a mile, Marlyebone still behind her, when she heard a low thrashing in the trees off to her right. She stopped. Behind her, Marlyebone stopped. She listened.

There it was again. Then she heard a moan. And a curse. Marlyebone pricked up his ears and bounced his head twice, nickering softly.

Melisande's heart raced again. Could it be Bellingham? Perhaps he'd been unseated and was lying in the forest injured. Should she go and try to help? But what help would she be? And then he would have caught her.

She wrestled with her conscience. Half of her desperately wanted to flee, but the other half could not let her leave a man obviously wounded in the woods with no one to help him.

That's just what he did to that servant girl, she

reminded herself. Left her alone to die, tied to a tree. Perhaps this is merely divine retribution.

She stood awash in uncertainty, biting her lips. If she were to leave whoever it was in the woods wounded, perhaps direly, they could die. And if she left them and they died, it wouldn't be God's will, it would be hers, for she would have had the opportunity to try to help. She knew what her responsibility was. She must help, if she could.

Unable to concede this to herself fully, she decided to go forward as silently as she could and try to assess the damage. After all, it could still be someone else—someone who'd stolen the horse, which would not make it advisable for her to help—or he could only have minor injuries.

She stepped slowly into the undergrowth.

Chapter Five

Flynn groaned again and held his head. Leaves tickled his cheek, and cold from the damp soil seeped through his clothes. He hadn't thought he could get any colder, but lying there in the dank forest, he found himself trying to remember what death by hypothermia was reputed to be like.

"You!"

Flynn nearly jumped out of his skin. He scrambled to a sitting position, his head spinning, and looked around for the source of the voice.

She stood next to a tree, the woman from the window, one of her hands braced on its trunk and her dark hair half-pulled up, half-streaming around her face. He blinked at her.

"You *stole* Lord Bellingham's horse? Are you *mad*?" She glared at him, outrage and incredulity on her face.

He glanced past her and saw the demon animal from Merestun a few paces behind the woman.

"You keep that thing away from me," Flynn said, his voice gravelly and his head splitting with the sound. He backed up against a tree and shot the animal a look of pure malice. "If I never lay eyes again on that insane son of Satan, it won't be long enough for me." He followed this up with a string of obscenities he believed perfectly suited to describe the wretched creature.

Her face took on a look of disgust.

"The damn thing stole *me,* not the other way around," he continued, incensed. "I was just trying to get away from the lunatics at Merestun." He paused, realizing that though he'd apparently escaped from the lunatics at Merestun, her presence confirmed that he was still in the bizarre dream he'd awakened to from the fountain.

"Why are you following me?" Her voice was calm this time, her eyes cold, her chin haughty. "Did *he* send you? Did you tell him you saw me leave?"

Flynn laughed slightly and shook his head. "Believe me, I'm not following you. That devil Bones was, maybe, but not me. Trust me, I had no say in the matter whatsoever."

"What did you have to escape from at Merestun? I thought you were a guest."

He glanced up at her and saw the flash of sarcasm on her face.

"I thought I was too. But that old fart on the patio thought differently. After pulling a knife on me, he called his buddies and tried to have them teach me some sort of lesson. I don't normally run from a fight, but when it's six to one ... well, I'm not a fool.'' He exhaled deeply and looked up through the tree branches, the steady rain plummeting onto his face. ''You know, I didn't even want to come to this wedding.''

''So why did you?''

''My mother ...'' He trailed off, lowering his eyes to her. It sounded pathetic; he could see it on her face. ''I felt ... obligated.''

One corner of her mouth lifted. ''Surely you could have told your mother you didn't want to come. Or do you still cling so tightly to her apron strings?''

Flynn grimaced and shook his head, studying her.

''Why are you here?'' he asked.

She looked surprised. ''I beg your pardon?''

''I mean, why are you even talking to me? It's obvious you don't want to, so what are you doing here?''

''I ... I heard you moan. I thought you might be injured.'' Self-possession returned quickly. ''Are you?''

He scoffed. ''Just mentally.''

Her dark eyes were steady upon him.

''Look,'' he said. ''Like I said, I don't know what's going on here. I'm not—I'm not from here ... I'm not sure what to do, everything is so ... weird. You've treated me with nothing but contempt, so I don't expect much; but I'm thinking maybe ... maybe what I should do is go to London and try to find my way home from there. Can you help me with that? Can you at least point me in the right direction?''

The moment stretched long while she thought

about it. "I am going to London," she said slowly, watching him.

He wasn't sure how excited to get about this. She certainly didn't look pleased at the prospect of them heading in the same direction.

"Are you?" he prompted, half-wondering if she might deliberately mislead him.

She nodded. "Perhaps, if circumstances permit, we could be of some help to each other."

He nodded back, massaging his ankle. "Yeah, that's what I thought."

"It would be best if I did not travel alone. London is but a day and a half's travel by coach, but it would look exceedingly improper for me to venture forth without assistance. I'd planned to hire a maid and footman in town, but I'm afraid word might spread and then Lord Bellingham would know where to find me. I have the means to pay your way as well as mine."

"So we'd travel together for London," Flynn said, feeling the first touch of optimism since this nightmare started. "That's fine, that's great." This girl didn't think much of him, but she at least wasn't going to have him arrested, or beaten up, or whatever else they'd planned at Merestun.

And once he got to London surely things would be normal. Nina would be pissed, but even that would be welcome. Besides, there was not much he could do about it now. Cubby would take care of her, he was sure.

"You can be my manservant—"

"Your what?"

"—and we can take Marlyebone and turn him in

at Tunbridge. We'll say we found him, and they'll return him so Lord Bellingham won't come after you for thievery. We can hire a coach at Tunbridge. I think traveling with a manservant would be appropriate.''

She bit her lip, thinking. Then she smiled, and Flynn felt the bottom of his stomach drop out. Christ, she was pretty.

''You're taking this costume thing a little seriously, aren't you?'' he said. ''Why don't we just rent a car?''

She gave him a brief, odd look, then looked him over from head to toe. ''We'll also get you some clothes. Something appropriate for my servant. Pity we can't get livery so you would appear to be my footman, but no matter. Now, you get Marlyebone and we'll start for Tunbridge. It must be very late by now so we must hurry—''

''Oh, no,'' Flynn said, rising slowly to his feet. Every muscle in his body hurt, and he must have sprained his ankle because it throbbed like mad. He groaned.

''I beg your pardon?'' she said.

''I said no. I don't know what the hell you're talking about with footmen and maids, but if we go on this little venture together, *I'm* not going to be any servant. I've suffered enough indignities for one day.''

He looked at her, an unsettled feeling in the pit of his stomach. She wasn't kidding around about all this, he could tell. And if he hadn't just had the experience with the patio man and his thugs, he'd think she was deranged. But as it was, reality seemed to be bending in her favor.

"What do you propose?" she asked warily.

"Why don't *you* be the servant, huh?" Even as he spoke the words, he feared he was allowing an unnatural set of circumstances to take over his life. But something urged him on, something in the way things were going indicated he might really need this girl. "In fact, if you're looking to stay incognito, you acting like *my* servant would work much better, don't you think?"

"Be serious," she said, frowning. "I couldn't possibly travel as a servant. If anyone were to find out, my reputation would be in tatters. It's out of the question."

"Come on, it's perfect," he continued, angered by her superiority. "Who would believe an uptight little snob like yourself would play the servant? It's the ultimate disguise."

She drew herself up. "That is no way to talk to a lady. You should know as well as I do that someone of my station could not recover from a scandal such as that."

"*Your* station? What about mine? I mean, I've got some pride too, you know. Not to mention that I don't owe you a thing, least of all hard labor all the way to London."

"Fine, you have your pride. But I see no other option. If you do not travel as an inferior, people shall assume the worst about us and that is unacceptable." She paused. "Which, unfortunately, would leave you on your own for finding London."

He looked at her with reluctant admiration. "Why, you clever girl, you. That's blackmail, that's what that is."

She shrugged, unashamed, but not proud either.

"I think a compromise is in order. I'll play your brother," he offered. "Since you're so worried about appearances, it's the perfect solution. No one would suspect your own brother of wanting to jump your precious body."

He wasn't sure in the dark, but he thought she blushed.

"I don't have a brother. People would see through the charade as soon as we arrived in London. And then they really would think the worst."

"We wouldn't use it in London. And if you haven't really got a brother, that means nobody'll be coming after me for impersonation."

She laughed cynically. "No, they'll just be coming after you for thievery. Bellingham will probably notice the absence of his prize stallion before he'll notice *my* absence. And then you'll be in trouble. No, it's much better for you to travel as the servant."

"I don't see how that would help me any. Besides, did you ever think Bellingham might assume *you* stole the horse? After all, you're the one making the great escape. I'm just some nut passing through that he's probably already forgotten about."

The girl's face went slack and her hands rose to cover her mouth. She stared at him. "I . . . I hadn't thought of that," she said in a small voice. "Surely not . . ."

Something inside Flynn went soft with pity. She looked truly horrified. Maybe he should mention that no less than six men saw him take off on the horse. But then she might abandon him because they'd be chasing *him*. He wondered what she was afraid the pompous Bellingham would do to her.

"Look, if we both just get the hell out of here, Bellingham won't be either of our problems. Let's just get to Tunbridge and hammer out the details there, all right?"

She nodded slowly. "Yes, I suppose at this hour there won't be any who would recognize me. I'll just be a gentleman's daughter who met with a mishap on the road."

"Sure, we were in some kind of accident."

"My maid . . . perhaps my maid was injured and taken to a nearby cottage. I'll have to hire another tomorrow."

"Fine, whatever. Let's go."

Flynn brushed himself off and thought greedily of a warm bed. To drift into unconsciousness in any sort of bed, or anything far from the back of a wild stallion, struck him as heaven. With some luck, he'd wake up tomorrow in his room at Merestun with Nina beside him and all of this just a weird, bad memory. Of course it would be an angry, seething Nina, but even that would be all right. All he wanted was out of this crazy nightmare.

The girl looked around her, then sighed and put her hands to her temples.

"What's the matter?" he asked.

"My bag," she said. "I dropped it when you galloped by. I fear it's gone now. I have no idea where I was at the time."

"Do you know where you are now?"

She looked around at the blackness and trees surrounding them. "Not exactly."

"Then how are you going to get us to London?"

She pulled her cloak closer around her and crossed her arms under it. "If we find a road, I can find London. See here, there's the path I was following when I found you. Surely it leads somewhere."

They started walking, the horse's hooves crunching behind them in the underbrush.

"By the way, what's your name?" Flynn asked.

She looked startled, then laughed sheepishly. "Oh! You're quite right. I am Melisande St. Claire."

She said it so prettily, Flynn repeated it. "Nice to meet you, Melisande St. Claire." As he extended his hand, she actually bowed her head and curtsied to him. "Flynn Patrick," he added, taking the hand she offered, palm down, and shaking it. "So what do people call you—Mel? Melisande is quite a mouthful."

She gave him an odd look. "Perhaps it would be best if you called me 'Miss St. Claire,'" she said, the icy tone creeping back into her voice.

"Perhaps it would be best if I called you Miss Smith, wouldn't it? Isn't the point that you don't want to be recognized?"

"Oh, yes. Good thought. I shall be Miss Smith then. And you shall be—"

"Mr. Smith."

She opened her mouth to protest, and he added firmly, "Your brother."

She closed her mouth and he laughed. "Don't worry. I have no desire to present myself as your husband, be thankful for that. No, I think your brother is a good compromise. No bedroom rights, but no sleeping in the servants' quarters either."

"Sir," she said breathlessly, "I'm going to have

to ask you to please refrain from using such talk in my presence. I really find it most . . . dis . . . turbing.''

He'd thought for a moment she was going to say ''disgusting,'' but she'd obviously thought better of insulting him. Apparently she was so worried about either her reputation or her safety, she didn't want to jeopardize his accompanying her to London. How interesting, he thought. She solicited his help despite the fact that she felt threatened he might jump her body at any moment. How would that help her reputation?

He shook the confusion off. No matter what, he needed her help, so it worked out fine.

''Okay, okay, I won't talk about bedroom rights again. Though I have to say I think you're being pretty prudish about all this. I mean, who in this day and age is really going to comment whether we share a room or not? Are people so old-fashioned around here? I mean, we are almost into the twenty-first century.''

He knew as he said the words they would produce a response, but he did not want to think what it would be or why. He guessed he'd known all along the theme of this dream, but he hadn't wanted to confront the gist of it until now.

She turned her head and looked at him as if he'd grown another head.

''What did you just say?''

''Only that we could be boyfriend and girlfriend, you know. Significant others. A couple traveling through the country. What difference would it make to anyone?''

She turned squarely in front of him, and before he knew what she was about she'd slapped him hard across the face.

"What the—Why the hell did you do that?"

"I am a *lady,*" she ground out between clenched teeth. "And you would do well to remember it. You will therefore treat me with the respect my position deserves or we shall part here and now. I don't care if you *are* mad, I will not be treated like a common strumpet. My reputation is spotless and shall remain so or *you* will pay dearly for it." She took a moment to breathe in anger. "And another thing, you will watch your language around me. Perhaps you speak coarsely in front of ladies in America, but I will not tolerate it. Nor will any decent soul worthy of keeping company with me in England. So, you will not touch me, you will not speak ill in front of me, you will rise when I enter a room and bow when appropriate, you will help me in and out of carriages, you will carry my bag, and you will generally act as unlike the natural savage you are, or you will not be permitted to accompany me. Furthermore, if you cannot abide by these rules, I may feel compelled to turn you in to Bellingham himself once I arrive in London."

Flynn stood speechless for a full half a minute.

"And finally," she said, looking at him askance, "you know perfectly well it is the dawn of the nineteenth century. I don't know why you talk the way you do, but I do not believe you are as deranged as you pretend."

Flynn felt the blood drain from his head. "The dawn of the nineteenth century," he repeated in a flat voice.

"The year of our Lord eighteen hundred and fifteen." She looked at him suspiciously. "Which you know perfectly well."

He laughed, feeling his head spin, and put a hand to his brow. "Well, I have to say, this isn't totally unexpected." For some reason he felt he had to keep talking or he would pass out. "I mean, I haven't seen a car for miles. No lights, no airplanes. The way you're dressed . . ." He motioned toward her gown. "And the nut back at Merestun." Images of the couples dancing in the ballroom, the realistic costumes, the sharpness of the patio man's blade. He closed his fingers over the drying cut on his palm. "This is by far the weirdest dream I've ever had."

She looked at him, leaning slightly away from him. "I feel compelled to confess, I do not understand what you say. You use a great many words I have never heard before. Are you . . . that is to say, you're not . . . you're not *actually* crazy, are you?"

Flynn felt the beginnings of hysterical laughter hit his throat. He suppressed it and smiled instead. "I'd be the last one to know that now, wouldn't I?"

She shrugged, taking a step backward.

"Listen, Mel, I'm not crazy, but I'm having kind of a . . . weird problem. You'll probably *think* I'm crazy when you hear it, but I'm not."

"What is it?" she asked with obvious reluctance.

"Well, you see, I seem to have, somehow, traveled backward in time. Strange as it sounds, I live in America in 1998. Where I come from there are cars and airplanes and computers and microwaves . . ." Noting the look on her face, he stopped. "Well, never mind. Suffice it to say, I'm a little surprised to find myself in the early nineteenth century, as you said. So I'm going to need some help getting around, apparently. Do you understand?"

"You *are* mad." Her face was stony.

He sighed, then shook his head. "Maybe. I don't know. But that's the situation, okay? Just so you know."

They walked for what seemed like hours after that, mostly in silence, with the horse plodding behind them. They came upon a road after a time, and Melisande turned decisively in one direction. Flynn wasn't sure if she actually knew where it led or if she was putting on a show of confidence for his sake. In any case, he was too tired and too confused to bicker about it.

Flynn's mind turned over the events of the day and the layer upon layer of evidence that this was, somehow, 1815, until he felt he could no longer think about it. From here on out he was going to react, pure and simple, knowing that this whole scenario couldn't possibly be real. In fact, it was so impossible he ought to just have fun with it.

But that resolution didn't last past the subsequent musings over whether he was seriously insane or the victim of some mind-altering drug. This couldn't be a dream, he kept thinking. It was too real, too long, too painful.

Flynn's ankle was swollen and numb by the time they arrived in Tunbridge. To call the place a "town" would be to use a massive overstatement, he reflected as he hobbled along the one muddy road that ran between about eight houses. From the smell, Flynn assumed it was a farming town with the animals allowed liberal use of the street as their toilet.

No lights shone, no cars were in evidence, and no telephone poles or electrical wires were in sight,

Flynn noted again. The town was as primitive as he imagined deepest, darkest Africa to be. In fact, several of the houses had thatched roofs and what looked like mud walls.

Thankfully, the establishment at the end of the row was a larger building of wood with a faded, swinging sign over the door proclaiming itself an inn. The "Tunbridge Inn," not surprisingly.

"You tend to Marlyebone," Melisande said in her dismissive tone. "I'll procure the rooms."

Flynn ran a hand over his eyes. "You know, I think he likes you better. Why don't you tend to him and I'll get the rooms?"

"Because . . ." She paused, obviously wanting to add "you idiot." "I have the money."

"Okay. Here's the problem. This horse hates me and I have no real affection for it either. I also don't have any idea how to find, or even get it into, a stall. So you can give me the money and I'll get the rooms or we can do both together."

Melisande took a deep, pained breath and walked back toward him, past him, and around the side of the inn to a covered paddock. Bones went directly to the hay scattered meagerly in the bin and began eating. Melisande took a rope from a nail on the wall and casually placed it over the horse's head, tying the other end to a post.

She turned to him with a bland look.

"Okay," he said, "so it was easier than I thought it would be."

At that she nearly smiled. He could tell she suppressed it.

"Come along," she ordered.

They traipsed back around to the front of the inn.

The inside was dim, dank, and decidedly unwelcoming. Dark wood floors and walls were naked of any rug or decoration. A small, scarred reception counter backed up to a wall with a closed door. Flynn got a creepy feeling from the place, as if the building had been deserted for some years after a grisly murder.

Melisande picked up a bell from the counter and swung it heartily, shattering the silence without batting an eye. The two of them stood in the silent aftermath of the bell and listened. A distant shuffling sounded from behind the closed door. Flynn glanced at Melisande. She wore a determined expression, staring at the door as if she could will whoever it was to come to her.

Eventually the door creaked open and a man who resembled no one so much as Rip Van Winkle emerged. His clothes were rumpled, his long beard and hair matted, and he walked with a stoop-shouldered limp. If he wasn't so tall, he could have been one of Snow White's dwarfs. Stinky, maybe.

"Good evening," Melisande said coolly.

The man grunted in return, barely looking at her.

"We require two rooms."

"For the whole night?" the man asked in a surprisingly high voice.

Flynn understood what he meant and started to smile, but Melisande looked down her nose at him and said, "Certainly," as if he must be a half-wit.

The man mumbled something, and Melisande pulled a heavy string purse from her cloak. Flynn could hear the substantial *chink* of coins inside, and noted that the man behind the counter could too. The old geezer looked into her face with much more interest as she slapped two small coins on the counter.

"Thank you, mum. You sure you won't be staying but one night?" he asked solicitously.

"I'm sure." She tied up the purse and pulled it back under her cloak to store in some unknown location. "My—brother"—she pushed out the word with visible distaste—"and I have no luggage."

Flynn grimaced, realizing that he would be wearing this damn tuxedo—which was handsome and relatively comfortable when pressed and dry—for at least another day.

"We were involved in a carriage accident some distance down the road," Melisande continued. "My maid was injured and taken to a nearby cottage. I shall require another. Perhaps you know of someone who could help me?"

"Aye, mum. I'll see about a girl for you." The man moved the coins around in his hands like worry stones.

"How far is it to London?" Flynn asked the proprietor.

The old man, who had bent over to retrieve the room keys, straightened abruptly and stared at him. "Where you from, guv'ner?"

"The States," Flynn said. Then, at the man's bewildered look, he added, "America."

The milky eyes widened and the man whistled between his teeth, sending a couple of wisps of beard aflutter. "All the way *here* from America?" Then he gave Flynn the once-over and showed a gap-toothed smile. "That what they wear in America?"

"As a matter of fact, yes," Flynn answered testily.

"If they're very rich and very well-dressed, that is."

The man wheezed a sound something like a laugh. "Well, I've to say it makes you look a bit cakey to me. Look as if you come from the clothmarket, you do, though that's where you be going now." He bent over again and picked up the keys, chuckling to himself.

"What the hell is he talking about?" Flynn muttered, and saw Melisande suppress another smile.

The old guy led them both up a set of bare wooden stairs, and put Melisande in a room at the top of the landing. Next he led Flynn down the hall to a room at the opposite end of the building.

Flynn frowned. "Don't you have something closer?"

"Nope." The man smiled as he opened the door, his jaws working as if he chewed something. "Full up tonight."

"Hm." Flynn entered the room and looked around suspiciously. "Convention in town?"

"What's that?"

"Nothing. Listen, you got any heat in this place?"

The man nodded his head. "Aye. I can build you a fire but that'll be extra. And it'll take some time as the wood's prob'ly damp."

Flynn looked at the bed, which, while rather lumpy-looking, had a thick blanket on it. "Forget it." He looked at his watch. Nearly four A.M. What time had he left the party? Ten? The night had seemed longer than that.

"What's that you got there?" the old man asked.

Flynn looked at him askance. He didn't like the expression on the guy's face. It was the same look he'd had when Melisande had pulled out her purse.

"Nothing," he said, shaking his head. "It's for my wrist. I broke it a few months ago."

"Ah." The man nodded and made no move to leave. "Ain't got any bags, eh?"

"No." Flynn moved to the bed and pushed down on it. Soft as a pile of leaves. His back would be in agony tomorrow, he knew. And he further knew the chances of finding a chiropractor in this outlandish dream were going to be nil.

He turned and saw the old man watching him.

"Has that door got a lock?" he asked pointedly.

The old man laughed that wheezy laugh again. "What for? Worried someone's gone steal your fancy duds?" His withered hand gestured derisively toward Flynn's ragged Armani.

"No," Flynn said deliberately, taking several slow steps in the man's direction. "I want to make sure no one stands in the doorway and stares at me while I sleep."

"All right, all right, I'm going," the man said, throwing up his hands and turning out the door. "Just wanted to make sure the room were done up to a cow's thumb for you."

"We've got the cow's whole hand here," Flynn said, shutting the door firmly in the laughing proprietor's face. He made a mental note never to step so close to the man again, as "Stinky" would indeed have been an appropriate name for him.

He turned back and looked around the room. Spotting a rickety, straight-backed chair in the corner, he picked it up and brought it back to the door, shoving it under the knob. The chair, tilted at a steep angle, promptly slid down the door and clattered onto its back on the floor.

Why did that trick never work the way it did in movies? Flynn wondered. He hung the thing from the knob by one of the rungs on its back. At least that way it would make some noise if someone opened the door. Not that he was in danger of losing anything, as the old man had so tactfully pointed out.

He was just getting into the wretched bed when he realized the old guy hadn't told him how far London was. He'd have to ask again in the morning, he thought, and drifted immediately off to sleep.

Melisande woke with a start and stared at the barren room around her. Shivering she pulled the covers up to her chin and let out a breath. It fogged in the air.

As the reality of her surroundings penetrated her sleep-hazy brain, she began to feel her heart accelerate in panic. Good Lord, what had she *done*? Terror propelled itself right to her brain, and she realized with the clarity of morning that she had made a dreadful, dreadful mistake. Last night, watching Lord Bellingham with her father, and having that experience with him in the parlor before the party, then hearing Daphne's story and seeing the incident with Lady Carmine on the terrace . . . well, it had seemed as though she'd had no other choice but to leave. And her plan to go to her aunt had seemed so *logical*.

But now, in the cold light of day, she realized how foolish she'd been. In the eyes of the world she had spent a night unchaperoned. Even if she hired a maid today, it could still be reported that she'd shown up at an inn with a strange man—a man everyone would *know* was not her brother once they made it to town—and had spent the night there.

She would have to pay the maid to lie, she thought, her face burning with shame at the thought. She would have to hire someone trustworthy and convince her it would be right to lie about last night.

But there would still be her flight from the house. How, people would ask, had she gotten from Merestun to Tunbridge? Had she been alone? For sixteen whole miles? They would question whether she might not have met with highwaymen, or gypsies, or unscrupulous ramblers. Which, upon reflection, was exactly what had happened. Oh, what had *possessed* her to trust that awful man by the fountain? For certain he was handsome, and bore an uncanny resemblance to the prince from her dreams, but he was clearly insane. Lord knows what *he* would say once they got to town.

She pulled the covers up over her head and pressed the heels of her hands to her eyes. No, it was *she* who was insane! How much better it would have been to have stayed at Merestun and in the morning pleaded with her father to break the match. Surely he would have relented had she told him what she knew and what she'd seen. And if she'd begged—how could he have refused her?

But something inside her knew he would not have relented. He would have brushed Daphne's story off as idle gossip, and told her not to worry about the earl's dalliances *now,* as he was not yet married.

The certainty that he would have been unsympathetic gave her a small measure of comfort. No, if she had stayed at Merestun, she would be betrothed to Lord Bellingham today. As it was, she had escaped before the announcement and saved them all a good deal of embarrassment. At least she'd saved Lord Bellingham some embarrassment. For herself, she would still have many uncomfortable questions to answer when she arrived in London.

She pushed the covers from her face and sat up. She had much to do today. She had to hire a maid and a coach and get them all on their way to London. If she could do all that within the next two hours, it would still be all day and part of the night before they arrived in London.

She got out of bed and stepped into her traveling gown, teeth chattering and skin prickled with gooseflesh. She reached for her cloak and wrapped it quickly around her. Then she went to the bed and shoved her hands under the mattress for her purse.

Nothing met her fingertips. She pushed her arms further under, then forced them in up to her shoulders and spread them wide. Nothing.

Her heart hammered in her chest and she stood bolt upright. Breathing hard, she forced herself to swallow and stared down at the bed. Then she grabbed the mattress and with all her strength heaved it up, flinging it to the other side of the bed. There was nothing under the mattress.

There was nothing under the mattress.

A cold sweat broke out on Melisande's forehead. Her throat closed up, and she opened her mouth as if to scream. But she knew it was hopeless. Her money was gone. *Gone.* All of it. Her money was *gone.*

Chapter Six

There was no going back. She'd spent the night alone on the road. No, worse than alone. She was with that stranger. That *man*. She had no money to hire a maid, and certainly none with which to convince her to lie about last night. What would she do? Oh, God, what would she do?

Panic bubbled up her throat and sent prickles of dread all across her skin. She took short rapid breaths, and for a second thought she might faint.

No, she thought. No. I must be smart. There must be a way out of this.

But in her heart she knew there wasn't. She was a fool, an idiot. She thought back to last night, not even twelve hours ago, and the dread she'd felt at marrying Lord Bellingham. Compared to the way she felt today, that was nothing. She would have been much better off to have stayed at the party, to have taken her chances with her father, even to have married Lord Bellingham!

For she was ruined now, she thought, the blood frozen in her veins. *Ruined!* She plunked herself down on the bed frame and put her hands over her face. She could not even cry, her panic was so deep.

She wished she could turn back time. It was so close, last night was. She felt as if she should be able to take two steps back and have this whole situation be untrue.

She could claim to have been abducted, she thought with a brief, wild flash of hope. But her emotions crashed again; she would still be ruined. Everyone knew when a young woman was abducted, the first thing the criminals did was rob her of her virtue.

Her future was lost. Her bright, beautiful future was gone. Twelve hours ago she was to be a duchess. It was a triumph, a match beyond her wildest dreams, a match that would have been beyond her wildest dreams even if she were titled. Who cared if Lord Bellingham chose to dally with other women—perhaps he would have left her to herself, and how bad would that have been? And what if he over-disciplined his servants? She would not cross him. No, she could have stayed alone in her ducal palace, with her status and her reputation to give her comfort. Why had she not thought of *that* last night as she was climbing out that blasted window?

Someone knocked on the door.

"Hey, Mel?"

Melisande felt tears of frustration spring to her eyes. To top it all off, she was stuck with that lunatic man. She should have risen early and escaped without

116

him. She didn't need him, what had she been thinking? And he *was* insane, he'd as much as admitted it to her.

He knocked again. She wiped the tears from her cheeks but sat motionless. Maybe he would think she had left, and would take off in pursuit.

"Mel? Come on, open up. I know you're in there. The guy downstairs said you didn't leave yet." He knocked again, harder. "I'm going to open the door and come in in a minute, so you better tell me if you're not decent."

Melisande felt a strange calm come over her. A quiet, hollow emptiness. What would it matter if he did come in? She was ruined. She could be sitting here stark naked when he came in and she would not be further compromised than she was already. In fact, if society knew that she'd associated even this closely with such a low-bred, unbalanced fellow, she would surely be taken down.

He tried the door but it was locked. She noted this with dull interest. How had the thief gotten in? She had assumed she had forgotten to lock the door . . . unless it was that mangy-looking proprietor who'd come in with a key, taken her purse, and left, locking up after himself. In which case she would have no choice but to summon the constable, which would require her to face the very authorities who were no doubt searching for *her*.

"Now I *know* you're in there, Mel. Why else would the door be locked?"

Anger began to simmer in Melisande's stomach. She jumped up, unlocked the door, and flung it wide.

"Don't you *ever* call me by that hideous name

again, do you understand me?'' she said, fury pouring from her eyes, her voice, her very skin.

The lunatic took a step back, his handsome face slack with surprise. And it was a handsome face, she noted in the light of day. His blue eyes were brilliant, his facial features strong, his teeth white, his lips firm. His chest was broad and muscled, she could see now that he wore only the strange white shirt, open at the neck, that was under his coat last night. The shirt hung out over his black pants, making him look even more the madman, as disheveled as he was. But his face and his dark, reckless hair were dramatic and captivating.

The fine lips curved up in a displeased smile. ''Fine. Miss Smith then. What took you so long?''

''That's none of your affair.''

He took a deep breath. ''All right. When do you want to leave? I wanted to be sure I didn't miss you.'' With this, he smiled cynically. ''Something told me I'd better get up early. Just in case you were in a hurry, that is.''

She smiled coldly back at him. ''Good thinking.''

His cockiness failed him for a moment; she could see it in his eyes. A moment of uncertainty, or disappointment that he'd been correct in thinking she might leave without him.

''Okay,'' he said slowly. ''Well, while you were thinking of ditching me, I was telling Mr. Hospitality about the horse we 'found' last night, and I also got us a coach that's going to London. It'll be there late tonight.'' He laughed at this, for some mad reason of his own. ''I also told the guy to have some breakfast for us in about fifteen minutes.''

Melisande swallowed. "My, you've been busy," she murmured, thoughts spiraling through her mind. She couldn't pay for all of that. She couldn't pay for *any* of that. "I don't suppose you took the liberty of compensating the man for all of that, did you? Or did you assume I was going to provide everything for you?"

His eyes narrowed. "I assumed that was our deal, yes."

Her heart thundered apprehensively as she felt her way through each decision. "Well, it is not. Tell the proprietor we won't be needing any breakfast. And cancel the coach. I've decided it would be too easy to follow."

"What of it? By the time they find us we'll be in London."

"No." She shook her head. "I don't want them to know where I'm going."

He ran a hand through his already tousled hair, the movement strangely familiar to her, and glanced down the hall. Then he turned his face back to her. "You're not thinking of taking that beast we brought with us, are you? Because they'll follow that too, I've gotta tell you. And there's no way in hell I'm getting near that bastard again."

Melisande winced at his language and gave him a stern look. "We're not going to take Marlyebone, if that's what your crude blathering is about."

"Good. Yes, that's what it was about. So what are we going to do?"

"We're going to walk," she said decisively, feeling not anywhere near as confident as she sounded.

He looked at her incredulously and laughed. "Walk? To London? Are you crazy?"

Indeed she was. It would take them forever and her reputation would be irretrievably lost. But what choice did she have? Her only hope was to get to her aunt as quickly as possible and hope that Felicity would, possibly, lie for her. If she claimed Melisande had arrived immediately and with a maid, no one would question her.

"From here on out, I shall leave the insanity to you, Mr. Patrick. From my point of view, walking makes infinitely more sense. No one will look for us walking, and we won't be confined to the roads, which Bellingham and my parents will certainly be searching, if they are not already."

"Listen, yesterday I rode in a car, going sixty miles per hour, and it took me close to an hour to get to Merestun. And that was just from the train station. Walking would take us days."

Melisande swallowed hard and lifted her chin. "I don't know why you persist in talking. You make no sense. Talking is about communication and yet yours only confuses. Or offends."

He laughed slightly. "As opposed to yours."

"Now please cancel breakfast and the coach before we are charged for them. By then I should be ready to depart."

"You do know it's raining outside," the infuriating man said.

Melisande mentally cursed her luck. "Of course."

"And you still want to walk."

"What I *want*, Mr. Patrick, is to be in London, sitting by a fire with a cup of tea and all my troubles behind me. What I *have* is a very long journey with the added difficulty of required anonymity. You are here to help me, as I am to help you to get to London. Is this arrangement no longer satisfactory to you?''

''As far as I can see the 'arrangement' keeps changing. I am supposed to be your brother, but you still treat me like a servant. You were going to foot the bill, now you won't even spring for a couple of eggs. What's going on with you?''

Melisande's eyes darted apprehensively down the hallway. ''I don't know what you mean. Now please, do as I say and keep your voice down.''

''You don't know what I mean? 'Do as I say,' she says, and she doesn't know what I mean. Get the coach, cancel breakfast, walk in the rain—*that's* what I mean.''

''Those are the actions any true gentleman would perform for a lady.''

He rolled his eyes toward the ceiling. ''The question is would any true gentleman perform them for such a bi—'' He stopped himself and looked at her narrowly. ''For such a cranky lady?''

''The crankier the lady, the more superior the gentleman,'' she said archly. ''Now, will you do as I ask or shall we argue some more and risk discovery by Lord Bellingham? While that scenario is not attractive to me, I do not risk being held in his dungeon while the magistrate considers whether or not I should be imprisoned as a common horse thief.''

She was bluffing, of course. After all, he could always turn that threat back around on her as he had before. Chances were Bellingham would sooner believe Melisande took the horse in her effort to escape than some crazy wanderer. She had always been a superior equestrienne. For some reason, however, the threat had the desired effect on him.

"Fine," the man said, stalking down the hall. "I'll just get right on that, *sis*. Nothing I'd like better than a good long walk in the rain." He stomped down the steps. "Hopefully the weather'll hold for days. And to do it on an empty stomach. Well, now, *that's* a treat."

His voice faded with the distance. She turned back to her room and shut the door.

Flynn marveled over the extent of his misery. He'd thought nothing could be worse than yesterday, but here it was, a new day, and he was every bit as unhappy has he'd been last night. His ankle still hurt, he was soaked through again, and he was tramping through country that looked neither familiar, nor apt to produce a town any time soon. Furthermore, *Miss Smith* had been silent for nearly two hours now.

He looked at her discreetly. Her hood was drawn up over her head and she hunched her shoulders against the drenching rain. How could she stand this? he wondered. She who had a choice. She must be sorely afraid of this Bellingham jerk to be willing to subject herself to this, prissy little thing that she was.

But as he studied the slice of profile visible beneath her hood, he thought she must have a core of steel. While he had complained incessantly through the first hour of their walk, making clever, sarcastic comments hoping she'd relent and pay for a coach, she had trudged stoically on.

She looked as miserable as he felt, and yet her resolve had not weakened.

And, he thought—purely objectively, of course—she was still one of the most beautiful women he'd ever seen. Even soaking wet and muddy to the knees.

"Say, Mel," he said, thinking to jar her out of her silence with the name she hated, "you hungry at all?"

For a long time he thought she wasn't going to answer. Then finally, he heard a weary "Of course."

He brightened. "Well, then, let's say we stop and get a bite to eat somewhere."

He raised his head against the rain and looked out across the road and the empty fields that lined it on either side. Rain came down in sheets over the miles of farmland, landing with a soft *shhhh* in the grassy fields and peppering mud puddles all along the road. Not a house was in sight.

He glanced over at Melisande, and saw she was watching him.

"Do you see anyplace you like?" she asked with one raised eyebrow.

He thought for a moment. "Not yet. Though we've passed quite a few watering holes." He laughed heartily at his own joke, and wondered if he'd finally lost the one marble he had left.

She didn't laugh.

"Get it?" he asked. He'd feel a lot less miserable if she weren't so morose.

"Of course, but I don't see what bathing has to do with eating."

"Bathing? What are you talking about?"

"You said watering places," she said irritably.

"No, watering holes—like bars, uh, pubs . . . now do you get it?"

She pursed her lips. "It's still not amusing."

"Do you think anything's amusing? Ever? Or are you always this droopy?"

She turned on him and they both stopped walking. He couldn't tell if her face was wet from tears or the streaming rain. Certainly the tragic expression on her face made him believe it was tears, but he hoped to God he was wrong. He hated it when women cried. It made him feel helpless, which usually pissed him off and made him act like a jerk.

"Mr. Patrick," she began in a voice that confirmed his fear of tears. "You have no idea what sort of trouble we are in." She paused, sniffed, then drew up her head. Her eyes looked tortured. "What sort of trouble *I* am in. You see. . . ." She seemed to be trying to make a decision. "You see . . . my money, all of my money, was stolen back at the inn in Tunbridge."

He laughed once, in disbelief. When her expression didn't change, he sobered rapidly. "Stolen?" he repeated. "That purse thing?" He remembered the solid *chink* of coins as she'd put it down on the counter at the inn. It had looked heavy.

She nodded, biting her lips.

"Well—" He threw a hand out to the side in exasperation. "Jesus, why didn't you say anything? Why didn't you tell me, or tell that old man? Holy sh—" He grabbed his head with his hands. "I can't believe you just let us leave without saying a word. Somebody might have been able to do something."

"If I'd said something they would have called the constable."

"That's right," he said with great exaggeration. "As they should have. Maybe they could have caught the guy. Did you lock your door? Where was your purse? Maybe you just mislaid it." He kicked at the ground in frustration. "Jesus, I wish you'd told me. I could have helped you look. I'm sure I could have found it."

She was shaking her head. "My door was locked and I'd hidden the purse. It had to have been the proprietor. Truth to tell, he didn't look reputable to me from the start."

"I'll say," Flynn agreed. "He was eyeing that sack of change you had from the moment you took it out. And that's all the more reason you should have said something. I could have beaten the crap out of him and gotten it back."

For the first time all day she smiled.

"What?" he demanded. "What's so funny? You don't think I could have taken him? That old man? Hell, I could take him with one arm tied behind my back. In fact—come on," he said, turning abruptly around. "We're going back."

"What?" she squeaked.

He heard her running footsteps squish through the mud behind him, then felt her hand on his arm.

"What on earth are you thinking? If we go back there and raise a commotion about my purse, who do you think they will summon?"

"The police?" he said, sarcastic again. "The men who put people in jail for robbery?"

"The constable," she said firmly. "The man who apprehends criminals for wrongdoing, such as robbery, or horse theft. . . ."

He stopped walking.

"Not to mention that the first person my parents

125

and Lord Bellingham would have informed of my absence is the nearest justice of the peace, who would no doubt have informed the constable. If we were to return and raise a great hue and cry over my purse, we would be apprehended immediately. Do you understand me? This would all have been for naught.''

Flynn felt irritation gnaw at his gut. He would have loved to have taken that scrawny old man apart, limb by limb, for this trick. Smug, sleazy bastard. He rubbed his hands over his face.

''Holy God,'' he groaned. ''What are we going to do?''

She took a deep breath. ''I'm not sure.''

He dropped his hands and looked at her. No wonder she'd looked so bereft all morning. She was in deeper trouble than he was. As ridiculous as this whole thing was for him, it was just one more inconvenient aspect to a nightmare that got more inconvenient the longer it went on. But this, to all appearances, was her life. Her *real* life. She was not going to wake up from this one.

''Okay,'' he said in a calmer voice. ''All right. This is not so bad.''

''It's not?'' She looked up at him with such hope in those deep brown eyes that he felt something melt inside him.

''Well, I mean, it's not like they're in hot pursuit right now. We do have our freedom.''

The thought didn't appear to comfort her much. She frowned and looked at the ground.

''And even if we're moving slow, we're still on our way to London.'' He started walking in the direction they'd been moving all morning. "What's in London for you anyway?"

She straightened her shoulders and picked up the pace beside him. "My Aunt Felicity."

"Well, great!" he said. "Old Aunt Felicity. That's great. Are you close to her?"

He caught a slight smile from the corner of his eyes, and felt a rare satisfaction. He'd had a woman on the brink of tears and he'd made her smile. That was something.

"She's hardly old," Melisande said. "In fact, she's very beautiful. And yes, we are quite close."

"There you go," he said. "She can help you out of the scrape you're in, I bet."

Her brow furrowed. "That is what I am hoping."

"Well, of course she can. So we get to Aunt Felicity's in a couple of days and she explains everything to your parents. No problem. Who's she related to, your mom or your dad?"

"She is my father's sister."

"Even better," he said. "She'll be able to talk some sense into your old man, explain that this Bellingham guy just wasn't right for you. And I'd be willing to put in my two cents. I mean, any guy who was doing what he was doing out there on the porch with that other woman shouldn't be getting engaged. Shoot, if your father had seen that, he probably would have gotten out his shotgun and run him off himself."

"I doubt that very much."

"I don't. If it were my daughter, engaged to a scumbag like that. . . ."

She was definitely smiling now, and even the rain seemed lighter than before.

"Well, I wouldn't want *any* woman I knew marrying a guy like that."

"I would like to see you with a daughter, Mr. Patrick. Perhaps she would be able to make a gentleman of you, as nothing else could."

"Hey, listen, I'm a gentleman. I just don't want to spread it around too thin, you know? I only let my inner gentleman out on special occasions."

"Your 'inner gentleman'?"

"Yeah, you know, like your inner child? All that psychobabble stuff."

He glanced over at her. She was looking at him with that "Oh, no, he really is crazy" look on her face, so he smiled.

"That was . . . kind of a joke. Something we say in America. Never mind."

They walked on and though they were silent again, Flynn felt a modicum of camaraderie. He was starting to really like this girl. She was strong, she was smart, she was beautiful. If he were in his right mind—his right *time*—he'd be looking at her with a whole different eye. As it was, however, his admiration stopped there. She was an interesting, perhaps extraordinary, person, but he was *not* getting involved.

Hours later, Flynn's stomach was rumbling constantly. He hadn't eaten since the wedding reception that now seemed a lifetime ago, and he was actually feeling lightheaded. His pace had also slackened considerably. The rain, however, pummeled the earth as steadily as it had all day. He was going to catch pneumonia for sure.

"Look." Melisande's voice broke the silence, sounding strangely close in the empty landscape.

Flynn looked up and followed the direction she pointed with his gaze. Smoke drifted upward from among some trees down the road to the left.

"It must be a cottage," she said.

"Thank God. Maybe they'll give us something to eat."

"Do you think so?" Her eyes stayed wonderingly on the smoke on the horizon.

"They'd better. Or I'm going to pass out in their doorway and they'll have to haul me away."

"Yes, I'm feeling a bit weak myself."

He looked at her. She did look tired, her face pale, her eyes shadowed.

They started across the field toward the line of trees, feet sucking into the damp, loamy soil. A couple of times Flynn was afraid he would lose a shoe as he pulled his foot free of the mud.

When they got into the trees, the relief from the steady rain was immediate. Walking all day with that pecking at his head had been like suffering under Chinese water torture; only he didn't realize it until he was under the protective awning of tree limbs.

They marched through leaves and pine needles, following the scent and direction of the smoke, until they saw the house, tucked away in the forest, with nothing but a narrow dirt road running up to it from the opposite direction. A small shed stood beside the house, surrounded by a pen with several pigs in it. All in all, the place looked pretty shabby and poor. The house couldn't be more than one room, Flynn thought. Fat chance these people would have any food to spare.

"You wait here," Melisande said. "I'll go to the door."

"No. If I'm your brother it makes more sense that I should go. Besides, you don't know who lives here—it could be some sort of maniac."

She smiled wanly. "Hard to believe there could be two in one county."

"Trust me, they're everywhere," he said, taking two steps before he realized she had insulted him. He turned and looked at her. "Very funny."

She shrugged.

He advanced to the door and rapped soundly on it. It was opened immediately. A stout woman in a kerchief and long gown stood wiping her hands on her apron and gave him the once-over.

"Aye, what can I do for ye?"

At that moment he realized he had nothing to say. Nothing convincing, that was.

"Uh," he began. "My sister and I . . ." He turned and gestured toward Melisande, standing darkly in her cloak under the trees. "We were on our way to London when we were robbed." He paused a moment, hoping for some sympathetic remark. None came. Instead, he was studied by two expressionless brown eyes in a bland face. She put her hands on her hips.

He pushed on. "And we were wondering if there was any chance you could spare a little food and maybe a place to sleep tonight."

"Where are you from?" The eyes narrowed and she crossed her arms over her ample chest.

He smiled. "Well, I'm from America, but Me—my, uh, sister is from here, from sort of over near Merestun."

Eyebrows the color of pencil lead shot up. "Near Merestun? You've traveled a spell then, ain't you? And tell me how it is you're brother and sister from two different parts of the globe, eh?"

"Well." He chuckled forcibly. "It's the same old story, you know, ma'am. We're from a broken home. I lived with Dad in the States and she grew up with Mom here. Our parents divorced when we were very young." He gave her a confidential, you-know-how-it-is look.

The look she gave him in return was scathing. "*Divorced?* Good heavens to Betsy. Roy! This 'un says his parents *divorced*! Have you heard of such a thing? D'you know of a woman living near Merestun what got *divorced*?"

A low voice from the shadows muttered, "Nope."

"Saints preserve us, what a scandal that must have been," she continued, looking at him with lurid interest. "Probably spent your whole sorry life suffering for their mistake, eh? Well, that explains your odd way of looking, I suppose. Your sister, you say? Well, tell her to come on over here. I guess we got a little something to offer, but the best I can do is give you the hayloft in the shed for sleeping, and even at that you got to help Roy in the morning with the pigs."

Flynn stood uncertainly for a moment, unsure what to make of nearly everything the woman said—what he could make out, that is. Her accent was the oddest one he'd ever heard.

"Well, go on then, call her over," the woman insisted, and turned back into the cottage.

Flynn turned slowly to Melisande and shrugged, then waved her over. When she neared, he said, "I

131

don't know what we've gotten ourselves into, but I think she said they'll give us some food and a place to sleep."

Melisande hesitated, peered around at the cottage, and looked up at him. "What did you tell them? Did you tell them we're brother and sister?"

"Yeah. I said our parents divorced when we were young, which is why I grew up in America and you grew up here, near Merestun."

Melisande's mouth dropped open, and she looked at him with an expression of horror. "You told them *what*?"

He gave her an exasperated look. "It's the only thing I could come up with. And I didn't know where you—"

"You told them our parents *divorced*?"

He nodded. "Why not?"

"What did she *say*?" Her eyes were aghast.

He frowned. "She actually looked an awful lot like you do now. What? What's wrong with that? Plenty of people get divorced."

She took a deep breath. "Maybe in America they do, but not here. I'm surprised she'll even let us in."

"Because our parents were divorced? That's the worst sort of prejudice I've heard yet."

"No doubt she thinks we're just as profligate as they are. I'm surprised she doesn't think we're running from the law or something."

"That's crazy. Of course we are," he added as an afterthought.

"Are you coming in or aren't you?" The woman's voice was shrill. "There ain't but one fireplace in here, and it ain't fit to warm the whole outdoors."

Flynn gestured Melisande inside ahead of him. She entered, still shaking her head.

The cottage was dark and smoky. One smelly candle burned on the rough-hewn table in the center of the room. To the right was a narrow bed, half-concealed by a curtain. To the left, a row of clay pots and dried plants lined a short counter supported by spindly legs. Directly ahead of them was the fireplace, glowing red and issuing a good deal of smoke into the room, as well as up the chimney. A thin man, hunched over on a chair, sat before it.

The woman stood next to the fire spooning something soupy out of a kettle that was nestled into the embers on one side.

"What are your names? Mayhap we've heard of your mother."

"Doe," Flynn supplied, with a mental smile. "Jane and John."

Melisande gave him an annoyed look.

"We're the Clydes," she said "I'm Mary and this is Roy."

"Nice to meet you," Flynn said, nodding at Roy, who glanced up from what appeared to be whittling.

"How do you do?" Melisande said, inclining her head.

With her words, both Roy and Mary turned to look her full in the face. Her eyes widened, and she looked at Flynn in alarm.

"My sister went to a very nice school. It was the last thing my mother did before she, ah, died. She hoped Mel—uh, Jane could get some kind of job, you know, a secr—"

"A governess," Melisande said quickly, shooting

133 ·

him a quelling glance. "I am on my way to London, to fill a position for a very respectable family. In Mayfair."

The woman's eyebrows shot up again and she said mildly, spooning out a second bowlful of whatever burbled in the kettle, "My, my."

The Clydes weren't much for talking after that. Mary eyed Melisande curiously through the meal, but Roy didn't budge from his chair by the fire.

Flynn found that whatever the food was he was eating—some kind of stew—it was far better than he'd anticipated, though that could have been due to extreme hunger. Potatoes and onions were the primary ingredients, but there were a few pieces of meat floating in the salty broth—bacon, he thought. The bread was a bit stale, but he found if he dipped it in the broth, as the Clydes did, it went down fairly easily. Flynn thought he could practically hear the food hit the bottom of his empty stomach.

He consumed his meal with gusto, and it was a while before he noted that Melisande only picked at her food, occasionally bringing the spoon to her lips but just taking the barest sip from it. The way Mary Clyde's look turned from curious to wary told Flynn she believed Melisande considered herself too good for their food. Flynn wasn't at all convinced that wasn't the exactly the case either.

The meal ended quickly, and Mary cleared the dishes from the table, eyeing Melisande with growing hostility when she emptied her bowl back into the pot. Flynn elbowed Melisande in the side, motioning for her to get up and help, try to endear herself to the woman. He received a haughty look in exchange.

"Well, follow me," the woman said. "I'll show you to the shed. It ain't much but it's dry."

"The shed?" Melisande repeated, clearly horrified.

Flynn knew it was a spontaneous response, but Mary turned with her hands on her hips and those raised eyebrows and glowered at her, as if this was just the remark she'd been waiting for.

"What's the matter, missy?" she asked sharply. "Our shed ain't good enough for you? *You,* near bastards that you are, and begging for a meal. You're lucky I didn't turn you away the moment I laid eyes on you. Putting on airs like you're some kind of princess, taking food off the plates of hardworking people—"

"Please stop," Melisande said, her hands out as if to ward off the barrage. "You've misunderstood me."

But at her tone and her choice of words, Mary Clyde's anger only grew.

"And now you're as good as calling me simpleminded. I've half a mind to turn you out right now, I do. I don't need no holier-than-thou coming into my—"

"Mrs. Clyde," Flynn said, taking her arm and steering her away from Melisande in the tiny cottage. He grasped her hand in his. "Please, let me apologize for my sister. She's—how can I put this? She's a little . . ." He tapped his temple with a forefinger and gave the woman a pained look.

Mary narrowed her eyes and grunted noncommittally.

Flynn lowered his voice conspiratorially so Mary had to lean toward him to hear. "My sister's had it in her head for some years now that she's actually a very fine lady. I think when the folks divorced it put her over the edge, you know, made her a little . . . off. So she's always overcompensated some, pretended like she came from somewhere else, some other family. She doesn't mean to offend you, it's just her way of trying to forget the pain of the divorce. I'm sure you understand. . . ."

Mary Clyde's expression was anything but understanding, but she nodded her head slowly.

"It's been a hardship for me," he continued, trying to look pitiful. "They sent for me from over in America, because they needed someone to look after her. It was that or an institution, you know. I didn't have much money but I came . . . and then we were robbed . . . and, well, I won't bore you with the details. I'd just really appreciate it if you'd overlook her, ah, attitude." He gave her his most confiding smile and squeezed her hand.

"We-ell," Mary said, looking at him appreciatively. "I'll overlook it this once, as you're having such a time with her. But you ought not to let her get away with such behavior. It might look bad for you, you know, and you're a clever boy. You could do something with yourself, maybe." She winked at him. "Handsome too. That always helps."

Flynn smiled, looked at the ground, and actually shuffled his feet a little. He stopped just shy of saying, "Aw, shucks."

"I appreciate that, ma'am."

She patted his cheek with one callused hand and moved around him toward the door. "You two follow me then," she said, but couldn't stop herself from shooting a hard look at Melisande on the way past. "I'll show you to your bed for the night."

"*Our* bed?" Melisande breathed.

As Mary walked from the cottage, Flynn wrapped an arm around Melisande's shoulders and clapped a hand over her mouth.

Chapter Seven

"Don't you ever touch me like that again," Melisande said, once they were alone in the hayloft of the shed.

The loft was small, about the width of a double bed, Flynn noted, with a ceiling too low for him to stand up straight under, but to his weary eyes it looked comfortable enough. In fact, it looked as if someone slept here fairly regularly. Probably Roy, Flynn thought. He couldn't imagine the Clydes' marriage bed was particularly inviting to either of them.

"And what did you say to that woman?" she added, obviously annoyed.

Flynn took off his jacket, knelt down, and laid it, regretfully, on the hay. If Armani could see his creation now.

"Nothing you should worry about. I just told her

you were a little nuts and to ignore everything you said."

He glanced up to see how horrified Melisande's expression was with that, and was amply rewarded.

"I told her you were unhinged by our parents' divorce." He grinned wickedly.

"Oh, my God." Melisande slumped to a sitting position on the other side of the loft from him. She bent her head into her hands and rested her elbows on her knees. "I cannot believe that I have sunk so low. And now . . ." She raised her head and looked around the loft. "To have to sleep here. With you."

"Hey, you're welcome to sleep downstairs with the pigs," Flynn said, stretching out on the jacket and propping his head up against a bale of hay. He had to tuck his feet in behind where Melisande sat.

She sighed, her mouth turning down at the corners. "You just don't understand."

Flynn thought for a second, worried that a second bout of tears was imminent. "Here's what I understand. We both need to get to London. Neither of us has any money. And it's a long trip. The way I see it, whatever we have to do to get there is whatever we have to do."

"But my life will not be worth living once it's known what I had to do to get there."

Flynn crossed his arms behind his head and studied her. "That's a little dramatic, don't you think?"

"No, I don't," she snapped. "You obviously have no idea what life is like here for a woman of my position. And I don't feel like explaining it to you. Again."

"Okay," he said. "I just wondered what happened to your spunk, that's all. It doesn't matter to me any anyway."

She sniffed and looked away. Not to be coy, he knew somehow, but because she was ashamed of her tears. "I know."

He was silent a minute, considering. "All right, that's not completely true, what I just said about it not mattering. I do care that this is so hard for you."

"No, you don't."

He sat up, brushing hay from his hands. "Yes, I do. I don't want to, but I do. I like you. I just think you're making a mountain out of a molehill. I told you, I'm sure your Aunt Felicity won't have any trouble coming up with a viable explanation for how you got there. Nobody has to know we spent the night together."

He saw her shiver.

"And," he added slowly, "it's not as if anything were actually going to *happen* between us." He cocked his head, trying to see into her averted face.

"Of course not," she said, staring into the hay. She looked very, very tired.

"So let's let tomorrow take care of itself. Right now we're doing all we can do. Right?"

She nodded.

"Okay." He leaned back against the bail of hay. "Now, spread out your cape and lie down. It'll be cold tonight, so why don't you lie down right here, next to me, and we'll keep each other warm. Body heat, you know, that's all."

"*Next* to you? Oh, no." She eyed him suspiciously

and shook her head. "I'll just sleep over here, just like this."

She curled her knees to her chest and pulled the cape around herself.

Flynn sighed. "All right, but you'll be cold." He lay back down on the hay. "And I'll be cold," he muttered, folding his arms over his chest and closing his eyes.

He was conscious less than a minute.

Hours later, he guessed, he woke to hear hay shuffling nearby, and a second later Melisande crawled over to lay down next to him. His sleep-puffed eyes could just make out her outline in the dark, but he thought he saw her trembling. A moment later, as she exhaled deeply, he heard her breath shaking with the cold.

Flynn moved slowly, realizing as he woke that his hands and feet were freezing, and the tremors he thought he detected in Melisande shook him from the inside out as well.

He edged closer. She didn't move, though he was sure she was awake enough to feel his nearness. Since she didn't object, he snaked an arm around her waist and pulled her close.

It took only a second before her warmth infused him with comfort. He spooned tighter against her, his face so close to her hair he could smell its fragrance. Some kind of flower scent, he guessed. Her body was lithe and fit snugly against his, and even though he spent a delicious moment wondering what it might feel like naked, he fell immediately back to sleep.

What seemed like five minutes later, he was awakened by something. His alarm clock, no doubt, he thought. He spent a second trying to remember what day it was, if he had a meeting this morning, and prayed it was the weekend. He kept his eyes closed against a dim light, and realized groggily that someone lay against his chest, his hand was curled in a soft abundance of hair, and he was hard as a rock.

His lips curved, and he turned toward the sweet scent of the woman, putting his other arm around her waist and pulling her toward him. Somewhere in the back of his mind he knew this wasn't Nina. But it had been not-Nina before and no harm had been done.

She cuddled close and he lightly kissed her lips, running his hand up her side to her breast as he nuzzled her neck.

He had a brief moment to wonder why they were both wearing so many clothes before the woman beside him bolted straight up in bed and hissed, "What in *God's* name are you *doing*?"

Flynn's eyes opened, and he felt a wild panic in his chest before he figured out where he was. He blinked hard and swallowed, disorientation making his head swim.

Loud clattering sounded in the shed below them. Flynn's eyes shot toward the sound, then moved swiftly around the loft. The dim light came from cracks between the wall planking, and Melisande, her hair tumbled around her shoulders and down her back, glared at him with furious eyes and scalding pink cheeks.

"I'm—I'm sorry," he said, his voice rough. "I forgot where I was. I forgot who I was with. I'm sorry."

"With whom did you think you were? Some *harlot*?" Her cape lay beside him on the hay, so he could see her chest rising and falling rapidly beneath the dress she wore. The neckline was cut so that he could see the pale rise of her breasts, sumptuously round and soft-looking despite the lacy scarf she wore tucked into the edges of it. He felt his loins throb at the same time he registered a profound disappointment that he was still here, still in this odd, unending nightmare.

She slapped a hand to her chest. *"Don't look at me so!"*

He jerked his eyes away.

It wasn't a nightmare, he thought, sitting up stiffly. He rubbed both hands across his eyes and then up through his hair. It had gone on too long to be a nightmare. Not to mention that he'd just slept and woken up and he was *still here.* Disappointment dragged at his heart the more clearly he realized this.

"Sun's nearly up!" The shrill voice came from below, followed by a distinct *thud* on the floorboards beneath them as Mary Clyde obviously jabbed something against the boards to wake them up. "Mr. Doe? Roy's ready to tend the pigs!"

Flynn felt his emotional balance tip first one way and then the other. At this last statement, though, he had to come down on the side of laughter. *Pigs,* he thought, wondering if this was indeed madness. *Pigs!* He laughed out loud.

He imagined himself sitting in some psychiatrist's office in D.C. right now, laughing and saying "Pigs!" over and over again, for surely he wasn't where he thought he was. He was just crazy, dwelling in some back corner of his mind. Reality—the twentieth century—no doubt swirled around him unperceived.

He wiped his eyes and stopped laughing. "Just when you think things can't get any worse," he said, feeling another hysterical chuckle bubble up inside him as he thought about his mother watching him through some two-way mirror. For some reason it struck him as terribly funny that his proper, appearance-is-everything mother would have to watch him sit in a corner screaming "Pigs!" No doubt she'd have him locked up and tell everyone he'd died. The *shame* of having a mentally disturbed son would be too much for her.

Melisande looked at him as if he were crazy. As usual.

He calmed himself. "Oh, relax, honey." He pushed himself to his feet, feeling every muscle protest. "At least I touched you *before* I tended the pigs." He laughed again, and wiped his eyes. "Oh, God," he breathed. "And I was worried I had a meeting today."

He picked up his jacket and, stooping over to save his head from the rafters, moved to the ladder and descended.

Melisande sat back against a bale of hay and touched her lips with her fingertips. She'd been kissed before, once or twice in a dark corner of a balcony at a ball, but never a slow, sensual kiss like the one she'd just gotten. And never had she been lying down, her hair loose around her, and her body pressed hotly against a man's as his hands moved over her.

Her hand drifted down her neck. His palm had held her breast, his thumb had touched her bare skin. She felt again the tingling of pleasure that started at her core and melted downward. For a moment, at the edge of waking, she had wanted that hand to move inside her clothing. For a moment, her entire body had longed to push up against the hard, male body next to hers, to feel him along her torso, her limbs, to clutch his back and pull him into her.

She shook her head roughly and jumped to her feet. This was terrible. This was why unmarried women were not supposed to be alone with unmarried men. He'd put her under some sort of spell, some sort of *sensual* spell, she thought with horror. Had she been a little more sleepy, what awful liberties he might have taken with her.

She felt again his hand in her hair, the way he'd cupped the back of her head, and his warm breath along her neck. Spine-tingling sensations of pleasure wound through her again now, as they had when he had been here.

She pressed her hands to her cheeks, which burned with the memories. What might it all have led to? For a second she imagined him pulling down the bodice of her dress, his fingers touching her *there,* and she felt herself go breathless.

Swallowing hard, she picked her cloak up from the floor and shook the hay from it. Then she sat on the bale, pulled the pins from her hair, and started to pick pieces of hay out of the tangled mess. She reflected that this was *exactly* what they said about profligate young serving girls. She remembered hearing Cook once say that they'd let a kitchen maid go because she'd "taken a tumble in the hay with one of the stable boys." Melisande hadn't thought twice about it then. But now she wondered . . . had the maid felt that same tidal wave of desire that *she* had felt this morning? Melisande suddenly felt a flash of compassion for the young woman. And fear for herself.

She finger-combed her hair as best she could, braided it, and wound it into a severe bun at the back of her head. She tentatively touched her temple, where she'd struck her head yesterday, and found it sore, but the skin felt barely broken. Then she donned her cloak and tied it securely at her neck. Then she sat back down on the bale of hay.

What was she to do? If she left the shed, where would she go? She couldn't imagine herself going to the cottage to sit at that dirty, rough table and make conversation with that awful Mary Clyde. Especially, she thought with ire, remembering, now that the woman thought she was crazy.

She moved to the wall and looked through one of the cracks. Thankfully, it looked like the rain had stopped. She could walk outside. Yes, that's what she would do. Because she certainly couldn't stay here. Not so close to the place where she had so nearly lost her senses and done something shameless. If she had let him kiss her again . . . one of those soft, gentle kisses, with his warm, masculine body pressed up against hers . . .

She threw her leg over the edge of the loft and descended the ladder.

He was working in the pigpen when she emerged from the shed. His shirt was off despite the chill air, and his hair hung into his face as he shoveled a load of what she thought must be manure into a wooden cart over the fence.

Despite her recent shame, she could not help gaping at the bare skin of his chest. He was lean and strong, she noted in surprise. For some reason, she hadn't noticed it through those odd clothes he wore. And the hair spreading across his chest and descending to a line at his hard, flat belly accentuated the fine shape of his torso. He looked like one of the sculptures at the museum.

Roy Clyde worked in the pen also, and the pigs huddled in the opposite corner. But Melisande's eyes barely left the man she had just slept next to. She felt, inexplicably, a bond with him amongst these strangers. She watched him move, his dark hair somehow thicker and wavier with his sweat as it bounced against his forehead and clung to the nape of his neck.

He was, she had to admit, dreadfully handsome.

As soon as she had the thought, as if she'd shouted it out across the yard, he straightened from what he was doing and looked right at her. The brilliant blue of his eyes stood out against his work-flushed face as their gazes met. With his bare chest exposed and the memory of that morning's illicit kiss in her mind, he looked like a dangerous animal. A dangerous, *attractive* animal.

Like Satan, her mind told her. He was tempting her in the most base, carnal way.

She turned abruptly away. She had to get away from him. How had he changed so quickly from the harmless lunatic to the dark seductive being he was now?

Suddenly she remembered her dream. She whirled back to look at him. He'd gone back to work, but the memory of his eyes haunted her. They were the color of a finely tempered blade. That clear blue-to-silver of the sharpest metal. This man *was* her prince. How could she have forgotten? Especially after the encounter by the fountain that was almost exactly as she'd dreamt it months ago?

But this man was certainly no prince, that title she had made up about him for Juliette and Daphne. And now she remembered the hidden discomfort of those dreams, the vague sensation of a threat beneath the love and desire she'd thought she'd felt for the man in them.

The threat, she realized suddenly, *was* her desire. The immoral, lustful desire she'd felt that morning. Perhaps the dreams had been a warning. Perhaps the reason she'd felt so unsettled by them was the moral imperative they'd conjured. She desired someone physically that she must deny herself absolutely.

She turned away again and walked toward the cottage. She had to get away from him. But how? And how would she get to London on her own? The thought was terrifying. She could meet with any number of hazards along the road all alone. At least with this man—this man who had *apologized* for his behavior, she reminded herself—she was not at risk of being forcibly accosted.

No, her conscience said, with this man she was at risk of being willingly debauched.

Melisande shivered and walked toward the cottage.

"Well, the princess has waked up, has she?" Mary Clyde said as she came through the doorway. "You and your *brother* looked mighty cozy up there this morning when I come out to feed the hogs."

Melisande turned on her heel and walked out.

*   *   *

148

"You know," Flynn said as they traveled the muddy road once again, "you could have been nice to her long enough to get some breakfast."

"She was a horrible, low-class, ill-bred woman. I wouldn't have tolerated her had she given us a ten-course meal."

Flynn laughed. "Hell, I'd have gotten down and kissed the ground she walked on if she'd given us a ten-course meal."

"You dispense your kisses rather carelessly then, don't you?" Her chin was held higher than usual.

Flynn grinned. "Still thinking about it, huh?"

She flushed red, and he laughed.

She turned angry eyes on him. "Of course I am. It was a disgusting, horrid thing for you to do. You— you took advantage of me while I was sleeping."

"Actually I think it was you who took advantage of me."

"Me!"

"Yeah." Flynn stuffed his hands in his pockets and kicked a rock out in front of him. The sun had broken through the clouds and he was feeling pretty good. Maybe because he was finally dry and warm and had eaten something, but he actually felt a little resigned to the fact that he was temporarily stuck in this strange place. At least here he had no real responsibility. And if he were insane, at least nobody was waiting on him to finish a damn speech. This could prove to be the best vacation he'd ever taken.

If, that is, he could figure out how to return someday.

He shook the thought off.

"Yeah," he repeated. "As I recall, it was you who

came cuddling up to me in the middle of the night. And you didn't exactly resist this morning when I—in a sleepy, confused state myself—accidentally kissed you.''

"I was unconscious!'' She stopped and stomped her foot with the word.

Flynn couldn't help it. He laughed.

"Don't you dare laugh at me,'' she fumed. "And how do you *accidentally* kiss someone?''

"I thought you were someone else.''

"Who? Your wife?''

"I don't have a wife.''

"Who then?''

"I'm not sure. Just someone other than you.''

She looked appalled. "You mean you just woke up and assumed whoever it was asleep near you was there for your pleasure?''

"Now why else would they be in my bed?'' he asked calmly.

"We weren't in your bed!''

"But I *thought* we were. See?''

She started walking again, her skirt flipping about her legs as her long stride took her forward.

"I can't talk to you,'' she said when he caught up. "You're immoral and depraved and I don't trust you.''

He was silent a few steps. Then said slowly, "Okay . . .''

"And why do you keep saying that? *Okay, okay, okay*—what does that *mean*? I just don't understand you. And I've met other Americans before. I didn't have any trouble understanding them. It's just *you* I don't understand. *You* are making me crazy!''

150

Her arms flew out from her sides as she stalked forward.

"Calm down," he said, looking at her with concern. "Okay just means all right, yes, I agree. It's sort of slang, I guess."

"*Slang,*" she spat. "Language of the low-born."

"What's with this 'low-born' stuff, as long as we're grilling each other? 'Ill-bred,' 'low-born,' 'low-class'—you're a real dyed-in-the-wool snob, aren't you."

"Snob?" she repeated derisively.

"Yes, snob. Pompous, pretentious, self-important, affected, conceited—get it, *Miss Smith*? You put so much importance on *breeding* and your precious reputation, but you've got the worst manners of anyone I've ever met. Nobody who was really polite would be so rude." He paused, cleared his throat, and added, "Obviously."

He ran a hand through his hair. Jeez, he hadn't realized he was so angry with her. Maybe it was because she made him feel the same way his father used to, as if he wasn't good enough, smart enough, tough enough, just wasn't *enough*.

He exhaled.

She walked silently beside him.

He knew he should apologize, but he couldn't bring the words to his lips. She'd been pretty awful to him, he thought, justifying his behavior. Treating him like a servant despite their agreement. She hadn't even *thanked* him for shoveling out that pigpen for their meal and lodging this morning.

As he wrestled with himself to say something nice, she slowed her pace. He was just thinking he would kill for a ten-speed bicycle when she stopped and turned toward him, her eyes on the ground.

"I'm sorry," she said. She crossed her arms under her cape. "I have been ungracious. You're perfectly right to upbraid me for it."

"Well . . ." He wasn't quite sure what to say. "You're under a lot of stress."

She nodded.

"And I wasn't upbraiding you," he said, guessing at the meaning and hoping he meant what he said. "I'm just frustrated. You don't understand the situation I'm in any more than I fully appreciate yours. I guess we've got to expect some disagreement. We're pretty different people, from pretty different places." And times, he thought, but he decided not to push that point.

She nodded again, turned, and started walking. "Tell me about where you're from, Mr. Patrick."

"Flynn, please."

She glanced at him. "I don't think I should call you by your given name." But she smiled to temper the words. "Where I am from that is considered improper until—" She broke off, blushing. "Well, just improper."

"So I should call you Miss . . . what's your real name?"

"St. Claire. Yes, you should call me Miss St. Claire."

He put his free hand in his pocket, and their pace shifted to a stroll. "All right, but what about in private? I mean, like now, when there's nobody else for miles." He swept his hand out to encompass the rolling hills and farmland. "Can't I call you Mel now?

152

Miss St. Claire seems awfully, well, cumbersome.''

She thought about this for a minute. "The problem is, it would become a habit, and then you might slip sometime in company and people would make assumptions about our relationship."

"You mean they might assume we slept together . . . maybe shared a kiss?"

He smiled when she looked up sharply.

"Just kidding," he said, grinning.

To his surprise, she let a smile play at her lips. "Actually, yes, that is what I'm afraid they will assume."

"Okay, I'll try. But I might already have developed the habit. And it's Washington I'm from."

"Yes, you told me that. Have you any family there? You said you have no wife. What about brothers and sisters? Parents?"

"My mother is there. My father died about a year ago. No family other than that."

"I'm sorry about your father. Were you close?"

"No." He felt the vestiges of that earlier anger and the memory of how his father had felt about him. "What about you, any siblings?"

"A sister. Juliette." She smiled. "We are very close, though she is quite a bit younger than I."

"And how old are you?" he asked, looking at her pretty, unlined face. She was much more mature than the age she looked. And while she wasn't anywhere near as rail-thin as Nina, she had a beautiful, strong body.

"I am nineteen."

"Nineteen! Hah! Jailbait, for sure," he said, laughing, but actually feeling something like disappointment. He was thirty-three years old to her nineteen. He suddenly felt ancient.

"What on earth do you mean?" she asked, smiling. "Jailbait?"

"Well . . ." He looked at her and decided against explaining. "It's just an expression. Meaning you're much younger than you ought to be."

"Do I look so much older then?"

"No, it's just that *I'm* so much older."

Her smile broadened. "And how old are you?"

He eyed her askance. "Thirty-three."

She laughed, that delighted laugh she'd had on the patio at Merestun, the one he'd found infectious. "Are you hoping I shall look at you paternally, Mr. Patrick? Come now, you are really five and twenty, admit it."

"No, and I wouldn't go back to twenty-five if you paid me," he said.

She sobered and looked into his face. "You are not serious? Three and thirty?"

"It's not so old," he said defensively.

"But my goodness," she said, looking genuinely put out. "You really don't look it at all. You haven't a gray hair on your head. And your physique—"

She cut herself off, and he saw that crimson blush again. Lord, but she was pretty. Even if she was almost young enough to be his daughter. Biologically she *was* young enough, if barely. He grimaced before he realized what she had been about to say.

He raised his brows. "My physique, you were saying?"

She took a breath. "You're just very physically fit. I noted it this morning. For thirty-three."

"Well, I work out."

"You work out of doors?" She was obviously grateful for the seeming change of subject.

He laughed. "No, I *work out*. I exercise. Go to the gym. Lift weights. That sort of thing."

"The jim?"

"Gymnasium, you know, a place to exercise."

"Oh, yes." She nodded. "And do you work? That is, what sort of work do you do? You are not a gentleman of leisure. . . ."

"I wish. I'm a writer."

"A writer!" she exclaimed, apparently delighted. "So you read!"

"Of course I read. What do you think I am, an idiot?"

"Of course not, I just . . . many people don't read. What is it that you write, Mr. Patrick?"

"Well, I used to be a journalist, but now I write speeches. For senators mostly."

She frowned. "They don't write their own?"

"Not if they want to sound intelligent."

She laughed. "There are many MPs who could use your services too, I vow. Though I don't believe that's a tradition that will be adopted on this side of the Atlantic. No one would be willing to admit they haven't the skill themselves."

"Nobody at home does either. They just claim not to have the time."

"I see. How clever. So you must have had some schooling to be able to write a speech for a senator. How were you educated? And were your parents educated people?"

"Sure. I went to college, same as my parents. I

guess you could say we're among the better-educated people in the country, yes.''

"So you must speak several languages. French, perhaps?''

Flynn shook his head. "No. I took some Spanish in college, just the prerequisite, but I can't remember anything but how to order meatballs in a restaurant. *Donde esta las albondegas?*''

Her brows furrowed. *"Estan,"* she corrected. "So you speak *no* languages then? Do you read Latin and Greek at least?''

Flynn laughed. "Yeah, right. The day I learn to read Latin, look for pigs to take flight.''

"No Latin! So you are not a man of information." She sounded disappointed.

"A Man of Information?" He laughed. "Sounds like 'The Man from Uncle.' Uh, never mind. I read the newspaper every day. Is that enough information for you?''

She scoffed. "The newspaper. No real information is contained there, unless you wish to know the latest fashions.'' She looked him over pointedly. "Which I doubt. Or perhaps you are a society person, in which case you must peruse the gossip columns daily.''

"I don't give a rat's—'' He glanced at her. "I don't care about gossip.''

"Well, that's something. And you do not ride horses?''

He shook his head, remembering the awful night he'd spent on Old Bones. "Not on purpose.''

"Do you fence?''

"What, you mean swords? God, no.'' He laughed again. "Only the sissies took that in school.''

"Surely you can dance at least?"

"I don't like to."

"But you know how."

He looked at her, beginning to get that not-good-enough feeling again. "Probably not the way you know how."

She sighed, looking bothered.

"You're not getting pretentious on me again, are you, Mel?" he asked. "Because I want you to know that where I'm from, I'm quite a catch. I've got money, a good job, a nice car, a big house. I'm a smart guy."

"Yes, I can see that," she said morosely.

"I don't know what difference it makes to you anyway," he said angrily, sensing that she'd wanted to admire him and didn't. "With any luck at all I'll be back home in the morning."

She looked at him doubtfully. "Surely you know there is no way to get to America by morning."

He looked at her cynically. "Don't worry. I'm not that stupid, I'm just in a situation you could never understand. Hell, *I* don't understand it. And for all I know I could wake up tomorrow and be home. Not just in America, but in America in the year 1998. Call me crazy, but *that's* my home, Melisande. I don't have any idea how I ended up here, but I'm from a future so distant you'll never even see it."

Chapter Eight

"You have said that before, and unless for some reason you *want* to be taken to Bedlam, I suggest you stop saying it."

Melisande could barely contain her frustration. She didn't know what she'd expected by asking about his background, but to have him be so hopelessly uneducated, so far from being a gentleman, so unequivocally beneath her, was a severe disappointment.

Perhaps she hadn't wanted to admit to herself that she'd been attracted, even momentarily, to someone so unrefined. She'd been carried away by his appearance, it was as simple as that. She never would have thought it possible of her to be so frivolous, but, she reasoned, it was not worth donning a hair shirt over. Many women were swept away by a man's appearance, and didn't realize until it was much too late that the fellow had none of the qualities they desired in a husband. Melisande nad merely suffered a tiny lapse that no one but herself need know about.

The thought gave her some comfort, and she dwelt on it as they continued walking. The day felt somewhat warmer than the preceding one as the sun broke through the clouds and lay across her back like a shawl. She looked up into the sky, and decided that it would be blue before the day was out.

Yes, she felt much better, she told herself. And it was only a good thing that she now knew exactly what sort of man he was. Low-born, somewhat fanciful, charming, yes, but not of her ilk, her breeding, her class. They would do each other this favor—perhaps she would even give him a reward for his service when she got to London—and then she would never see him again. Once the devil was out of her midst, she would have no worries about succumbing to any vile temptations.

From the corner of her eye she noticed her companion's grim expression and glum pace. His brow was furrowed—his *handsome* brow, yes, she could admit this freely now, objectively, she thought with some satisfaction—and his eyes were shuttered, as if he looked inward at something he wasn't quite pleased with.

"Come now," she said, feeling conciliatory, "there is no need for such a long face. We shall be in London by tomorrow night, I vow, and then all will be well."

He grunted. "I'm sure we'll be in *your* London. Not mine."

They walked several more paces.

"And while we're on it, I'm not shoveling any

more crap,'' he added grumpily. ''You got it? That meal we had last night was hardly worth an hour and a half's slopping around in a pigsty this morning. This time *you* work for the food.''

''Me? What on earth would I do? I don't know the ways of poor people as you do. I would be completely inept.''

He turned an incredulous look on her. ''What are you talking about? I don't know the 'ways of poor people' any better than you do. In fact, I probably know a lot *less* about these people than you do. Because not only is this my first time in England in twenty-seven years, I've never even *visited* a farm, let alone one in the nineteenth goddamn century.''

''Your language, Mr. Patrick,'' she reminded him. ''It just seems to grow worse every day.'' She decided not to mention the comment about the nineteenth century. The more she encouraged talk on that subject, the more likely he would be to fabricate further stories to support the contention. No, she was best off ignoring all mention of it, though she did not have it in her to ignore his deplorable manners and reprehensible language.

''You shouldn't think you're so far above manual labor, Miss High and Mighty,'' he said, pointing aggressively at her. ''I think a little of it would do you some good. In fact, from what I can see, this whole trip will probably do you some good. Let you see how the little people live.''

''I know how the little people live, Mr. Patrick. I visit my father's tenants on a regular basis. I bring food and medicine to those who are sick or injured, and I report anything that needs repair on their homes to my father's bailiff. How many people less fortunate than yourself do *you* help, Mr. Patrick?''

He was silent for a time, and Melisande smiled to herself.

''I went to a soup kitchen once,'' he said finally.

She sighed. His odd phrasing was another irritating thing, though she was not about to admit she understood barely a third of all he said. Most of the time she could guess what he meant from the conversation's context, but not this time. ''A soup kitchen?'' she repeated.

''Yeah, a place where they feed the homeless. A girl I was dating worked at one, and that's where we spent Christmas Eve one year.''

''Once?''

''And I give money to charity—I give a lot of money. To the Heart Association. The Arthritis Foundation.'' He cleared his throat and gesticulated again. ''But this is not the point. The point is, I worked for our food last night, you can work for tonight's. That's the point.''

''Fine,'' she said.

It didn't matter, she thought. She was sure any help she might be able to offer would procure them very little in the way of food or shelter. No doubt he would end up having to do something manual no matter what she did. And no matter what he said, he had to know more about poor people than she did, since he was so obviously one of them.

Look at his education, she told herself. His dress. His coarse language. His *accent*—it positively grated on the ears. No, he was mistaken if he truly considered himself well-educated. Though perhaps he was, compared with his American compatriots, she realized. She'd always heard that the Americans were a bunch of savages.

"You're just saying that," he said. "You're not really going to do anything, are you?"

"That's right. I honestly don't know what service I could provide to these sorts of people that would make them want to part with good food and a place for us to sleep."

He gave her a dry look. "You could wash a few dishes. Help someone clean up, make up a bed or something. You're not an invalid, are you?"

"Of course not."

He nodded. "There you go."

She shook her head. He was impossible. He was not even worth arguing with, she told herself. She had no idea why she entertained his foolish ramblings.

They walked on.

Toward evening they came to a small town—quite bustling compared to Tunbridge, Flynn noted. The cottages on the outskirts looked far more prosperous than the one they'd stayed at the night before. Most of these had gardens to the side or in back, though they were fallow now, and what looked like fruit trees in neat rows nearby. A couple of them had small stables with ponies or cattle in them, and almost all had a pig or a couple of goats. They were also a little bigger and the yards were cleaner than the lodging of the night before.

Smoke rose from the chimneys of the houses they passed, and lights glowed from the windows into the evening dimness in which Flynn and Melisande walked.

"How far do you suppose we are from London?" he asked. His voice sounded strange to him in the quiet surrounding them. They'd barely talked the last few hours, both of them lost in thought. Flynn had mostly been thinking about his feet and how he'd give half his fortune to be able to sit in an easy chair with a pair of slippers on for a month.

"I'm not sure. If the Clydes were correct, this should be Quails Head, in which case we should be no more than twenty-five miles or so."

"Hmph," Flynn said. "Twenty-five miles, is that all?" Eight hours, he figured. A little more, if they walked the human average of three miles per hour. Eight more hours of walking in dress shoes.

They came to a slow stop in the middle of the main road. Cottages lined the streets and several shops, closed now, displayed their goods for an absent public.

Melisande's hands rose to her hair and pushed some stray locks back into the bun she wore. Smoothing her palms down her cape, she looked at him.

"How do I look?"

The question surprised him. "Fine," he said, then realizing that was never enough for a woman, he added, "You look good. Especially considering . . ." He stopped himself.

She smiled wryly. "Considering I've been wearing the same gown for two days and slept in a haystack last night?"

He smiled back. "Well, yes, frankly. Why? What are you planning to do?"

163

She gazed down the street, caught sight of something, and pointed. "I'm thinking I'll go to that inn and see if the proprietor won't . . . extend a little credit. If I explain to him that once I get to London I shall have all the money I need with which to pay him, perhaps he'll let me send him the fee for the room."

Flynn raised an eyebrow at her. "Hmm."

"You don't think he'll let me?"

He cocked his head to one side and exhaled. "If it were 1998, I can tell you he wouldn't. But who the hell knows now?"

Her expression turned dark. "Mr. Patrick—"

"Okay, okay." He held his hands up in surrender. "Sorry! I forgot. No bad language."

"It really is *most* unseemly. And this talk of the future must cease also. You won't be fit for any company at all if you persist in talking so."

"All right, I get it. I'll remember next time."

She looked at him dubiously.

"I will." He gestured toward the inn with his head. "Now, go on. Once he turns you down, we won't have much time to find something else."

She glared at him, and he laughed. "Go *on*," he repeated.

She turned on her heel and stalked toward the inn. Flynn stood in the middle of the road and looked around. After a moment he wandered over to one of the shop windows. Inside, propped up on stands, was a selection of small, leather-bound books. He leaned close to read the titles, and could make out a small book of Shakespeare's sonnets, a small book of Byron's poems, and some book in three volumes called *Evelina*.

No John Grisham here, he reflected, as if he needed anymore proof that this situation was not a joke, nor a movie set, nor a dream. He'd fallen through some kind of black hole into another time. And when he was perfectly honest with himself, and didn't dwell on the question of whether or not he would ever get home again, he had to admit he felt better than he had in years. Less stressed, more open-minded, healthier. Aside from the fact that he hadn't eaten in almost twenty-four hours, he'd been exercising more and getting more fresh air. Part of that had to be doing him some good.

He stepped to the next window, and saw bolts of fabric and ribbons and lace lined neatly for passersby to see. Some ridiculous-looking ladies' hats stood in the background.

He looked down at his ruined suit. He had to admit he would love to get out of this suit and into something else, even if it meant putting on what he'd seen men wearing on the road. The high boots, cotton pants and shirts, and heavy jackets looked infinitely more comfortable than this tuxedo, even if he had ditched the tie and cummerbund miles ago. And the shoes, well, if he never wore another pair of dress shoes again, it would be too soon.

Moments later he saw Melisande emerge from the inn. He could tell nothing from her expression or body language. In fact, she was always so composed that she was a mystery to him. No doubt that was the major part of his attraction to her. He was always attracted to women before he really got to know them.

Then . . . well, suffice it to say he was not a man built for commitment.

"Where should we look next?" he asked as she approached.

"Nowhere," she said, with what could only be called a triumphant smirk. "The proprietor and I have reached an agreement."

His brows rose. "Really?"

She shrugged nonchalantly. "Really."

"You got us rooms?"

She inhaled slowly. "Yes. I, ah, got a room."

"*A* room," he repeated. "So . . . I'm sleeping on the floor."

She frowned. "Not exactly."

He crossed his arms over his chest. "What does that mean, not exactly."

"I told the man we were brother and sister—to be consistent, you know. But he thought it might be best if you were to sleep downstairs. They have a back parlor, very small, for the servants. He said he would be happy to provide a blanket and pillow."

"So I'm sleeping in the servants' quarters after all."

"Yes, but—"

"On the floor."

"Yes—"

"While you sleep in a bed in a private room."

"That's true but—"

"And will I be shoveling shit in the morning too?"

She glared at him. "You promised you would clean up your language."

"Will I?"

166

"I have no desire to speak with someone so crude." She turned away from him.

He grabbed her by the arm and turned her back, letting go quickly when she jerked her arm away. "Answer me."

"No," she said finally. "I've made other arrangements."

"What other arrangements?"

"Nothing that involves you."

He narrowed his eyes. Surely she wasn't thinking... "Why do I suspect you're hiding something?"

"I'm not. I—I'm going to teach the proprietor's son to dance."

Flynn's eyes opened wide. *This* he had not been expecting. Laughter burst from him. "What?"

"It's not funny. I'm going to teach the proprietor's fourteen-year-old son to dance. And if you're smart, you will pay close attention as I do. Nobody who wishes to be considered a gentleman should be unable to dance."

"I take it the proprietor doesn't know how to dance either. Is he expecting a lesson too, Miss Melisande?" The idea of watching Melisande dance was not at all unappealing. In fact, he couldn't think of a better way to spend the evening, aside from sitting in a La-Z-Boy recliner and watching a fight on TV with a beer in one hand and a plate of French fries in the other.

She looked disconcerted. "No. I don't know. It doesn't matter."

"I guess we'll see then, won't we? Is he going to throw in dinner with this deal?"

"Yes."

"Thank God."

"Mr. Patrick!"

"What? What was wrong with that? Can't I thank God?"

She gave him a narrow look. "You were perilously close to using the Lord's name in vain."

"Hey, I'll praise him from here to kingdom come if we get something hot to eat," he said, striding for the inn.

"And remember," she said, catching up to him, "we are the *Smiths*."

"No, no, now you must go to my left. That's right. And back. Then you wait for the other couples. There should be at least three or four other couples." Melisande stood in the center of the chilly parlor while the inn's proprietor and his youngest daughter clapped to the rhythm of what should have been music.

Mr. Patrick—Flynn, as she allowed herself to call him in her mind—lounged on the settee, watching her with those clear eyes that made her skin warm all over.

Jeremy Porter, the innkeeper's son, was a tall, gangly lad of fourteen with freckles across the bridge of his nose and an engaging smile. His father was anxious for him to deport himself like a gentleman, but Melisande feared that his lack of grace would keep him from ever dancing very well. Someone with his coordination, or rather lack thereof, should have been started on this at a very young age.

"Once the couples have passed and it is our turn, you take my hand, lay the other upon my waist—

lightly, Mr. Porter, if you please. I am not a horse to be led about.''

Jeremy smiled sheepishly. "Sorry, Miss Smith."

"That's all right. You're doing well."

The clapping continued, and she endeavored to lead the boy through the steps while giving him the illusion of leading. All the while she could feel Flynn's eyes upon her.

He didn't clap. He simply lounged, his eyes at half-mast, watching her like the cat that had just lapped up all the cream.

"And now," she said, drawing away from the boy, "you bow to me—*slowly*. That's right. And I curtsy to you."

Jeremy bounced up from his bow and spun to look at his father. "How'd I do, Papa? I got through the whole dance this time without messing up real bad, did you see?"

The innkeeper smiled a gap-toothed smile, his eyes crinkling appreciatively at Melisande. "I saw, son. Aye, you did real good. Didn't mash the miss's toes once this time, did you?"

"Let's do it again. Can we, miss?" Jeremy turned back to her, big hands at the end of bony arms outstretched.

Melisande smiled. He *had* improved, she thought, and felt some satisfaction at having started with nothing and created, well, not a dancer exactly, but someone who knew the steps.

"Very well. One more time, and then perhaps we should try a different one."

Jeremy's face fell. "A *different* one? You mean there's more than one?"

Behind her, Melisande heard Flynn laugh. She turned slowly to him.

"I shouldn't be so amused if I were you, Mr. Patrick," she said.

His eyes widened, and he glanced pointedly at the innkeeper. She frowned at him. What was he about now? Then she drew in a sharp breath.

"So, Mr. Patrick *Smith*," she corrected herself quickly, "*you* shall be next." She turned to Jeremy. "My brother never learned to dance either, Mr. Porter. So you see you are in good company, though I doubt he will pick it up as quickly as you have."

Jeremy blushed and smiled. "You mean you don't dance neither, sir?"

Flynn shot Melisande a severely displeased look, but smiled at the boy. "Nor do I intend to."

"You don't intend to?" Jeremy asked. "Whyever not? Papa says that a man mayn't be called gentleman if he can't dance. How come you can't dance, Mr. Smith?"

"Ah, my brother grew up in America," Melisande supplied, noting the innkeeper's strained look. "They apparently have different customs there."

"But now you're here you'll be wanting to learn, I bet," Jeremy said. "You got to be a gentleman here too, or you won't get nowhere, my pa says. Id'n that right?"

Flynn's eyes moved from the boy's face to the innkeeper's. "Sure. That's right," he said evenly.

The innkeeper smiled. "You see, son? Everybody knows a gentleman's got to dance."

"It's fun," Jeremy said earnestly to Flynn. "Really. I didn't think it would be either, but it is. Why don't you go 'head and take a turn with your sister. I'll clap.'' Jeremy flopped into a chair and put his hands on his knees.

Melisande turned to Flynn and held out a hand. She could not help smiling a little snidely.

"Mr. Smith?" she offered.

He made a sour face and did not move for a long moment. Melisande was gratified to see his smug expression of a few minutes ago replaced by something close to embarrassment.

"You've been watching us now for a while," she went on. "So we won't be starting quite from scratch. Come, I think this is a good lesson for you."

Finally, he rose. She felt a fluttering beneath her breastbone, and told herself it was mere appreciation of his grace. The fact that all he'd done was stand up was irrelevant. Grace showed itself in all motions.

He took her hand in his, flesh against flesh, as she had no gloves, and squeezed it slightly. His hand was warm, her fingers icy.

"Now," she said, glancing to the floor and setting her feet just so. "You stand across from me. Not so close. Just so that our extended arms might touch."

Inexplicably, she felt her cheeks flush.

"Before the dance, I curtsy and you bow." She curtsied, keeping her eyes raised to see him bow stiffly. He raised his eyes and their gazes met. Melisande paused.

He looked at her so intently. What was he thinking? Did he not care that the innkeeper and his son were watching? Not to mention the little girl.

"Clap!" she said suddenly, turning on the two Porters. They jumped at the word, and the little girl

171

laughed. Haphazard clapping ensued, finally settling into the correct rhythm.

She took a deep breath and looked at Flynn. "Now, follow my actions. Take two steps forward, clasp hands, now let go. And step back. . . ."

He picked the steps up easily, no doubt from spending the last hour watching her and Jeremy. He faltered when they had to circle each other, going the same way she did and causing a minor collision. He grabbed her to steady her, his hands hard on her arm and waist, but he let go quickly.

They continued, with Melisande calling out the steps like a circus ringleader, until the clapping stopped, then commenced in appreciation of their dancing.

"Well done!" the innkeeper said. "Well done, Mr. Smith. You done that before, I vow."

"You looked almost as good as me after an hour's practice!" Jeremy added, enthusiastic but looking not altogether pleased.

Flynn bowed to them all and turned back to Melisande.

"Now, sister dear," he said, a devilish look in his eyes. She had a moment to dread what he had up his sleeve before he continued, "Let me teach you a dance. Here's one we've been doing in America for years. My mother taught it to me when I was about Jeremy's age. Little did I know when it would become useful." He smiled into her apprehensive eyes, and her stomach did a little flip-flop.

His hand closed again on hers, encompassing it in warmth again. "Come here," he said in a low voice that thrummed along her nerves. And his hand drew her to him.

Their bodies nearly touched when she stopped. He placed his other hand around her, so that it touched the small of her back, and she had difficulty keeping her breathing even. They were so close, his arm almost enveloping, she thought she could feel the heat emanating from his body.

His eyes dropped to her lips, and she realized they were parted breathlessly. She closed her mouth and lifted her chin, returning his steady gaze.

"We call this the waltz," he said.

Her heart tripped a beat. "I—I have heard of the waltz. It is . . . scandalous, they say."

His brows drew together. "I'll never understand this world," he muttered low. His arm tightened slightly around her. "Now," he continued, smiling, in a tone not unlike her own had been. "Here's how it goes. One-two-three, one-two-three," he counted without moving. "That's the beat. Are you ready?"

She nodded stiffly.

"Okay, follow me." And he swept her into a circle, dipping slightly on the "one" and turning on the "two-three." Before long the Porters took up the rhythm with their clapping, Jeremy having to scoot quickly out of the way as their circles grew wider, and Melisande felt positively breathless with the dance. It was a heady mix of closeness and motion, spinning and stepping, forward and backward movement.

She clasped his hand tightly, her other hand holding his upper arm for balance. She had no idea if he did this well, but she found it exhilarating. Immodest as it was, she felt delirious and brazen, and she did not wish it to end. She thought she could spin like this forever without a care in the world. And the longer they danced, the tighter his arm became, until she was pressed up against him like a shameless hussy, her legs brushing between his and his breath in her hair.

When he finally slowed to a stop, she could not help laughing with the thrill of it.

"Oh, Mr. Patrick," she said, clutching his arm and his hand though they'd stopped. "That was *wonderful*!"

He gazed down at her, into her eyes, into her smile, and she felt as if he'd spoken to her in a language she never knew she spoke. He held her tightly, and memories of that morning when they'd awakened together in the hay flitted deliciously through her mind.

He wanted to kiss her again—she could tell by the way he looked at her—even though now he was wide awake and knew exactly who she was. She felt his heart pounding through his odd American shirt, and God help her, she wanted him to kiss her too.

All too soon the Porters' applause ceased and Flynn eased back, letting her go. Reluctantly, she thought, their eyes still locked, for his hand slid from around her back, touching her side, her waist, a portion of her stomach before leaving her.

"I daresay they won't let you do that with someone who ain't your brother, eh?" The innkeeper laughed.

Melisande tore her gaze from Flynn's and clasped her hands in front of her.

"No, I daresay they wouldn't," she agreed. "It is most improper."

"But you liked it, didn't you?" Flynn asked, decidedly smug. He approached her, picking his jacket up off the chair back and swinging it over his shoulder with one finger. He moved close and leaned toward her as he passed, saying quietly near her ear, "You're not so *proper* after all, are you?"

Chapter Nine

"This is most generous of you, Mr. Porter," Melisande said, climbing tentatively onto the back of the hay wagon. The sturdy old vehicle was piled high with bales of hay, so scaling it was no small feat.

When he gave her a leg up, Flynn caught a glimpse of heavy white stocking over a shapely calf as she pulled herself up onto the stack.

"Are you sure we'll be quite safe up here?" she asked, her voice reedy with worry.

"Oh, aye," Mr. Porter said, doing something complex to one of the horse's harnesses. "We strapped them bales on there good. And we won't be takin' any corners real fast like." He laughed.

Melisande sat gingerly on the top of the stack, folding her legs under her and grabbing the string on two bales with her fingers.

Flynn climbed the stack and grinned at her. "Pretty

nice view from up here. I'll give a quarter to the first person who sees London. My parents used to do that when we went to the beach.''

"A quarter what?'' she asked, clutching the hay.

He looked down at her fingers, bloodless around the string binding the hay. "We're not even moving yet, Mel.''

"I know,'' she said defensively.

"Then why are you holding on so tightly?''

She looked away from him, keeping her eyes on the horizon. "I don't like being up high. It makes me nervous.''

He bent and looked over the side of the wagon. "We aren't that high. Shoot, you could probably fall on your head off of this thing and get nothing worse than a nasty headache.''

"I know,'' she said testily.

Mr. Porter clambered onto the wagon, followed by Jeremy up the other side. A sharp whistle, the crack of the reins, and the wagon lurched forward.

A little gasp burst from Melisande's mouth and she bent lower over the hay, apparently trying to make herself smaller, or sturdier, or something.

"Why don't you lie down?'' Flynn asked, stretching his legs out and sliding so he had enough room to lie back. "You'll feel steadier.''

"Then I won't be able to see what's coming. A—a curve, perhaps, in the road.''

He laughed. "Melisande, you could sit up once an hour and tell what's coming. We're not moving that fast. Porter says we won't be in London till seven, and that's if the roads are good.''

She took a deep breath and tried to scoot her legs

out from under her. It was difficult since she wouldn't let go of the bales and her skirt kept getting tangled with her feet.

Flynn watched her struggle for several minutes before he sat up and took her by the shoulders. "I can't watch this anymore. Come on." He lifted her upwards, over one of his legs, so she sat between his legs. "I've got you. Now straighten out your dress or whatever it is you need to do and lean back against me. I can guarantee you I'm not going to fall."

She did as he said and leaned back into him, her hands clutching his thighs.

"There now. Feel better?"

He watched her head move in a nod.

"You know, you really surprise me sometimes. One minute you're one of the boldest women I've ever seen, and the next you're cowering over a ride on a hay wagon."

"You have not seen me at my best, Mr. Patrick," she said. "I am normally quite refined." The wagon hit a rock and her fingers closed like vises on his legs.

"I'm not going to let you fall. Now come on, you're stiff as a poker."

After a moment's consideration, he felt her relax against him. He put an arm around her waist.

"What are you doing?" she asked, stiffening again. She obviously didn't dare move.

"Just holding on. I thought you'd feel safer this way. Don't you?"

"I don't feel as if I'm going to fall, but I wouldn't say I feel 'safer.' "

Flynn laughed. He could hear the wryness in her voice, and admired her for it. He'd known someone once who was afraid of heights, and he realized what it took to confront the phobia.

"Trust me, then, you're safe. If I haven't ravaged you by now, what makes you think I'm going to?"

"Opportunity, Mr. Patrick."

"I've had better opportunities on this trip than this one. You know that, Mel." He smiled, smelling her hair close to his face. She felt good against him. Soft and warm, somewhat voluptuous. At home, he'd always been attracted to the model types, the rail-thin ones who hung out at the gym ten hours a day and could beat the crap out of half the men they dated.

But Melisande was another story. He was attracted to her, there was no doubt about it, but she was different. Rounder, softer, but still strong. She looked the way a woman should, he found himself thinking. With curves in the right places and a seductive way of moving. She didn't walk as though she'd played volleyball in college. She strolled as if she knew exactly what sort of pleasures her body was capable of.

Though of course that was ridiculous. Flynn would stake his life on her being a virgin.

"I'll thank you not to mention those opportunities to anybody once we reach London," she said. She looked down at his arm and he felt her move his sleeve. "What is this?"

He twisted his wrist and looked over her shoulder. "Oh. My watch."

"Upon your wrist," she said. "How ingenious. And it's tiny."

"One of the marvels of the twentieth century," he said with a smile. "The band is about to break, though. I should take it off so I don't lose it. God knows where I'd get another one around here.''

He felt her back stiffen again. ''Once again, Mr. Patrick, I must ask you to refrain from saying such things. People will think you mad, and will look further down upon me as a consequence. When we reach London, I'm sure I'll be able to make it worth your while to keep silent about this whole trip.''

Flynn wasn't sure why this comment took him by surprise, but it did. As did the sharp knife of disappointment he felt inside. After all they'd been through, she still didn't trust him. Oh, he knew she didn't trust him not to put the moves on her, he accepted that. What woman would? But he thought she at least had confidence in his character. He'd helped her so far, keeping her secret and maintaining the charade for everyone around them. Why would she doubt him now?

He removed his arm from her waist and leaned back on his hands. Melisande lurched with his shifting weight and caught at his thighs.

''I'm sorry,'' she said quickly. ''I didn't mean to imply . . . that is, I'm sure you're trustworthy, it's just—''

''Forget it,'' he said roughly. ''You made your point. And don't worry, I'm still not going to let you fall.''

Her hands on his legs relaxed marginally. He watched her shoulders rise and fall with a deep breath as he lay back against a high, uneven bale. She sat stiffly between his legs.

They rode this way for a while before Flynn drifted off to sleep, happy that he was not walking and vowing to throw his shoes away the moment he could get some new ones. He imagined that Melisande's method of keeping him silent would be money, and he was anxious to buy some clothes. He wondered if she would continue to help him once they got to London and her precious reputation was under scrutiny, or if he would be on his own to negotiate what would undoubtedly be another sea of unfamiliarity. The thought made him uneasy. Not that he was a coward or anything, he explained to himself. He was just tired of having everything from sleeping to peeing be a challenge.

He woke sometime later, when the sun was high in the sky, to find Melisande asleep on his chest. She had leaned back into him, then turned so that her head rested near his shoulder and her legs were curled under her. He lifted his arm and put it around her shoulder, liking the feel of the contact without all the conflict that was present when she was awake. She nestled closer.

His other hand he moved to her head, feeling a strand of chestnut hair between his fingers. It was satiny soft, like a strand of corn silk. He laid his palm on her forehead and gently pushed the hair from her face, looking down to see the white skin at her temple, the dark end of an eyebrow, and the thick shadow of lashes against her cheek.

She looked perfect to him, and for once in his life he didn't question why, or how long he thought it would last, or what he was going to do about it. There wasn't anything he could do about it. He just looked at her and thought she was perfect.

Perfect looking, that is. She had a few qualities he'd get rid of if he had the chance, he told himself, or if he was going to be around long enough for it to make a difference, which he wasn't. Her snobbishness, first of all. And that was *not* simply because she looked down on him, he argued to his sanctimonious conscience. She *was* a snob, there was no doubt about it.

And her preoccupation with her reputation. What was that all about? Always worrying about how things *looked,* what people would think, appearances. She'd drive him crazy with that if he were around her for any length of time. Hell, she drove him crazy with it now.

He slid her hair through his fingers again and remembered how she'd looked when he'd waltzed with her last night. He'd botched the dance, but she had still looked radiant and graceful in his arms. She'd blushed, actually *blushed,* when he touched her. And yet she'd taken his hand and followed him through the steps of the dance, making it look as good as if they were dressed to the nines with a full orchestra playing Strauss.

Then he wondered if Strauss had even been born yet. Sure would have been nice, he thought, drifting off to sleep again, if he'd paid a little more attention in history class.

Melisande awoke to the sound of a hawker yelling, "Matches! Rags! Get your matches 'ere! Rags! Matches! Get your rags 'ere!"

They must be in London, she thought with both panic and relief. Daylight had given way to twilight, she saw as she stretched her legs and shifted her position. It was only when Flynn's hand slid from her shoulder that she noticed what she lay upon.

Carefully, so as not to wake him, she pushed herself up, noting as she did that his other hand was tangled in a thin lock of her hair. She disentangled his fingers and sat up, feeling the cool air against her side where her body had touched his. She looked at his face in the gloaming. Handsome, even in sleep, she thought. Then, such a shame.

She wondered if he had ever been married, since he said he did not have a wife now. It was rare for a man of three and thirty to never have been married. And if he had been, she wondered what his wife had been like. A poor woman, obviously, as he was. Yet she could not picture him with a working wife, one with calloused hands and a sun-lined face. Someone like Mary Clyde.

Most likely he would have married a governess, or some other respectable type of woman, though on second thought, he spoke too crassly to satisfy a governess. He was a puzzle, she decided. For though he spoke no languages and could not dance or ride or anything, he did not seem wholly uneducated. He could read, for example, and for the most part his vocabulary was good, even if he did occasionally make up a word and his accent was somewhat offensive to the ears. And it seemed to her he could do figures, though she could not remember what made her think so.

She looked at his hand, lying limp on the hay, and glanced up at his face. He looked dead to the world. She rested her fist in his palm a moment, and when his fingers did not clasp shut upon it, she lifted his hand onto her lap. No callouses, she noted, straightening his fingers and examining his palm. In fact, the nails on his well-shaped hands were very neatly trimmed too. Could he possibly be considered a gentleman in America? Could this strange clothing really be what they wore in that country?

She drew her fingers along the inside of his palm, feeling the heat of its center and the mound of muscle at the base of his thumb. This was the thumb that had touched her skin, she thought. That morning when he had kissed her, and touched her breast through her dress, this thumb had slipped through her fichu and skimmed her skin.

The wagon slowed, and she looked up to see a line of carriages before them. She did not recognize the area, but a few of the carriages looked fine enough that she suspected they neared Hyde Park. Thank God, they must have slept through the worst parts of town. When she'd given it half a thought earlier in the day, she'd dreaded going through the poorer areas of the city.

Flynn stirred, and she pushed his palm off her lap. His eyes opened and she busied herself looking forward, over Mr. Porter's head, to the carriages in front of them.

"There's some sort of jam," she said importantly, "but I'm sure we'll get through it in a moment's time."

Flynn's nose wrinkled. "What's that smell?"

Melisande smiled. "London."

"No, I mean the sh—uh, I mean the—"

"Dung?" she asked primly.

"Yeah."

"It's London," she said, not without satisfaction.

Despite the olfactory assault that she noticed every time she arrived from the country, London was the grandest city in the world, and Melisande felt some pride in it in front of this American. "It takes a while to get used to, like any city, but you will. And it's not nearly so bad in Mayfair, where my aunt lives. In fact it's not bad at all, except for some nights when there's a party and a lot of carriages come through."

"So it is dung," Flynn said, sitting up stiffly.

"Mostly," she said, not elaborating. He could surmise the rest without her help. "I've been thinking. Mr. Porter will drop us at Covent Garden on the way to the market. From there it is something of a walk to my aunt's, though we shall pass through no perilous neighborhoods. My concern is the servants."

"The servants," Flynn repeated, rubbing his eyes.

"Yes. If I am to simply show up at the door looking like this, it will be all over Mayfair by morning. Therefore, I think you should go to the back door with a note for my aunt. Give it to Cook to give to her and she will send a carriage for me. If I show up in a coach it will look much better."

Flynn looked at her dryly. "You don't think the servants will make the connection between me with a note and you showing up ten minutes later in a coach? I might also point out that it'll be obvious you don't have any luggage and you will still look, if you'll excuse me for saying so, like the ragged end of nowhere."

Melisande sat back and Flynn laughed.

"I can't believe it," he said. "You can even get offended at that. What, did you think that three days in the same dress, sleeping in haylofts and ratty inns, wasn't going to alter your appearance any?''

"You're saying I look terrible," she said, feeling suddenly self-conscious. She didn't know why she cared. In fact, she hadn't thought twice when he'd made a similar comment yesterday. She must be tired, she decided.

He shook his head, smiling. "Actually, no, you still look pretty good. But you also look as if you've been through the mill. If I were you I'd throw out that dress as soon as you get another one."

She looked down at her dress, the dark green fabric dotted with bits of hay and wrinkled from hem to sleeve. She turned her face to his.

"I suggest you do the same with your . . . ah . . ." She gestured disdainfully toward his suit. *"Clothes."*

"I intend to," he said, pulling off a shoe and emptying it of hay. "Starting with these." He waved the shoe at her. "I'd give everything I own right now for a pair of Nikes."

"Your entire fortune?" she said sarcastically. "Something tells me you are not referring to the goddess of victory."

"Who?"

She laughed hopelessly. "These Nikes must be extremely dear to prompt a man to offer so much." She did not even attempt to contain her sarcasm.

"They are," he said, replacing the shoe. "And do I need to tell you again that I have a lot of money? I just don't happen to have it with me."

"How unfortunate."

"I'll say." He turned and looked at the street around him. "You know, this doesn't look all that different from when I was here last time." He peered over the side of the wagon at the passing shop windows.

"I thought you said you'd never been to England before."

He glanced at her. "I meant . . . a couple days ago."

She raised a brow.

"You know, in my own time."

"Ohhh," she said, nodding. "That's right. What was it? Nineteen-ninety?"

"Ninety-eight," he said, ignoring her mockery.

"So you're saying that things won't change much in the next, oh, hundred and eighty-three years?"

"I'm saying the buildings will still be here. But it won't smell like shit."

She pursed her lips and looked away. He'd spoken so only to taunt her. No matter, she would be rid of him soon. Him and his strange, unpleasant ways.

She watched him as he perused the streets. His strong profile, his dirty hair, his odd suit, his broad shoulders, his fine hands. It truly was such a shame he was deranged.

She handed him the note after folding it carefully into eighths. Flynn pressed the tight square into his palm.

"There," she whispered, pointing down the alleyway. "You go to that yard, the third one down, and knock on the back door. Tell Cook you have an urgent message for her mistress. And please, try not to act too odd."

Flynn scowled at her. "I don't act odd. Just because you think I'm dressed—"

"I meant don't say anything stupid, like about

187

coming from the future or—or that your parents were divorced or anything like that.''

"My parents weren't divorced."

She rolled her eyes.

"They should have been," he continued equably, "but they weren't. I always wondered about it too. What made them stay together? I'm sure it wasn't for the 'good of the children' as people always say—"

"Mr. Patrick!" she hissed, grabbing his forearm and squeezing with no small amount of force. "*Please* be quiet. In fact, perhaps it would be best if you just handed the note to Cook and pretended to be mute. Yes, that's it—act as if you cannot speak. That will certainly appear less odd than if you actually open your mouth and spew something ridiculous."

"Okay," he said, holding up a finger, "I'm going to pretend you didn't just insult me, if you promise to buy me a new pair of shoes."

"*Please,*" she repeated, exasperated. "Fine, I'll get you anything you want. Just go. I am anxious to arrive. The longer we dally out here, the greater the chance of discovery. Now *go.*" She pulled the hood of her cape up over her head and backed into the shadow of the wall, watching him.

"That door?" he asked, pointing. "The one with the iron knocker on it?"

"Yes, yes. Just knock once or twice and someone in the kitchen will answer it."

"What if it's not the cook?" he asked. "If I ask for the cook my cover as a mute will probably be blown."

Melisande sighed heavily. "Hand it to anyone. My

188

aunt's name is on the outside. They'll take it to someone who can read.''

''All right.'' He took a few steps in the direction of the door, then turned back and returned to her. ''Do you think they'll give me something to eat?''

''*I'll* give you something to eat, if you'll just help me get in the blasted door!''

Flynn looked at her in surprise and laughed. '' 'Blasted'? That's like a swear word for you Brits, isn't it? Did you just swear, Miss St. Claire?''

''I'll do worse than that if you don't get moving.''

''All right,'' he said, and started off again. ''But I don't want to hear any more of that cursing. It's vulgar, you know. And it offends me. Deeply.''

Flynn chuckled as he walked toward the door, wondering if it was hunger that was making him this asinine. He'd barely eaten one meal a day for the last two days, and had not consumed a thing in nearly twenty-four hours. As he neared the back door of the townhouse, the smell of cooking food assailed his senses. His stomach woke up immediately, like an angry lion prodded with a chair, and his mouth literally watered. He trotted down the slate path to the door.

He knocked three times, and the door was opened at once by a girl in a cap and apron. She took one look at him and yelled over her shoulder, ''Cook! 'Ere's another one!'' She turned back to him. ''You just wait out 'ere, she'll bring you some soup.'' She started to close the door.

''Wait!'' Flynn stuck out a hand to stop the door, and the girl stepped back. ''That's not what I'm here for. Well, actually, I would like some soup,'' he added, lowering his hand. "But I've got a note for Mrs. Kesterbrook. A very important note."

The girl's face crinkled at him. "Good Lord," she said, grimacing at him. "Cook! Come 'ere. Listen to this one, eh? 'E sounds like 'e's from Australia or somewhere."

"America," he supplied. "But I have this note—"

"Now we're getting foreigners begging at our back door?" a grisly voice demanded, and a stout woman with iron-gray hair emerged from the warmth of the room. She wore a stained white apron, a faded brown dress, and a drooping white cap. "What's the world coming to, eh?" She looked Flynn over as she wiped her hands on her apron.

"You must be Cook," he said.

The moment the words emerged from his mouth, she giggled as if he'd just found the ticklish spot in her ribs.

"Oh, Lord, Rachel, you were right!"

" 'E says 'e's from America, not Australia."

The cook smiled at him, revealing four teeth, each leaning in a different direction like the rocks at Stonehenge. "All the way from America for a taste o' my soup?" She laughed at her own joke and slapped young Rachel on the back. Rachel laughed with her, obviously used to the abuse.

Flynn glanced back over his shoulder, wondering if Melisande had heard all the cackling and was now angry at him for not being a mute. He had to admit, this probably would have gone more smoothly if he hadn't opened his mouth.

"Listen, I have this note—"

"A note, you say?" the cook shot out a meaty hand and grabbed it from him.

"For Mrs. Kesterbrook," he said quickly, hoping she wouldn't open it up and read it on the spot. "A personal note. An important personal note."

The cook frowned at him. "From who?"

"Uh, that I can't tell you."

Her small, sharp eyes fixed on him. "Why not?"

The woman was as tough as Scotland Yard. He wondered if Scotland Yard was in existence yet.

"Because I don't know who," he said. "It was given to me by someone in a carriage, a real nice-looking one, and they said if I delivered it I might get something to eat." The cook was looking at the note skeptically. "They said this house was famous for its food."

She looked slowly back up at him. For a second he thought she was going to call him a liar and slam the door in his face, but she stepped back and motioned him inside.

"Come on in then, and have a seat at the table. Will you be taking an answer back?"

Flynn stopped. Had Melisande said something about an answer? He couldn't remember, he'd been so busy teasing her. But if he didn't take back an answer, what was he supposed to do, wait here for her? Once he finished the soup Rachel was laying out for him, he didn't think they'd just let him hang around.

"Well?" the cook barked.

"Uh, yeah," he said. "Yeah, I'm to take back an answer."

The cook giggled again. " 'Uh, yeahr,' " she mimicked, not coming close to his accent. "I could just listen to you all night, I could." She turned and made her way to another door, one that obviously led to the interior of the house.

"Come sit 'ere," Rachel said. She was a pleasant, round-faced girl, and she'd set a place for him at the thick round table in the corner of the kitchen.

As he took a seat, he glanced around the spacious room. Several female workers dressed the same as Rachel scurried about, hauling pails or chopping vegetables. They all did their best not to look at him, but Flynn could see their eyes flitting over to where he sat and then back to their work.

The room wasn't exactly sterile, he noted, but it looked clean enough. The floor was slate, obviously scrubbed frequently, and the counters that weren't empty had fresh-looking meat and vegetables in various stages of preparation piled around. On the interior wall was an enormous hearth with a healthy fire blazing. Shining copper pots and pans hung from the stones that made up the chimney, and a huge spit pierced the center of the fire. At the moment, a large black iron kettle hung from a hook to one side of the flames.

The place was cozy after the cold, drafty places he'd been the last two days, and he felt the warmth melt into his bones. He turned to the soup in the hefty, stoneware bowl in front of him. Large pieces of beef floated in a dark broth, surrounded by carrots and potatoes and onions. Then Rachel returned to the table and plunked a wooden cutting board full of crusty bread in front of him.

Flynn thought he might pass out from happiness.

He picked up the spoon and dipped it into the heavenly stuff, inhaling the heat fumes as they floated up from the broth, and closed his eyes.

He was just about to tip the first spoonful into his salivating mouth when the door behind him, the one the cook had disappeared through, burst open and all the kitchen workers gasped.

He spun in his seat to see a resplendently dressed woman, with dark hair piled high on her head and dark, flashing eyes, standing imperiously behind him. She looked like a confection, delicate and delicious, and very, very rich.

"Leave us," she commanded, her voice a honeyed testament to breeding and authority.

Knives clattered to the counters and pails clanged to the floor as the shocked workers bustled from the room. In seconds, the room was empty save for Flynn and the beautiful woman.

"Where is she?" she asked.

"Melisande?"

Her arched brows rose and she literally looked down her aquiline nose at him. "Yes. My niece. Melisande St. Claire."

Too late, he realized he should have stood up. He did so now.

"She's outside."

"Outside?" The single word brought home to Flynn an acute sense of negligence, as if he'd irresponsibly left a valuable item outside to be stolen, or worse.

"Yeah. She didn't want to come in. She said, you know, the servants. She didn't want them to see her and talk." He felt the same way he had when Mrs.

Reese had caught him in the girls room in fourth grade.

"Where are you from?" she demanded.

Flynn sighed. "You all don't get many visitors around here, do you? Why does everyone keep asking me that?"

"Because you sound like a braying mule when you speak."

Flynn laughed, embarrassed and angry at feeling embarrassed. "Don't sugarcoat it, honey, tell it like it is."

"Take me to her," the woman said, looking angrier herself.

Flynn drew himself up. "No." He stepped around the chair, away from the soup, so he did not feel so much a beggar. "That's not what she wanted. And that's not what's best. If you go out and bring your niece through here, what do you think are the chances nobody will see her, coming in the back door like she has something to be ashamed of? You parade her through the house like that and the whole world will know in a matter of days that she—"

"I understand your point, sir. But I want you to explain to me—"

"No again. Now, I suggest you send your carriage to wherever it is she said in her note, and then ask *her* to explain things to you. Because I haven't understood or been able to explain things for days and I'm not about to start trying now."

"What is your name?"

"Flynn Patrick."

She stood motionless, studying him, and he thought

he'd never seen such a beautiful woman look more intimidating.

"I feel like I should point out," he said, forcing himself to stare the woman down, "that the longer you stand here giving me the hairy eyeball, the longer your niece stands around outside waiting for your carriage."

She didn't move. She simply stood there, letting her eyes go from his face to his suit, to his shoes, and back to his face again. Flynn felt angry and uncertain, but most of all he felt nearly faint from hunger.

"I've sent the carriage," she said finally. "My niece said in her note we are not to let you leave, so you will stay here. I'll send Brayle to show you to a room. What I'd like to know before I leave you is why my niece feels you are due this service."

"I helped her out." He shrugged. "Did her a favor."

The woman laughed derisively, making Flynn feel less than worthless.

"You did her a favor. And what favor was that, Mr. Patrick? Abducting her from Merestun?"

Flynn was suddenly aware that the iciness in her tone was not authority, it was rage.

"Ruining her reputation and her future, and most likely her sister's as well, is that the favor you did her, Mr. Patrick? Is it to you we owe the destruction of her life?"

Chapter Ten

Melisande went straight to her aunt's room, despite the fact that she looked atrocious. If she didn't go, she knew her aunt would come to her.

She entered the sitting room tentatively, for some reason feeling a need to be as silent as possible, though hoping to go unnoticed was ridiculous. Her aunt was seated at her writing desk, penning a letter with an air of concentration.

Melisande stood silently near the door.

"Come in and sit down, dear. You've never been timid before. I'll be disappointed if you are so now."

Her aunt did not lift her head as she spoke, and her tone had been matter-of-fact. Melisande felt an inexplicable urge to cry. The open arms and warm cry of welcome she'd been expecting, or at least hoping for, were not to be had.

She moved forward into the room until she stood

in front of the desk. Her aunt's fine handwriting was too small to be read upside down and from this distance, but Melisande feared she knew to whom her aunt wrote so rapidly.

"You know that your parents are worried sick," Felicity said almost conversationally, but Melisande heard the steel beneath the words.

"Yes, ma'am. That is, I was afraid they would be."

Felicity nodded without looking up. "You realize that Lord Bellingham is livid."

"Y-yes. I knew that he would be angry with me."

At this, her aunt's head lifted and she looked Melisande dead in the eye. With her high, arched brows, Felicity looked the picture of disapproval.

"He's not angry with *you*, dear. He's angry at your abductor. The man who stole both you and his favorite steed out from under his very nose. He's apparently felt no small amount of embarrassment that this travesty took place in his presence. And the duke as well has suffered as the incident casts his home in an unfavorable light. To have brigands roaming one's grounds, you know, is simply not the *thing*."

Melisande felt her cheeks flush, and forcibly kept her hands by her sides to keep from fidgeting. The fact that her aunt showed no concern for her welfare told Melisande that she did not believe the abduction story any more than she should.

"I understand that," Melisande said quietly.

"Do you?"

"I—yes, now I do." She swallowed hard.

Her aunt said nothing.

"I had no intention of causing the duke any embarrassment," Melisande added to fill the silence. "I did not think of that . . . aspect of the situation. Nor did I wish to upset my parents.''

Her aunt laid her pen down and leaned back in the desk chair.

"You . . . ." Melisande began, then hesitated. "You know that I was not abducted.''

Felicity nodded again. "There was the matter of the bag found on the road to Tunbridge,'' she said. "Neatly packed with items an abductor would hardly have found necessary.''

"Does Lord Bellingham know of the bag?''

"No. Your parents thought it best for him to believe you'd been taken against your will. In such a case, they thought he would not be inclined to seek redress for a broken agreement, not to mention a public humiliation.''

"Aunt Felicity,'' Melisande said, her voice breaking on the words, "who else . . . that is, does everyone . . . ?''

"Everyone knows,'' her aunt stated. "It's been kept out of the newspapers, thank God and the duke. But there's been endless speculation. I heard at one point it was even considered that you would be best off to be found dead at the end of the ordeal.''

"Oh, God.'' Melisande sank into the chair behind her, her stomach roiling with sudden nausea and her breath too shallow to keep her head from spinning.

" 'Oh, God' is right. Now tell me, Melisande, about this—this *man* with whom you felt the need to run off. I want the truth. Who is he and what, exactly, is your relationship?''

Melisande jerked stricken eyes to her aunt. "Run off! I did not run off with *him*! And I have no relationship—he is insignificant, Aunt Felicity. You must believe me. I only employed him for protection on the road. It was pure chance that we even met."

"So you met up with this fellow on the road and decided on some sort of whim of self-preservation to travel with him?" Aunt Felicity's face was uncharacteristically flushed in anger. "He is nobody? A commoner from nobody knows where? Melisande, what *possessed* you?" This last was not said in supplication but indignation.

Too easily, Melisande saw the situation in the same light that her aunt did. The same absurd, unfavorable light. She saw so clearly all the mistakes she'd made, the foolish choice of leaving, the folly of trusting the stranger, the awful way everything *looked* despite the real and random circumstances. Which made it all so much harder to justify.

"I met him at Merestun," she began. "He claimed to be a guest, though I did not believe him. At first I tried to get away from him, but he followed me. Charged after me on Bellingham's horse, in fact." Melisande felt tears spill over her lashes and ignored them. "I thought he *was* Bellingham, and so I—I ran. By then I was in the woods and lost and—and he *seemed* harmless enough. He'd taken the horse by accident, you see. So there I was, alone in the woods in the middle of the night, and . . . he said he needed to go to London too. He asked for my help and he seemed, at that point anyway, rather . . . needy. So I made him an offer."

"You made *him* an offer," her aunt confirmed. "This stranger."

Melisande paused, looking at her hands, then said,

"That's right. My reasoning was, if he traveled with me, perhaps he could protect me from those who might be truly dangerous. But then at Tunbridge I was robbed, at the inn. And so, without money, I could not hire the maid or the coach I intended to make the trip respectably, and by then it was too late to turn back." She looked desperately at her aunt. "I had planned to arrive here in a manner that would be above reproach, Aunt Felicity. Truly I had. But circumstances . . ." She waved a hand hopelessly. "And then, once on the road, I thought perhaps, perhaps we could at least *say* that I did. Show up respectably, that is. But I didn't know, I didn't think, I didn't realize everyone would know I was missing. I thought I could get here in time. . . ." She choked back a sob and buried her face in her hands.

"You were gone three days, Melisande." Her aunt's voice was gentler now, though still not forgiving. "Your parents did their best to keep it quiet, but there was an investigation going on, to appease Lord Bellingham. Word got out after a day."

"Oh, God," she said again. Then, after a moment, her head shot up. "What have you done with him? You haven't given him to the authorities, have you? He was blameless in this. Truly, it was my plan, and mine alone."

Felicity studied her niece a moment. "He is still here, no doubt sleeping by now. I had Brayle ready a room for his use after he'd eaten. The reason he is still here is because he answered one question to my satisfaction. After that I did not see fit to call the authorities."

Melisande blinked away tears and sat up straight,

though she didn't look at her aunt. "Oh. So you spoke to him." Her tone was despondent. "He was supposed to play a mute."

At this, Felicity actually smiled. "Yes, I did speak to him. He is anything but mute."

"What question did you ask him?"

"I demanded that he take me to you and he refused. That might have alarmed me, but his reason was to safeguard your character. I knew without a doubt then that you had not been abducted."

Melisande's gaze dropped to her lap, where her fingers were braided together in a tight knot. "I have made . . . so many mistakes," she said quietly.

"Yes. You have."

The weight of her situation began to penetrate the haze of panic that had surrounded her for days, and with each breath she took she realized anew that she was ruined. She would never marry, never have children, never know the happiness of a normal life again. She might be pitied by some, as the story of her recovery was made known. But society would proclaim that she had been ruined and her life would be over.

"He is quite handsome," her aunt added, speaking slowly. "Your protector."

Melisande glanced up at her through her lashes, knowing now that that one shallow point had been instrumental in her trusting the stranger. As if good looks made for good character. She looked back down at her hands. "Yes."

"And what interesting clothing he wears. I'll have to show it to you closely. Despite its odd style, it is very finely made. The intricacy of the stitching and the quality of the fabric is quite breathtaking."

Melisande drew her brows together. "I did not notice it."

"His shoes are even shaped differently for each foot, did you notice that?" Felicity exclaimed.

Melisande shook her head. "How very eccentric."

"Yes. And did you see the watch upon his arm? I wonder where he got it. I wonder where he got all of it."

Melisande did not want to explain where Flynn had said it was from. Instead she merely said, "America, I suppose."

"Which brings us to that accent—atrocious!"

She frowned. "Yes, I know."

"He does not seem so very stupid, however. Where is he from?"

Melisande shrugged. "The capital supposedly."

"And what is he doing here? Does he have any education? Any money at all?"

Melisande scanned her memory, but realized she had never asked him what he was doing here, or what his plans were. She supposed it was because someone who believed he was here accidentally from the future probably had no plans. "I don't know. He has no money, it is quite obvious. But he only talked about getting to London, to try and get home." As he asserted he was from the future, she was not sure how he intended to do that. "I'm afraid he is not altogether right in his mind, however."

"What do you mean?" Felicity's voice was hard with concern.

"Oh, he's not dangerous or anything. It's just . . . sometimes he says very odd things. Impossible things. Crazy rantings. It can be"—she smiled ruefully—

"amusing at times. But he is not . . . normal."

Felicity folded her arms across her chest and studied her niece. "I see."

"Yes, well, you probably will, if you ever speak to him again."

"I'm sure that I shall." She cleared her throat and continued in a more conclusive tone. "In any case, we will endeavor to rectify what we can of this situation. All may not be completely lost, my dear. Right now you should go to your room and try to get some rest. I had Elsa run you a bath."

Melisande looked up. "By 'rectify,' " she asked hesitantly, "you don't mean . . . that is . . . Lord Bellingham?" She hardly knew whether to hope or dread the answer to the question.

Felicity issued a cynical laugh. "Heavens, no, child. He made it quite clear from the start that your betrothal was nullified, if, that is, you were found alive. He put it in the most suitable way, of course, vowing to see justice prevail and the blackguards who stole you hang from the highest yardarm. But he never failed to add that he would also see to it that your life was lived in the peace and solitude that would befit a woman who'd suffered such a painful experience, one from which she would no doubt never recover."

Melisande, to her own great surprise, found herself purely relieved. "You know he killed a servant girl," she told her aunt, eyeing her for her reaction.

Felicity's brows descended ominously. "When did you hear that? Surely you didn't believe that vile rumor."

She looked up at her aunt. "You *knew* of it? You

203

knew of it and yet said nothing as I was betrothed to him?"

"It is naught but idle gossip," she said, indignant, throwing out a hand as if to shoo the thought away. "One of but a thousand rumors circulating about the richest and most dynamic men. Why, I've heard Lord Fescue grazes on the lawn with his cattle. I've heard Admiral Corduron beats his wife with a cat-o'-nine-tails, and yet she appears at every party looking the very picture of affluence and satisfaction. I've heard Lord Renquill shot Lady Renquill's lover in their bed-chamber, but Lady Renquill continues to flirt outrageously at every outing. I've heard rumors about your own father that would curl your hair, and I know without question that they're not true. Now please tell me, Melisande, this bit of slander was not the sole reason you chose to leave."

Melisande exhaled slowly, suddenly too tired to think. "Not the sole reason, no."

"What were the others?"

Exhaustion overtook her. She slumped in her seat, but looked up at her aunt. "Surely you know," she said quietly. "It is the reason I came to you. I met him and knew I could never love him. He is . . . cold. He looked at me like a hawk eyes its prey. He made me . . . very uncomfortable."

"And yet you knew him only a matter of hours."

"I do not believe he would have improved upon knowing him longer—"

"But you don't know."

"Aunt Felicity," she said, her voice thickening, "I did not care for him! He frightened me. Surely *you* understand. I could not marry him. I *could not*." She sat up straighter and looked through defiant and tortured eyes at her aunt. "Even now I do not regret it. Even knowing that I am ruined—*ruined!*—I am glad I will not be his wife."

Felicity was silent, her face looking strained and older than Melisande had ever seen it.

"I could not go through with the match, no matter what," Melisande added, "and I knew Father would never understand, and would never let me out of it."

Felicity dropped her gaze. "And you came to me because I broke an engagement myself."

"That's right. That's why I was sure you would understand. Aunt Felicity, if you met this man, Lord Bellingham, you would see for yourself. He is not . . . kind." Melisande shook her head, the inadequacy of the words frustrating. But she felt she had reached her aunt, and looked at her with intensity.

"My engagement was to a merchant, Melisande." She looked back up. "Not an earl, who will someday be a duke. Lord Bellingham," she said slowly, "is a very powerful man."

Melisande felt the words as if they dropped onto her shoulders. She was doomed. Her life was irredeemable.

Once Flynn had eaten three helpings of the soup and felt his eyes drooping with every mouthful of the last one, the old man, Brayle, appeared and asked him to follow. Flynn dragged himself to his feet—warm for the first time in days—and followed Brayle from the kitchen. They wound through a labyrinth of narrow halls until they emerged into a large airy foyer. Potted palms waved from the corners, and the marbled floor was so shiny it reflected the paintings and huge mirrors on the walls.

He followed Brayle up the wide, curving staircase, watching the sober faces of the pictures on the wall watch him as he passed.

They reached the third floor and moved down a wide hallway that had a plush Oriental runner down the center. All around him were finely polished tables with knickknacks and ornaments that looked like the kind of expensive fare offered in the upscale antique shops of Georgetown.

At the end of the hall, Brayle opened a door and bowed for Flynn to pass inside.

"I believe you will find everything you need, sir," the old gentleman said. "If you require any assistance, the bell is here." He crossed the room to a swath of fringed velvet hanging from the ceiling. "The water closet is through that door"—he gestured toward a narrow door near the corner with a gnarled hand—"and Mrs. Kesterbrook has taken the liberty of supplying some clothing in the armoire." He walked to an ornate wardrobe that dominated one wall and opened one side. Flynn caught a glimpse of a selection of clothes hanging neatly before Brayle closed the door.

In the center of the room was an enormous four-poster bed with curtains drawn back at every corner. The thing was so high off the ground there was even a step-stool at the side of it. Two plush armchairs flanked a table at the far end of the room near a window, and either side of the bed sported a table with candles, books, and a decanter of liquor on the near side.

"There is a nightshirt on the end of the bed, sir. Do you need anything else at the moment?" Brayle asked, standing by the door.

Flynn shook his head, feeling exhausted and overwhelmed and intensely grateful for the comfort that surrounded him. He wished he had some money in his pocket because he would give this old man at least a fifty for leading him to this nirvana.

"I don't think so. Thank you." He moved to the bed and pushed down on it with an experimental hand. After a moment, he looked up to see the old man watching him with an inscrutable look.

"Very good, sir," Brayle said, nodding once. "Ring if you should think of something."

Flynn glanced at the bellpull and back at Brayle. "I will. Thank you."

The man nodded again, and backed out of the door with a slight, classy bow.

The man would put John Gielgud to shame, Flynn thought.

He turned and looked at the huge bed with relish. Across the foot of it lay the cotton nightshirt, the sight of which actually made him smile. Piece by piece, he stripped off the filthy tuxedo and threw the items to a corner, hoping against hope he would never have to wear any of them again.

When he'd stripped to the buff, he picked up the nightshirt and smelled it. The soft linen smelled of soap. He pulled it over his head. His body sated and his clothing clean, he felt more contented than he ever remembered feeling. If he could have had a hot shower, he believed he would be in heaven.

He crawled under the covers and pulled up the

heavy blankets. The mattress enveloped him like the hand of God and he closed his eyes. Within seconds he was asleep.

He awoke he wasn't sure how long later, but a tray with a silver coffeepot and cup sat on the bedside table. He stretched out a hand and felt the pot—still warm, though not hot.

He got out of bed slowly, stretching and feeling the grogginess of the first good night's sleep in days depart from him like a fog burned off by the sun. He heard the crackling of a vigorous fire. When he moved around the end of the bed, he nearly plunged into a huge copper tub filled with warm water. When in the world had this appeared? he wondered, touching the water with his fingers. It too was still warm.

He pulled the nightshirt over his head and stepped into the bath. Warmth enveloped him and though he had to bend his knees to fit, he slid immediately under, feeling the water drift through his hair like fingers, lifting away days of misery and cold. He found a bar of soap on a temporary table next to the tub, and lathered himself everywhere, going over his hair several times, until he felt cleaner than he'd been in years.

A thick towel greeted him from the tub and as he secured it around his waist, he moved to the wardrobe and opened the door.

"Oh, I see you're up, sir," a female voice said from the doorway.

Flynn turned to see a young maid in a cap and apron of sheerest white over a black dress curtsy to him.

"I come to help you, but I see you've just finished.

I'll empty the bath after you've dressed. Would you like me to send the valet for you?"

"The valet?" he repeated.

"To help you dress, sir."

Flynn laughed. "No, that's okay."

Half an hour later out of desperation, Flynn re-donned the towel and pulled on the velvet rope. When the maid appeared he said through the crack in the door, "I think I would like that valet, if you wouldn't mind."

Stifling a smile, the maid curtsied and moved briskly off.

Just as Flynn and the valet were finishing up the complex procedure of dressing—Flynn had felt almost indecent in the tight pants until the double-breasted long-tailed riding coat was presented—there came a knock on the door.

"Come on in," he called, adjusting the high, knotted cloth at his neck the valet had called a "cravat." The points of the collar poked him in the chin.

The door opened and the servant girl appeared again. He turned from the mirror when he saw her.

"Mrs. Kesterbrook requests that you join her in the front parlor," the girl said. "If you're ready I can take you there now."

"Sure," Flynn said, and with a nod of thanks to the valet, left the bedroom.

The beautiful woman he'd met the night before sat on the sofa in a perfectly appointed living room. She rose when he entered, and moved toward him.

"Mrs. Kesterbrook, I presume," he said with a smile, even though she wouldn't get the joke.

Her lips curved slightly. "That's correct. It would

be best if you bowed when you greet a lady, Mr. Patrick. It is our custom.''

Flynn laughed, embarrassed, and said, "Sure." He executed a deep bow.

"Very pretty," she said, "though you needn't bend so far. I'll have Brayle instruct you later. How did you sleep?"

"Like a log," he said, moving to shove his hands in his pockets and discovering that there were none in the skin-tight pants. Self-consciously, he placed his hands on his hips. "How about yourself?"

She ignored the question and moved back into the room. She was as beautiful in the daylight as she had been last night, though she was less formally dressed. The gown she wore today was not as shiny, nor as deeply cut at the cleavage, as the one she'd had on then, and her dark hair was drawn back into a thick bun. She turned at the sofa and indicated an armchair across from it.

"Please, have a seat," she said gently.

"Thank you," he said, following her.

He waited until she sat—some ancient schooling in manners telling him he should—then sat in the chair opposite her. She looked a little like Melisande, he thought. The same coloring, the same erect posture and dark, dark eyes. But Felicity Kesterbrook had an unmistakable air of maturity about her, exuding a presence that Flynn could only compare to royalty, though he'd never actually been in the presence of royalty. The evidence of her age was chiefly in this air, though some delicate lines were just visible around her eyes and mouth, and her body, while shapely, was just a bit thicker and did not have the lithesome quality that Melisande's had.

"Melisande tells me your parents attended university. Did you also?"

"Yes." Flynn nodded, feeling the odd compunction to gloss over his real past and exaggerate that which might please this woman. Obviously, she would think he was crazy if he told her what had happened to him, but some element of self-preservation told him he could and should stick with the parts of the truth that would be best received.

"This was in America?"

"Yes." He took a deep breath.

There was more at stake here than just pleasing a beautiful woman. Flynn knew that if he seemed too unworthy, too ill-bred, as Melisande might put it, they might kick him out of this lap of luxury, and then God knows what he would do. Though he didn't have any clue what to do next, he had the feeling he would need Melisande's help. She was the only person on earth who knew his story, though she didn't believe it. But there was something in him that demanded *someone* know it, and if that someone didn't ship him off to the loony bin and happened to be an incredibly pretty girl, then he was ahead of the game. There was something else too. He felt comfortable knowing he'd been completely honest with her.

"Actually, though, I was born in England," Flynn added, "somewhere near Merestun, as I understand it. My parents moved to America shortly afterward, though."

At this Felicity looked very interested, her eyes growing brighter and staying on him with even more intensity than they had last night. "Near Merestun? Do you know where exactly?"

He shook his head. "Sorry. My parents weren't big on talking about the past. Come to think of it, they weren't big on talking at all, at least not to me. Or each other."

"What was your mother's maiden name. Perhaps we could track some of her family, if there are no Patricks to be found."

He laughed. "I doubt it. She was American too."

Felicity looked thoughtful. "That's a shame. It would be most helpful if we could find some of your relations. How old were you when you left?"

He shrugged. "I'm not sure. Five, maybe. Six. I don't know. I don't really remember. Not long enough to keep the accent apparently." He grinned.

She smiled back.

"Why do you want to find my relations?" he asked.

Here she took a deep breath. "Mr. Patrick, do you have any idea of the situation my niece is in right now?"

"I know what she's told me. She didn't want to marry that Bellingham guy, she ran off, her parents are going to be pissed—ah, angry, and let's see, she doesn't want anyone to know how she got here or her reputation will be ruined." He said this last with a sarcastic flourish, and looked to Felicity to share his joke. Surely someone of her age knew how pointless it was to worry what other people thought about your actions.

She didn't, however, look as if she took the worry any less seriously than Melisande. In fact, she looked as if he'd just confessed to killing someone.

"I have to admit, Mr. Patrick, that I have never been to America, so I am not familiar with its culture. Your attitude may be perfectly appropriate to your home and your station there. However—"she held up a hand when he began to protest—"*here* there are very strict rules for young, unmarried ladies. *Very* strict."

"Let me guess. Melisande's spending a night or two in my company pretty much broke those rules, right?"

As Flynn looked at her, all the blood drained from Felicity's face.

"What?" he asked in alarm. "Didn't . . . I mean, I thought Melisande had told you what happened."

"She did. Briefly."

Flynn sat back, watching her warily. "Nothing happened. I mean, it was really only one night that we were actually *together* and even then nothing happened. If you understand my—"

"I understand," she said frostily. "And while I am glad to hear it, it makes no difference. The fact that these events took place robs my niece of her virtue as surely as if it had actually happened."

He began to scoff. "Her virtue is in—"

"Let me finish, Mr. Patrick," she commanded.

He laughed once in frustration. "Sure."

"May I be blunt?"

He shrugged and held out a hand, palm up. "Fire away."

"I believe you didn't touch my niece. But even if you had touched her—even if you had had *sexual relations* with her—the situation now would be exactly the same.'' She stared at him. ''Do you understand me?''

''You're saying that everyone will believe that we did, so we might as well have.''

She nodded. ''Exactly.''

For some reason, he felt as if the walls were closing in on him. He laughed once, to dispel the sudden sense of unreality that descended upon him, but it didn't work. ''And now,'' he said slowly, ''you're going pull out your shotgun and demand that I marry her. Is that right?''

Felicity sat back and folded her hands in her lap. Her face was dead serious. ''I'm hoping the gun will not be necessary.''

Chapter Eleven

"Marry him!" Melisande felt her heart nearly stop; then it took up a violent beat that threatened to burst from her chest. Her cheeks flamed as she stood before her aunt in the center of the sitting room. "Aunt Felicity, you can't be serious."

"You have no other choice, my dear. This is your only hope of ever being accepted into society again."

"What on earth do you *mean*?" Melisande's brain stuttered over the suggestion.

"I mean we will present the marriage as an elopement and say that you were married right away. For that's the only thing society might accept, you know."

"But what about Bellingham? He would be humiliated if it looked as if I preferred another to him—and such a man—a—a nobody, over a *duke*. He would destroy us."

215

Her aunt nodded sagely. "Bellingham will be dealt with."

"*How?*" Melisande knew her tone bordered on the hysterical, but there was little she could do about it. Though she'd slept like the dead last night, she'd awoken feeling more nervous and unsettled than she had since she'd begun this wretched course of action. "How do you deal with a man like that? He is ruthless. I am sure he would stop at nothing to salvage his pride."

"We will tell him the truth." She smiled. "Or some semblance of it. We will tell him we must tell this story to save your reputation. We will apply to his mercy, his compassion for a young girl's future. We will also, of course, tell him that the elopement was against your will. The man took advantage of you, then forced you to pay the parson so the marriage cannot be contested."

"Wait. But suppose the marriage *could* be contested—"

"You are thinking you could be free of them both. But no. If the marriage were annulled, Bellingham would still not have you. And if he would not have you, no one would. You would find yourself in the same position you are in now. That of a social pariah."

Melisande sat down in the straight-backed chair by the door. Felicity sat placidly with her sewing in the wing chair by the fire.

"What if he won't do it?" Melisande asked. It was her last, best hope. "Mr. Patrick, that is. What if he won't marry me?"

"He will do it." Her aunt calmly pulled a needle

216

through the material in her lap and pulled the thread tight.

"You've *spoken* to him about it?" Melisande stood. "You've already asked him?"

"Yes. He's agreed to do it."

Melisande's mouth dropped open. She didn't know how or why she was shocked. "Well, of course *he'll* do it," she said, collecting her wits. "*He* has nothing to lose!"

Her aunt's dark eyes moved slowly to Melisande's face. "Neither, my dear, do you," she said quietly.

Melisande sank again to the chair and felt her breath leave her. "This is so humiliating," she said, more to herself than her aunt. "I am having to be portioned off. Tell me," she added, her voice brittle, "did you tell him how wealthy he will be? How much convincing did you have to do after that?"

Felicity made several more stitches before answering. "I had to do a considerable amount of convincing," she said at last.

Tears spilled from Melisande's eyes. She wiped them from her cheeks in annoyance. "You mean he didn't want me even with all that money?" she scoffed, feeling particularly wretched at the thought.

"He never once asked about the money," Felicity said. "And I did not tell him."

Melisande waved that away with a hand. "He probably already knew I am to inherit. He was probably *waiting* for me outside on that terrace. He may have planned this whole thing! How do we know he didn't actually scheme to steal me off to Gretna Green? How do we know this wasn't his plan all along?"

217

"My dear." Felicity looked at her with the patient eyes of a schoolteacher. "Why would he have brought you here first?"

She could not argue with her aunt's logic. He had obviously had no plans to abduct her for any reason. She had known that all along.

"But what a bed of clover he finds himself in now, does he not?" she declared bitterly. "He is to be wealthy. All the men of his station will *admire* him for his leap above their heads. He will gain everything while I shall be reviled. Married to a *pauper*. We will probably not spend one minute in proper conversation our whole lives." She shook her head vehemently. "Aunt Felicity, you don't understand how awful this is. He is a man of no breeding, no background, no connections whatsoever—not even bad ones! How could he improve my lot, for who will have me even once we are married? Where will I ever be invited but to public balls and assemblies? And even there people will snicker and tell stories. I may as well not marry at all as endure that."

Unaffected by this speech, her aunt continued to sew. "You must marry him, Melisande."

"But *why*? It will do me no good. I would rather live out my days at home as a spinster than marry so far beneath me." Melisande thought of the quiet sitting room off her bedchamber at Browerly. Yes, she would much rather be there, alone, than married to that man—that wild, uneducated, *insane* man.

For a second she pictured him as he'd whisked her through that illicit dance—the waltz—at the Porters' inn at Quails Head. Those stunning eyes looking down on her, his lips so close to her face . . . her blood had fairly steamed.

"You do not have a choice, Melisande," her aunt replied implacably.

Melisande's stubbornness roiled up inside of her. "Why not? I shall be no worse off alone. And I will not risk some profligate spending all my money on unhealthy pursuits such as gaming and women. For that is what all low-bred people do once they get money. I would be risking my family's fortune! Why should I marry him if I would be better off alone?"

"Do you really not know the answer to that question, Melisande?" her aunt asked, dropping her sewing to her lap and looking at her with obvious disappointment.

Melisande looked at her hesitantly, but could not keep defiance from her voice. "What do you mean?"

"You have thought of no one but yourself throughout this whole ordeal," Felicity said, anger tinting her words. "You thought only to save yourself from a situation you suddenly found inconvenient. A situation, I might add, of your own making. No one forced you to accept Lord Bellingham's offer."

Melisande sat silent under the indictment. It was true. She had gotten herself into a mess, and then made an even bigger one trying to get out of it.

"It does not affect anyone but myself," she hedged, thinking that surely her parents would recover from this.

"Can you not think of others even now, Melisande? Can you not, for example, think of Juliette?"

The mention of her sister's name brought a sudden welling of poignancy to Melisande's heart. Oh, how she *wished* Juliette were here now. Though she was young, she always cheered Melisande no matter how down she was. And though Juliette knew little of the ways of the world, she listened to Melisande's problems and thoughts with the most sympathetic of ears and the most caring of hearts.

"With a sister ruined by her own actions," Felicity continued in a hard, uncompromising voice, "Juliette's chances of marriage would be equal to your own right now. She would be considered as dissolute, as immoral, as you will be if you do not marry. *She,* who has done nothing."

Melisande felt the shock of the truth open onto her like a Biblical deluge. She had anticipated the anger of her parents and the guilt of being a grievous disappointment to them both. She had anticipated Bellingham's anger and the guilt of breaking her promise to him. But she had not thought once of Juliette. She had believed the risk to be solely her own.

An appalling guilt, the likes of which she'd never known, fell like cannon shot in her stomach. Shame, mortification, and contrition braided in her heart and her tears fell freely again. Her aunt was right, she had no other choice. She had to marry the man. She had to do what she could to preserve Juliette's chances.

Her heart twisted painfully as she remembered Juliette's rapt expression during Melisande's stories about her dreams, the joy she took in the prince, and the childlike belief she had in love and chivalry and heroism. To have that all destroyed by a hand so dear to her heart . . . to be ruined by her own sister before she was even out . . . Melisande could not, *would* not, be the cause of that.

With deep resignation, Melisande knew she could only be glad she had at least one course of action open to her. She must try what she could to mitigate the disastrous effect of her bad decisions.

"Of course," Melisande said quietly and stopped. She had to clear her throat of emotion before she could continue. "Yes. Of course. I shall marry him then. As soon as possible."

Felicity sat back and smiled, her hands in her lap. "That's a good girl," she said, satisfied. "I knew you would do the right thing, Melisande. You only needed to see reason. You have made a mistake, but you can do something to right it. And I knew you would." Her tone was instantly warm, the tone of welcome Melisande had hoped for from the beginning.

Ordinarily, this would have made her feel better. But Melisande quickly found herself caught in a vision of a life not unlike that of Mary and Roy Clyde. Marriage to a low-bred, impoverished man who claimed to be from another time could only lead to a miserable life. She had been brought up to believe that if you married beneath yourself you would suffer immensely, and believe it she did. What would a man like Flynn Patrick do with the enormous fortune that would suddenly become his? He would squander it, of course. They always did, those people born to poverty. They did not know how to manage money, and she would be cooking stew over an open fire in a cottage before her life was half-over. Just like Mary Clyde.

"You know, I found him quite charming," Felicity was saying as Melisande emerged from the bleakness of her future. "Not at all unpleasant to talk to, once I became used to the accent."

"Yes, he can be . . . entertaining."

"And I am not sure he is so badly bred. His parents are both educated people. He can read and write and do figures. He has an engaging way of speaking his mind."

"But he cannot dance," Melisande supplied morosely. "He is afraid of horses. He knows no language other than English. And that," she scoffed, "is debatable. He cannot read Greek or Latin. He does not fence. He cannot shoot any sort of gun. Has never hunted. He curses like a sailor. And he will not stand when a lady enters the room."

Felicity eyed her niece with amusement. "You seem to know him quite well."

Melisande blushed and stood up. "I have spent an entire night with him. What more is there to know?" she said recklessly, fully expecting her aunt's anger to return.

Instead Felicity said mildly, "Yes, he mentioned that night."

"What?" She whirled on her aunt. "He did? What did he say?"

Felicity lifted a shoulder noncommittally and focused on her needlework. "Only that one of the nights was spent together, side by side."

Melisande's cheeks flamed so hot she thought it must surely damage her complexion. "Nothing happened! And no matter what he told you, that kiss was a *mistake*! His mistake, not mine, and one I did *not* participate in. I was asleep."

Felicity looked up at her, surprised.

Melisande's chest heaved with anger and she pressed her lips together. "He did not mention the kiss, did he?" she asked softly.

Felicity shook her head.

"Ohhh," she growled in frustration, turning to pace away from her aunt. "What did he say then?" she asked, spinning back.

"Only that you had slept nearby. Fully clothed. Including your cloak, he pointed out."

"That's *true*," Melisande declared, poking a finger at the ground.

"But what about this kiss?" Felicity smiled placidly.

Melisande stared at her, aghast. "How can you smile? How can you be so—so *casual*?"

"Well, it hardly matters now. You are to be married." Felicity took up her needlework again. "So he kissed you, did he?"

"It was a *mistake*," she repeated. "I was not awake. He thought I was someone else, apparently." Her tone was disgusted.

"Who would he have thought it was? Not a wife." Felicity looked concerned.

"No, he has never married. He didn't know who he thought it was. Just someone. Not me. Probably some doxy."

Felicity relaxed. "Was it a nice kiss? Did you enjoy it?"

Melisande's face was on fire, she was sure of it. Her whole body was. Her aunt, meanwhile, sat calmly with her sewing, looking the very picture of tranquility.

"How could I enjoy it?" she demanded, turning

away and pacing toward the door. "It was . . . it was unprovoked, and unappreciated, I can tell you that."

"That hardly answers the question."

"Would *you* want to be kissed by him?" Melisande asked, turning from the doorway and hoping her blush was less obvious from there. Perhaps her aunt would attribute it to anger, instead of the shame it really sprang from . . . the shame of knowing she *had* enjoyed the kiss, if only for a moment.

"That is too hypothetical. I am a married woman. I only wish to be kissed by Mr. Kesterbrook."

"You're taunting me," Melisande said finally.

"Melisande, I only want to point out that this marriage may not be as awful as you seem to think it will be. Of course, it's not what we hoped for you. It does not compare to being a duchess, for example. But he is not an unpleasant man, and he is not hard to look at. He is poor and a trifle strange, but that is better than some characteristics he could have."

Like believing himself to be a traveler from the future? Melisande wished she could add. But she didn't want it going any further than herself that she was marrying a lunatic.

"Your parents will be most unhappy about it, of course, but it's better than having to marry an actual criminal. Think about some of the commoners you see on the streets, Melisande. Let's face it, the situation could be a lot worse. And I have every confidence that your parents will come for the wedding, so you will have no doubts about their approval of the strategy."

Melisande felt physically ill at the thought of facing her parents.

"If they come for the wedding, will that not make it too obvious that we were not married on our way here?"

Felicity shook her head. "We won't tell people the wedding was here, simply a formal reception by your parents. I have already sent a note to Reverend Willy asking him to perform the ceremony, and you can depend upon his discretion."

"The problem is, once the strategy is employed and my future once again, God help me, secure, I shall be stuck with the cure for the rest of my life."

"Better than being stuck with the disease."

Melisande sniffed and sat back down in the chair by the door. "You have taken care of everything," she said, realizing the enormous debt she owed her aunt. "Thank you. Thank you for trying to help me despite all the pain I've caused." The words were hard to get out, but she knew they must be spoken.

"You've caused me no pain except that which is on your account. Your parents may view things differently, but they cannot argue with the logic of your marrying Mr. Patrick. I am sure they will approve."

Marrying Mr. Patrick. The very words sent a shiver of apprehension through Melisande.

"What choice do they have?" Melisande said. "What choice do any of us have?"

"Mr. Patrick has a choice," Felicity gently pointed out. "And he has chosen to marry you."

Flynn sat on the sofa and stared at the elaborate mantelpiece. The robust fire that burned in the grate was the only source of heat in the room. He was wearing leather boots that came to his knees, a high collar that poked him in the chin, and a wool jacket that, had it been made in his day and happened to be in style, would have cost a small fortune, so well-tailored it was.

Outside the front window, nothing stirred. No cars whizzed past, no planes roared overhead, no TVs sounded in another room, and no phones rang.

It was getting too real, he thought, feeling fully awake for the first time in days. The whole thing. Too real.

He was undeniably in the nineteenth century.

The nineteenth century. 1815. Eighteen hundred and fifteen. Hell, Napoleon fought sometime around now. Flynn sat up straight. Napoleon was probably still *alive*. What an incredible thought.

He sighed and looked into the flames, resting his chin in his hands, his elbows on his knees. He was staring into a fireplace that probably no longer existed. He was sitting in a room in a house that was probably a McDonald's by now. He was looking at, talking to, and socializing with people who'd been dead for almost two hundred years.

At first, when he'd thought he was merely dreaming or hallucinating, he'd been able to treat the whole thing like a joke. A bad, scary joke, but still . . . He'd been able to afford to go along with the charade—steal the horse, walk to London, tease Melisande. He could be who he was and shock people with his modern mores, say outrageous things, even talk about what had happened to him. He was not really a part of these people's lives.

But *now,* he thought with a tremor of apprehension, now things were getting sticky.

Now they were talking marriage.

He thought about Melisande, about her determination and fear. He pictured her beautiful hair and her warm living skin. He thought about the way she moved, the flash of her eyes, the way she laughed. She was *real*. And she was going to be asked to marry him . . . a man who she didn't even realize was little more than a phantom.

He drew the idea out further. Suppose he were to actually go through with this marriage—which, if he were not somehow transported back to reality, would take place in a matter of days. They would have to have a wedding night, which he imagined would be pretty traditional as it was 1815 and she was no doubt a virgin. So supposing then he slept with her, took her virginity . . . he felt an involuntary tightening in his gut . . . and suppose she got pregnant. What then?

If he was still here and knew about it, could he return to the twentieth century in good conscience? And suppose he'd already gotten back. How could she cope alone with a child? Alone with *his* child, he thought.

Flynn felt a sharp stab of possession, and denial. He could *never* leave a child.

Then he shook himself. What in God's name was he thinking? He couldn't stay *here*. This was madness. An illusion. He wondered if his family and friends were standing around some waiting room in a hospital, waiting to see if he chose reality or insanity. And here he was contemplating insanity.

Of course she would probably refuse to marry him, he thought, realizing the craziness of thinking that she wouldn't with something that wasn't quite relief. She thought less of him than dirt.

The door opened and he sat up abruptly. Felicity strode in, followed by Melisande. Flynn stood up.

As beautiful as Felicity was, it was Melisande who captured his attention and would not let it go. She had cleaned up, as he had, and now wore a white dress, cut low, with her hair piled on her head in some intricately feminine style. As alive as she'd been a minute ago in his thoughts, her effect upon him was ten times as tangible as he'd remembered. She was beautiful and alive and, he thought again with awe, *real*.

Her eyes were downcast as she came into the room, and stayed that way as she and Felicity curtsied. Flynn bowed, feeling foolish but not wanting to start this conversation with a reprimand from either one of them. They seated themselves on the couch, while Flynn moved to an armchair.

"Mr. Patrick," Felicity began.

"No," Melisande said. "Let me."

She raised her head and looked at him for the first time since entering the room. For a moment he thought she was going to jump up and exclaim that he was to leave the house and never return. She looked shocked, for some reason. Then he realized it was the clothes. She was so used to seeing him in the tux, it was probably disconcerting to see him in the clothes of her time.

He stood up again. "What do you think, Mel? Better than the Armani?" He turned around in a circle and grinned at her, hoping for at least that ghost of a smile he once in a while could provoke.

She closed her mouth and nodded hesitantly. "Y-yes. Quite."

Beside her, Felicity laughed. "You look quite the English gentleman now, Mr. Patrick. I suppose your American friends would think you a sight."

He looked down at himself and imagined the press room at the *Post* getting an eyeful of this. "You can say that again."

"Mr. Patrick, it is all arranged," Melisande said suddenly.

Flynn looked up, and Felicity turned her head toward her, both of them taken by surprise.

Melisande hurried on, without taking a breath, it seemed. Or taking too many.

"Our marr—our wedding, that is, for us to get married. It is arranged. My parents will be here tomorrow and we will be married in the evening, that is Thursday, and that will be that. We will not, obviously, have a wedding journey as the world believes we have already had one, albeit for only three days. I understand you have already agreed to this proposal— I mean this scheme. And I want you to know that I appreciate your willingness to—to do this, though as you know you will be well compensated for it as my family is one of the oldest in the country and you will hardly be doing yourself a disservice by connecting yourself with it."

She stopped and took a deep breath. He thought she had more to say, but she merely looked at him expectantly.

He shook himself. "Uh, right. Yes, your aunt and I talked about it. About why this is necessary. But I'm glad you came to talk to me, Melisande." He looked at Felicity. "Any chance I can talk to her alone?"

"None at all." Felicity smiled. "You may, however, take a turn about the room and I shall continue with my sewing."

"Take a turn about the room. What do you mean, dance?" He looked at her incredulously. "I just want a word or two in private. Holy cow, we're going to be married in a couple days. And it seems a little late to be worried about how it looks. Don't you trust us?"

Melisande stood up. "She means walk about the room," she said, frustrated. "Just . . . *walk*."

She turned and began to walk casually away from her aunt. Flynn followed, muttering, "This is ridiculous."

He caught up to her and stopped her at the far corner, turning her to him with his hands on her forearms. "Listen," he said, looking into her face. She kept her eyes averted, studying a china figurine on a nearby table. "Melisande, look at me."

She looked up, her eyes defiant.

He gazed at her intently. "Look, I just wanted to ask you," he said quietly, "if this is really what you want. Your aunt explained to me about society and your reputation and all that junk, but I want to know if this is really what *you* want, Melisande. From the look on your face, it doesn't seem like it. I know you don't think much of me, and you shouldn't. I'm a stranger to you, and I know I probably seem pretty weird on top of that. But if this is the best thing for you, I'll do it. What I want to know is if this is what *you* think is best. All right?"

She stared up at him, her mouth slightly open, her eyes dewy as if she might cry. Flynn braced himself.

"Is this really the only thing that will save you, Melisande?" he asked, squeezing her arms. "Answer me."

"Nothing will save me," she said, her voice low. He was glad she was not overtly crying. He wasn't sure what he'd do in that case. "I am doing this to save my sister."

He dropped her arms. "Your *sister*?"

She nodded. "Yes. You see, if I am considered ruined, then she will be as well."

"But she wasn't even *there*."

"It is guilt by association, Mr. Patrick. If one woman in the family is believed to be immoral, then the rest of them are too. So you see, because I love my sister, I really have no choice but to marry you."

His Grace, The Duke of Merestun
Park Lane, Mayfair
29 January 1815

Your Grace,

Please forgive me this imposition on our old friendship, a request I realize could be extraordinary in lieu of the recent unpleasant events which have transpired between our two families. I hope you will do me the honor of recognizing my continued esteem for you, despite the loss of that connection for which we all so fervently hoped, and read this missive in the spirit of good will with which it was written.

Kind sir, I have what I believe to be a spec-

ulation worthy of your consideration. I do not wish to enclose my suspicions, which are of a grave nature, in the unsecured confines of such a note as this, however. I hoped that perhaps instead you could send to me your trusted man, whom I know to be of the most scrupulous character, that I might convey through him the details of my conjecture. You might then investigate the theory at your option.

I write with regard to that unfortunate occurrence suffered at Merestun these twenty-seven years ago.

Yours sincerely,
Mrs. Miles Kesterbrook
Regent Street, Mayfair

Chapter Twelve

Melisande couldn't help it. She could not stop picturing Mr. Patrick in the clothes her aunt had provided for him. She'd thought him handsome before when he was wearing the odd suit, but clothed in the height of fashion, he was breathtaking.

It made her nervous.

She knew she should be thinking about her parents—they were to arrive at any minute. And she *was* anxious about seeing them. But whenever she tried to concentrate on how she would act with them, or what she might say to them, she got to the point of the wedding and got all tangled up in the vision of Mr. Patrick in tailcoat and buckskin.

If he was the devil, as she was beginning to suspect, why would he be tempting her now, when they were already set to marry? For tempting he was. When he'd pulled her aside from her aunt yesterday and spoken all those honeyed words about wanting only what *she* wanted—well, the allure of them had very nearly undone her. She'd had to mentally kick herself and steel her mind to give him the truth. And to remember the truth herself—that he was marrying her for her money and would probably never have let her out of the arrangement. He knew she had no other choice but to do it, and had made himself look good by offering her the out.

She was just drifting back into the vision of Mr. Patrick as he'd looked yesterday, and was beginning to wonder what would happen on their wedding night, when a carriage pulled up in front of the house. She heard the horses' tack jingling as the footman took them by the bridle, and got to the window in time to see her father alight from the carriage. A footman then helped out Juliette, who was followed by Melisande's mother and Daphne.

Melisande's insides went to jelly at the sight of her father. His expression told her nothing, though he did look grim. She told herself the fact that they hurried to the door could have been because of the cold and not necessarily the shame of being looked upon as the parents of the "stolen heiress," as she'd been dubbed by the public.

She stepped back from the window as they entered, and she heard them being divested of their coats in the lower hall. She straightened her hair and gown, and stood primly near the fire as they entered the room.

When the door opened, any hope of a dignified greeting was lost as Juliette barreled through the opening and ran to her sister.

"Melly!" she cried, running with open arms to clasp Melisande around the waist and lay her head on her chest. "Oh, I'm so *glad* you're *alive*! Everybody spoke of you as if you had died, and I went to sleep every night praying for your survival. And look at how God has answered my dearest prayer!"

Melisande felt a lump of emotion rise up in her throat, and she choked back tears while hugging her sister. "I'm so happy to see you, Juliette. And I'm so sorry for the worry I caused you."

"It wasn't *you*!" she said, standing back and bathing Melisande in an adoring, compassionate look. "It was that awful man. And now, oh, Melly, you have to *marry* him!"

"That is enough," her father snapped. "Juliette, we told you to be silent on the subject of your sister's marriage, did we not? Did you not understand the situation?"

Juliette's eyes lowered and she clasped her hands behind her back. "Yes, Papa. I'm sorry. I just thought since we were alone with her—"

"We are never to speak of this marriage—whether alone or in public. We must never forget that to the world it was an 'elopement,' do you understand?"

"Of course," Juliette said.

"Good," he said. "Your very future depends upon it. Remember that."

Melisande's stomach turned to stone as her father's stern gaze left Juliette and moved to herself. She had never seen him so severe.

"Elinor, perhaps you should take Juliette up to her room." Her father glanced at her mother and jerked his head in the direction of the door.

Melisande glanced at her mother, and got an inscrutable look in return before her mother turned and left the room.

Her father closed the door behind them and turned back to Melisande. He moved slowly toward her into the room. Melisande's nerves quivered, and she wondered if she visibly shook where she stood, as she felt she must.

"I do not even want an explanation," her father proclaimed, fixing her with the coldest eye she'd ever seen from him. "I believe I can assume correctly that you did not want to marry Lord Bellingham after all and took it upon yourself to plunge us all into this nightmare. Is that correct?"

Melisande swallowed, and feared for a second she would choke as her throat closed with anxiety. He was angrier than she'd ever seen him. She took a deep breath. "Truly, I did not think it would become such a nightmare."

He closed his eyes and nodded. "So you admit this was willingly done, this *abduction*." He said the word with complete disdain.

"I did not intend," she began quietly.

"What?" her father boomed. "Speak up."

Her eyes whipped to his, and for the first time in her life she felt afraid that she had actually lost her father's love. Gone was the genial man he had always been, replaced by someone whose disappointment was palpable.

She cleared her throat. "I did not intend to be accompanied by Mr. Patrick. It just—happened." No vision of Mr. Patrick was going to save her now. In the eyes of her father she was ruined as surely as she was in the eyes of society.

"And so now," he continued, outwardly calm, "my eldest daughter will be married to a stranger without land, without position, without education, without merit of any kind, and with the reputation of a criminal, though of course we can press no charges as he is to be your *husband*."

"Only for Juliette's sake, Papa," she said, her voice emerging desperately weak. "Surely you know I do not *wish* to marry this man."

"I would that you did, Melisande, for that is all you shall have."

She swallowed hard, suddenly aware that he had other designs than demonstrating his shame or anger with her by conducting this meeting alone. He had something important to tell her.

"You're a bright girl, Melisande," he continued, looking at the floor, his hands behind his back, "so you must understand that I cannot give you what has always been your birthright. Because of the events of the last several days"—he hesitated but a second before proceeding—"I have had Mr. Clement, my solicitor, draw up a new will naming Juliette as my sole beneficiary."

Melisande's stomach plummeted to her feet.

He cleared his throat and added, "She does not know it yet and I would appreciate it if you did not tell her. We will inform her at the appropriate time."

Melisande was frozen where she stood, every limb suddenly icy cold and motionless. "So—I am—destitute?" The words quaked from her throat, making her sound like a very old woman. Only through sheer force of will could she remain standing. If she moved one muscle, she knew she would crumble to the ground in pieces.

But while her body was paralyzed, her mind spun out of control. She *would* be living in a cottage like the Clydes, she thought desperately. Without her inheritance, they would have no way to live. Mr. Patrick would be useless as a provider. But even if he weren't, she would be married to a man who had to work in order to put food on the table. The life she'd always known would be utterly and completely gone.

"I have made arrangements for a small living to be granted you and your husband," her father said, looking at the floor again. He actually looked sad as he said the words that destroyed her entire life. "You may maintain a modest house here in town with it, perhaps in Cheapside, or you may prefer the retirement of the country. Anticipating this, your mother has found a cottage you can let in Derbyshire for a reasonable amount of money. It is on the estate of a baronet. One . . . Sir Thomas Cromley, I believe."

Melisande realized as her head began to swim that she had forgotten to breathe. As she parted her lips, she found herself inhaling sharply and stumbling to one side as the lack of air undid her equilibrium. Darkness edged into her vision and then her knees crumbled.

She had just hit the floor—jarring herself awake as pain shot through her knees and shoulder—when the door opened. She tried to right herself, but the feeling of airlessness would not leave her. Dizziness kept her scrabbling for balance.

"Good God, man, why don't you help her?" a

voice demanded, and before Melisande could gather her wits enough to look up, she heard footsteps pound across the floor toward her. Strong arms encircled her and pulled her against a protective chest. She didn't have to look to know she was in the embrace of her husband-to-be.

For a second she wished to sink into that broad chest and be held, comforted, the way her parents never would comfort her again. He held her firmly but with surprising gentleness, and placed a cool hand on her forehead. She was surprised he did not jerk it back from the heat. For she knew she was flushed with shame to be situated so in front of her father.

As soon as Flynn had helped her stand, Melisande pushed away from his chest. She couldn't look at him, and yet she could not look at her father either.

"Were you going to just let her lie there?" Flynn demanded. "Jesus, don't you care about her at all?"

Melisande felt humiliation to her core at the combative, derogatory tone he used to her father. Her *father,* who held their fates in his hands.

"Mr. Patrick," she protested, choosing to look at him instead of the outrage she knew would be on her father's face. "Curb your temper, please. It was nothing. I'm afraid you do not know to whom you are speaking—"

"I know who it is," Flynn said, more calmly but without a trace of respect. "The same man who coerced you into getting engaged to that bastard Bellingham."

"Mr. *Patrick,*" she said with a gasp, grabbing his forearm with all of her strength. "*Please.* I am begging you to stop."

239

Flynn turned to her, looking large and angry and powerful, as she imagined Lucifer would appear in a battle for one's soul. His pale eyes pinned her where she stood, but the expression in them for her was not uncaring. "Are you all right? Do you want some water? I think you should lie down a minute."

Melisande felt her chin quiver at his solicitousness. Kindness was a powerful weapon.

Summoning her last reserve of strength, she said quietly, "I would like to introduce you to my father. Mr. St. Claire. May I present to you, Father, Mr. Flynn Patrick?"

The two men eyed each other like enraged stallions for a long moment, standing opposite each other across the docile expanse of sitting room.

"*Bow*," Melisande hissed to Flynn.

He turned his face to her, his expression the same as it might have been had she asked him to stand on his head.

"*Please*," she whispered, on the verge of tears.

He took a deep breath, turned back to her father, and executed the shallowest bow possible. Her father nodded his head once.

As Melisande scoured her mind for something to add to this, the door blessedly opened again and her mother and Juliette appeared. Melisande was aware of the concerned expression on her mother's face as she made the introductions, and was gratified to see Flynn bow civilly to her mother and sister, both of whom curtsied as they would have to any new acquaintance. Juliette looked at him with wide, terrified eyes, and immediately moved next to Melisande and held her hand.

It was not until her mother ushered them all to sit down that Melisande noticed Flynn's clothing—much fancier than he'd worn yesterday and that much more handsome. She was grateful for the small favor that she would not have to be ashamed of the way he looked. If she could only get him to stop talking.

She imagined Brayle had helped Flynn choose the clothes, for it was obviously suited for the ceremony that was to be performed this evening. But even as she looked at him, she began calculating what the cost of such garments would be. Prohibitively expensive for those with the restrictions of a "small living," she knew. Once they were married, he would never be able to afford such clothes, and she found herself hoping her aunt intended for him to keep at least the two suits he'd already worn.

Conversation was strained and consisted mostly of superficial pleasantries between her mother and herself. Then Felicity arrived home from her morning calls to find them all grouped together in the front parlor like a bunch of estranged relatives at the reading of a will.

"Well, I see we've all met one another," she said, breezing into the room and kissing her brother on the cheek. She might as well have kissed Michelangelo's David for all the response she got. "Elinor, it's lovely to see you again."

"Thank you, dear," Melisande's mother said, and they kissed each other's cheek. "I only wish it were under happier circumstances."

"That's as it may be," Felicity said, sitting across from Flynn and smiling at him. "Things could be worse, you know, they could always be worse."

"They could always be better too," her father added, glaring at Flynn.

"Why, Cornelius," Felicity said, "that sounds positively optimistic."

"You know what I meant," he growled.

As Felicity carried on the conversation, mostly one-sided, with Melisande's parents, and Flynn sat stewing over whatever thoughts boiled in his mad brain, Melisande sat in a state of numbness, thinking about the night to come. They would take their vows in a mercifully short ceremony, Felicity had assured her. Then they would eat a small dinner and retire. They would stay in the luxurious gold room, Felicity said, and Melisande's things, the dresses and personal effects her parents had brought for her, would already have been moved there.

Melisande tried to imagine going up to bed with this strange man. Then she tried to imagine getting undressed in front of him. And the more unsettled her thoughts became, the shallower her breathing got, until she thought she might pass out again.

Juliette elbowed her in the ribs.

Melisande took a sharp breath and looked down at her. "What?" she whispered with unintentional irritability.

"He looks like the prince," Juliette whispered back, pointing one small finger discreetly at Flynn.

Melisande glanced at Flynn, who in his dove-gray coat and black pants certainly looked the picture of affluence. Princely even, she thought, if she forgot that he was crazy.

"Look at his eyes," Juliette prompted, as if Melisande might not have noticed them. "Like a sword blade. Just as you said. Did you not recognize it—the similarity? Do you not suspect it could be him?''

"I, yes, I did notice the similarity," Melisande said carefully. "But dearest, he's not a prince."

Juliette gave her a patient look and explained, "But dreams are not always exact, you know, Melisande. You could have made that part up."

Melisande almost smiled, but could not. Indeed, she wondered if she would ever really smile again. Then she shook herself. That was pure self-pity, which she loathed.

"But I suppose he must be awful," Juliette continued, wrinkling her nose, "to have taken you away like that, just like you were a painting or a necklace to be stolen away."

At that, Flynn's eyes shifted to Juliette and he looked at her with intensity. Juliette squirmed next to Melisande and squeezed her hand. Then his eyes moved to Melisande and something sparked within their steely depths.

The painting! The thought burst into his brain like water through a dam. In Cubby's house, the painting of the seductress, the young, beautiful woman—it was *Melisande*. He could picture it perfectly and it was her.

The revelation brought with it a thousand implications. If there was a portrait of Melisande St. Claire hanging in the modern-day Merestun, then she must somehow have redeemed her reputation. He couldn't imagine a scenario that would have that painting hanging in Merestun right now, but he would ask her later if one existed. If not, then the one he'd seen had yet to be painted, and therefore had yet to be hung in the hallowed walls of Merestun.

As he recalled, in the painting she might have looked a little older, certainly not younger, than she did at this very moment. He tried to remember the dress she'd had on in the picture, thinking maybe the style could tell him whether it had been painted already or would be in a few years. Not that he would know anything about fashion, but he could ask her. He was fairly certain it had been some color, like green or red.

He shifted his gaze back to Melisande's sister. She would be a beauty too, he'd bet, though she was very young now. He guessed her age to be about eight, maybe ten. She was fair where Melisande was dark, but her hair could grow darker with time. Still, she didn't look enough like Melisande for him to think it might have been her in the portrait.

The little sister looked uncomfortable under his perusal, and whispered constantly to Melisande, so the next time she darted a look at him, he smiled. She blushed to the roots of her hair, then smiled tentatively back.

Well, at least there was one member of the family who might not hate him for all time. Which brought him back to the portrait. It *had* to mean Melisande would eventually take her rightful place back in the scheme of things.

The thought was profoundly comforting. This bizarre trip he was taking couldn't possibly cause that much diversion from fate without it having major implications for history. And he found it hard to believe he could have any sort of real impact on history. So the fact that Melisande would end up worthy of the fine-quality portrait he'd seen still hanging in Merestun in 1998 gave him the peace of mind he'd been struggling to find ever since he'd agreed to marry her.

Perhaps his deeds were not irrevocable, he thought. These actions they were taking probably amounted to nothing more than a blip in history, a snag in time's tapestry. It was most likely that once he found his way back home, he'd be presumed dead here and Melisande would marry, ultimately, whoever it was she was supposed to marry to begin with. He felt better just thinking about it.

After half an hour's agonized conversation, the St. Claires decided they should get themselves ready for the wedding ceremony. Melisande and Juliette left too, to change into their clothes, and Flynn was left sitting with Felicity again.

"I heard what you said to my niece yesterday," Felicity said.

Flynn turned his eyes from the closing door to her. "Thanks for the moment of privacy."

Her gaze was steady upon him. "I was impressed with your approach to her."

"It wasn't an approach. I just didn't want her getting railroaded again. Though it looks like she has been anyway."

"Railroaded?"

Flynn laughed—amazing how language changed with every new technology. "You know, backed into a corner, forced into something."

"Melisande is the victim of her own actions. It's you I'm thinking of, Mr. Patrick. Are you sure you haven't been . . . railroaded?" She smiled.

He shrugged. There was no way he could explain that this was all temporary for him. That his actions didn't really mean a thing, except where they affected others.

"There's something I think you should know," she continued. "Before you go through with the ceremony this evening."

"What's that?"

She eyed him carefully. "Her father has disinherited her. He wrote me about it, and from the look on Melisande's face he probably just told her."

"Jesus," he muttered, remembering how he'd found Melisande in a near faint on the floor. Her father had disinherited her and she'd almost passed out. "He's a real prince, isn't he?"

"Who? Mr. St. Claire?"

"Yeah. That father of hers," he said, throwing out a hand. "First he engages her to a sleaze like Bellingham. Then when she doesn't want to do it, he takes away her inheritance. After all she's been through. What a jerk." Flynn felt anger on Melisande's behalf rising up inside of him. It seemed he and Melisande had something in common—fathers who were selfish, controlling bastards. "I should have hit him this afternoon when I had the chance. How much could he love her?"

"I'll thank you to remember he is my brother. And he loves her very much. That's why he wanted her to become a duchess. She would have been honored the rest of her days."

"Oh, she'll be honored," Flynn said, feeling smug in his secret knowledge. "Mark my words. She'll find her place in history. With any luck she'll leave a diary or something telling everyone how she did it despite a manipulative father.''

Felicity's expression was puzzled. ''I wonder how you feel, Mr. Patrick, knowing that the woman you're going to marry this evening is to become virtually penniless.''

Flynn was about to exclaim that he wouldn't take a dime of the old man's money even if he offered it on a silver platter, when he realized the purpose of Felicity's revelation. In fact it was probably the whole reason she'd stayed behind to speak with him once the others had left. She wanted him to know he couldn't marry Melisande for her money.

His lips curved and he looked at her appreciatively. ''You took kind of a chance telling me that, didn't you?''

She tilted her head to the side. ''Did I?''

''Sure. If I were a run-of-the-mill kidnapper I'd probably be out the door right now. Is that what you're thinking?''

''And are you? A run-of-the-mill kidnapper, that is?'' She watched him.

He smiled and rubbed the back of his neck. ''No, I don't think you could call me a run-of-the-mill anything right now. And yes, I will still marry her.''

The smile that blossomed on Felicity's face was triumphant. ''I knew you would. I had a feeling about you from the first moment I saw you.''

''Well, it couldn't be too accurate or you'd be running for your life right now,'' Flynn said.

True to her word, Felicity had Reverend Willy perform the shortest ceremony Melisande had ever heard.

247

Melisande had argued with herself for the two hours between talking to her father and the appointed time for the ceremony about telling Flynn about her disinherited state. She felt in all fairness she should tell him and give him the opportunity to renege on the wedding if he should so decide. After all, the mistakes made were not his, they were hers. And there was no reason he should suffer for the rest of his life.

On the other hand, if he *should* decide not to marry her, her scandalous reputation would be beyond repair. And while at this point she could see herself living the life of a spinster somewhere all alone, she could not see sentencing her sister to a similar life.

She was still debating when Felicity knocked on the door and told her it was time. Melisande knew she could probably steal a moment to talk to Mr. Patrick alone, but when Juliette came into the room, dressed in her gown of white with a floral wreath on her blond curls, Melisande knew her decision was made. This beautiful, innocent girl required any sacrifice Melisande could make. And despite the drastically altered circumstances Melisande would have to accept, they were probably still better than anything Mr. Patrick might have achieved on his own.

So she had gone through with it. God help her, she'd said the words—albeit in not a very strong voice—and she'd married the man. In front of her family and several trusted servants, she and Mr. Patrick, in a considerably stronger voice, had sworn to keep each other for the rest of their lives. Her signature, even now, lay drying on that dreaded certificate. And here she stood with a plate full of food in front of her and no appetite.

Her mind was blank. She stared down at the Portuguese ham, sausage, boiled potatoes, and cauliflower, and thought she would never eat again.

It was a while before Melisande looked up, across the table of muted conversation, to see her husband—the word sounded peculiar even in her head—talking with Juliette. His head was bent toward her and he said something that actually made her giggle. From there Melisande's gaze traveled down the table, past her mother, Mr. Kesterbrook, her father, to Felicity and an older, balding man on her right whom Melisande had assumed was one of the servants, but his position at the table disputed that. And the intimate tone of his conversation with Felicity created a spark of curiosity in Melisande.

As she watched, the two spoke softly and glanced frequently at Flynn. Her aunt looked calm, but the gentleman to whom she spoke—she remembered now being introduced to him, Lourds, she thought his name was—looked increasingly agitated.

A burst of laughter from Flynn and Juliette arrested all other conversation and everyone turned toward them.

Flynn looked mildly abashed and flashed a look around the table. "Sorry," he said, sounding anything but. "I just—we just . . ." He chuckled again. "She just said something funny, is all."

Melisande wondered how long he would be laughing like that once he found out he hadn't married the fortune he'd anticipated. She wasn't sure if she looked forward to or dreaded that conversation, but she did know his seeming unconcern with the gravity of the day annoyed her.

"Mr. Patrick," she declared across the table. All heads turned to her.

He looked at her, a smile playing about his lips. "Yes, Mrs. Patrick?"

"I—" The name tripped her up. Her heart skipped a beat, and whatever she had been going to say along with every other viable thought fled her mind like a flock of frightened birds. How could he call her such in front of everyone? It was ... unseemly. As if he were *proud* of what they'd just been through, what they'd just put *everyone* through.

She stared at him, speechless.

Obviously sensing her loss of composure, the others started conversation up again at the table, leaving Melisande to look helplessly into her husband's amused countenance.

"Was that all?" he asked, leaning forward over the table so he could direct the question solely at her.

Melisande dropped her gaze and stabbed a fork into her ham, forcing a piece down her dry throat.

Swallowing, she muttered, "Never mind."

He nodded and let his gaze linger on her, before turning his attention back to Juliette.

The old man who sat next to Felicity at dinner left when the ladies did, taking quiet leave of the company in a way that reinforced his remarkable air of dignity. For some reason Flynn had liked the old man immediately, though they had not spoken directly to each other at all. He guessed it was the old man's seeming serenity coupled with a kind, fatherly face. He wondered who he was and why he'd been invited.

Flynn was not surprised, however, when once the

group dwindled to just himself, Mr. St. Claire, and Mr. Kesterbrook—a docile, gray-haired man of astute eyes and very few words—that Kesterbrook made his excuses and departed for his office, leaving Flynn alone with Melisande's father.

Flynn had been watching St. Claire since the incident in the parlor, and thought he was trying very hard not to cave in to a strong desire to kill this man who had "abducted" his daughter. And though Flynn understood his reasoning—as Felicity had explained it to him, Mr. St. Claire blamed Flynn for his daughter's ruin, even though the fact that she was gone three days would have ruined her whether she was with a man or not—he thought it pretty ungrateful of the man to overlook the fact that Flynn hadn't *had* to marry Melisande at all.

St. Claire had the look of a nice guy who, while master of his own universe, had no very great knowledge or understanding of the world or human nature. Flynn's guess was that he had never been crossed before, and now found himself caught between an inattentive love for his daughters and a provoking combination of anger and indignation.

Now Melisande's father sat staring at him as if trying to decide if he should stab or shoot the man who had just married his daughter, and whether or not before doing either of those things he ought also to torture him.

"You know," Flynn said, deciding to break the silence, "you could look at this whole situation in another light than the bad one you've chosen. I know you're not happy about my role in this affair, but if your daughter had traveled all the way to London on her own without me, she'd be *looking* for a husband right now instead of saddled with one. And from what I understand, that could be a tough business after all the talk of her disappearance.''

St. Claire's eyes narrowed, and Flynn was pretty sure the man had decided on disemboweling him, with some intense torture to start with.

''You're quite right, Mr. Patrick,'' the man said, ''about my not being happy with this situation. Which is why I wished to speak with you alone.''

Flynn touched the glass of ruby-red port in front of him and spun it slowly on the tablecloth, watching the alcohol coat the sides of the glass.

''Go on,'' Flynn said.

St. Claire cleared his throat, like a great orator about to speak. ''We are all aware that this marriage is a tragedy. A tragedy for all involved. As you should already have discerned, Melisande was born for superior things, for a prosperous life, for an exalted status befitting her beauty and birth. But all of that is irrelevant now that she has married you. Though these circumstances are particularly unfortunate for Melisande and her family, they are unfortunate for you as well.'' At this the man's eyes took on a satisfied sort of gleam. ''You see, if you had hoped to better yourself through Melisande's misfortune, then you have been foiled.''

Flynn took a slow sip of the port, thankful for the warm calm it spread throughout his chest. The man's daughter had just had her life turned upside down and all the jerk could think about was his money and the possibility that someone was after it. It made Flynn want to slug him. Many times.

''Are you talking about the fact that because of her

misfortune you chose to disinherit your daughter, making the situation that much worse for her?" Flynn drilled the man with a frigid look. "Is that what you're leading up to?"

St. Claire looked momentarily nonplussed, but he collected himself quickly. Obviously he'd wanted to be the one to give Flynn the bad news. Flynn silently thanked Felicity for her foresight.

"So you knew, did you?" Melisande's father asked.

Flynn nodded, raising a brow and allowing a slight smile. "I knew." He sipped his port.

"And you married her anyway. Why?" St. Claire demanded, more angry than before.

Flynn continued to look at him. "Because if I didn't, Juliette would have been the big loser, and Melisande would have blamed herself for the rest of her life. At least this way, even though I know Melisande hates this marriage almost as much as you do, she'll be able to tell herself that she did all she could to help her sister."

"You'll forgive me," St. Claire stated, his lips curving into a sneer, "if I don't believe your motives were so purely disinterested."

"No," Flynn said, shaking his head and looking at his glass, "I had some reasons of my own for going through with it." Not the least of which was that he had no other place to go and no way to get there if he did.

"Do you mind if I ask what those are?"

"Yes. I do." Flynn's eyes shifted to St. Claire and fixed on him. This was not so different from facing down the president's press secretary over a particularly sticky policy point, Flynn thought.

St. Claire did not look happy with this answer.

"But let me tell you this," Flynn continued. "I believe this whole situation could have been avoided if one person had acted differently. And that one person is you, Mr. St. Claire. If Melisande had felt that she could get some understanding and some sympathy from her father, she might have gone to him first with her concerns about Bellingham. But she knew you, sir." He said the word with disdain. "She knew that nothing would stop you from sacrificing her for the money."

St. Claire's face turned beet-red with anger. "I don't care about any money. She was to be a *duchess*. As an American you can't possibly understand what that means, but to us it is unparalleled success. Yet even aside from that, though you apparently wish to vilify me in this, it was *her* decision to marry Bellingham. I forced her to do nothing." He leaned forward and narrowed his eyes, one fist on the table between them. "But she was right that I would not have had sympathy for her, not at the late date she decided to change her mind. She had pledged herself to Lord Bellingham and she had a duty to fulfill. And now, look what happens when one reneges on one's word."

"She hadn't married him yet," Flynn said, sitting forward also, his grip tightening on the port glass. "There was no vow to be broken."

"She had *promised* to marry him." St. Claire's fist came down on the table, rattling what was left of the dinner plates and glasses. Then slowly, without relinquishing Flynn's gaze, he leaned back and added, "It is the same thing."

Flynn scoffed. "I don't think so. I think what she did was disappoint you, Mr. St. Claire. Imagine! Your own a daughter a duchess," he said facetiously, then sobered. "But look what happens when one gets greedy and reaches too far. One ends up with a Mrs. Patrick instead of a Lady Bellingham."

St. Claire stood up so quickly his chair bounced backward onto the floor.

"You are a *brute*," he breathed. "The lowest, most despicable sort of opportunist."

"I am your son-in-law," Flynn countered.

St. Claire seethed before him. "There is but one thing I wanted to say to you before you went to my daughter. And that is to be aware that she has led a sheltered life. She was bred for gentility. To be married now to someone of your class, someone boorish and uncouth, with the manners of a rustic, is going to be a shock to her. So I'm asking you to be"—he stopped, looking at the table and regulating his breathing—"*careful* with her, in the . . . in the . . ." He waved a hand as if expecting Flynn to supply the words. "In the marriage bed. I'm asking you to think of her as something fine."

Flynn stared at the man. "What do you mean?" he asked slowly, feeling the insult all the more because the man was perfectly serious in his concern. "What, are you afraid I'm going to jump her like a stray dog?"

St. Claire colored and glared daggers at Flynn. "For all I know."

Flynn exhaled hard and shook his head. "I don't

even know how to answer that. Your pomposity—the word doesn't even fit, it's too mild. Your arrogance, your patronizing—it's beyond me even to tell you how blindly self-centered—no, self-*aggrandizing* you are. Just because I'm from a different place, because I act a little differently than you do, does *not* make me an animal. And since you're suddenly so concerned, I'll tell you—Melisande will have the choice whether or not to sleep with me. And if she chooses not to, then I'll be the last one to—''

''No!'' St. Claire's outburst startled him. ''Melisande has a duty—a marital duty—to perform. She must not be given the choice not to fulfill it.''

''A *duty*? It is her *duty* to sleep with me? I would never do that to a woman. I would never *want* that from a woman and I can't imagine what kind of disgusting man would. No, I believe you intend for it to be further punishment for her disobedience. That's what I think. You're the despicable one, St. Claire.'' Flynn felt nauseous. Did they really think he would go up there and just *take* her, as if she had no say in the matter?

''She has a duty to this family,'' St. Claire continued as if Flynn hadn't spoken, ''to continue the line. Do you understand me, Mr. Patrick? As much as I might despise you—and I do—it is *your* progeny who may inherit all I have, all I have worked to maintain and strived to make flourish. If Juliette should prove barren, or God forbid, die without issue, all will go to your children, yours and Melisande's. You should be thankful for that, Mr. Flynn Patrick from America.''

Flynn scowled. ''I don't want your money.''

"*You* won't get it."

Flynn paused. He shouldn't argue too strenuously against the bequeathal for it could be one answer to Melisande's inheritance problem. It was the one good thing that could come of her possibly becoming pregnant by him.

"All right. Fine," he said, wanting suddenly to be out of this conversation. The old-fashioned morals people generally thought of as quaint were appalling in reality. But as anxious as Flynn was to be away from Melisande's father, the next conversation he had to have had every likelihood of being worse than this one. For next he had to go talk to Melisande and—devil take her father—he had to give her the choice to either have him or not.

Chapter Thirteen

For Melisande, dinner had been both unbearably long and frighteningly short. The moments had ticked by with interminable tedium, but before she knew it dinner was over, the men were enjoying their port and cigars, and her aunt was taking her upstairs.

"Do you have any concerns you wish to talk with me about?" Felicity offered quietly as they ascended the stairs.

Melisande knew what she meant and had a thousand questions, none of which could be answered by her aunt.

"I don't believe so," she replied.

"You do know what will likely take place tonight?" her aunt prompted.

Apprehension shuddered through Melisande's body. "I must give myself up to him," she said simply. "To that strange, homeless man."

"That strange, homeless, *handsome* man," Felicity corrected.

"Good looks can only give so much pleasure," Melisande said. "True happiness comes from shared lives, common backgrounds, similar beliefs. Mr. Patrick and I have none of those things."

"Neither would you and Bellingham," Felicity pointed out.

Melisande said nothing, but thought to herself that at least she and Bellingham would have in common that they sprang from the same century.

Not that she believed Mr. Patrick's outlandish tale.

Felicity helped her undress and change into a white linen and lace night rail. Then Felicity brushed out her hair, tucked her into bed, sitting up against a profusion of pillows, and left her with a sympathetic smile.

Melisande sat perfectly still listening for the sound of footsteps on the stairs. Her heart pounded too rapidly in her chest and her palms sweated. She sat rigidly for so long her muscles began to ache.

Was he never coming up? Could he be nervous too? she wondered.

Her eyelids were just drifting shut when a gentle knock sounded on the door.

Flynn felt the cool brass of the knob in the palm of his hand, and paused before turning it. This action would be the first he took that felt inexorable. Everything else, including the brief wedding ceremony, was playacting. He'd merely been participating in something over which he had little or no control.

But *this* . . . this he had control over. Once he slept

with this girl, she would be forever changed in this world. She would be truly married, no longer a virgin, no longer eligible for a proper marriage in the way young ladies of this time should be, from what he could gather. Therefore she would be altered irrevocably in the eyes of her peers.

Did that mean her portrait would not end up in the gallery at Merestun? Of course it would, he told himself. He'd seen it there himself. He couldn't change that now. It already *was*. But . . . wouldn't that have to mean she'd marry Bellingham after all?

There were too many questions he didn't know how to answer. The last one being, could he really do this?

Of course he *could,* he thought wryly. She was gorgeous. But should he? Suppose he were to be swept back to the twentieth century tomorrow?

Well, then, she would be eventually declared a widow, his rational side said. It wasn't as if she were in love with him, he reasoned, and would be distraught at his absence. He thought he should laugh at the notion, but he felt far from amused. If anything, she despised him for getting her into this mess simply by being in the right place at the wrong time.

He bit the inside of his cheek. Truer words than that were never spoken. Right place, wrong time.

He took a deep breath. She didn't have to do this, he would tell her. No one needed to know if they didn't sleep together, not even her damn father. But then if they didn't have sex, he countered, and she had no children who could inherit, what would become of her after he disappeared? Would she remarry? *Could* she? This world was so strange he wasn't sure what would happen to her.

He would leave it up to her, he decided. It was the only thing he could do. Figuring out why he was here and what he should be doing was bad enough. Trying to figure out what might happen to others was beyond him. So far events had carried him along with them. Perhaps he should just continue to go with them. Chances were better than good that she would accept his offer to live celibately until he found a way to get home, and the problem would then be solved.

While he was not completely satisfied with this course, he turned the knob and opened the door. She was sitting straight up in bed, her reddish-brown hair long and thick, framing her pale face and falling over her shoulders.

"Hi," he said, standing in the doorway with one hand on the knob.

Her voice was barely audible. "Hello."

He found it hard to look at her. She had never looked so vulnerable. He turned away and closed the door carefully behind him, then took his time turning back. She was scared to death, he could see it immediately. She was scared to death of *him*, of what he had the right to do to her. Her fear made him feel sick—as if she thought the same thing her father did, that he was an animal and would take her like one.

He began to untie the complex cravat the valet had secured that morning, his fingers fumbling in the fabric, and walked to the opposite side of the room. He tried to be casual about undressing, but he felt her eyes on him with every movement. Wide, terrified, deer-in-the-headlights eyes.

There is nothing to worry about, he told himself. If she decides she wants you, it will have been her choice. You know you're not going to justify the fear on her face, so stop acting like you might be the beast they accuse you of being.

Besides, the one rational part of his mind continued, even if you sleep with her, if it weren't you initiating her into the world of sex, it would be someone else. But immediately upon having that thought, he realized the idea was unbearable. People were probably so sexually backward in this day and age that some other man might not know to show her how she could gain pleasure from the act. Flynn knew he himself could not be further from the animal her father accused him of being. In fact he was probably the one man in this whole damn country who could show her how to feel good.

It wasn't that he couldn't stand the thought of her with another man, he told himself. No, of course not. It was that he couldn't stand the thought of any man treating her roughly.

He finally got the stupid cravat undone, and threw it on the chair with a little more force than necessary. He turned back to her as he unbuttoned his shirt. She continued to watch him, her eyes large and uncertain.

"Listen," he said, looking down at his hands as they worked so as not to embarrass her, "I know you're probably nervous, so I'll get right to the point. We don't have to do this. We can put on an act like everything's normal, but we don't have to go through with it. If that's what you want, then I'll do it. It's up to you."

She was silent. He couldn't bear to look up, didn't

want to see the relief on her face. His ego had taken too much of a beating since he'd been here, he told himself.

"Because there's the chance," he continued, "that you would get pregnant, and then if I ever made it back to my time, you'd be stuck here, alone, with my kid. I wouldn't want to put either of us through that."

He had gotten his shirt unbuttoned, but felt uncomfortable taking it off, so he sat on the chair and pulled at his boots. "I know you don't like me much, but it would be easy to act as if the marriage was all right in public. I just don't see the point of putting us both through the hassle of putting on the act in private."

He yanked the second boot off and let it thud to the floor before looking up at her.

Her eyes were downcast, her hands clasped in her lap, and she looked as if she were about to cry.

"Mel?" he said, standing and moving hesitantly toward the bed. "What, uh, what do you think of all that?"

"I think you've chosen a most delicate way of telling me you do not want me."

He sat gingerly on the side of the bed. "Hey," he said. "That's not true. You know I didn't mean it that way. It's not that I don't want you." He chuckled ironically. "Let me make one thing clear. I *want* you. But you know my situation. Or at least, you know what I've told you my situation is, whether or not you believe it."

"I know you are not in your right mind," she said, and turned her face away, "to think you are from the future. And I suppose I should thank you for reminding me of that and sparing me the unpleasantness of—of having to lie with you.''

He studied the side of her face, the pink cheek and ear, and the knotting of her hands in her lap. Could it be that she really *wanted him*? Despite all she knew about and how little she thought of him? What else would explain her mood? She clearly was not happy with his proposal that they merely pretend to have slept together.

When he looked at her in the virginal white nightgown, with the low scooped neckline that exposed a generous swell of bosom, his pulse jumped at the opportunity of sleeping with her even as his mind railed that it would be a mistake.

She probably didn't actually want him, he thought then. She was probably thinking of the fact that her children might inherit her father's fortune where she no longer could. Maybe that was what she wanted. But he couldn't ask her. For some reason, bringing the topic of money into the workings of the bedroom went against every passionate impulse he had.

He slid closer to her on the bed and took her by the chin to turn her face toward him. ''Mel, be honest with me,'' he said as she faced him. Her eyes were still downcast. ''What's really got you so down? I know it's not that you're secretly in love with me.'' He tried to laugh at the lame joke.

She glanced quickly up at him. ''Of course not,'' she said, ''It's just . . .''

A muscle flexed in her jaw. He let his fingers loosen from her chin and caressed the spot with his fingers. Her chest rose with a deep breath.

Keeping his eyes on her face, he let his fingers trail

down her neck, touching the soft skin as a bonfire ignited in his loins. He reached the crest of her breasts and trailed a finger along the edge of the nightgown.

She shivered and parted her lips.

"Melisande," he said so quietly it emerged as a whisper.

Still, she did not look at him.

He let his fingers drop lower, over the material of the nightgown, to the peak of one breast. The nipple stood hard and as he touched it, she inhaled sharply.

He stopped. "Tell me you at least want me," he whispered. "Don't make me do this without knowing that."

She couldn't possibly say such a thing to him. She would be unable to get the words out, she knew, so she would not even try. But she *did* want him. Oh, she did.

When his fingers had touched the skin at the top of her nightgown, she'd felt flutters of excitement all through her body. This was not the simple, relaxing pleasure she used to feel when her mother rubbed her back with those same light fingers. This was pleasure bordering on torment.

But now he touched her breast. Even through her gown it was a place nobody but herself had ever touched. She felt as if he held the string to every sensation in her body and dextrously made them all quiver, like a skilled marionette master.

Up and down his fingers played, making the nipple harder and more erect. Every breath she took grew more unsteady.

Part of her wished he would kiss her, simply and

softly, as he had that morning in the Clydes' hayloft. That had been pleasure illicit enough. This touching of her private area was doing things to her insides she was not sure was healthy.

She lifted her eyes to his and found him looking straight at her. He was so foreign, so alien to her. No matter that she'd been looking at him for days. Here, in her bed, with his shirt unbuttoned and his hands upon her, he looked like a predator—handsome, seductive, dangerous.

"I . . ." she began hoarsely. She swallowed. "I believe it is our duty to—to complete the wedding night in the usual fashion."

His expression darkened. Her nerves thrummed.

"I don't want to hear about duty, Melisande," he said in a low voice. "I want to hear about desire. Tell me you want me, or tell me you don't. I need to know."

She opened her mouth, but could not get a sound to emerge. How could she say, *I want you*? How could she get those words past her lips? They were a harlot's words. She wanted only to do her duty.

"Tell me, Melisande," he said.

Then he removed his hand. The touch had been so riveting she nearly gasped at its sudden absence. Her heart thundered in her chest and her eyes whipped to his.

With audacity she didn't know she possessed, she leaned forward, put her hand around the back of his neck, and pulled his face toward hers. Their lips met as her fingers registered the feel of his soft hair. His hands rose to her shoulders and he pulled her closer, sliding toward her on the bed so her body lay flush against his. At the same time his tongue slipped past her lips.

The surprising sensation produced a shock of desire so powerful it blasted along her limbs. Her other arm rose and wound around his neck, pulling him closer to her as she opened her mouth and experimentally touched his tongue with hers. She let it move against his, feeling their breath combine into one, joining their bodies, feeding one force. The feeling was incredible.

He moved his lips from hers to kiss her cheek, then her neck. Ripples of pleasure washed over her, shimmering across her skin as his mouth moved to her collarbone. She tilted her head, and felt her hair shift and fall to her other shoulder, covering her arm.

The sleeve of her gown succumbed to his hand, dropping over her shoulder as his lips descended further, down her chest, following the edge of the fabric. She inhaled deeply, wanting the pleasure never to stop, urging him onward, downward, arching her back until his fingers fumbled with the buttons of her gown and finally freed her breast.

His lips found the hardened nipple. Melisande's body turned to liquid. She felt it, hot and moist between her legs. She pulled his face against her breast and threw her head back.

This must be what they said was so evil, she thought. This exquisite desire must be what they warned young women about.

His lips pulled at the nipple and she gasped with pleasure, her heart pushing the blood to race through her veins.

Their movements grew more frenzied, his mouth,

her hands, his arms, her body, until he abruptly let go and sat up, yanking his shirt off and rising up on his knees to work at the buttons of his trousers.

She felt suddenly exposed, alone and untouched on the bed. Her breast felt cool in the air, so she pulled the fabric of her nightgown over it. She did not know where to look, what to do with her hands as he worked at his own clothing.

"Damn," he muttered, ripping a button off his pants.

She turned her eyes up to him and a smile curved her lips. She wanted to extinguish the light, wanted only to feel, but then she looked at his chest, at the muscles in his arms, and she knew she wanted to see what was beneath the fabric of his breeches.

With the same nerve that had surprised her before, she reached toward him and gently pushed his hands aside. She undid the buttons remaining on his pants, his hands suddenly still beside them as she did so. But she did not have the courage to look into his face. His fingers combed into her hair as she pushed his pants down over his hips to his knees as he knelt there.

The sight of his manhood simultaneously embarrassed and intrigued her. She had never seen a man's member before, though she'd certainly felt a few pressed against her leg during a stolen kiss or the brief contact of a dance. This one, however, was upright and hard. She touched it tentatively with one hand.

After a second, a little groan emerged from Flynn and he closed his hand over hers on himself. Slowly, he moved her fist in a gentle motion that she could see gave him great pleasure. Without thinking, she leaned forward and kissed his chest, their clasped hands between them.

He stopped then, moved so that he could kick his pants off completely, then lay her back on the pillows. She looked up, accidentally, into his eyes and found them intently on her face. The pale blue depths captured her gaze and seared her with their intensity. She could not look away.

His hands pulled her nightgown from her shoulders, then drew it down across her body and off. Cool air settled onto her skin as she lay naked before him. But for some reason she felt no shame, only desire to have him touch her again.

His hands skated up her body, starting at her thighs, to her hips, and to her breasts. He lowered his mouth to suckle them again. In spontaneous response, her back arched to meet his lips and she held his head against her.

One of his hands slid down her side to her hip, then across to the nexus of her legs. Gently, his fingers pushed between her thighs and she parted them, unsure what would happen next. His mouth slowed on her nipple as his fingers probed, then found that hot, wet spot.

Instinctively, her legs closed on his hand.

"It's all right," he murmured against her skin. "I've got you. It's all right."

And then his fingers probed deeper, until they were actually inside her and moving.

She took a deep, quavering breath and forced herself to relax. It only took a moment before her hips were rising to meet the thrust of his fingers.

He rose up, then, and balanced himself over her.

His eyes captured hers once again, and he lowered his organ to the spot his fingers had just left.

Her breath came rapidly and she melted into the heated look in his eyes. She felt the tip of his manhood touch her again and she wanted—*something*. Her hips rose toward him and he pulled back, nudging her gently again when she lay back.

"Oh," she heard herself sigh as if from a great distance, as his manhood slid a fraction of the way in where his fingers had been.

"What?" he whispered.

She grasped his shoulders and moved her hips toward him. He pulled slightly out of reach again, then pushed against her as she lay back, entering her slightly.

"Please," she whispered, and looked into his eyes.

He was smiling, his eyes half-closed. She might have been angry, or humiliated at his teasing, but she could think of only one thing. She *wanted* him. She wanted his manhood to push into her the way his fingers had, every portion of her body cried out for it.

"What," he whispered again, shifting one hand so that his fingers touched the front of her heat while his manhood pushed against her center.

"Oh, oh," she breathed, arching her back. "Oh, God, I want you." Her words emerged in a rush, and then she could not stop them. "Please, Flynn."

He pushed deeper into her, slowly, and paused. "It'll hurt for just a second," he said quietly, lowering his mouth to her ear. "But it'll pass, I promise."

She barely registered what he said, so close was he to what she wanted. She pushed her hips toward him at the same time he thrust forward and she felt a sharp pain, as if he had gone too far. She gasped and drew back. His lips found her neck.

"It's all right," he said into her ear.

"No, no," she breathed, pushing against his chest.

But his hips moved forward again, and this time it did not hurt. This time it was deeper, and she felt him trembling with desire against her. Her hips lifted of their own volition. He pushed into her, then out, again and again, until pretty soon the pain was forgotten in the whirlwind of fulfillment and desire that coursed through her.

He pushed himself up, still moving inside her, and his fingers returned to her core, doing something, something she did not want him to stop. And before she could think what might be next, her body exploded into a glittering haze of ecstasy. She arched her back and cried out, digging her fingers into his thighs, and was dimly aware of his own moan of pleasure as he pushed deep inside her and stayed there, pulsing even as she pulsed, their bodies slick with sweat, their hearts thundering like the sound of a thousand galloping horses.

Chapter Fourteen

Melisande awoke slowly. Her limbs were stiff and she felt too heavy to move, so she only opened her eyes a sliver. The covers were tucked in up to her chin and she felt warm and rested in a deep, all-encompassing way she had never felt before.

She turned sluggishly onto her side, aware of a stickiness between her legs, and opened her eyes.

Mr. Patrick was gone. The pillow next to her was wadded into a ball and the covers were tucked around her. The other side of the bed was empty.

She took a deep breath and stretched her legs, pointing her toes under the warmth of the covers, then relaxed. She was glad he was not here. She was not sure she could have looked him in the eye first thing this morning. In fact, she was not sure she would ever be able to look him in the eye again. What they had shared last night was so fantastical, she could not think of it without her breath catching in her throat and her insides going all liquid once again. She could hardly believe it had been she herself who had become so wanton, so brazenly consumed by passion. He had done something incredible to her, something wicked and holy all at once. Even now the memory of it electrified her.

So *that* was the marriage act, she thought with a small, privately delighted smile. It was no wonder married ladies never spoke of it, or else they would never be able to keep the unmarried ones from trying it. It was too delicious, and she could not believe she was to be allowed the pleasure of it whenever she wanted. She had a husband now. She was *supposed* to do it.

She turned onto her back, looked up at the lace canopy, and thought about getting up. She imagined herself getting dressed and joining her parents and her aunt and uncle—her *husband*—for breakfast, and suddenly wondered how in the world she would face them all. Heavens, every one of them knew what she had just done. They would look at her differently; she would blush scarlet every time she met their eyes.

She sat up and pushed her hair out of her face. *Where* had Mr. Patrick gone? At the thought she realized how foolish it was to call him Mr. Patrick, even in her mind, after what they had shared last night. Oh, it was all too confusing! She had to go downstairs and pretend nothing had happened. Maybe the others would think that she and her husband hadn't done anything after all. But that would be almost as embarrassing. It was one thing to make a bad marriage, but to make a bad marriage and live like a nun would be intolerable. Especially knowing what she now did about the marriage act.

What was she to do? She couldn't stay up here forever.

Slowly, she got out of bed and rang the bell for a bath. She would consider how to encounter them all one step at a time. First, she had to clean up and get dressed. Then she would be able to face them. She hoped.

At least she had done the right thing, she consoled herself. She had married the man and made things all right for Juliette. Perhaps things would get back to normal now, or at least close to normal anyway. How could anyone fault her now that she had gone so very far to make it all appear right?

Her self-assurance that she'd done the right thing was not to last long, however. Once she'd made it to the dining room and greeted her mother and her aunt as composedly as possible, without directly meeting their eyes—the men having gone off to various locations early—she saw the newspapers. They were full of Melisande St. Claire's scandalous wedding. She read them in horror, every one of them.

The gossip columns were bad enough, but there was even a complete article that talked about Gretna Green and detailed her supposed flight there with her new husband. They characterized him as "an American, without connection in the city." Subtle as it seemed, that one phrase told the world—*her* whole world—that he was nobody, picked up from nowhere, with no other purpose than to save what was left of her reputation.

They didn't mention her aborted betrothal to Lord Bellingham, heir to the Merestun dukedom, no doubt because the duke was able to quash the story, but she knew the simple mention of her name was likely to anger the earl all over again. And the Earl of Bellingham angry was not something she wished to think about.

Evidence that the Patricks were not to be accepted even remotely into society came in the form of total quiet that morning. No cards arrived, no visitors stopped in, not even friends of Felicity who would have come on an ordinary day showed their faces. The quiet, coupled with the suddenly sinful memories of last night, reinforced Melisande's humiliation.

After breakfast, which she merely picked at, Melisande retired to the parlor with her mother and her aunt, awash in feelings with which she did not know what to do. Memories of the night before assailed her, bathing her in remembered sensations of corrupt pleasure and chaste contrition. She was suddenly certain that to enjoy the marriage act as she had was immoral.

He—Flynn—had done something to her that had made her feel as if her whole body had burst into a million sunlit pieces, sparkling as they descended once again into her earthly body. His hands were magic—or sinful—but unearthly, and they'd found her most secret spots and exploited them, waking them into purveyors of pleasure. And now, guilt.

Could all of that be wrong? It couldn't, she argued mentally. She had only done her duty as a wife. The problem was, it had not felt like duty. She must be wrong to have enjoyed it.

She longed to ask her aunt about it, but there sat

her mother to whom she could never voice such thoughts. Wrestling with the problem, she found she could believe her aunt might enjoy the act as well, for she and Mr. Kesterbrook were affectionate with each other, touching when they thought others were not looking, kissing one another good-bye even when they only separated for short periods.

Melisande's parents, on the other hand, barely spoke to one another, except to exchange information vital to performing their duties throughout the day.

But that was not the point, she reminded herself. It did not signify whether or not she enjoyed Mr. Patrick's—Flynn's—caresses. What mattered was the fact that no one had come to call. Not one person. Not her oldest, dearest friends who always called the moment they knew she was in town or if they came to the country. Not her aunt's legion of society friends. Not her parents' considerable connections. She happened to know that yesterday her mother wrote notes informing her friends of her arrival and inviting them to visit, saying she would be "at home" today. Not one of them had come.

And so this was how it would be, she told herself. From this day forward she would languish in obscurity. No, it would be worse than obscurity. She would be reviled. She wondered if she were to go walking in Hyde Park, would people avoid walking even in the same direction as she, the way she'd once seen a woman treated who had disgraced herself?

Undoubtedly. For she had not only disgraced herself, she had on top of that married terribly. It would have been one thing if she'd disappeared, then turned up married to someone of her own station or above.

But the shame of the union with Mr. Patrick would have been enough to destroy her even without the three-day disappearance and the so-called "elopement."

She was just about to pick up another newspaper to hide tearing eyes from her aunt and mother, when the parlor door opened and the butler entered.

Expecting him to pass her by on the way to her aunt, Melisande only followed his movement with the periphery of her vision, but when he stopped beside her chair she looked up in confusion.

"Note for you, Madam," the butler said, bowing so she could see the note on the silver server.

It was penned on heavy vellum with a thick, blue seal. On the front it read "Mrs. Patrick." She took it up in a trembling hand. Her eyes darted to the butler's inscrutable face.

"Thank you," she said.

He bowed again and departed.

She looked closely at the seal and felt her composure desert her. It was the Merestun crest. A reprimand from the duke, for certain. The note felt leaden in her hand.

She glanced up to see both her aunt and her mother looking at her expectantly. Her mother took one look at her face and sat forward in her seat, her brow furrowed.

"Melisande, what is it? Who is it from?" her mother asked.

Melisande's eyes shifted to her aunt, then back down to the letter. "It is from Merestun." She swallowed, holding the envelope as if it might struggle to get away and she would gladly let it. "I am sure it is a rebuke. I do not wish to open it."

"You don't know that," her aunt said. "Open it."

Melisande pressed her trembling lips together. She wanted nothing more than to break down crying like a child who has fallen and needs her mother's help. She looked up at her mother, pleading with her eyes for her to understand, to save her from this humiliation, but her mother only nodded her head toward the note and said, "Open it, dear. If it is a rebuke, then you'd best read it and get it over with."

No, Melisande thought. She would be best off to run and hide from everyone right now, before this degradation went any further. She would go to Sir Thomas Cromley's cottage and live out her days there in solitude. She didn't care. As long as she didn't have to suffer any more reproach from good, high-minded people who had never been in a position to have to choose between marriage to a murderer or a nobody and a life outside all of good society.

Of course, no one believed Bellingham to be a murderer, according to her aunt. But Melisande did. Melisande had looked into his eyes and seen no soul.

She took the note in both hands and gently opened the seal. Extricating the card, she looked at the dark, tremulous handwriting. The old duke must have written it himself, she thought with a start. But because it was so short her dread lessened.

Every muscle tensed, she read the contents.

The words took her breath away. Her eyes flew to her aunt, then her mother.

"I don't believe it," she whispered.

"What is it?" her mother asked, moving to the

edge of her chair as if she might pop up and snatch the note from her daughter's hand.

Melisande's eyes trailed to her aunt, whose expression, in contrast, showed a quiet confidence.

"He's invited us to tea." She held the note in her outstretched hand, at which point her mother did take it from her. Melisande looked at Felicity. "The Duke of Merestun has invited Mr. Patrick and me to tea."

Her aunt smiled. "How wonderful."

"Am I dreaming?" Melisande asked. Then her heart skipped a beat and she said, "Or could it be that he wishes to reprimand me—or both of us—in person?"

"That is hardly the duke's style," her aunt said mildly.

"It's true," her mother marveled. "He asks them to tea tomorrow afternoon. I can scarcely believe it." She held the note like a cherished bird in her hands. Melisande could see the edges quivering in her grasp.

"Do you know him so well then, Aunt Felicity," Melisande asked, "that you would know him unlikely to want to berate me face to face?"

"I know his character," her aunt answered. "It's highly unlikely he would invite such unpleasantness into his home. And while he can be severe, I have never known him to have a bad temper."

Melisande looked at the note in her mother's hand. "But . . . I cannot imagine he wishes to congratulate me on my marriage, considering it was his own nephew, his heir, that I . . . well, you know. Still, what other reason would he have to invite *me* to tea? I have never even met him."

"You must go and find out," her aunt said.

279

"I shall hardly know how to act, what to say. Should I apologize? I would hate to bring up the subject if he had some other objective in mind." She paused, thinking. "You do not think . . . that is, he is not senile, is he?"

Her aunt laughed. "My dear, you amuse me. No, he is not senile."

She frowned. "But when was the last time you saw him? He is very old. Look at his handwriting."

"I'm sure that's not his handwriting. It is most likely his man, Lourds, who wrote the note. I have seen the duke recently enough to know he has his faculties about him."

"Extraordinary," her mother murmured, still looking at the note. "Tea with the Duke of Merestun."

Flynn returned late in the day, having been out with Mr. Kesterbrook's valet purchasing clothes, according to Felicity. Melisande was surprised to hear that her father had actually paid for the équipage, then realized that it would bring as much shame upon him as Mr. Patrick himself for her husband to be seen in the strange clothes in which he had arrived.

Melisande, in the front parlor, heard him return, and studiously kept her eyes on the book in her lap without reading a word while he entered the house and was divested of his hat, coat, and gloves. He joined her immediately.

"Hey." He strode into the room with that casual greeting and a broad smile upon his face.

Melisande glanced up from her book.

"Hello," she said. She had purposely kept but one lamp lit so as to hide the blush she knew she'd have when she saw him. She returned her attention to her book.

He sat on the sofa across from her and rested his elbows on his knees.

"How are you doing?" he asked in a confidential tone, cocking his head to one side.

She looked up again, feeling the strange thrumming along her nerves she'd felt last night start up again. "I am well. How are you today?"

"Great." He grinned again. He seemed to be feeling no awkwardness at all. "I just bought a bunch of new clothes, all on Papa St. Claire."

She frowned. "I must admit that surprises me. Papa was . . . quite angry with you. With both of us."

"Yeah, well, I guess he wanted to make sure I at least *look* respectable. And he did say something about being paid back someday. But now you won't have to be ashamed of me anymore."

Melisande felt an unexpected lump rise to her throat. But she *did* have to be ashamed of him, she reminded herself, though increasingly when she looked at him she found it hard to believe. He was nobody, a pauper, and they would be living off the charity of her father. Good society would have nothing to do with him.

But somehow, as he sat across from her, smiling that charismatic smile, those blue eyes so clear in the lamplight, it was hard for her to remember why that mattered. What should matter is that he was kind to her, she thought. It had been lost in the excitement last night, but now that she thought about it, she realized he had been very gentle and cautious of her feelings. He was so caring, she found herself thinking, she could almost believe he was in love with her.

But that was ridiculous. She shook herself out of the reverie. "I am glad to hear it. That is, I know you were not comfortable in your old clothes. Tell me, how do these feel to you? Better than your others?"

He looked down at himself. "Actually, yes. I can't believe it, but this getup is pretty comfortable. But maybe it's because that tux wasn't meant to be worn wet."

She followed his gaze. "You do look very good."

The pleasure on his face made her smile.

"I have some news." She closed the book on her finger and rested her other hand on top of it. "Something extraordinary, I really can't fathom. We've been invited to tea. . . ." As he tried to look impressed, she drew the announcement out. "At the Duke of Merestun's townhouse."

At this he did looked surprised, then his brows drew together. "Merestun. You don't mean Bellingham. . . ."

"Oh, no." She shook her head, trying to look positive about the event. "He is the heir to the dukedom. But the old duke, Lord Merestun, is still living and he is in town. He sent a note earlier asking us to tea. Of course, I answered in the affirmative immediately."

"What's he want?" Flynn's expression was concerned. "He can't be happy about everything that's happened, can he? Is there something I'm missing?"

"No . . . that is, I don't think so." She opened the book on her lap and smoothed its pages with her hands. "I too had some concern at first, but Aunt

Felicity assured me that he is not the type to . . . to be angry . . . outwardly.''

"Not the type to be angry outwardly."

"No. So we must go and find out what he wants."

Flynn steepled his fingers and looked down into them. "Hmm."

"I don't believe it will be anything bad."

He looked at her. "Yes, you do. I can tell by the look on your face. You're dreading this."

"I am not."

"Melisande, come on. Why lie about it—"

"I'm not lying!" She closed the book with a hard *clap* and dropped it on the table next to her. "I am merely trying to be calm about this." She stood up and moved to the fireplace. "Aunt Felicity has assured me," she said again, trying to modulate her voice to keep the quaver out of it, "that Lord Merestun is a fair man."

"A fair man with an heir like Bellingham? Hard to believe."

"That is a familial obligation," she said stridently. "One cannot always choose one's heirs. He must leave the title to a male relative. As it happens, Bellingham is the closest one."

"I have to believe a duke has more choice than that."

"You don't know a thing about it. There are no titled people in America."

"One more reason to want to get back home," Flynn muttered.

The words sent a shot of panic through Melisande. It had never occurred to her that he might want to return to America. Heavens, suppose he intended to

take her with him. She couldn't go. She *wouldn't* go.
She couldn't imagine leaving Juliette, and Daphne,
and her parents and Felicity. Not mention her friends
. . . but then she had no friends any longer, she realized. No one would associate with her. And what was
the difference between being relegated to Sir Thomas's cottage and shipped off to America?

She couldn't help it, her eyes teared and she inhaled, high and shrill. "I won't go, do you understand?" she said in a voice not her own.

Flynn stood up. "Where? To tea?"

"No! To America. I won't go, I don't care if you
are my husband. You can do what you like to me, but
I won't leave my family. This is my *home*."

"Melisande," he began.

"Don't tell me it's my obligation. I never even
thought. I mean, I knew you were an American, but
it never even occurred to me that you might want to
go home. But this is *my* home, don't you see? And I
cannot leave it."

He took two steps toward her. "But I never asked
you to go to America," he said gently.

She turned blurry eyes to him. "What?"

"You couldn't go home with me even if I wanted
you to," he said. "Remember what I told you, about
1998 and all? I know you don't believe me. You
can't. It's crazy. But you can't go home with me, so
don't worry." He came to her and took her hand in
his, peering into her face with such calm concern, it
was all she could do not to melt into his arms.

Of course, he was crazy. She brought herself up
with the reminder. Even now he spoke of being from
the future. How could he seem so sane in some ways

and yet persist in such an obviously deranged belief?

"But," she said, "you cannot get back there—to this future you keep speaking of. Can you?" She didn't know what he could possibly be thinking about that, but she couldn't imagine being left behind, alone, exiled to the countryside without even a husband. The double humiliation of marrying him and having him leave her would be too much to bear.

He put an arm around her shoulders, and she relaxed against his side. "Calm down. Where did all this come from anyway? One minute we're talking about tea and the next I'm carting you off to America."

"Oh, I don't know. I'm losing my mind, I think." She certainly was, to be comforted by a madman.

"You're under a lot of stress. Come on, come sit down. Do you want a glass of wine or something? What do you people drink recreationally?"

She smiled at his wording. If you got over its incorrectness, it could be considered quite charming, she thought. "Sherry mostly. Though the gentlemen will drink brandy most often." She took a deep breath and pulled away from his side. "But I don't need anything. Thank you. I am better now."

"Well, I do. I think I'll have a brandy. And if you're worried about tomorrow," Flynn said with confidence, "just let me do the talking. Trust me, I'm good with powerful men."

"I hardly think that would be wise," she said, "considering your . . . delusion."

Flynn stopped on his way to the brandy decanter. "My delusion?"

"Yes, you know, about the future." She straightened her skirt and sat down on the sofa. Then she looked up at him, concerned. "You never answered my question."

"What question?"

"This 'future' you talk about, you won't go back there, to wherever it is you think you're from, will you? You are here now, to stay, are you not?"

"Melisande," he said gently, coming back and sitting in the chair across from her. "I know you don't believe me, like I said before, but you do have to believe one thing. And that is that I must go back to where I came from eventually."

Panic sliced through her chest again. It was not that she couldn't do without *him*, she told herself. It was the idea of being abandoned that had her rattled.

"You plan to leave me?" she asked, her voice higher than normal and a degree of panic showing through it. "Why on earth did you marry me then?"

He looked at her, confusion evident on his face. "Because you needed me to."

"But now you will just disappear? *Abandon* me?" She felt hysteria threaten. She could not be alone in this misery. She could not.

He sighed. "I have to go back. I don't see how I can't. You have to admit I don't fit in here."

She stood up, frightened more than she'd ever been, even when her aunt had told her there was no saving her reputation. She would be a pariah, alone. She would grow old, alone. Even Juliette would not be able to come visit very often once she found a respectable husband. Melisande would become an old woman, a crone.

"Thank you very much for telling me this now!"

she cried, channeling all her energy into anger. "After the wedding—and *after* last night. You've probably got a wife somewhere and *that's* the reason you've made up that ridiculous story about traveling through time. You're *despicable*. You're a low, common, heartless beast of a man!"

Flynn stood up too. "Maybe I did owe you an explanation," he said, anger tinting his words, "but I notice you didn't mention to me that you'd been disinherited. Correct me if I'm wrong, but you believed I was marrying you for your money. How convenient that you forgot to mention you wouldn't have any."

Melisande felt the blood drain from her face. Guilt swept over her, clouding her anger. "Who told you that?"

"Felicity. Do you deny it?"

She gritted her teeth. His arrogance was infuriating. Here he was threatening to leave her—no doubt because there was to be no money—and he was berating her for lying. His very actions confirmed the necessity of the lie. "No. I do not deny it."

He folded his arms over his chest. "Then it seems we both had our little secrets, doesn't it."

The ride to the duke's house on Park Lane was excruciating for Melisande, Flynn knew. It was the only reason she spoke to him. After the argument last night she had locked the bedroom door to him, so he'd slept in the sitting room next door. He wasn't sure he blamed her, though, and thought maybe it would be best she did stay angry. At least then she might be glad when he left.

She could not keep her eyes from the carriage window, claiming to feel the public's eyes upon them every step of the way. Unfortunately, the day was warm so a lot of carriages were out and on their way to Hyde Park, according to Melisande. And the closer they came to it, the more plentiful the onlookers became.

A couple of times Melisande tried not to look out the window, but she could only sit back a moment before glancing out again. At one point she claimed she actually saw someone stop and point at them. Then several carriages stopped and Melisande was sure she could see the occupants of an open phaeton tittering behind their fans.

"Oh, this is intolerable," she said, gazing out the window again.

Flynn looked out his window and could see nothing but a bunch of carriages heading down the street. Occasionally someone looked their way, but he didn't feel as though the world was waiting to see what they would do.

"No doubt these people are all thinking we're planning to ride through the park," she continued. "And they're just salivating at the opportunity to cut me the moment they get the chance. Oh, I've always hated London. All the gossip and the meddling. Well, all I can say is I hope every last one of them is watching when we pull up in front of the Duke of Merestun's townhouse."

They turned onto Park Lane and, Flynn had to admit, traffic literally stopped as they slowed to a halt in front of the duke's residence. Flynn got up, as she'd instructed him, and got out of the carriage when the footman opened the door. Then he turned and held out his hand to assist her.

She looked incredible, he thought, in a fancy white dress and a fur-trimmed cape. He even felt pretty spiffy, though the outfit that he wore—complete with gloves—made him feel all the more as if he were pretending. Indeed, he *was* pretending. He was going to put on the best show he'd ever put on, in the hope that his being found respectable might help Melisande in the future.

They ascended the stairs to the duke's house, and the door was opened before they could even knock. An auspicious beginning, Flynn thought, and turned on the stoop to wave at the crowd of onlookers before entering. He smiled as one, obviously without thinking, waved back.

"May I take your wrap, Madam?" an ancient, stoop-shouldered butler asked.

Melisande inclined her head and removed the cape. Flynn was captivated once again by the sight of her in the sheer white dress. It clung to her curves and pushed up her bosom so that the creamy skin drew the gaze as surely as any one of the world's natural wonders. The hat he could have done without. It was a huge feathered affair that made her look as if something wild had landed on her head, but she removed that as well when the butler had laid her cape over his arm.

Flynn was so engaged in looking at her that it wasn't until the butler cleared his throat that he remembered to take off his own hat and gloves and hand them to the man.

"His Grace will be right with you. If you

would like to sit down." He led them to a living room that was huge, with fifteen-foot ceilings at least, and an enormous hearth with a fire burning robustly. Along the walls were paintings, oils, Flynn thought, that even to his untrained eye appeared a cut above the typical. One was a portrait of a woman with nearly black hair, sitting in this very room, it looked like, with a child standing beside her, his hand on her arm.

The butler left. Melisande and Flynn stood silently in the center of the room.

"Pretty nice place," Flynn said, looking around at furnishings and ornaments that looked not only costly, but breakable. He was almost afraid to sit down in any of the finely carved chairs.

"Exquisite." Melisande approached the painting of the woman and studied it. "She is beautiful, is she not? I imagine that was his wife."

Flynn looked at the painting, happy they were at least having a civil conversation. "Yes. She is beautiful."

He came closer, a feathery kind of feeling in his stomach. The woman in the painting had high, arched eyebrows and a mouth that seemed about to curve into a smile. The boy, next to her, was somber, his hair the same color as hers but his eyes a brilliant blue.

"What happened to her?" he asked.

"Oh, she died. Years ago. As did the little boy." She cocked her head. "So sad, isn't it? It's said that the duke was desperately in love with her."

The door opened behind them, and they turned to see an old man in a wheeled chair being pushed into the room by an equally old man. After a second,

Flynn realized the man pushing the chair was the same one who'd been at their wedding and had sat next to Felicity at dinner. So, he thought, the plot thickened.

"Your grace," the man who'd been at their wedding said to the man in the chair, "may I present Mr. and Mrs. Flynn Patrick." He turned watery eyes to them and said, "Mr. and Mrs. Patrick, His Grace, the Duke of Merestun."

Melisande dropped into a deep curtsy and Flynn, catching sight of it from the corner of his eye, bowed respectfully.

When they'd risen, the gentleman in the chair held out a gnarled hand toward a dainty sofa and said, "Please, sit down," in a strong, cultured voice.

Melisande moved gracefully to the sofa and sat. Flynn sat beside her, having to stand back up immediately to move the tails of his coat before sitting again. He glanced at the duke and saw his brow raise slightly.

Flynn felt uncharacteristically self-conscious. The duke's eyes—an unnaturally pale blue with an unsettling intensity—never left him, even though Flynn sat next to what he had to believe was one of the most beautiful women in England, not to mention the one who had jilted his heir.

"It's an honor to meet you, sir," he said into the ensuing silence.

The duke's eyes narrowed. "Mr. Patrick," he said in that voice that commanded attention, "I would like to know where it is you are from."

He resisted the urge to sigh at the now-common question, and reminded himself he wanted to impress this man. "America, sir. The nation's capital."

"Washington," the duke said, watching him.

"That's right."

"How old are you?"

The question surprised him. "Thirty-three."

The old man nodded. "And when is your birthday?"

He decided that the truth, as far as he could stick to it without appearing crazy, was the best course. "I'm not sure. My parents told me it was September sixth, but they couldn't know for sure either."

The duke and the old man behind him exchanged a long look. "September the sixth, you say?" the old man asked.

Flynn shifted his attention to him, more comfortable talking with the servant. "That's right. I'm sorry, what was your name again? I know we met at the wedding."

The old man bowed and said, "Lourds, sir."

"Mr. Lourds. Nice to see you again."

"And you too, sir."

The old man's eyes were so watery they looked almost teary, Flynn thought. He wondered how he could see out of them.

"About September the sixth," the duke continued. "Why would your parents not know your date of birth?"

"I was adopted. The sixth was they day they found me, or so they said."

The odd eyes drilled him. "*Found* you?"

Flynn took a deep breath. He had a sudden pain in his chest, the same one he always got when talking on this subject and the same one that always made him wonder if he might be having a heart attack. If he was, he knew he'd be dying right here—nineteenth-century medicine consisting mostly of leeches and midwives, if he could trust what he recalled of history class.

"Yes, they found me. Somewhere near Merestun, in fact. They believe I must have been born near there. But nobody claimed me, so my parents took me back to America."

Melisande was staring at him. He could feel her eyes on the side of his face.

The duke frowned. "This is absurd," he said gruffly to Lourds. "The man has been instructed."

"Sir, *look* at him," Lourds said, close to the duke's ear. "But perhaps you cannot see it . . . ?"

"I see it," the old duke said irritably.

Melisande and Flynn exchanged a glance, and Melisande's eyes strayed to the paining behind him. Flynn began to suspect there was more happening here than he knew.

"Where did you get your name?" the duke asked, piercing Flynn again with those pale eyes.

"Patrick was my adopted father's name."

The duke shook his head. "No, no, I meant your given name. Why did your parents call you that?"

"Flynn?" He took a deep breath. He just absolutely hated revisiting this subject. "That was apparently what I called myself when I turned up at . . . when my parents found me."

Lourds made a strangled sound and all eyes turned to him. The man turned away, however, pulling a handkerchief from his pocket. After a second he turned back. "Excuse me. The spring weather has affected me."

"Allergies," Flynn commiserated, nodding. "I get them in the fall."

"Allergies?" Lourds repeated, puzzled.

"Pollen, from the trees, you know. It makes your eyes itch and your nose run." Too late, Flynn realized nineteenth-century doctors had not yet discovered what allergies were.

"What the devil are you talking about?" the duke snapped.

Flynn's eyes jerked back to the duke. An uncertain feeling, as if he were doing something wrong, swamped his stomach. "Never mind. It's just . . . something I heard once."

The duke looked at him, obviously displeased. "I despise mindless conversation. How old were you when your parents 'found' you?"

Flynn shrugged. "Five or six. No one was sure."

"Do you remember anything," Lourds asked, "from the days before you were adopted?"

Automatically, Flynn answered, "No."

"You answer very quickly," the duke said. "Have you never tried to remember?"

Flynn inhaled slowly. He hadn't anticipated that by sticking to the truth the questions would become so involved. It had been a long time since he'd thought about the years before becoming Neil Patrick's son. A long time since he'd made the effort to put those memories behind him. He didn't believe he even had them anymore, and he did not want to start looking for them now. He had to keep his wits about him.

"No, I never have. What's past is past. I don't

believe in dwelling on what can never be solved.''

Lourds and the duke exchanged some low words Flynn could not hear. He hoped they were finished with him, and wondered if Melisande's grilling would then begin. For surely they were more interested in her—the one who'd dumped the heir—than they were in him. Maybe this was just some sort of intimidation technique.

''We'd like you to attempt it now, Mr. Patrick, if you don't mind.'' The duke's expression conveyed anything but room for refusal.

Flynn shifted uncomfortably in his seat. ''I don't understand why,'' he said steadily. ''With all due respect, your grace, they are *my* memories. I don't see what makes them any business of yours.''

The duke studied him through those too astute eyes. Flynn decided the creepiness of them was that they were so sharp and clear in such an aged face.

''Humor an old man,'' the duke said then, settling back in the wheelchair and folding his hands over his stomach.

Flynn forced himself to hold the duke's gaze. Most of what he remembered involved his move to America and the feelings of unfamiliarity there. But he knew if he tried to explain his mystification over such things as the swing set, he'd only get embroiled in a lengthy discussion about playground equipment. A lesson that was likely to benefit none of them.

''I remember . . .'' He took a deep breath and raised his eyes to the ceiling. After a minute he looked back at the duke, then glanced at Lourds, and at Melisande, who still watched him as closely as the other two. ''You know that none of this will seem very interesting. After all, I was only five or six. What sticks in the head of a toddler can't be taken with any seriousness.''

The duke inclined his head. "We understand that."

Melisande nodded at him, then moved her hand to his arm and squeezed. "Go ahead, Flynn."

This act of support so surprised him after their argument the previous day that for a minute he just looked at her. What was going on here?

"I remember bushes," he said then, hopelessly. Despite their rapt expressions, he knew they were bound to be disappointed. "I remember crawling around through bushes mostly."

Lourds was nodding vigorously. Flynn was afraid the old man was becoming a bit addled to be so excited over this first paltry offering.

"All right," the duke said. "What else?"

Flynn crossed his arms over his chest and stared into the fire. "I remember a big, stone hearth. With . . . I don't know . . . something above it. You know, on the stone over the fireplace." His hands gestured as he spoke, painting the hearth in the air, but his eyes focused inward. "I don't remember what, but I remember being very interested in it. I remember sitting on that hearth and looking up. Seems like it was a picture—or no." He shook his head, pulling the image from his deepest memory. "A . . . a head. You know, a hunting trophy, a bear or something."

Lourds was smiling now.

Flynn thought of something else. "There was also . . . a floor, a marble floor, with sort of blue-gray swirls in it. Very cold. I remember tracing the pattern with my finger."

For a long time he was silent, traveling through corridors in his mind that were dark and hazy, but real. He was not making things up, even to fool himself, he realized. The more he thought, the more came back to him, but they were still fragments of the time, isolated pictures of what the whole must have been, like a tiny corner piece to a giant jigsaw puzzle.

"Do you remember any people?" Lourds asked quietly, as if guiding him through a meditation.

Flynn shook his head. "But I remember a . . . bird."

The duke sat forward in the chair, his elbows gripping the armrests, and Flynn refocused his eyes on him.

"What sort of bird?" Lourds asked.

Flynn glanced at Lourds. This was not the part he would have considered interesting, if any of it at all could be considered interesting. "A blackbird. Like a crow or something. It seemed very large, at the time. I remember it standing on the hearth. It must have gotten into the house somehow."

The memories faded now as he looked from Lourds to the duke. The duke watched him and Lourds watched the duke.

Flynn turned to look at Melisande and shrugged his eyebrows slightly. "That's all I've got. It's all true," he said to her questioning look. "It's not much, but it's true." He turned back to the duke. "Is that all you want to know?"

Lourds gripped the duke's shoulder. "You see?" he said urgently. "It is him. I had the feeling just from looking at him, but the bird, your grace. He *remembers the raven.*"

Chapter Fifteen

"Wait a minute." Flynn felt suddenly queasy. "What are you talking about? What do you mean?"

Lourds straightened and looked at him, but said nothing.

The duke sat back in his chair and studied Flynn. "How long have you been in England?"

"About a week."

"Is this your first return here?"

"Yes."

"Why do you come back now?"

This was a tough one. Flynn shifted his eyes to Melisande and found her staring at her hands in her lap.

"I didn't really have a choice," he said finally. "I . . . my father died recently, and my mother wanted me to come back. I'm not sure exactly why. But I did it to appease her."

"She knew," Lourds said softly to the duke. "Perhaps she had a fit of conscience."

"Did she instruct you to come to me?"

Flynn laughed. "To you?" He chuckled again. "No. No, she didn't."

The duke's brow descended and an ominous expression overtook his face. "Why do you laugh? My questions are not intended to be humorous."

"Well, yes, I know that. Sir. But the idea of her telling me to come to you strikes me as funny. I'm sorry if that offends you."

"Did anyone instruct you to come to me?"

One side of Flynn's mouth kicked up, and he glanced toward Melisande. "*She* did. Yesterday, after getting your note. She said we had to come. So here I am."

The duke's eyes grazed Melisande and returned to Flynn. "You would not otherwise have come?"

Flynn felt the desire to laugh again, but squelched it. He pressed his lips together and shook his head. "No."

Silence reigned for a moment in which the four of them sat still in the opulent room.

"Mr. Patrick," the duke said, exhaling slowly. "Many young men over the years have come to me, claiming to be my lost son. You are familiar with the story of how I lost my son?" He raised his brows at Flynn.

Flynn glanced again at Melisande, who was giving him a significant look he could not translate. Or maybe didn't want to translate.

"I," he said slowly, "understand he died when he was young."

"He was presumed dead, Mr. Patrick. He was playing a game with Lourds during which he ran out onto the terrace. That was the last anyone ever saw of him."

Flynn's heart pumped wildly in his chest and beads of sweat broke out on his forehead. "Was he kidnapped?" The words emerged a near-whisper.

"We didn't believe so, at first. Lourds had thought he'd heard a splash, indicating the boy might have fallen into the fountain, but no trace of him could be found." Lord Merestun looked down at one hand where it gripped the armrest of his wheelchair. "His name was Norflyn Bellamy Hamilton Archer, and we called him 'Flyn.' "

Flynn tried to take a deep breath, but it caught in his throat. He exhaled on a cough. "That's . . . quite a coincidence."

This was insane. Of all the insane things that had happened so far, *this* was truly insane, Flynn thought.

One of the duke's brow's rose. "Do you think so?"

"I—yes, of course."

He couldn't let them believe this, Flynn thought. It was too much. And yet the coincidences were incredible. The two men seemed almost convinced. Indeed, Lourds seemed already convinced Flynn was Merestun's long-lost heir. But that was crazy.

What these men didn't know, and what Flynn couldn't possibly tell them without being committed to an asylum for sure, was that he was from 1998 and there was no possible way he was this little Lord Norflyn, or whatever his name was, who had disappeared thirty years ago. He was Flynn Patrick, staff speechwriter for Senator Irving Strand. Columbia graduate.

High school all-state running back. General all-around, all-American kid.

"Flynn, listen to them," Melisande said quietly, looking at him with such an expression of awe that he was almost tempted to go along with the story. But looking back at Lord Merestun and Lourds, two old men whose lives were almost over, whose hopes had run away with them, whose last chance to find their rightful heir seemed to be at hand . . . he just didn't think he could take advantage of them like that.

"My son disappeared," the duke continued in a steady voice, "on September the sixth, Mr. Patrick."

Flynn felt the breath leave him as if he'd been punched. He stood up abruptly and turned away from them. But he found himself facing the portrait of mother and son, staring into the brilliant blue eyes of the boy.

As if from another lifetime, Nina's words floated distantly in his head. *Gypsies have dark eyes. His are too blue, too pale.*

Plenty of people had blue eyes, Flynn told himself firmly. Sure, the duke did. But so did Flynn's mother. Even his father, Neil Patrick, had blue-gray eyes, whose cold depths he used to intimidate people on a regular basis.

And plenty of things happened on September sixth. People were born, people died, people moved, people got married. This was not such an irrefutable coincidence.

"Would it be such a bad thing, Mr. Patrick," Lourds's voice interjected gently, "to be discovered as the missing heir to Merestun?"

Would it? Flynn wondered. Aside from feeling like

301

even more of an impostor than he already did, the benefits could be overwhelming—and not just temporarily for himself. If he were acknowledged as the heir, and therefore the future duke, Melisande's future would be assured. In fact, he thought suddenly—could this be how her portrait happened to be in the halls of Merestun?

Flynn turned slowly. "Of course it wouldn't be a bad thing," he said carefully. "I just find it hard to believe, to say the least. And I don't," he added truthfully, "want to be the cause of any more pain on the subject than you both have already endured. If it turns out I'm not this Norflyn Bellamy whoever, how hard will that be for you to swallow? And how will you ever know for sure?"

"Very noble of you," the duke said, eyeing him shrewdly. Flynn wasn't sure if he was sarcastic or not. "You are right that we must be sure. However, whatever 'pain,' as you characterize it, we may have is irrelevant. The prime concern, the *necessity* of leaving the title and the estate to a man of noble blood, a man of *Archer* bloodlines, is our purpose in pursuing this possibility. I have not the womanly need of succor or affliction of sentimentality you seem to think."

Instinctively, Flynn looked to Melisande, expecting the bristling at this characterization that he knew Nina would have felt and reacted with. But she sat placidly, attentive to the conversation—intensely—but unoffended by the duke's comment. What surprised Flynn most, then, was that *he* was offended for her. And for himself. Ironic, considering how he used to blow that sort of feeling off as paranoid nineties political correctness.

He turned back to the duke and said in a controlled voice, "I hope it is not solely the woman's domain to love a son."

Lourds took a step forward. "Nobody ever loved a son better than His Grace," he burst out, looking at Flynn with a mixture of anger and misery.

The duke held up a hand to silence him.

"I'm glad to hear it," Flynn said, "I don't know who would want to be claimed by a man who didn't."

"You speak your mind with a great deal of self-assurance," the duke pronounced.

"I'm nothing if not self-assured," Flynn said.

The duke turned to Melisande. "Is this the quality you found attractive, Mrs. Patrick, when you married him?"

Melisande looked startled at the sudden attention. "I—I . . ." she fumbled.

The duke smiled coldly. "Of course not. You find nothing about him attractive, do you? How could you, when the inglorious criminal stole you from your betrothed?"

Melisande started to respond, glancing desperately at Flynn. He shook his head almost imperceptibly. She closed her mouth and looked uncertainly back at the duke.

"The details of our elopement," Flynn said, "are not significant to the matter at hand."

"Aren't they?" The duke raised an eyebrow again. "Everyone knows them, in any case. I hardly think it behavior suiting a ducal heir to abduct a young woman."

Flynn smiled. "I wasn't aware I could be a ducal heir at the time."

The duke's eyes darkened. "You make light of a very serious situation."

"Frankly, I don't know what else to do with it."

"Perhaps you would enlighten us on your reasoning in the matter. What would prompt a man to steal a woman from a celebration of her betrothal?"

"The circumstances were . . . unusual."

"Unusual? Is that so? I'm afraid I have to disagree. I do not find greed an unusual circumstance, unfortunately. For I have to believe it was greed—why else would a penniless man abduct an heiress and then marry her?"

Flynn found himself reacting in anger again to the man's dictatorial presumptuousness. It shouldn't matter, he told himself. He was here to save Melisande. He had to keep that in mind.

"For reasons you would never understand," Flynn said. "And no, I don't care to enlighten you. Now, you called me here for a reason, apparently to determine if I might be your long-lost son. Have you determined it? And if not, what do you intend to do with us?"

"He is very direct, is he not?" the duke said to Lourds, keeping a speculative eye on Flynn. The look made Flynn feel like a specimen at a zoo, and he suspected the duke realized it.

"Yes, your grace," Lourds said. "Much as you were at the same age."

The duke turned an amused eye to his man, then turned it back on Flynn. "You can, I imagine, see where Lourds stands on this issue."

Flynn didn't answer, but he moved his eyes from one to the other of them.

"And perhaps Lourds would know best," the duke reflected. "He spent a great deal of time with the boy before his disappearance. We had a nanny, of course, but the two seemed to prefer each other."

"How did you think to invite me here?" Flynn asked. "I mean, I know Lourds was at our wedding, and I see now it was something of a reconnaissance mission for him, but what made you send him to the wedding?"

"You don't know?" the duke asked.

Flynn took a deep breath and expelled it, restraining the many caustic comments he could have made. "Obviously not."

"Do you not also wonder then why I persist in accusing you of stealing Miss St. Claire from her rightful groom, when I am one of the few who knows your wedding did not take place in Gretna Green, as is widely reported, but here, *days* after Miss St. Claire disappeared?" He turned cool eyes to Melisande.

"Please leave her out of this," Flynn said firmly. She looked terrified every time the duke's attention turned to her.

"Why? Is she so innocent?"

"She is," Flynn said.

"No, she is not." All heads turned to Melisande in surprise. She stood up with the words, her hands fisted in her skirt on either side, her eyes fervent. "Your Grace, I beg leave to explain to you what really happened—"

"He *knows* what happened, Melisande," Flynn said. Dammit, she didn't need to protect *him. He* was protecting *her.* She didn't realize, didn't believe, how truly untouchable he was in this situation.

"No. He believes you to be the villain," she said strenuously. "When in fact he is the hero," she told the duke. "I left the ball voluntarily, your grace. I do not think I can apologize enough for the offense to yourself, which I certainly did not intend. But I could not marry your nephew. I went about it terribly. In an immature and self-centered way that I should be punished for and will regret for the rest of my days. But you must know that Mr. Patrick married me to help save my reputation—or what was left of it. He has selflessly done all he could to help me."

Silence greeted this confession. Flynn wracked his brain for a way to contradict her that would not sound like a lie.

"She is saying this, your grace, in a generous effort to save me from your wrath," he said finally. But he knew, and could see the duke knew, that her confession had the ring of truth.

"Why would she want to protect her abductor, I wonder," the duke speculated.

Flynn didn't have an answer for that. She wouldn't. If he had actually kidnapped her, he knew for a fact she wouldn't have married him in a million years, let alone stood up for him like that. And one probably didn't need to know her character very well to guess that, Flynn thought. She had shot herself in the foot without knowing it. He could easily have taken the blame, without much consequence, but she didn't know that. And now, the only way left to save her was to become the duke's long-lost son after all. If he could.

But something told him he could. And something told him it wouldn't be very difficult.

"Mrs. Patrick's aunt wrote to me with a suspicion about you." The duke waved a hand at Lourds. "So I sent Lourds to discover if there was any merit in what she said."

"Aunt—" Melisande began.

"Felicity?" Flynn said at the same time, surprise rocking him to his core.

"Mrs. Kesterbrook," the duke confirmed.

"What in the world did she say? What could have made her think of this wild scenario?"

The duke didn't answer. After a minute he said, "I would like for you to come to Merestun. As soon as possible."

Merestun, Flynn thought. *The fountain.* He needed to get back to the fountain, for it could only be from there that he'd be able to get home.

"I can do that. What good do you think it would do?" he asked. If he got too acquiescent now, it would be suspicious.

"Consider it a test of sorts," the duke said. "If you are able to remember something significant, something definitive, your position in life could change dramatically."

"What could possibly be proof enough?" Flynn asked.

"That, Mr. Patrick, remains to be seen."

Melisande unlocked her door that night. Flynn turned the knob with a mixture of desire and dread. He knew she'd started to believe what the duke and Lourds had proposed, and he could see no reason to lead her on about it, other than the selfish one of taking advantage. No, he had to tell her his motives in going along with the theory, because the next day they were all packing up to go to Merestun.

The duke had insisted. Flynn was to return to the supposed place of his birth and see what he remembered. But while it didn't seem likely that he would be able to remember—or rather fabricate—something conclusive enough to be proclaimed the missing heir, he knew he had to try, for Melisande's sake. Then, while he was there, he needed to get back into that fountain and try to get home.

The idea of it, however, sent a shiver of fear through him. He still remembered, all too vividly, the sensation of drowning he'd felt when he'd first arrived here. Not to mention the blind outright terror of knowing, really *knowing,* he was going to die. He wondered how close to death he'd actually come. And whether, in attempting to return, he would take the same risk.

Melisande was reading in bed when he entered. Maybe it was the fact that he knew he wouldn't be here long, but he believed he'd never seen a prettier scene.

The lamplight brought out red highlights in her dark hair, and her skin glowed like pale, sun-warmed sand in contrast. She wore the white cotton nightgown with the lacy sleeves thrown back at her delicate wrists as she held the book. Around her were a profusion of fat white pillows and the heavy comforter.

She looked up at him and smiled, her eyes gleaming in the low light, her cheeks turning a pale pink.

"Hi," he said, crossing the room slowly while he worked at the cuffs of his shirt.

"Good evening." She followed him with her eyes.

"I'm sorry about last night. I was overwrought. And . . ." Her eyes lowered, the lashes thick and dark above her cheekbones. "I'm sorry I didn't tell you that I'd been disinherited. There is no excuse, really, but I have to tell you I didn't want to trick you. I simply . . . I simply worried. . . ." She closed the book on one finger and folded it and her arms across her chest. "I want to be completely honest with you."

"Melisande, it's okay," he said, sitting in the chair where he could see her.

"No. I must tell you. I wasn't sure I needed to, but I *did* deceive you. I knew that I should tell you, that if I made the effort I could find a way to speak with you alone and tell you about my inheritance, but then there was Juliette." She held up one hand as he started to interrupt. "Please let me finish. If you had decided not to marry me, she would certainly be ruined. But I do not implicate Juliette, for it was not really *her* account on which my actions were founded. I had to do this, I had to save her, so that I could live with *myself*. So you see, it really was not for her at all."

Flynn thought the picture could not have gotten any prettier, but as she'd made her recitation, confessed her secret, she had grown even more beautiful to him. If he wasn't careful, he thought, he'd end up falling completely in love with her.

"Do you think," she began, studying her fingers. Then he could tell she forced herself to look him in the eye, her chin a little bit too strained. "Do you think you can forgive me for that lie?"

He got up from the chair and moved to the bed.

Settling one hip on the mattress, he took her hand in his.

"I have a confession," he said, a ghost of a smile on his lips.

Her brow furrowed.

"I knew about the money. Or the lack of it. *Before* the wedding. Felicity told me."

The change in her face was amazing, he thought, renewing his fear that he was perilously close to falling for her. Her eyes widened, her lips parted, and her expression radiated such surprise and emotion he could not help but smile.

"You *knew*?" she whispered. "You knew and you married me anyway?"

He nodded, feeling a little ashamed of wanting to revel in the impression the gesture made.

Her fingers tightened on his hand. "Then you did it just for me. Just to help me, didn't you." Her eyes were bright upon him, and his conscience felt scalded by the look of gratitude in them. "You are," she said slowly, with great conviction, "a good man. I suspected it all along, but you have confirmed my finest suspicions of your character."

Flynn's skin heated, and he realized he was blushing. She leaned forward then, kneeling on the bed, and kissed him softly on the cheek. Then she raised one hand to the spot and looked him in the eyes.

"Thank you," she whispered. Then she touched her lips to his.

Desire blasted through him and he raised his free hand to the back of her head, pulling her lightly against him and into another kiss. Then he kissed her once again with more urgency.

Her lips parted beneath his and she leaned into him. His fingers spread in her hair as his tongue found hers. The heat they generated was immediate. Flynn felt a waterfall of desire plunge through his system. He wanted this woman badly. He wanted her and he could have her. She was his wife.

But she was kissing him because she believed he'd made a great sacrifice for her, believed he had a character he did not really have.

Regretfully, he knew his brief tenure as a "good man" was at an end.

He pulled away, his eyes lowering, and moved his hand from her hair to place it over their clasped ones. He knew her eyes were upon him, bewildered. He could feel the touch of her rapid breathing on his cheek.

"I'm sorry," he said, swallowing, "but I can't have you sleeping with me because you think I'm someone I'm not. I'm no hero, Melisande. I did a nice thing, maybe, but at very little cost to myself."

"But you might have married well," she said quietly, her hand squeezing his. "You married me, knowing I had no money, when you could have married another. You have great charm, when you want to." She gave him a sly smile with the jibe. "You might well have married another woman who had some small dowry, had you gotten the proper clothing and tutelage."

He suppressed a smile at that, then sobered. "No, you don't understand. One reason it was so easy for me to marry you, even knowing you would have no money, was because I know—and I know you don't believe me—but I know I must return to my own

311

time. I also believe," he continued in the face of her darkening expression, "that I may be able to do it from Merestun. From the fountain. Which is how I got here to begin with."

Regretfully, he saw the muscles around her mouth tighten.

"Mr. Patrick—" She stopped. "Flynn. You seem to be an intelligent man, so you must understand that what you say about coming from the future is impossible. What purpose would it serve, for one thing? It is against every religious principle. God gives us birth, life, and death. You must believe that. You cannot live before you are born."

"A week ago, I would have agreed with you completely."

"All right," she said purposefully, setting aside her book. "If you are from the future, you must know something that's going to happen. Predict something amazing and I might then be compelled to believe you." She looked at him with the same sort of tolerant expression she might use for a child.

"The only things I can accurately predict," he said, "are things you will never live to see. Like . . . like, cars. Everyone will have these vehicles, made of steel and rubber and plastic, that will run without horses, and go ten times as fast. Faster than trains, even, which maybe you don't have yet either." His hands sketched out his words as his eyes visualized the twentieth century. "And there'll be airplanes, in the sky. Men—and *women*—flying across the ocean in a matter of hours. And televisions—boxes with TV shows, ah, plays, little theaters right in their homes. And computers . . ." God, he didn't even know where begin describing a computer. But when his eyes descended to hers again, he saw she looked simply amused.

"Melisande," he said firmly. "I'm not telling you this for your entertainment. These things will happen. A man will land a rocket on the *moon* in 1969, for chrissake."

At that she laughed outright. "Mr. Patrick! You really ought to sell your stories. I begin to believe we won't be penniless after all."

Flynn looked at her in frustration. "I only wish you would live long enough to see it. I wish I had a picture . . . which is *another* technology coming our way. Photographs. Actually, you may live to see that, come to think of it."

"Flynn, please. This is a serious problem. You mustn't persist in this—"

"Okay, wait. Is Napoleon still alive?"

"Of course. He is in exile on Elba."

"Good!" he exclaimed. "Because I can tell you what will happen to him."

Her expression became skeptical in an instant. She raised her brows.

"He's going to escape from Elba."

She laughed. "I've heard that a dozen times if I've heard it once."

"Okay, how about this then. Once he does, there'll be another war and they'll call it The Hundred Days War."

She looked at him dubiously. "A hundred-day war? Are we to be so weak then, or is he?"

"He is. He'll be defeated, at place called Waterloo, and then he'll be imprisoned on St. Helena. I'm not sure . . . what year is this? 1815?" He thought a minute. "I don't know, but it must be this year, if he's already been exiled. It wasn't long after that, I don't think. Then again, it's been a while since I sat through a history class."

She studied him a long moment. "I don't think you should tell anyone else this. It could be misconstrued as treason. They may think you plot to free him."

He laughed. "Yeah, I'm going to free Napoleon."

"Please do not be light."

"Fine, I'm only telling you. And only because I want you to believe my story. In fact, here." He picked up a piece of paper from the bedside table and handed it to her. "Write it down. So when it happens you have proof of what I told you. It may be next year, though, I'm not sure." He looked around for some kind of writing utensil.

She leaned back, set the paper aside, and crossed her arms over her chest. "I shall write it down tomorrow. There is plenty of time. That prediction could unfortunately take a great while to confirm. In the meantime, how can I believe such an outlandish tale?"

He shrugged, thinking he knew now how God must feel, always being asked for a miracle. "I don't know. You may just have to trust me. Sorry."

"Haven't you anything else? Surely this era is not so unremarkable in the future annals of history?"

"Actually, I think it is. Unremarkable, that is. But what do I know? I barely made it through high school history." He let his eyes rest on her, propped prettily among the pillows and looking at him assessingly. He wondered why he even bothered trying to convince her. It wasn't as if her believing him had anything to do with whether or not he could go back.

Maybe, he thought, he wanted her to believe him so she would know he wasn't simply abandoning her. Especially now that she had no money.

"That's a pity, isn't it," she said, "for if you could tell me something remarkable I would have no other choice but to believe you."

"Melisande, listen to me. I guess it doesn't matter whether you believe me or not. Once I'm gone, the reason won't make much difference. That's why this trip to Merestun is important."

"So that you can get back to your fountain and leave me?" she asked archly.

"No. So that I can convince the duke I'm his son and leave you with some security."

Her eyes widened. "So you admit you are his son?" she nearly whispered.

He shook his head. "It's impossible. I wish I were, but it can't be true. I told you, I'm from the twentieth century."

She started to roll her eyes, and Flynn's frustration got the better of him.

"*Listen* to me, dammit," he said, taking her by the shoulders.

She stiffened.

"Do I seem crazy in any other way?" he asked desperately. "You saw my clothes when I arrived, they were soaking wet. And they were odd, you said so yourself. Your *aunt* even said so, remember? And this." He punched his arm out so that his sleeve drew back and the watch was visible. "You said yourself you'd never seen one of these before. 'Ingenious,' you called it. Melisande, *I am not crazy.* Somehow I was thrown back in time. And it's important you remember that because I *don't want* to leave you." As the words came out of his mouth, he realized how true they were. He took a slow breath and put a hand to her cheek. "I really don't. But I'm afraid I'm going to have to."

She was silent a long time, her expression somber. Finally, she said, "I must admit, in all other respects you seem normal. I . . . I remember Aunt Felicity's fascination with your clothing. The fine, even stitching and the good-quality material. Your shoes . . . the way they fit each foot individually. Your belongings do speak of a vastly different culture, with advanced methods of making clothing."

He sighed heavily and looked down at the bed. "It's not just a different culture."

She would never believe him. And he didn't blame her. Maybe it was best that she didn't or she might be tempted to regard him as some sort of prophet. With his sketchy knowledge of history that could be dangerous.

"Flynn." She touched his arm and he took her hand in his. "What will happen," she asked slowly, "if you return to Merestun and the fountain does not take you back to the future? Will you stay then?"

He raised his head and looked at her. It was something he hadn't wanted to consider, not being able to get back. But sitting here looking at her, he thought he could stay. In fact, he wondered if he thought about it long enough whether he could talk himself into not even trying.

"If the fountain doesn't work, Melisande," he said, holding her gaze steadily with his own, "then you're stuck with me."

Chapter Sixteen

The following day the front table was littered with cards. Melisande looked at them in awe. She had never received so many in her life. To all appearances, she and Flynn had become some of the most sought-after guests in the city.

Almost as soon as they'd left the duke's house, rumors had begun flying about what the meeting had been for, Mr. Kesterbrook told them. Some people speculated, as Melisande originally had, that the purpose of the meeting was a face-to-face reprimand. But many others thought it was a public acceptance, and therefore were hastening to make their amends to the couple.

There was no time to make the rounds and rub their noses in it, however, much as Melisande would have liked to, because they were to leave for Merestun on the morrow. Both her parents and the Kesterbrooks were also invited on this mission that was to determine whether Flynn Patrick was really Norflyn Bellamy Hamilton Archer.

"I have to admit," she told her aunt in the parlor that morning, as the servants packed their trunks and readied the carriages, "the possibility that Flynn could be the heir is stunning. Just think of the irony. I left the supposed heir, only to end up marrying the actual heir by accident."

"The moment I saw him I was reminded of the duke in his younger days." Felicity sat with her sewing, obviously enjoying the happy turn of events. "Then the more I spoke with him, the more convinced I became. I am sure they will discover he is the missing boy. The resemblance is simply too uncanny."

Melisande's needlework lay next to her on the sofa. She couldn't concentrate on anything else with the possibility of Flynn being the duke's missing son in the air. She would be nearly delirious with anticipation if it weren't for the fact that Flynn still spoke of leaving her. Every other possibility was brought down by that.

Of course, it was crazy, what he'd said about returning to the future. But then, there was something very *sane* about him. She could not believe he was somehow so unbalanced as to have made up such a thing.

"There is something in the set of the features," her aunt was saying, "and of course the eyes, that directly mirrors the duke. For the duke was quite a handsome man in his day."

"Yes," Melisande said slowly. "While we were in

Lord Merestun's parlor, looking at that painting of the little boy, I had such an eerie feeling. The eyes were the exact same shape and color as Flynn's. And the hair was the same color too. But even more striking than his similarity to the boy, was his similarity to the *duke*. It was spellbinding. The more I looked from one to the other of them, the more alike they seemed. Even some of their mannerisms were the same. The timbre of their voices, the shape of their faces, their *hands*."

"It's quite extraordinary," Felicity agreed. "And when I heard he was a foundling from Merestun! Well, I knew then I had to speak with Lourds."

"Indeed. Lourds looked quite emotional on a number of occasions yesterday."

Felicity nodded. "He would. He and the boy were extremely close, he told me. And not only that, he's been convinced all these years that the child's disappearance was his fault. He'd been playing a game with the boy. One of those 'hide-the-toy' games, and he'd hidden a little horse, I believe it was, behind a loose brick in the wall of a fountain on the terrace. Then next thing he knew, he heard a splash and the boy was gone."

Melisande nodded, having heard the story yesterday, but after a second the words penetrated her mind in a way they hadn't before. She brought her eyes up and stared at her aunt. "The boy disappeared *in the fountain*."

"Yes, that's what they thought at first. But Lourds came out moments later and couldn't find the child anywhere. He searched the fountain, then had the staff search the grounds. Lourds said there simply hadn't been time for the boy to have gotten far. They did a comprehensive search of the house. But still, he was gone. Vanished without a trace. They even drained the fountain, but of course that was hours later. And he was not there anyway. He must have been stolen, though you would think the kidnappers would have tried to ransom him at the very least.''

Melisande's heart thrummed in her chest. She knew it was wrong to even entertain the thought, but if Flynn was right about coming from the future through the fountain, could he not have gone to the future as a child the same way?

"What's wrong, dearest?'' Aunt Felicity said.

Melisande's eyes focused on her aunt's face. "Oh, nothing. I'm sorry, did you say something else?''

"I was saying, it will be interesting to discover what your husband remembers about Merestun. Has he confided anything to you about his feelings on the subject?''

"He said he doubted it was true,'' Melisande said.

Said it was impossible since he was from the future, she added to herself. But he didn't know everything, she thought. If one crazy thing could happen, why not two?

"Your father is being obsequious as hell,'' Flynn said under his breath to Melisande as he handed two bags to a footman. The footman threw them to another man on top of the coach who strapped them onto a pile of trunks. "Ordinarily I'd like that, but it's driving me crazy today. He did say one good thing, though. Because we're newlyweds he said we should have his coach to ourselves. He and your mother will go with the Kesterbrooks.''

''He believes you are to be a duke someday.'' Melisande stood by the door of the carriage, her hands tucked into an enormous muff.

Flynn grimaced and looked around at the bustle of footmen scurrying to and from the two carriages with boxes and trunks and bags and packages. So much activity and nothing for him to do but wait.

He moved his hands toward his pockets. After a minute, he cursed, crossed his arms over his chest, and said, ''I'm going to have someone sew me some damn pockets.''

''If you were a duke they would do anything you said.'' She smiled dryly. ''No matter how coarsely you said it.''

He glanced at her. ''Sorry.'' He smiled, his eyes warming with the sight of her face. She just couldn't be any prettier, he decided for the hundredth time. Why couldn't he have run into an ugly girl? Leaving would be so much easier. ''And what about you? Will you be as compliant as your father if they decide I'm in fact the next Duke of Merestun? What's his name? Norflyn Archer? There's a Poindexterish name if I've ever heard one.''

She slanted her eyes at him. ''If you are the next Duke of Merestun I'll do whatever you say,'' she said with a sultry smile. ''As will everyone else. Now, however, you are Mr. Patrick, so help me into this carriage before every one of these footmen knows you for the ill-mannered clod you are.''

''Oh, sorry again,'' Flynn said, suddenly realizing that was why she'd been standing there so expectantly. He handed her into the carriage and got in behind her, closing the door.

Thank God St. Claire had decided they should be alone, he thought. Ever since the man had found out he might be a duke, Flynn had had to suffer through uncountable apologies that ranged from quick assurances of respect to interminable blathering excuses for treating him as badly as he had. Flynn hadn't wanted to start an argument, so he'd settled for merely mentioning that it was Melisande the man should be apologizing to and not himself, but Flynn doubted that would happen.

Hours later the landscape began to look familiar. Flynn guessed it was because they were traveling the route he and Melisande had walked, but still, he found himself kind of enthralled with it.

"Sure is refreshing to make this trip on wheels," Flynn said, thinking how gratifying it would be to travel the road in his Porsche, going ninety.

"Yes." Melisande looked out the window. "I wonder if the Clydes are at home today."

Flynn laughed. "Hey, did you remember to send the Porters some money? Or were the dancing lessons enough?"

"I sent them a generous sum, I believe. Or rather, Miss Smith sent it to them."

They looked at each other and smiled. Maybe it was because of all they'd been through together, but Flynn had a feeling of closeness, of camaraderie, the likes of which he'd never had before. Not with a woman anyway. Added to the other feelings he had for her—or *could* have, he amended—the package was becoming irresistible.

Flynn reached over and took her hand and a comfortable silence descended again, each of them looking pensively out their respective windows.

It wasn't long before Flynn realized the reason things looked familiar was because he had just made this trip, not on foot, but in a car—just days before and hundreds of years after this moment. The landscape was farmland, separated by some hedgerows and groves of trees, so it was not exactly unique. But though it was not raining now, he had a strange sense of déjà vu with the day he and Nina had arrived from London. The neatly parceled land, the cottages tucked into the trees, a man with a horse-drawn plow . . .

He leaned forward and craned his neck to follow the sight of the man with the plow. He had *thought* he'd seen just such a sight that day in the car with Nina, he remembered, but then it had only been a pile of deadwood in some other field. Or so he'd thought at the time.

Chills snaked up his spine.

He sat back in the seat and, letting go of Melisande's hand, clasped his two together. The palms were damp. Melisande was dozing. He took a deep breath. This was getting strange, he thought, with mild panic in the pit of his stomach. Not that it wasn't already, he thought wryly.

His eyes strayed to the window again. The land was not passing with the blur it had from the car, but it was passing nonetheless. And it was looking increasingly familiar, the way it hadn't on the trip in the car. The road was dirt now, the cottages real, with real smoke coming from their chimneys. Winding circuits of footpaths criss-crossed many of the passing fields, and slow-moving sheep dotted distant hillsides.

He swallowed and looked ahead, nearly pressing his face against the glass to see up the road. The route turned a ways in front of them, around a stand of old trees, and it was beyond that Flynn knew Merestun stood.

"We're almost there," he said, touching Melisande's shoulder. He wanted her awake and with him. He needed her to be watching this with him, to make sure it was all real, to make sure *he* was real.

They rounded the trees, and there, across the lawn, stood Merestun. And there, in front of the house, in the wide, circular drive, stood a big black carriage and four dancing horses. A man in peacock blue livery sat on the box, with a whip straight as a fishing rod beside him.

Flynn's head began to swim. It was just as before. Just exactly as he'd seen it the first time, only all the strange things he'd only *thought* he'd seen before were now real. Powerfully real.

Good God, he thought, his pulse racing, had he somehow *foreseen* all of this?

Footmen worked around the carriage—which did not disappear when Flynn glanced away as it had last week—and Flynn realized that the duke must just have arrived.

The pond Nina had commented on, which Flynn had inexplicably said was new, was non-existent. No old willow tree beside it.

"Goodness!" Melisande yawned. "I can hardly believe how quickly this trip went."

"Next time we'll walk the last couple miles,"

Flynn said, amazed that his voice emerged as strong as it did.

Melisande laughed, and his muscles relaxed a fraction.

While Flynn watched, the man atop the carriage flicked the whip and the horses pulled forward. The carriage rolled past the front door, then took the right-hand curve in the drive around the house toward the back.

"Lord Merestun has just barely beaten us," Melisande said. "We gathered three families in the same time it took him to gather himself."

"He's a stubborn old goat," Flynn said, feeling very certain of the words. "He probably waited to be sure we were coming. In fact, he probably sent poor old Lourds to hover around Regent Street all morning, waiting."

Melisande looked at him, a smile on her lips. "You like Lourds, don't you."

"Why do you say that?"

She shrugged. "You're very nice to him."

"I've barely spoken to him."

"Then you don't like him?"

Flynn frowned at her. "Okay, I do. Is there something wrong with that, Miss Manners? Should I not notice him because he's a servant?"

"There's nothing wrong with it. And I believe Lourds is rather more than a servant at this point. He's been with the duke for over forty years. Since he left the military."

Flynn turned to her, but did not see her. He saw instead the flash of a small painting in his mind's eye.

A soldier in a red coat and white breeches, a sword swooping from his waist.

"He was in the army," Flynn said. "A knight in the service of the king."

"Yes. Though he is not a knight." Melisande straightened her cape around her and pulled up her gloves. "Apparently he used to tell little Norflyn soldier stories."

A hollow echo of marching feet sounded in Flynn's head, a remembered imagining. He blinked hard as the carriage they rode in pulled around the drive and came to a stop in front of the house.

A liveried footman in peacock blue opened the door and Flynn forced himself to his feet, trying not to think about the fact that that shade of blue had always been his favorite.

Lourds met them at the door. "The butler will show you to your rooms, my lord," he said with a bow.

"Don't call me that," Flynn said, wanting to physically straighten the man from his bow. How could he deceive these people, this man, the duke, even with the best of intentions? "We don't know anything yet."

"With all due respect, sir," Lourds said with a calm assurance, "*you* may not know anything yet. But I know all that I need to."

Flynn shook his head. "I would hate to be the one to disappoint you, Lourds."

"You never have, my lord."

Flynn blew out his breath. Beside him, Melisande smiled placidly, her hands in her muff.

The butler met them and took their coats, while

Lourds went to inform the duke of their arrival. They should meet for tea, he said before exiting, in two hours. The duke would be waiting in the salon.

Flynn looked around the great hall. It looked much as it had the night he'd first arrived—*after* the trip through the fountain—except for the table full of food. He wondered how Melisande felt, returning, as it were, to the scene of the crime.

"How are you doing?" he asked as they followed the butler up the stairs. "You okay?"

She smiled at him, but he had caught the intent expression on her face a moment before. "I'm fine. Thank you."

"No . . . anxiety over the last time you were here? What was it supposed to be, an engagement party?"

She shook her head, this time looking amused. "No, I'm not anxious. And yes, it was a ball in honor of my betrothal to the heir of Merestun." She laughed lightly. "And see how I have married the right man after all."

Flynn laughed uncomfortably. "Don't get too confident, Mel. The game has only just begun. Let's hope I don't do something stupid to blow it."

Melisande preceded him into their bedroom with a smug smile. "I don't believe you could."

Melisande decided to take a nap before tea, but Flynn was too wound up to sleep. He told her he was going to walk around some. He wanted to see what else had changed besides the great hall since he'd come for Cubby's wedding.

He exited the room and looked both ways down the hall. An Oriental runner lay the length of the corridor, with small semicircular tables holding various vases and knickknacks between doorways. He turned to the right, away from the stairway they'd ascended, and quietly passed the closed doors to all the other bedchambers.

When he reached the end of the hall, a portrait of a huge vase of flowers hung over a narrow table. He stared at the picture, remembering its place in the great hall at the modern-day Merestun. It was across the hall from the one of Melisande. He leaned forward and touched the tiny rip in the canvas near the signature with one finger. It was not nearly so well repaired as it had been in the twentieth century.

He brought his hand back and ran it through his hair. Had he remembered the tear then, in the twentieth century? Or had he simply noticed it? He remembered it now, however, and had a flash of vision—a steel blade poking through the picture and a terrible feeling that trouble was to be had over it.

He took a deep breath and wiped his hand over his forehead. It was damp with sweat.

"There was quite a row over that," a voice said from behind him.

Flynn turned to see the duke, stoop-shouldered but standing, leaning heavily on a cane.

"Young Flyn fenced with his cousin, and there was a mighty argument over whose blade actually made the damage." He came forward slowly. So slowly, in fact, that Flynn was tempted to offer help. But he knew instinctively the duke would be offended.

"I'm sure it was his cousin's," Flynn said with a slight smile.

The duke raised a brow, but Flynn could see the amusement in his eyes. "So he said. He and his cousin were frequently getting into such trouble together. Most of the time it ended up in a fight between the two of them.''

''I hope Flyn won.''

''Rarely.'' The duke shook his head and turned, obviously expecting Flynn to follow. ''His cousin was several years older than he was and, as such, quite a bit bigger. Flyn had trouble remembering that when he was angry. Have you much of a temper, Mr. Patrick?'' The duke managed to eye him skeptically as they inched down the hall.

''I used to,'' he admitted. ''It got me into too much trouble, so I gave it up.'' He thought of the fights with his father, one ending in blows, which he had lost. It had shocked him at the time that even in anger he couldn't bring himself to hurt Neil Patrick, despite all the awful things his father did, especially to his mother. He'd decided later that he was probably afraid of getting carried away and actually killing him.

They reached the top of the stairs, and Flynn could not stop himself from offering his arm. If he didn't, he was sure the old man would topple down the stairs and wind up nothing but a bunch of matchsticks on the floor below.

Surprisingly, the duke accepted the help, and the two made their way down the steps, the old man's grip strong on Flynn's forearm.

''I used to take these stairs three at a time,'' the duke said. ''Seems to me it was just last week.''

The old man chuckled and Flynn laughed with him, thinking morbidly that just last week for *him,* this duke had been dead probably 180 years.

At the bottom of the stairs, the duke crooked a gnarled finger at him and said, "This way."

They walked down a hall and paused at a set of double doors. But as the duke handled the knobs, Flynn looked farther down the hall, feeling a twinge of something curious at the back of his mind.

"Just a second, your grace," he said, touching the duke's narrow shoulder before moving toward the end of the hall. He knew the duke watched him, but he felt so drawn to the end of the corridor he did not want to not stop, the way one follows the feeling of having been somewhere before to see how long it will last.

The hall dead-ended at a door that led outside, but that was not what intrigued Flynn. He took a couple of steps back and looked at the wall, upon which there was a long piece of molding at the top and bottom with solid wood paneling in between. He stopped at one of the creases in the paneling and pushed his fingernails into the crack. Then he looked down and to his right, and touched his boot to a piece of the toe molding.

He glanced back at the duke, who had moved closer, his eyes unblinking and intense. "Go on," the duke said, nodding toward him.

Flynn looked back at the paneling, hardly knowing what he did, but following the memory of his hands as they flattened on the wall. He pressed his weight onto his foot and down the piece of molding went. The wall swung open in front of him, nearly knocking him backwards, to reveal a narrow dark staircase.

Flynn stared into the blackness in shock.

How had he known this door was here? Had Cubby

mentioned it? But that would not explain the familiarity his fingers had felt, Flynn thought, and the certainty with which he'd followed his feelings to this spot. A nervous shaking began in his stomach and radiated outward along his limbs.

He had known this door was here. And he had known about the rip in the picture. He turned and looked at the duke.

"Where does this lead?" he asked.

The duke looked at him steadily. "To the upstairs hall. Near the painting you were just examining."

Flynn closed his eyes. "To the right of it, as you look at the picture."

He opened them again. The duke was nodding, looking at him through—Flynn was not altogether sure in the dim light—watery eyes.

"Come with me," the duke said, his voice still gravelly. He turned and moved back to the set of double doors. They entered a huge, well-appointed room, on the opposite wall of which stood an enormous stone hearth. Over the fireplace hung a boar's head, prominently displayed with gleaming fangs and glass eyes. Just the thing to intrigue a small boy . . .

It was a one-two punch Flynn couldn't withstand. He nearly staggered into the room and sat down hard in a chair just inside the door.

The duke stood looking at the boar. "Is this what you remembered?"

Flynn dropped his head in his hands and nodded, his eyes tightly closed. "Jesus Christ," he whispered to himself, then repeated it several times over.

His stomach knotted and a lump grew in his throat. His limbs trembled and he felt nauseated.

"There is one last thing," the duke said.

But Flynn didn't feel that he could move. He didn't even want to open his eyes. He felt as if his whole world were becoming something interminably strange. Even the past, the time in the twentieth century that had seemed so normal, was off now, a lie, a figment of his imagination.

"Please."

The duke's low-spoken word was enough to raise Flynn's head. He did not look at the man, though, but gazed across the room at a heavy wooden table for two, upon which sat a chess set.

He glanced at the duke, who nodded. For some reason Flynn did not want to get up, did not want to go look at the table to see what he might find. But the longer he sat there, staring at the distant rows of pawns and rooks and kings and queens, the more certain he became.

Finally, without rising, he looked up at the duke and said, "The knight is missing."

The old man didn't flinch, but stood straighter than Flynn had yet seen him, staring into his eyes.

"Is that right?" Flynn asked, his voice hard. "The black knight?"

The duke glanced over at the set, as if gauging whether or not Flynn could have seen it from where he sat. Then he turned back and nodded.

Flynn took a deep breath, remembering all too well the feel of the piece in his hand. Like a worry stone, he used to carry it everywhere.

"I had it as a child. My mother said I had it with me when they found me. A small horse, straight and true . . ." He paused. Was that the beginning of a rhyme? He shook his head. "Made of black marble."

"Lourds had hidden it for you." The duke's voice emerged quiet but strong. "It was a game you liked to play with him. Do you remember it?"

"The loose brick," Flynn said, trancelike. "At the base of the fountain."

Silence held them in its spell for a long time.

"And the bird?" Flynn asked. "The black bird? It was a pet, right?"

"Yes."

Flynn closed his eyes, and recalled how on the day he'd first returned to Merestun with Nina, he'd watched a black bird fly parallel to the car for a long, long way.

Finally, the duke said, "We have a lot to talk about. I think perhaps this is enough for today. We should save the rest for tomorrow."

Flynn looked up at him, his chest tight with emotion. What must the man be feeling, he thought in a strangely detached way, to have suddenly found his son? Was the duke as removed from paternal feeling as Neil Patrick?

But the duke's lips were pressed hard together, as if warding off emotion, and his eyes appeared small and bright.

"Tonight," he said, striking his cane once upon the floor, "tonight, we will celebrate."

Chapter Seventeen

Flynn awoke the following morning with the sure signs of a hangover. His head pounded, his mouth was dry, and his eyes felt pasted shut. But worse than any of that was a feeling of displacement so overpowering he could not make sense of it. Why feel so misplaced now, he wondered, when he'd been in this strange country, this strange time, for over a week.

He knew what it was. Since he'd come to this world from the fountain he'd had one goal, one direction to think about, and that was getting back home. None of what happened here was relevant or important because his real life was in the future. But now "home" was a concept he couldn't decipher and the life that was his "real" one was no longer obvious.

Even to Flynn it was apparent, in an unreal way, that he had been to this place before. In fact, if it

334

wasn't so personal, he would have no trouble con-
cluding from the evidence that he must be this missing boy, the duke's lost son. But when he tried to put
that together with his life in the twentieth century,
this turn of events was simply too dreamlike to be
taken seriously.

Last night he had eaten and drunk and toasted with
the rest of them, even feeling, once the champagne
had set in, that this was a miraculous set of circumstances. Life had looked rosy in the glow of the candles and the smiles of the people around him. He'd
even felt, or told himself he felt, a sense of belonging
that he'd never felt in the twentieth century, in that
life so fraught with neuroses about his father, constant
stress in his job, and lack of commitment in his personal life.

But then, part of his feeling of calm was because
he hadn't been looking any further down the line than
last night. Melisande's future was assured. The duke
was happy to have found his son. And last of all,
though he hadn't known he craved it, the mystery of
his own birth had been solved.

In fact, the whole time he'd been here he'd simply
been living one day at a time—something every book
on stress he'd ever read said to do, but which he'd
never been able to achieve. Until now.

Today, however, with last night's champagne bub-
bles pounding inside his head and a set of tough decisions to make, he wondered if he would have been
better off to have just been faking the connection to
the duke. The fact that it was real made his decisions
that much more important.

Could he go back? *Should* he? Did he have an obligation to stay in this time and be the next Duke of Merestun? The idea was almost laughable. He, Flynn Patrick, a duke. It was ludicrous. What did he know about being a duke? He was probably the least qualified person in the world to be in a position of power in this era.

Then he thought about his father—or rather, stepfather, Neil Patrick. How he would laugh to discover his son, the reckless, undependable, irresponsible Flynn, had become a duke. For a second Flynn indulged the thought of ordering Neil Patrick's head lopped off, but he guessed only kings could do that. And besides, it wasn't Neil's fault his son had been a rakehell, not really. Flynn had just been living in the wrong time.

The thought startled him and he sat up, sending the room spinning. He bent his head and clutched it with his hands.

That was what had been missing, he thought with uncharacteristic clarity. All those years of rebellion and the anger all those therapists his mother'd dragged him to had told him he'd been harboring were born of the simple fact that he'd been living in the wrong time. And the thing he'd been missing— or rather *not* missing—since he'd been here was that irritated anxiety. That constant underlying feeling of nothing ever being *enough* or *right* had been gone. He'd been living in the moment and he'd been happy.

Yes, he thought, he'd been *happy*. Walking from Merestun to London, dealing with absurdity and discomfort at every turn—he'd been *happy*. He thought about his vexation with traffic and noise and work and *people* at home, in the twentieth century; he'd been a continual ball of nerves. But here, *here* he'd dealt with constant inconvenience and he'd taken it one moment at a time.

And, he had to admit, he'd had *fun*.

He swung his legs over the side of the bed and shuffled to the wardrobe.

What if he didn't go back? he let himself think. What if he never tried the fountain—would that be so bad? Would he always wonder if he'd done the right thing? Would it hang there like some unanswered question? His own personal Sword of Damocles?

Probably, he admitted to himself. But he could stand that. Because when he thought of going back, of popping up and trying to sort out what had transpired in his absence and how he would explain what had happened to him, he got that same old anxious, aggravated feeling in the pit of his stomach.

Melisande was already up, so he knew he must have slept beyond everyone else again. He pulled his clothes out of the wardrobe, handling them with renewed interest, and tried to imagine showing up in 1998 wearing them. How could he possibly pick up the pieces of his twentieth-century life and forget all that he'd experienced here?

Forget, he thought with a kind of shocking accuracy, both his wife and his father.

He had to talk to Melisande. She was the only one who knew, though she didn't believe, his incredible story. She was the only one he could talk to about it.

He dressed quickly, went downstairs, and found Melisande and her aunt in the breakfast room. On a sideboard was a buffet line of food unrivaled by any restaurant he'd ever seen, with a selection of foods huge beyond reason. Meats—sausage, bacon, beef, ham—and cheeses and vegetables of all description. He wondered if they intended to feed the entire countryside.

He caught Melisande's eye and smiled at her. She smiled back. She had gone to bed far earlier than he had last night, and when he'd gotten there he'd known he was too drunk to awaken her to say any sort of emotional good-bye. But now, maybe he didn't need to say good-bye. Maybe he could stay and build a life with her, sleep with her and not worry about leaving a child here in the past, because he would be here to raise it. To raise it with the love and support and belief that he'd gone without.

As Felicity chattered on about something to Melisande, a stout, gray-haired cook entered with a covered tray. She wore a blue dress with a white apron, and she moved to him directly.

"Your breakfast, milord," she said with smile. Her eyes were watery, but crinkled with the smile as she lifted the lid of the tray.

Flynn was about to make a sarcastic comment about there being enough food for a month of breakfasts when he caught sight of the apricot tart on her tray.

His mouth salivated automatically, like one of Pavlov's dogs, and he raised his eyes to the old woman's face.

"I can't believe it. This . . . this was one of the only things I remembered," he said quietly, reaching out to touch it, but drawing his hand back before he did.

"When people asked me, I told them all I could remember was a woman in a blue dress with an apricot tart."

She smiled. "It was your favorite," she said, setting it at his place on the table. "You asked me every morning would I make one for you. Course I could only do it when we had the apricots. But I would do it. You just loved 'em so."

Flynn sat down and picked up a fork. The old lady watched him. The first bite was like an instant memory. The apricot flavor exploded in his mouth and he couldn't contain his smile. He turned his face up to her. "It's incredible."

She smiled sheepishly. "I'm so glad. I thought it'd be the best welcome home I could give you."

"It's perfect," Flynn said.

She smiled again. "You always was a kindly child. I'll make you another'n tomorrow. We got plenty a apricots right now." She curtsied and backed out the door.

Flynn watched her leave. The evidence was becoming overwhelming.

He turned to Melisande. She shifted her gaze to him, her smile turning to an expression of concern at the intensity of his gaze. He looked pointedly out the window and inclined his head that way.

She nodded and slowly put her fork down on her plate.

Felicity spoke on for several more paragraphs before Melisande was able to interject, "It's such a lovely day, Aunt Felicity. Would you mind if I left you to explore the gardens with my husband?" She folded her napkin next to her plate and got up.

Felicity smiled at the two of them. "Ah, so finally he is your husband. I believe that is the first I've heard you say it, Melisande."

As Flynn looked at her, Melisande colored. "I'm certain that's not true, Aunt Felicity. I know I've said it before."

Felicity looked at her skeptically and then waved them away with a napkin. "Very well, go on then. Though I know Lourds wished to be with Mr. Patrick—heavens, we can't verily call you that anymore, now can we? Lord Archer, perhaps, though I'm sure your father will bestow one of his lesser titles on you until such time as you are the duke. In any case, you might wait for Lourds before venturing too far."

They promised to stay close to the terrace and left.

"Did you need to speak with me about something specific?" Melisande asked.

Flynn noticed she turned away from the fountain when they reached the terrace. Did she believe him then? he wondered.

"I did, yes," he said, "but I don't really know where to begin."

They walked silently toward a wall of high hedges.

"Perhaps," she began tentatively, "you might tell me your feelings, now you have been confirmed as the duke's son. I know you did not believe it possible before. Do you think you are the heir now?"

Flynn took a deep breath. "I . . . yes, I think so. Though it's really hard to believe. On any kind of deep level, you know. But I don't suppose I could be any worse than Bellingham, could I?"

Melisande smiled as she looked at the ground.

They moved toward a break in the hedgerow.

"Melisande, I'm . . . I'm thinking of not going back. Of staying here and trying to take my place in this world—"

She instantly turned to him with such joy and excitement in her eyes, he nearly forgot what he was going to say. He took her hands.

"Hear me out," he said fervently. "You of all people, Melisande, must understand how difficult this is going to be for me. I'm a complete klutz in this world, you've said it yourself a hundred times. But if I stay, there is one very important thing I'm going to need from you."

"What?" she asked immediately. "What is it you would have from me? You need only ask."

Flynn examined her face. She was so completely for him, her hands tight on his, her eyes direct and energized.

"You have to believe me," he said quietly, expecting her eyes to shadow at any moment. "You have to believe what I've told you about the future, about where I came from. If I stayed here with you believing anything else, I don't think I could stand it."

"Yes, but Flynn," she said urgently, her eyes relentless upon his, "I've been thinking about that. Did you know the story of how the boy—how *you*—disappeared? You remember Lourds said he heard a *splash* when the boy went near the fountain. That means you must have fallen in. Could you not have gone to the future as a child, as surely as you came back here as an adult?"

Flynn's eyes searched her face. Did she believe him? Could she really? "Melisande, when I was here at Merestun in the future, I saw a portrait of you in the gallery. There wouldn't be one there now, would there?"

"A portrait? At Merestun? No." She shook her head. "I have had my portrait done but once, as a child, and that is in my home at Browerly."

"The picture I saw had you sitting in a . . . a red dress." He closed his eyes to remember. "Kind of low-cut but with little . . ." His hands moved to his shoulders. "Puffy, short sleeves." He looked at her. "And you had a little umbrella. A, uh, what do you call it—a parasol, you were leaning your hand on, and it had a lion's head on the handle."

Melisande had stopped walking and was staring at him, her mouth agape.

"What? What is it? Have you had this painting done? I thought . . ."

"No," she said, shaking her head. "I have not even seen that dress. But I ordered one exactly as you describe two weeks ago for my trousseau. And a parasol with the Merestun lion's head upon the handle."

Flynn inhaled deeply. "And the only way that portrait would be hanging in Merestun in the twentieth century was if you were at one time the Duchess of Merestun. Since we know you didn't marry Bellingham . . ."

"Flynn, you saw a portrait of me? You remember seeing *me*?"

He nodded, and laughed slightly. "My girlfriend was jealous because I was so drawn to it. I thought," he said quietly, "that you were the most beautiful thing I'd ever seen."

Their gazes held for a long moment before Melisande broke into a broad smile. She jumped on her toes and threw her arms around his neck. "Oh, Flynn," she said, her face buried in his chest.

His arms came around her, feeling her body pressed against his and suffering that same overwhelming desire he felt each time she touched him. How could he leave this? How could he leave *her*? he wondered, feeling a certainty he never thought he'd find with a woman.

Their lips met and she opened to him, more willingly than she ever had before. He cupped her head in his hands, kissing her lips, her face, then her neck.

"I love you, Melisande," he whispered close to her ear. The words had had to come out. They'd been building up inside of him for days, and the feeling he had upon saying them was like a release. He'd never spoken the words before, he thought. He'd never spoken them and meant them with every fiber of his being.

She drew back and looked at him gently. For one panicked second he feared she meant to let him down easy, tell him she didn't love him. But her lips curved into that sultry smile he'd first seen in the portrait and she said softly, "And I love you. Truly. I think I've loved you since that first moment on the terrace. Perhaps before," she added with a mysterious smile.

His kissed her again then, deeply. Her body answered his, pressing against him with the same urgency he felt himself. He raised his head to see where they were, thinking he might take her right here and damn anyone who happened to see them.

Melisande raised her head and looked around too. She pushed away from him and turned around. "Flynn, look where we are," she said with a laugh. "We're in the center of the maze. How funny that we found it by accident."

Flynn looked at the high enveloping hedgerows and the number of openings they had to choose from to get back. He felt an instant familiarity with the surroundings, and suddenly noticed the smell.

Boxwoods. *These* were the bushes he remembered crawling around in. This must have been why Lourds had looked so pleased at the memory. He used to beat the old man in races to the center by crawling under the high, thick bushes.

He began to laugh. Melisande laughed with him.

"How are we ever going to get out of here?" she asked, smiling.

He raised a brow at her and took her by the hand. "Never fear, my love," he said taking her toward another exit.

"But we came in over here," she protested.

He looked at her again, a smile playing at his lips. "Never fear."

Melisande thought she'd never been so happy as she was following her husband as he unerringly made his way out of the maze. The day before the ball at Merestun she had tried to wind her way through these bushes and had gotten hopelessly lost. A footman had had to come get her after hearing her own and Juliette's calls.

But now, here she was, the future Duchess of Merestun, and she was completely in love with her husband. He was, she decided, her prince after all.

She was still smiling as they exited the maze, and she was laughingly congratulating him on finding the way, when he stopped walking. Frozen where he stood, he had locked his eyes on something on the terrace. She turned and followed his gaze.

Bellingham.

He stood with one foot on the wall of the fountain, his cane dangling from his fingers, his dark eyes hard upon Flynn.

"So, the *impostor* succeeds," he said, his voice every bit as cold and soulless as Melisande remembered it. "I knew I should have killed you when I had the chance."

Flynn moved forward, his hand tight on Melisande's. She thought about stopping, drawing him back with her to the maze, for she had a bad feeling about Bellingham's presence. He was not going to suffer the loss of his inheritance lightly. Indeed, she feared what he might be capable of doing.

"I don't remember you ever having the chance," Flynn said.

"No?" Bellingham asked. "You do not recall my blade at your heart on this very terrace?"

"Sure, I remember that. But you wouldn't have killed me. In fact, I think you're a lot more bluster than you are brawn, Bellingham."

Bellingham's eyes narrowed, and Melisande felt her blood chill. She wanted to warn Flynn about taunting him, but she knew at this point it would do no good.

"Did you come here expressly to steal my position, Mr. Patrick?"

Flynn laughed and leaned his foot on the wall of the fountain as well. "No, that was just an added bonus. I actually came here to steal your fiancée."

"My *betrothed*"—he sneered the word—"you can have. I would not have her now if she came with all of Midas's gold. But I'm afraid my inheritance must remain mine. You see, we cannot have a man without Archer blood running through his veins occupying the seat of power. I'm afraid it's up to me to dispute the veracity of your claim to the title."

"Dispute away," Flynn said. "A couple of days ago I might have helped you out. But now I'm not so sure. And no matter what kind of duke I make, I'm sure to be a better one than you."

"Bold words for a peasant."

Flynn shrugged. "I don't know how you're going to convince the duke I'm not his son. He and Lourds are convinced I am."

Slowly, Bellingham drew the long, razor-sharp blade from his cane. "It will be simple," he said.

Melisande gripped Flynn's hand, but the expression on his face was not worried. In fact, he looked as if he'd just had some kind of revelation.

"Wait a minute," Flynn said wonderingly, "*you're* my cousin. You're the cousin I used the play with, the one I was always fighting with."

Bellingham smiled coldly and came toward Flynn, circling the blade in the air nonchalantly. "I was Norflyn Archer's cousin, but I am no more. He died twenty-seven years ago."

"You put the hole in the flower painting," Flynn

said. Then he laughed. "Seeing you now with that sword, I remember it perfectly. Even then you weren't a very good swordsman. Of course, you blamed it on me."

Bellingham stopped when the blade reached Flynn's chest. He flicked Flynn's cravat with the tip of it. Flynn let go of Melisande's hand and folded his arms across his chest.

"So what are you going to do now, run me through right here?" Flynn asked. Melisande couldn't believe how calm he sounded. "I hardly think they'll hand you the title if you do that."

Bellingham shook his head. "No, I intend to prove once and for all that you are not who you claim to be. Years ago, when young Flyn was alive, he suffered a burn. Right . . ." He circled the tip of the blade at Flynn's shoulder, then poked him with the point. "Here. It was a sealing-wax burn that took weeks to heal, as it became quite infected from the dye, they said. He was left with a distinctive scar that I must believe would still be in evidence, especially considering the blue dye that had penetrated the wound."

Melisande watched Flynn's chest near the blade's tip rise and fall with his steady breathing. She could tell nothing from his face. Whether or not he still had this scar, she could not divine. He appeared neither nervous nor assured.

"It was you who burned me," Flynn said. "Wasn't it? You were always doing things to hurt me. Perhaps you wanted me dead even then."

"Flyn Archer died without my aid," Bellingham

said. "If I was happy at the circumstance, who could blame me?"

"*I* could," Melisande burst out. "You are a cold, heartless man with no soul. I could see it the moment I laid eyes on you. I would not have married you if you were to be king."

Bellingham's black eyes turned on her. "Don't think I don't know that you were behind all of this, Mrs. Patrick," he spat. "You were determined to marry a title and you would do whatever you could to get one, would you not?"

"Why would I not have married you then?" she countered, adrenaline giving her courage she was sure she would have lacked otherwise.

"Because you could not control me," he said silkily. "Not like you can *this* puppet. But let me show you how I shall prove him to be an impostor. And then you and your *husband* can go live in the infamy you deserve."

With that he slashed apart the sleeve of Flynn's jacket. Another flick of his wrist and the shirt fell away too, revealing a long bloody graze where he had, perhaps, misjudged the distance.

Melisande gasped and covered her mouth with her hands.

"You see my fencing skills must have improved, or you might well have lost your arm just now," Bellingham said.

Flynn barely flinched as Bellingham slashed his clothing, and stood perfectly still as the man deftly pulled away the bloodying fabric with the tip of his blade.

Melisande leaned toward him, drawn against her

will to look for the scar. Bellingham could easily have been lying about the burn, she told herself. It would mean nothing if the scar was not there.

But as she took a step closer she saw the unmistakable stain of blue in a deep silver scar just above the fresh cut on his shoulder. It was perfectly round, the exact shape and size of a sealing-wax press.

She turned triumphantly to Bellingham, a laugh upon her lips. "Impostor indeed!" she cried. "It seems it's been *you* who has been imposing all of these years."

Bellingham's brows descended and his black eyes flashed with fury. "You put that there intentionally," he snapped.

"How on earth would I have known that story?" Flynn asked calmly, pulling up the sleeve of his shirt to dab at the shallow wound Bellingham had just inflicted. "It seems to me you and I were alone at the time. And you claimed I had done it to myself."

Bellingham's eyes widened.

"But *you* had done it," Flynn continued, "saying that all future dukes must carry such a brand."

The look on Bellingham's face froze Melisande's heart. Then, with an inhuman, animal moan, he yelled, *"Nooooooo!"* and lunged forward, the blade targeted straight at Flynn's chest.

Melisande screamed as Flynn twisted and the blade buried itself in his upper chest, near his shoulder. But as he turned, and Bellingham extricated the sword, Flynn's foot caught on the base of the fountain. He fell backward into the pool.

*   *   *

Flynn's back hit the water with a *slap*. Panic shot through his veins as water folded over his face. The impact of the cold and the instant fear of disappearing back into the future hit him like an electric shock. He didn't want this, he thought frantically. He did not want to go back.

He struggled in the cold water and pushed his arms backward, searching for the bottom of the pool. But a searing pain bolted through his chest and down his arm, curtailing his movement. The pain was blinding, causing his vision to darken as the water swept over his face and penetrated his clothes to his skin. In the ensuing moment of blackness he saw the fountain as he had when he was a boy.

Cascading through his mind like a waterfall, memories fell deftly into place. He remembered finding the marble knight behind the loose brick. But then the bird—*his* bird, he recalled—the black raven that was his pet, the one he'd remembered seeing on the hearth, flew out of the house and landed on the head of the stone boy in the center of the fountain. He remembered crawling onto the wall of the fountain and reaching out for the bird, calling to it to come to him. He had been so afraid it would fly away. But as he'd leaned toward the statue, his eye firmly on the flat dark eye of the raven, he'd lost his balance and toppled headlong into the water.

Flynn couldn't recall the trip to the future, the way he recalled the terror of coming back, with the fear that he was drowning and the momentary acceptance of death he'd felt. But he knew he did not want to make the trip again. His place was here. He knew it now, never more strongly than he did at this moment when it looked like all was lost.

But could this event be so haphazard? Was there no plan to this traveling through time? Did he really have no choice?

He punched his legs outward and felt his feet hit something solid. He twisted onto his side. With his good arm, he reached for the bottom of the pool and, to his amazement, found it. He pushed himself up and out of the water, coughing and clutching his other arm to his chest. With a quick jerk of his head, he flipped hair and water out of his eyes. His disoriented gaze searched for Melisande.

Lord, please let him be home where he belonged, he prayed fervently, in the Merestun of the past.

Before he could get his bearings, a shot shattered the air, followed immediately by a scream. He twisted. Melisande, her eyes huge with fear, jumped into the water of the fountain and before he knew what was happening, she threw her arms tight around his neck. He grabbed her as she careened into him and they clutched each other, both of them standing solidly in the knee-deep water.

"You didn't go," she said in a small voice over and over. "Oh, thank God, you didn't go."

Flynn held her securely against him, barely noticing the pain in his chest, and turned to see Lourds holding a smoking gun. Their eyes met briefly before Flynn's gaze dropped to see Bellingham lying on the flagstone, a flower of blood blossoming across his back.

Flynn shifted his look back to Lourds. The old man

slowly lowered the pistol. His arms shook, but the look on his face was resolute.

"I had to do it," Lourds said.

Flynn nodded, his breathing ragged. "You did the right thing."

"Yes, thank God," Melisande said. She turned to look at Lourds, but held onto Flynn as if he might sink away from her at any moment. "Thank God you were here."

"I had to do it," the old man repeated, his eyes watery again. He smiled wanly at Flynn. "Because I couldn't let it happen again. I had to save you this time, my lord."

"You did, Lourds. And I thank you." Flynn smiled back, pulling Melisande's warm, trembling body closer. "You saved me. From a fate worse than death."

Epilogue

Melisande awoke with the sun, as usual, and stretched in the warm, early morning air. Summer had finally arrived, and with it had come the Earl of Brandleigh's move to one of the Duke of Merestun's estates in Derbyshire. The new earl had taken his young wife, the former Miss Melisande St. Claire, to the estate along with a core staff of loyal, well-trained servants who were instructed to assist him in learning the customs and duties of a man of his station, all most respectfully, of course.

Flynn had been doing quite well, Melisande reflected. But then, when one was born to nobility one had certain instincts bred in the bone.

She turned onto her side to curl up against her husband, but found that he was gone. She sat up. This was unusual. Flynn was never up before she was. She looked at the clock on the mantle—7:30 A.M.! This was too strange.

She jumped out of bed, her heart racing. It never failed, she thought miserably. If Flynn was not where he was supposed to be, she was thrown into a panic of ridiculous proportions. What if he had gone back to where he'd come from? her mind would ask. Oh, she knew he no longer wanted to go back, but what if he was dragged there, the way he'd been as a child? Or the way he'd been brought back? She knew that on both of those occasions he'd had no desire to be swept out of his life.

She dressed quickly, leaving her hair in the long braid in which she slept, and slipped out of the room. She was to sit for her portrait today, she thought, in the red dress she'd ordered months ago that Flynn had remembered seeing in the future.

Oh, Lord, she prayed silently, please let me find him. Please, please, please, she chanted almost subconsciously.

She raced to the breakfast room, and nearly stumbled through the door as her toe caught on the threshold. He sat at the end of the table, a buttered roll in one hand and the newspaper in the other.

He grinned at her as she burst through the door, his gaze quickly becoming concerned at her breathless state.

"I'm here," he said calmly, standing as she entered the room.

She heaved a great sigh of relief and ran toward him. He dropped the paper and the roll and took her in his arms, his hand cupping her head against his chest, and his lips kissing the top of her head.

"You've got to stop this, Melisande," he said quietly, one hand running reassuringly up and down her back. "I'm not going anywhere. I promise you."

She breathed deeply of his scent, relishing the feel of his chest on her cheek. "I know," she said in a small voice.

"Plus I'm afraid one of these days you'll get so tired of wondering where I am that you'll actually *hope* I've gone, just to get rid of the headache."

She could hear the smile in his voice, but still, she pulled away and said solemnly, "That will never happen. You know that will never happen."

"And do you know that I love you?" he asked gently.

She nodded.

"Do you know that you're the most important thing in the world to me?"

She couldn't stop a small smile, and nodded again.

"Then why the hell would I leave?"

She rolled her eyes and frowned at him.

He laughed. "That's better. I'm much more comfortable with your disapproval than with your worry."

"I hope you don't speak that way when I'm not around," she said sternly.

"Of course not. I save it all for you, darlin'," he said with a grin. "Now have some breakfast. And look, the mail is here. There's a box for you."

She picked up the box and sat down in the chair next to his. A servant filled her cup with tea and set a fresh plate of rolls on the table in front of her.

As she untied the string on the package, she realized what was inside. It was Flynn's watch back from London. When the leather band had finally broken a month ago, she'd sent it to a jeweler to attach a gold chain to the face. Now he could use it as a pocketwatch. As a fob she had ordered a small golden knight, fashioned just like the one from the chess set.

"Shoot, all this worry has made me kind of regret the surprise I have in store for you," he said, watching her.

She set the box aside. A freshly ironed newspaper lay across her plate, she saw as she picked up a roll.

"What sort of surprise?" she asked warily.

Sometimes his surprises were less than joyful things. She remembered one time he'd surprised her by taking her out "jogging." A more ridiculous way to spend time she could not imagine. It had been torture, despite his assurances that it would be fun. He'd even gone on to claim it was just the thing to promote good health. But for days afterward she'd felt as if she'd been injured beyond repair, and she'd refused to go with him again after that, though he went almost daily.

In exchange, she remembered with a smile, she had tried to teach him to ride. Which he'd said had made him feel about the same way she'd felt after "jogging."

He nodded his head toward the newspaper. "Read the front page."

She put down the roll, picked up the paper, and scanned the headline. "Napoleon has been defeated!" she exclaimed. "And so quickly. That's wonderful news." She glanced up at him and noted his smug expression. "Were you directly responsible for this?" she asked wryly. "Is that why you're looking so proud?"

"There's more." He inclined his head toward the table.

She looked down to see a sealed envelope on her empty plate. She picked it up tentatively, eyeing him as she broke the seal. When she pulled out the piece of notepaper, she was surprised to see her own handwriting. "What . . . ?"

Then she remembered. His prediction. The event he had forecast when she'd asked him to prove he was from the future. She glanced again at the newspaper. The Hundred Days War. Napoleon had been defeated at Waterloo.

She looked up at him, butterflies circling in her stomach. This proved it, without a doubt. There was no way anyone could predict how long a war would last or which battle would end it. Not to mention that Flynn had been correct about Napoleon's escape from Elba and the approximate time in which it would happen.

"And did you see where they're putting him? Napoleon, that is?" he asked, looking more than a little self-satisfied.

She nodded. "St. Helena."

"Look at the note," he encouraged, gesturing with his hand. He looked absurdly happy with himself.

She couldn't help it. Despite her worry, she smiled. "I saw."

"And . . . ?" he asked.

"And you were right."

"And what else?"

She looked down at the paper, controlling the fear fluttering in her stomach. "And I believe you."

She blinked rapidly to stem the tears that sprang to

her eyes. This evidence just added more fuel the fire of her apprehension. He really *was* from the future. She supposed she'd slowly started believing him somewhere along the line, because right now she did not feel shocked so much as terrified that he would someday be taken from her, the way he'd been taken from the duke when he was a child.

"Melisande, I can't tell you how much it means to me to hear you say that."

"I'm glad." She looked at him and made herself smile. "But Flynn, how do you *know* you won't somehow be taken back there? When you disappeared as a child, you didn't want to go. And when you came back, you didn't intend to either. How do you know, now, that it will not happen again?"

He gazed at her, his cocky expression melting into one of concern. After a second he got up and knelt by her chair, looking up into her face. "Melisande, it didn't work. You were there. I fell into that fountain and nothing happened. I don't think I could get back now even if I wanted to. And I *don't* want to."

"I know. But who's to say it won't someday happen again, in some other way perhaps?"

He shook his head. "I don't know. We may never know. The only thing I can tell you is that I feel, somehow, deep in my heart, that this is where I'm meant to be. I feel . . . at peace here, in a way I never did in my other life. It was there that I was an impostor."

She nodded, then smiled to ease the anxiety on his face. It would have to be good enough, she thought. Knowing that he didn't *want* to leave would have to assuage her fears. At least for now.

"I have a surprise for you," she said with forced cheerfulness.

He looked delighted. "For me? What?"

She handed him the box. He recklessly tore through the paper and opened it, unwrapping the puff of jeweler's tissue inside. The watch tumbled out into his hand, the gold face polished and the horse fob dangling from the end of a long chain.

From what Melisande could see, it looked as if the jeweler had done a good job. And from the look on Flynn's face, it appeared that she had chosen the gift wisely.

"This is . . ." He stopped, his hands reverently handling the watch. "This is incredible." He narrowed his eyes and studied it. "It looks . . ." He glanced up at her. "It looks great."

"When the leather broke I thought you might prefer it on a chain. And here, look at the fob."

He laughed. "It's the knight." He smiled into her eyes. "You're amazing. I don't know how I got so lucky." He leaned forward and kissed her. "Lady Brandleigh, I love you. Completely."

She didn't have to force the smile that came to her then. "I love you too. Completely."

Flynn was standing in the west wing, fingering the fob of his new watch and directing a crew of workmen in how to construct a proper bathroom, complete with a toilet that operated with a cistern from the roof, when it hit him. The proof that he was here to stay.

He whipped the watch from his pocket and stared at it again. All morning he'd been obsessed with the thing, but he hadn't been sure why. It wasn't just because it was beautiful, or because it was so caringly designed by his wife, though those things meant a lot to him. It was because it had brought back a strange, murky sense of déjà vu.

Now, though, the reason it had so captivated him dropped into his mind the way the solution to a problem magically emerges when you're in the shower.

He handed the foreman the plans he was explaining, told him to study them and get back to him with questions, then ran through the construction of the new master bedroom to find Melisande.

She was sitting for the portraitist today, he remembered—wearing the red dress and holding the parasol—so he made his way to the solarium, where the painter claimed the light was best.

"I've got it," he said after bursting into the room.

Melisande looked up at him in surprise, and he gazed back with his heart in his throat. For she sat before a background of deep blue in the exact same position he remembered from the portrait in 1998. For some reason it took him by surprise, the precise replication of that picture, and the whole scene made his revelation that much more obvious to him.

She smiled broadly at him. "What have you got, my love? Something tells me it's important."

He laughed. "It is, Mel. It's about . . ." He glanced at the painter, who mixed colors on his palette with a studied motion. "What we talked about earlier. I know that I'm here to stay."

Her eyes grew somber. "What? How do you know?"

"Remember how I told you about this portrait, and what you would wear?"

She nodded.

"Well, the same day I saw another portrait, of an old man—a *very* old man," he said significantly, "who had a strange pocketwatch in his hand."

He watched as a smile dawned on her face.

He nodded. "It was this one, Melisande," he said with certainty. "I remember the face looking so small. And the horse fob. It was *me*, Melisande." He laughed, thinking about it. He'd seen a picture of himself as an old man—and he'd been trying to send himself a message. Why else would he have posed with a chess set? He wished he'd looked closer at the painting because he'd just about bet his life that the set had been missing one black knight.

"Do you really think so?" Melisande asked, her face alight with hope.

He laughed incredulously. "I'm sure of it. I've been looking at this thing all morning, trying to figure out why it looked so familiar, and then it hit me. It was in that portrait."

She laughed with him, bringing her hands up to her mouth and gazing at him with sparkling eyes. "Thank goodness you visited that portrait gallery."

"I'll say. Melisande . . ." He moved toward her and took her hands in his. She looked up at him, joy radiating from her face. "I'm here to stay. There's no question in my mind now."

Her laughter quieted and as she gazed at him, the hint of a smile played on her lips. Her eyes were alight with love and desire. He was about to suggest they give the painter the afternoon off when the man abruptly stopped his paint mixing and exclaimed, "That's *it*! That's the expression, my lady, don't move a muscle." He followed this with some rapid sketching.

Flynn looked back at Melisande. At that moment, the déjà vu was complete. He knew, with absolute certainty, that the look on her face that had so drawn him to the painting way back in 1998—the one that had seemed to undress him with her eyes—was the very one she wore now.

It was no wonder he couldn't resist her. He'd been in love with her even then.

Elaine Fox
Untamed Angel

Bestselling Author of *Hand & Heart of a Soldier*

With a name that belies his true nature, Joshua Angell was
born for deception. So when sophisticated and proper Ava
Moreland first sees the sexy drifter in a desolate Missouri
jail, she knows he is the one to save her sister from a ruined
reputation and a fatherless child. But she will need Angell to
fool New York society into thinking he is the ideal
husband—and only Ava can teach him how. But what start
as simple lessons in etiquette and speech soon become
smoldering lessons in love. And as the beautiful socialite's
feelings for Angell deepen, so does her passion—and finally
she knows she will never be satisfied until she, and no other,
claims him as her very own...untamed angel.

___4274-6 $4.99 US/$5.99 CAN

Storm
NORAH HESS

"Norah Hess not only overwhelms you with characters who seem to be breathing right next to you, she transports you into their world!"
—*Romantic Times*

Wade Magallen leads the life of a devil-may-care bachelor until Storm Roemer tames his wild heart and calms his hotheaded ways. But a devastating secret makes him send away the most breathtaking girl in Wyoming—and with her, his one chance at happiness.

As gentle as a breeze, yet as strong willed a gale, Storm returns to Laramie after years of trying to forget Wade. One look at the handsome cowboy unleashes a torrent of longing she can't deny, no matter what obstacle stands between them. Storm only has to decide if she'll win Wade back with a love as sweet as summer rain—or a whirlwind of passion that will leave him begging for more.

_3672-X $4.99 US/$5.99 CAN

Janeen O'Kerry
QUEEN OF THE SUN

Riding along the Irish countryside, Teresa MacEgan is swept into a magical Midsummer's Eve that lands her in ancient Eire. There the dark-haired beauty encounters the quietly seductive King Conaire of Dun Cath. Tall and regal, he kindles a fiery need within her, and she longs to yield to his request to become his queen but can relinquish her independence to no one. But when an enemy endangers Dun Cath's survival, Terri finds herself facing a fearsome choice: desert the only man she'd ever loved, or join her king of the moon and become the queen of the sun.

___52269-1 $4.99 US/$5.99 CAN

Dorchester Publishing Co., Inc.
P.O. Box 6640
Wayne, PA 19087-8640

Please add $1.75 for shipping and handling for the first book and $.50 for each book thereafter. NY, NYC, and PA residents, please add appropriate sales tax. No cash, stamps, or C.O.D.s. All orders shipped within 6 weeks via postal service book rate. Canadian orders require $2.00 extra postage and must be paid in U.S. dollars through a U.S. banking facility.

Name_____
Address_____
City_____State_____Zip_____
I have enclosed $_____ in payment for the checked book(s).
Payment <u>must</u> accompany all orders. ☐ Please send a free catalog.
CHECK OUT OUR WEBSITE! www.dorchesterpub.com

Fancy

NORAH HESS

After her father's accidental death, it is up to young Fancy Cranson to keep her small family together. But to survive in the pristine woodlands of the Pacific Northwest, she has to use her brains or her body. With no other choice, Fancy vows she'll work herself to the bone before selling herself to any timberman—even one as handsome, virile, and arrogant as Chance Dawson.

From the moment Chance Dawson lays eyes on Fancy, he wants to claim her for himself. But the mighty woodsman has felled forests less stubborn than the beautiful orphan. To win her hand he has to trade his roughhewn ways for tender caresses, and brazen curses for soft words of desire. Only then will he be able to share with her a love that unites them in passionate splendor.

_3783-1 $5.99 US/$6.99 CAN

Dorchester Publishing Co., Inc.
P.O. Box 6640
Wayne, PA 19087-8640

Please add $1.75 for shipping and handling for the first book and $.50 for each book thereafter. NY, NYC, and PA residents, please add appropriate sales tax. No cash, stamps, or C.O.D.s. All orders shipped within 6 weeks via postal service book rate. Canadian orders require $2.00 extra postage and must be paid in U.S. dollars through a U.S. banking facility.

Name_____

Address_____

City_____State_____Zip_____

I have enclosed $_____ in payment for the checked book(s).
Payment <u>must</u> accompany all orders. ☐ Please send a free catalog.

THE FOREVER BRIDE — Evelyn Rogers

"Evelyn Rogers delivers great entertainment!"
—*Romantic Times*

It is only a fairy tale, but to Megan Butler *The Forever Bride* is the most beautiful story she's ever read. That is why she insists on going to Scotland to get married in the very church where the heroine of the legend was wed to her true love. The violet-eyed advertising executive never expects the words of the story to transport her over two hundred years into the past, exchanging vows not with her fiancé, but with strapping Robert Cameron, laird of Thistledown Castle. After convincing Robert that she is not the unknown woman he's been contracted to marry, Meagan sets off with the charming brute in search of the real bride and her dowry. But the longer they pursue the elusive girl, the less Meagan wants to find her. For with the slightest touch Robert awakens her deepest desires, and she discovers the true meaning of passion. But is it all a passing fancy—or has she truly become the forever bride?

_4177-4 $5.50 US/$6.50 CAN